Kitty Casino

Kitty Casino

Kim Cayer

TAMARIND TREE
Toronto

Tamarind Tree Books Inc.,
Email: info@tamarindtreebooks.com
OR
Kim Cayer,
Email: kimscharacters@bell.net

Library and Archives Canada Cataloguing in Publication

Title: Kitty Casino / Kim Cayer.
Names: Cayer, Kim, author.
Identifiers: Canadiana 20210355441 | ISBN 9781989242056 (softcover)
Classification: LCC PS8605.A9385 K58 2021 | DDC C813/.6—dc23

Cover image: i.Stock.com/bennymarty

Dedicated to Nanny. We didn't always see eye to eye,
but there is one thing we could both agree on....
You sure loved casinos.

CHAPTER I

"We have nobody here with that name," the receptionist informed me.

I was at Better Days Ahead Retirement Centre, the latest "home" where I had deposited my mother. This was the third place she'd lived over the past year. In the last two fine establishments, she had been asked to leave. The reason? Unruly and disruptive behaviour.

I assumed the previous senior homes had been acceptable. Online, they looked terrific. I took it a step further by having my eldest child, Rain, personally check them out.

"Looks great, Mom," came his reply to every retirement centre. "Nice place, nice people. And they say she can afford it."

Each time, Rain had to adjust his schedule to help his grandmother make the move. It wasn't like he was an important executive at a busy company…he was simply a boy in his second year of gruelling studies at university. In addition to school, he was holding down two part-time jobs.

Rain wasn't my only child. I also had twin daughters, Tatum and Sadie, both in their first year of university. All three of my kids had to end up being smarty-pants and choose to attend four year courses at various schools around the country. Rain was taking pharmaceutical studies in Hamilton and was the family member living closest to my mother. Tatum, learning about sports injury recovery, was in Vancouver. Sadie, as close as she was to her twin, chose the opposite coast. She was in Halifax to study accounting.

The person who lived the farthest away from Mom was me. For the past fifteen years, I've been on the road. However, due to circumstances beyond my control, I was recently forced to move back to Toronto. Since daughter dearest was back in town, the least she could do was look after her elderly mother.

"Are you sure you don't have a Katherine Canseco here?" I again asked the receptionist.

"I'm just filling in behind the desk until Marta finishes lunch," the girl relayed. "But I've been working here awhile now. I pretty much know everybody but I never heard of no Katherine Canseco."

"You're joking with me," I said, a mild panic starting to flutter in my gut.

She shrugged. "You sure you have the right name?"

"I think I know my own mother's name!" I replied…OK, shouted. Hearing a loud voice in the well-groomed lobby caused a lady to run out of a room, sandwich in hand.

"Whoa, what's the commotion?" she asked, giving me the eye. "I don't recognize you. How can we help?"

"Actually, you guys called me. My name is Tammy," I replied, trying to be pleasant. "You said you wanted my mother out of this place, the sooner the better. But your girl says my mom's not here. So where is she then?"

"Your mother's name?" the head receptionist, Marta, asked.

"Geez, how many old ladies are you kicking out?" I retorted. "Katherine Canseco already."

"I told her we didn't have her registered as a resident," the helpful temp added.

"Did you look in the files?" Marta asked her severely.

The temp shook her head. "But I know everybody here," she offered.

Marta "tsk'd tsk'd" and looked back at me. "We call her by a different name here. Maybe that's why Lolita was confused."

"A different name? Like what? Mrs. Canseco?" I was not amused.

"Actually, we call her Kitty Casino," Marta replied.

"Say what?" I interjected. "That sounds dumb."

"Not if you get to know her," Marta said. I gave her a look, one that read 'You're kidding me, right?' Marta caught it. "Sorry, what I meant was that ever since she got here, Kitty…I mean, Katherine….has been, well, a certifiable nuisance. She shouts, she harasses other residents, she's even had us on the verge of calling the mental health department! And then one day she signed up for a casino outing."

"Is that why we have so many casino trips?" Lolita asked.

"Exactly," Marta affirmed. "We discovered Kitty....sorry, Katherine...but she prefers to be called Kitty...."

"Go on," I ordered.

"Well, we discovered Kitty was a totally different person that day!" Marta exclaimed. "I'm telling you, it was astounding! We had even hired an extra staff employee to shadow your mother, make sure she behaved. He said she was an angel! And we saw it for ourselves when the bus picked us up. She was docile, content, went to bed without an issue. Even the next day was bearable with her."

"And then?" I asked.

"Then she got moody again! And whiney. And complained so much that one morning, we decided on an impromptu casino trip. And it was the same story; she was a doll. And that was the day Katherine Canseco became Kitty Casino."

"She likes to gamble, you say?" I mused. "That's news to me. So she goes to the casino, she's happy for a few days....and then it's time for another visit there. Why can't you handle that?"

Marta sighed dramatically. "Maybe she's happy for one day after the visit, but you have no idea what she's like when she's NOT happy. For the sake of Better Days Ahead, you have to remove her."

Better days ahead? Hah! Not for me, I feared.

CHAPTER II

Born late in life, and unexpectedly, to Katherine and Johnny Canseco, I was never what you'd call a 'good child'. Katherine raised me alone, after my father's death. That event had been foreseen. Following a cancer diagnosis, my father spent five years slowly succumbing until his eventual demise. Mom didn't like to talk about it. She kept saying we were robbed. When I asked her if she meant we were robbed of money, she'd wave off that suggestion.

"I meant I was robbed of a husband and you of a father," she'd explain. "Don't worry about money. The government did their thing and made sure to take care of us." When I asked about their life together, she said she worked hard to put him through engineer school. After he graduated, he got a lowly job in his field, so she kept working. He eventually moved up as an engineer in research and development with the space program, earning enough so that she could quit her job. They moved into a big house where she spent her days taking care of the joint while her husband worked long hours.

Mom said they were planning their first vacation ever when they got news of Dad's cancer. They still went on the cruise and I remember her stories about the ship's nightlife, the entertainers, the onboard casino, the exotic ports of call. More than anything, I heard that I was conceived on that boat - to a 44-year old woman and her equally surprised husband.

Maybe I was neglected the first four years of my life. Perhaps that would account for my later behaviour. How could I blame my mother though? In between feeding and changing me, she was doing the same for my father. As I progressed from babyhood, he regressed to that state. It was pitiful but somehow my mother managed. More than anything, I give her credit for extending my dad's life from the doctor's estimated two to three years. Through her constant loving care, he lived a further five years.

I missed Day One of junior kindergarten because of the funeral. Within a week, my mother received the first of many letters from the school. She would have seen more had I not hidden a few dozen. This letter was just to inform Mrs. Canseco that her daughter, Tammy, had not been at school on Thursday. They were wondering, since Katherine did not call in my absence, what the reason was?

The reason remains crystal clear in my mind. It was a beautiful summer morning and I was headed for my third day of kindergarten. Back in those days, if you knew where you were going and how to get back, parents let their kids walk anywhere at the age of four and a half. Walking to Beaver Creek Public School should have taken no more than six minutes. That day it took me almost four hours.

Already I felt that school wasn't for me. It seemed like we spent the first hour just learning how to line up. Then we sang the alphabet song for an eternity. Next we spent time learning how to print our name. For crying out loud, I already had a SIGNATURE, already knew cursive writing, and was just learning the multiplication tables when my father passed. I'm the daughter of a rocket scientist, for God's sake. Even though he didn't live to see me start school, it gave him joy to the end to fill my little noggin with all sorts of educational tidbits.

On this day, I figured it wouldn't hurt to miss that nonsense at the beginning of my kindergarten class. I did want to get there in time for recess though. Instead of taking the direct route to school, I went into a back alley where I heard a loud mewling. I followed the sound to an opening between two garages. A torn black garbage bag full of old clothing lay there. An orange cat, looking barely old enough to be a mother, had a big belly half the size of her. As soon as our eyes connected, she let out another painful "Meowrrr!" and a tiny kitten suddenly popped out of nowhere.

"Ohhh, you're having a baby!" I cried in delight. The cat didn't seem as pleased. She lay panting and then let out more of a groan than a meow. A second kitten popped out and slid down the black plastic of the garbage bag. "Another one?" I asked the poor thing. I picked up the second kitten, which lay mewling and squirming on the ground. School flew out of my mind as I became a midwife to Orange Cat.

Between Orange Cat birthing her six kittens, I rearranged her bed as best I could. I made it more level with a well in the middle to enclose her brood. After it appeared she was finished having babies for today, I found a cardboard box in a neighbour's garbage and used it to create overhead shelter. Once Orange Cat was settled and her kittens nursing, I stayed to watch out of curiosity.

With a start, I remembered I was now a student and had to get to school. I ran as fast as I could but as I rounded the corner, I could see the kids lining up to leave the schoolyard. The kindergarten bell sounded the end of the day. I just turned around and went back to my house.

The next day I had to come home with the note. I told my mother the truth and she told me I had to tell the school what happened and deal with the punishment. I did, my head hung in shame. The teacher laughed and thought it was so cute. The principal commended me on my compassion in dealing with the pregnant cat. I got off scot-free.

A couple weeks later, another note. I was caught kissing Geoffrey Taylor. Actually I was trying to get him to show me his penis. He said he would, but I had to kiss him first. That's how grown-ups did it, he claimed. I agreed to it, as a means to an end. It was good that Mrs. Bronwyn caught us then and not a minute later.

Once more I told my mother why I did what I did. I just wanted to know what it looked like. "But why the penis?" my mother asked with a sigh.

"Because you never see it; it's always covered up," I explained. "I wanted to see if it looked flat and smooth like my Ken doll."

"Then you tell that to your teacher," she ordered me. And I did.

"Natural curiosity," the principal decreed.

"She's displaying an awareness of the human body," the school nurse analyzed.

"Well, I'm glad it didn't come to that," Mrs. Bronwyn said. "I'll just ask her to keep her hands to herself."

That was it. I went from junior kindergarten through to high school breaking all the rules, usually getting off with a reprimand or a threat that a negative comment would go into my file if I continued my behaviour. Sometimes I would get detention and a couple times I did get suspended. All in all, the school system was quite lenient with me.

What was with me back then? I skipped school more often than I attended. Thankfully, though I was nowhere as smart as my Dad was supposed to have been, I managed to pass my tests. I just hated the regiment of attending classes, of having to always be at a certain place at the exact time. Instead I'd go to malls or movies or to the homes of other kids who were skipping. We'd play video games or just watch TV. Sometimes I'd even go to high school but not attend my classes. I'd sit in the cafeteria or hang out on the school bleachers and get high.

Speaking of those bleachers, that's where I conceived Rain when I was fifteen years old. Under the bleachers, to be more specific. No love story there. I was hanging out with a fellow wayward kid named Riley. We were walking back to the school after lunch when we got caught in a big rainstorm. We ran to the sanctuary of the bleachers, where we hugged each other to keep warm. One thing led to another and voila - I became another teenage pregnancy statistic.

Once I gave birth to my son, I went back to my old ways. Sometimes I attended school, sometimes I spent time with my boyfriend. Rarely did I look after Rain - I had no idea what to do with a baby! Mom took care of my lack of parenting skills by quitting her job. I had enough sense to fret over that; how would we afford diapers and formula?

"Don't worry about it," she consoled me. "It's only temporary."

"But how will we get by?" I wailed. "We don't have any money! We're poor!"

"Why would you say that?" Mom asked.

"You never spend any money, you don't buy new clothes, you never go places…"

"I'm careful with my finances," my mother said quietly. "It wouldn't kill you to learn a few things about money."

That was a conversation I'd heard many times over the years. How to put ten per cent away. Save for a rainy day. By now, I'd heard it so many times, the information went in one ear and right out the other.

"And we're a single-income family with a new baby!" I concluded. "So how long do you think you can stay unemployed?"

"The government will take care of us," Kitty said. "Let me take care of Rain and you go to school. This time stay out of trouble."

Missing two weeks to have a baby didn't strain my grade average too much. I hoped to pass Grade Eleven with a decent mark. Trouble came in the form of my new boyfriend, Reg.

I met Reg while I was in the hospital having my baby. Reg worked there part-time as a member of the cleaning staff. He visited me quite often during my three-day stay, but only during the night since that was his shift. On the last night, he took down my phone number and we necked a little.

About a month into the relationship, things went to hell in one single morning. Instead of going to school, I decided to visit Reg. We'd made plans for him to pick me up at lunch but I wanted to see him before that, simply to ask if he could tidy up a bit. When we first met, he'd been a real hunk in my eyes. Lately though, his hair was greasy, his body smelled, he didn't shave. I wanted the former Reg to be the one my girlfriends would see for the first time.

As I approached his apartment, a lady held the front door open for me. Another held the elevator. I got off on the seventh floor and crossed the hallway to Reg's suite a few feet away. The door stood ajar, a bag of garbage holding it open.

I could hear Reg cooing and giggling into the phone, though I couldn't make out what he was saying. I quietly opened the door and lifted the garbage bag back inside. Too late to catch the end of the call, I saw Reg hang up the phone, sigh, and turn around with a goofy grin on his face. Oh, as well as a raging hard-on in his boxers.

I was only sixteen and had never felt jealousy before. It was not a pleasant feeling. "Who was that?" I coldly asked.

"Who, that?" Reg pointed at the phone. I nodded. "Oh, that!" I waited. "That was my mom!"

"Your mom? Really? You're telling me you were talking to your mom just now?" I desperately wanted him to tell me that actually.

"What's the matter, honey pie?" Reg came over and took me in his arms. "You know I love you. Give me a kiss."

I leaned in and gave him a kiss that had no passion in it, just so he could see I was a little miffed.

"Come on, sweet cheeks, you can do better than that," Reg murmured, pulling me in even closer. His erection was obvious; it was like a ruler the teacher used to keep us all a foot apart at dances.

I pushed him off. "I gotta get to school," I said. "I just wanted to drop by and say hi real quick."

Maybe Reg didn't hear me. He cupped my breasts and squeezed them. "Oh, they're still so big!" he enthused. "Let me at them."

"Oh, you're gross!" I yelled as I slapped his hands away. He quickly grabbed my hands in his and placed them on his penis.

Moaning, he begged me to squeeze it, jerk it, eat it. Seeing as how I hadn't even had breakfast yet, I told him I wasn't interested. "Besides, Reg," I pointed out, "I'm not supposed to be having sex for another two weeks at least."

In the next moment, Reg had me on the bed and his hands were pawing at my sweat pants. "That's just a bunch of baloney," he stated. "I work in the hospital, I know these things. Really, you can have sex the minute after you have a baby."

So I let him. Mind you, I did say "I don't think we should" and "I'm not comfortable with this" and "No, Reg, no" a few times. He was so insistent though, his cock stabbing me everywhere, hoping to make penetration, that it just seemed easier to let him have his way.

After the act, which took all of ninety seconds once he got going, Reg jumped up. "I'm first in the shower!" he shouted and ran into the loo.

I remained in the bed, feeling Reg's semen slide out of me. Looking around for tissues, I spotted a box on his dresser. I pulled out a few and started cleaning myself off. Reaching for more, I noticed the box rested on a sheaf of papers. I slid the papers forward to see what they were.

Prescription pads? Why would a janitor have prescription pads? My radar went up and while the shower was running, I did a quick search of the bedroom. When Reg strutted out of the bathroom, I was dressed and ready to go to school, smelly twat and all.

"Now that we've done the nasty, I don't see any reason to meet for lunch, do you?" Reg asked, towelling his hair. I didn't answer so he removed the towel and glanced at me. "Is that a problem?"

Stepping away from the dresser, I pointed to three items. "Prescription pads? Are you selling these? And all these pills! Either you're seriously sick or you're selling those too. And three pairs of panties? You're probably going to tell me they belong to your mom but I figure you're cheating on me."

Walking to the front door, I picked up my school bag from the kitchen counter, where his mail was sitting. I saw a Visa bill addressed to a Mr. Reginald Dwyer. I didn't know that was his first name. "As far as I'm concerned, RegINALD, we're through," I tossed off.

"NOBODY CALLS ME REGINALD!!" Reg screamed as he came running at me, one arm cocked back, ready to throw a punch. My eyes had also lit upon the letter opener amongst the mail and I swooped it up.

"Jesus, Reg!" I yelled, brandishing the blade between us. "You're freaking over your actual name? You overreacting psycho! Stay away from me forever!"

Happy to be done with that potentially abusive man, a couple months later I discovered I'd probably have ties to him for the rest of my life. I was pregnant with his CHILDREN! Not just one but two fetuses were discovered in my belly.

I did finish Grade Eleven but there was no hope of me getting a complete high school education. As shallow and self-centred as I was, I didn't intend on dumping three children on poor Kitty. The plan was for me to stay home and help my mother raise my offspring.

Funny how things don't always go according to plan.

CHAPTER III

I stayed home long enough to see my three kids start school. Rain was in senior kindergarten and the twins in JK when I disappeared.

It wasn't enough of a shock to my mom that she'd file a missing person's report. There were enough signs for her to understand I wasn't cut out to be a mother. I'd spend days away from home and it didn't matter whether I was with friends or foe. I just didn't want to be with family. Don't get me wrong - I loved my little devils. I just didn't understand why babies needed so much non-stop attention. I wanted them to hurry and grow up and run to the corner store for milk if they needed it so badly.

"They're progressing at just the rate they're supposed to," my mother assured me.

"Well, why has Sadie been walking for a month and Tatum is still crawling?" I whined. "I'm sick of carrying them around. If Tatum wants to go anywhere, she better start walking. And I mean today."

"You can see she's going to start walking any day," Kitty countered. "You have to lighten up on the poor child."

"They have to lighten up on me!" I bitched. "And I'm so so so sick of diapers! And sick of Rain not saying his words right. Pudd-o instead of puddle, lidd-o instead of little…"

Mom interrupted me. "He's barely two years old, Tammy," she scolded. "He's just learning how to talk! And speaking of diapers, when was the last time you even changed one? Maybe you'd like to change one now?"

How dare she!? After I just told her how much I disliked diapers.

(Perhaps I assumed I was the only one in the world to despise the task?) Off I'd storm to a coffee shop or Gerry's Hangout or my pot guy. I'd meet up with a friend and we'd go somewhere else, maybe a party or to a club. One time I ended up stranded in Pennsylvania. Mom came to my rescue, three toddlers in tow, and brought me back to Toronto.

Gerry's Hangout was Ground Zero of my eventual exit from the city where I'd spent my entire life. It all began on my nineteenth birthday, the day when I became old enough to legally drink. A group of us decided to go to Gerry's Hangout to celebrate. It wasn't my first time going to a pub but it was the first time with my own identification.

That night, three live bands were playing. The second act, a rock group called Screw U, should have been the headliners. They played a sound that the whole crowd grooved to, including myself. I was dancing in front of the stage, making googly eyes at the singer while I extra-shook my booty. My fate was sealed when he stepped up to the microphone and said, "This song goes out to the hot chick in the rockin' red tube top." That bird was me.

As soon as Screw U's set was over, the singer - Axel - jumped off the stage in front of me. "You're coming with me," he said, taking my hand. I simply let myself be led into their dressing room. There were a couple other gals in there, girlfriends I believe, but I ignored them completely. I only had eyes for Axel.

It took me about six months to make Axel my boyfriend for real. During this time, I hung out with him every chance I could. Mostly I'd see him at band practice, which was held in the basement of Gerry's Hangout. Often there was another girl there - Roslyn - who I first recalled seeing in the dressing room the first night I met Axel. It turned out she was the reason it was taking me so long to lock in on Axel.

The bitch was Axel's girlfriend! Or should I say, ex-girlfriend who wouldn't let him go. They'd break up but then a week later, she'd discover she was pregnant with his child. When she wasn't showing after awhile, she'd claim she lost the baby. They'd break up again. Or she would show up at his house with a lame excuse and he'd give her sex because he was horny. She'd take that as a sign they were back together. The worst part was that Roslyn was the drummer's sister. Axel claimed he didn't want to start band problems by dumping the sibling of the best drummer Screw U ever had.

Half a year later, when Axel realized he could be getting steady sex from me and that Roslyn may be half-crazy and a band from the USA nicked Screw U's drummer, things turned in my favour. Axel finally severed ties with Roslyn and made me his steady girlfriend. That resulted in me spending even less time at my house. Much nicer to sleep in until noon with blackout curtains and nothing to wake me but my own body clock.

Axel wasn't the best of boyfriends. He really didn't know how to treat a lady but maybe he didn't see me in that light. He wasn't one for showering me with gifts or taking me out to dinner or even sharing endearments. I was more like a sidekick; it wasn't until he wanted to get laid that he might change tactics. When I'd hear Axel call me 'Babycakes', I knew it was the signal to start undressing.

On the plus side, being with him kept me out of the house. My own house, that is, where my mother and my three children managed without me. And Axel had a more exciting life than mine. No pushing kids in swings, no visits to McDonald's PlayLands, no reading irrelevant children's books to wide-awake toddlers. No…. Axel got to play a different club every week, the band was busy making an album, there were stage clothes to buy…As the steady girlfriend, I got to tag along everywhere. Hell, I was expected to be at his beck and call!

The turning point in my life began with that man. One day I woke up, ate a Pop Tart and then decided to wake Axel and break up with him. Things, in my opinion, had become quite staid. It didn't take me long to realize I was hugely attracted to Axel when he was performing. He presented a persona that was sexual, dangerous, commanding. But once he stepped off the stage, he resumed his normal wishy-washy indecisive self.

On that afternoon, I walked into the bedroom to rouse my boyfriend. Axel was already up, sitting on the bed, the sheets bunched around his lower body. His ear was pressed to the phone. I was about to say something when he quickly lifted his arm and raised an open hand. Sign language for "Ssshh!", the most commanding thing he'd done since the night I first met him.

"I'm in, I'm in," I heard Axel say. "Make the deal." He hung up the phone and then turned to me, stone-faced. "The day has come."

I assumed he was referring to us. "Yeah, Axel, I guess it has," I began. "So where do we go from here?"

"Fucking Detroit Rock City!" he yelled. "In two fucking days!"

"I don't get it….." Then realization hit me. "Oh, you got a show in Detroit?"

"Not just one show, Screw U is going on tour!" He jumped out of bed, his scrawny body racing to his dresser. He started to open a drawer but turned back to me. "No, you gotta do this. Pack me enough clothes for six weeks on tour."

"Six weeks!" I exclaimed as I walked over to him. "You don't have that many outfits. You're going to have to rotate them."

"Will I have to clean them too?" he whined.

"Well, somebody has to," I replied.

Axel began digging through his supply of hair products and male make-up. "You know, they said we could bring our girlfriends. I know Vinnie is taking BiBi. I don't know about Kevin; he's still single."

"I'm pretty sure he's gay," I stated.

"Nah, he told me he's still looking for the right one," Axel said. "You know how finicky Kevin gets. Everything always has to be just perfect."

"He did wear a cape the other night, just saying," I threw in. I wasn't about to start a fight; I was waiting for the big invite to join the tour.

"So it looks like I'm going to be needing some help on this gig," Axel decided. "Thing is, the girlfriends all have to pay their own way." I nodded. Not that I had money but I figured Mom would lend me some. "K, as long as you know," Axel continued.

I nodded again. Silence from Axel as he moved on to his collection of belts and scarves. With an innocent look on my face, I asked, "Do you want me to go?"

"Look at it this way," Axel countered. "If you don't go, what if I get horny? There's always groupies at these clubs. I might get tempted. If you're there, it'd be easier to just do you."

Ah, romantic as ever. I risked this trip of a lifetime to ask, "So you want me there to stop you from cheating?" Axel nodded. "And so you have clean clothes?" Again he nodded. I waited about two seconds before giving him an answer.

"OK. I'm in."

CHAPTER IV

Screw U was the opening act for the most famous Canadian band in recent history - The Noise. This was the biggest thing to ever happen to both rock groups - a six week tour in the USA. Not all fifty states but at least six of them.

For a big break, things seemed to be done on a small scale. Both bands plus their girlfriends, as well as most of the roadies (who were not allowed to bring romantic mates) travelled in one bus. We were followed by a truck that carried two more roadies and all the equipment. The hotels we stayed at were not AAA-approved and almost every meal was eaten at some roadside diner.

I loved it all. There were laughs a-plenty, new people to discover, a curiosity about what lay around the bend. Every show was different, always something to catch our eye, create a memory. Even the little dramas along the way (couples fighting, getting lost) held interest for me. I was away from that little burg called Toronto and I was finally living! Of course I did see my family before my departure. I let them know Mommy would be gone a long time - six whole weeks! None of my kids seemed bothered. Rain asked, "Will anything be different, Grandma?"

"No, I'll still be taking you and your sisters to school," my mother told my son. "And I'll still pick you up and make you your three square meals a day...."

"Oh! Speaking of eating," I interrupted, "I need some spending money on this trip. You know I rely on you for cash...."

"How much?" she asked.

"Gee, I don't know. Six weeks of food and, you know, birth control…"

Kitty winced. "You make sure you buy that before food, please."

I continued. "Hotels are paid for but I may need other stuff."

"Marijuana?" Kitty asked. "I'm not paying for that."

"Just give me what you think I might need," I said.

"I'll give you a thousand dollars," she said. "And I think that's too much. I just know I'm buying marijuana."

"You're not buying marijuana!" I told her. I'd be the one buying it.

"What does Mary wanna do?" Rain asked.

"Rain!" I turned to my son and pleaded, "Articulate! It's not 'wanna', it's 'want to'. What does Mary WANT TO do?"

"Tammy, go pack for your trip," Kitty butted in. "You can use the nice big suitcase I bought for my cruise. It's only been used that once."

Sadie glanced up from the colouring books she and her twin had scattered on the kitchen table. "I want to go on a trip," she announced. "Tatum and me want to go to outer space."

"So did your Grandpa Johnny, bless his soul," I said. Kitty made the sign of the cross. "Listen, kids. Even though I'm going to be gone a long time, Mommy is going to call home every few days. Got that?"

Seems I didn't get that memo. The tour was doing a gig in Toledo, Ohio when Axel got a visit from an ex-girlfriend who now lived there. She showed up with her adorable daughter, Kenzie. This perfect specimen of a child made me remember I had kids of my own. I couldn't wait to get back to my hotel room and call them.

After a few words with Kitty, I hastened her to put the kids on speakerphone. "Hey, guys," I cooed. "It's Mommy! Do you miss me?"

"Hi, Mommy," said Tatum. "Are you at Axel's house?"

"No, but I'm with Axel," I replied. But not for much longer, an inner voice told me. "We're on a job."

"Are you planting trees?" Rain asked. "We learned that in school today. That's the job I'm gonna do…."

"Going to," I sighed, the old exasperation sneaking out. "Going to do."

"Rain had a big poop today," Sadie piped up. "Grandma Kitty said it was the size of a baseball."

"Did not!" Rain denied.

"That was you," Tatum said. "Grandma Kitty said you need more fruits and vegetables."

"Kids….," I tried to cut in.

"You need more fruits and vegetables in your face!" Rain yelled.

"Grandma!" one of the girls shrieked. "Rain just threw a grape at me!"

Kitty's voice came over the speakerphone. "Rain! Those grapes are to help move your bowels! You will not throw them, you will eat every last one of them."

"Or you're going to poop more baseballs," Tatum, or possibly Sadie, teased.

I hung up the phone. Maybe it would be another two weeks before I called again.

• • • • •

The tour was still in its infancy when I seriously knew the Axel-Tammy romance was over. It became obvious he thought I came along to happily be his slave. By day I ran his errands, by night I was his fuck toy. He was making a decent wage but wouldn't even buy me a cup of coffee. And while I paid my own way to come along, this was no vacation.

It could have turned into one big on-the-road breakup drama. Had I let it happen, I would have to get home on my own dime. As it was, the thousand bucks Kitty had lent me was dwindling fast. Buying dope off the various sellers in different cities wasn't cheap; neither were the after-show drinks. It was a nonstop party and I wasn't ready to go home. To keep peace among the travelling troupe, I continued the charade that I was still Axel's girlfriend. I made sure he was up in time for sound check, I tended to his stage costumes as well as his regular clothes, I fetched him his food and pills and rolling papers. Hell, I worked harder than any girlfriend on that tour.

By the fourth week, everybody knew that things weren't peachy keen between Axel and I. We were spending a week in the Chicago area and on the first day there, I strayed off the usual agenda. Instead of sitting through another sound check, I decided to visit a grocery store in the vicinity. Sick and tired of fried food, my body screamed out for something natural.

Stocked up on fruits and vegetables, I went back to the club. The Noise was nearing the end of their sound check. I went into the parking lot and saw a couple members of Screw U standing around the tour bus. A few teen-aged girls, as well as a couple of their moms, stood talking to the bandmates. One mom stepped in when Kevin reached out to adjust a teen's scarf. I knew he meant no romantic intention.

I reached the bus but didn't see Axel outside. I climbed aboard - no Axel here either - and stashed my bags of nutritious food. Grabbing an apple, I exited the bus. "Has anybody seen Axel?" I asked anyone who was listening.

"I think he's still in the club," Vinnie replied.

The front door was locked so I made my way around to the back. A horde of maybe fifty people, mostly girls, crowded the stage entrance. I pushed my way to the front, where my new pal Aapo was manning the door.

Aapo was a decent dude. He drove the equipment truck so I didn't get to see much of him. When we arrived at our destinations, Aapo was busy unloading equipment pre-show and loading it again after the gig. When he wasn't doing that, he was given assorted duties. At the moment, he was protecting The Noise from fandemonium.

Sometimes I'd see him at dinner time, more often at the after-show parties. He was always a gentleman with me and I'd only seen him talking to groupies. I never saw him mess around with any of them. I ended up spilling the beans to him about my romantic woes and he was a willing ear. I kind of wanted to sleep with him as well but didn't want to rock the tour boat even more.

Once Aapo spotted me, he gave me a wink. "Aah, the press has arrived!" Opening the door just a smidgen, he gave me enough space to squeeze through.

"Hey, Aapo," I whispered. "Have you seen Axel around?"

"Haven't seen him, cookie," he replied. I grinned at his endearment. It was a nice change from 'Babe' that all the rock stars seemed to use.

The Noise was wrapping up its sound check. As I passed the stage, the singer's voice came over the loudspeakers, blasting my eardrums. Instead of a lyric, I heard, "Hey there, what's that you're eating?"

I stopped and looked up at him. "It's an apple," I replied. My voice wasn't amplified but he still heard me.

"Where'd you get that?" he asked, as if I were eating an exotic fruit.

"At the grocery store," I said. "I bought a bunch of healthy stuff."

"Can you spare that one?" the singer - Bradley - asked as he placed his microphone on its stand. He held out both hands. That apple was mighty good and I'd only taken two bites out of it. But there were three more in my shopping bags, so I tossed it up at him. Perfect throw, perfect catch and we both laughed at the same time. "Babe, you're a keeper," he said. "Final song, guys," he told the band.

I made my way around the stage toward the back, where the dressing rooms were. Nobody was in The Noise's room, located right off the stage. I went towards the next room and could hear sounds coming from inside.

"Hhhm," I thought to myself. "Obvious sex noises. Do I walk in? What if it's not Axel? Oh shit, you know it is. So let the fun begin."

I quietly inched the door open and heard a female say, "C'mon already! I heard Bradley say it was the last song."

"One more minute, babe, just another minute," huffed the naked body who was pile-driving her. The voice didn't sound like Axel but I could tell by the half-finished musical note tattoo on his back that it was my soon to be ex-boyfriend.

I spoke up. "Bringing diseases home, my dear?"

The predicted shock and swift uncoupling took place. "Who are you?" the girl asked.

"I'm the girlfriend," I answered. "And you are…what? 15 years old? Get dressed. Get out of here."

"I'm not even here for this guy," she nodded toward Axel. "He's hot, but I'm into the Noise. Anybody from that band, I love them all!" she gushed.

I turned to Axel and gave him a withering look. More for the sake of his memory bank; the truth was I found I didn't much care this had happened. Even yesterday, the way I felt about Axel verged on dislike. Axel gave me a contemptuous look. "You weren't here, she was," he said in his defence. "I got horny. We talked about this."

"Oh, that's so lame," I replied, shaking my head. I walked out the door but turned and gave him the best I had. "I know you've probably heard this a thousand times before but Axel…you're an asshole."

• • • • • • • • •

I expected to be kicked off the tour from the moment I walked out of that dressing room.

Exiting the same way I came in, I again encountered Aapo. The crowd had doubled in size. Aapo, the tall burly guy that he was, actually looked a bit concerned.

"Check out the crowd today," he said. "They're getting bigger all the time. Americans love The Noise!"

"Are you going to be able to contain this?" I asked. "Maybe I should call the cops or get you some help?"

"Nah, the guys are almost done, aren't they?" he asked. I nodded in the affirmative. "Can you run back in and tell them to use the front doors when they leave? And get on the bus as fast as they can."

"I'm on it," I shouted over the din of the fans and did an about-face as I raced back into the club.

The first person I saw was Axel, heading toward the exit. I simply stepped around him. Walking into the dressing room of The Noise, I saw the same promiscuous girl playing up to the drummer. The rest of the band were just about to leave.

"Hey, hang on!" I commanded. "First of all, Stan, that girl is jailbait, like Grade Nine. Hands off." To the girl, I said, "Boy, you get around! How did you even get in here?"

"My daddy owns the club," she giggled as Stan disentangled from her embrace.

I turned back to the band. "Second thing. There's a shitload of fans out there, maybe more than we can handle. They're gonna tear you to shreds."

Bradley looked down at his shirt. "This is from Roots. I love this shirt. Nobody's ripping it."

"So we're going out the front door," I said. "Even though it's locked, we can still exit from the inside. And there's nobody waiting out front."

"Maybe we should go out the back," Stan suggested "That could be free publicity."

"True.....," Bradley considered.

"There won't be any publicity, just mayhem," I advised. "If you want publicity, let me think about it, maybe we can plan something. But let's get going right now. I don't know how much longer Aapo can hold back the stage door crowd."

We exited through the front door into the bright daylight. As one, all members of the band immediately reached for their sunglasses.

"The bus is in the parking lot!" I yelled. Leading the way, I was followed by the four members of the band. It was maybe a hundred yards to the bus and we ran full tilt.

A latecomer to the stage-door crowd spotted The Noise running. He yelled out, "I see them! Here they are! The Noise is out here!" Suddenly it became a conga line of me in the lead followed by four men in skintight jeans, trailed by sixty fans that seemed to materialize out of nowhere.

In retrospect, it looked like I was living the rock star life. But while it was happening, it felt like I was running for my life. Reaching the bus first, I yelled at the Screw U band to get on fast. They just continued to stare stupidly at the oncoming crowd. I yelled at them again and they hustled on, their heads all cocked to witness this tour highlight. I made sure The Noise's four guys got on before I jumped in and ordered the driver to floor it. I could see fingers almost being stuck inside the bus door when it closed shut.

As we swung around the side of the building, we saw the throngs of fans running into the parking lot. The driver swerved into the loading dock and beeped his horn. Aapo came out the club's back door and ran to the bus, a big grin on his face.

"Man, am I glad to see you guys!" he enthused. I moved over and patted the seat next to mine. Aapo dropped into it with a big sigh and then turned to me and ruffled my hair. "Good job, Tammy," he said. "Mission accomplished!"

I decided I was going to spend more time with this fellow.

•••••••••

That night, before the show, I found Aapo in the crew's dressing room. I think it was more of a storage area than a dressing room. Extra tables and chair were stacked against one wall. Lining another wall were boxes of old programs, upon which the crew settled their belongings. The third wall displayed bags of musty material which I assumed were old curtains. Against the fourth wall was a motley assortment of broken speakers and non-working cables. Aapo sat at the lone table set up in the middle of the room. He was staring at a video camera.

"The Noise is starting soon," I said. "I think they're going to need your help with security. It's a full house."

Aapo looked up morosely. "Brad wanted me to shoot some video of the band tonight," he muttered. "Went out and bought a camera and a case and everything."

"Did he remember to buy film?" I asked.

Aapo raised a cartridge. "That's not the problem," he said. "I don't know how to work these things! Give me a monitor, give me a sound board; I can probably figure that out. But a video camera?"

"Let me look at that," I said. In reality, I knew that type of camera quite well. A bunch of us kids used to mess around with one, shooting skateboarding and pot smoking scenes. When Kitty suggested we should get one to record the kids, I bought the newest version on the market. I had a lot of fun with that camera. Not much footage of Rain or the twins but I captured every square inch of Axel's nude body. The camera had been taken away from me as punishment when Kitty showed the neighbour what she thought was footage of the sand castle Rain created at the beach.

Within seconds, I had the camera up and running. I showed it to Aapo, saying, "The main thing is you have to use the power button. That gets it started." I pressed Record, shot a few seconds of Aapo's amazed face and then pressed Stop. I let Aapo watch as I rewound the tape, pressed Play and he saw his dumbfounded immobile look. It may as well have been a photograph instead of a video.

"Now you try it," I said, giving him the camera. He pointed it at me and I pirouetted, I blew a kiss, I curtsied. "Enough, shut it off," I said.

He pressed a button and I went to view his handiwork. There was the shot…er, footage of Aapo's face and then nothing but fuzz. Aapo did not succeed. I showed him once more how to hit the Record button and made a sweeping shot of the dressing room. I ended on his face (now looking nervous) and then showed him how to press Stop. Again with the Rewind and with Play. He grunted as I showed him each step, apparently absorbing the information.

I handed him the video camera again. "Now you try it," I said. This time I just posed for a few seconds, then waved and said, "Hi, Bradley." I told Aapo to hit Stop and he made a big stab at the button. I ran to his side to see if he'd captured my inner beauty.

Nothing but the footage I had shot. "I don't know what you're doing wrong, Aapo."

"It's my fingers! They're too big for those little buttons," he decided. "I can't do this." He looked up at me. "But you can, Tammy! You're like a professional with a video camera." I didn't correct him but really, I didn't take great videos. I just knew how to work the camera. "Would you mind taking some video of the band tonight?" Aapo pleaded.

At that precise moment, I did want to do something nice for Aapo. At the shabby restaurant earlier tonight, I'd entered late and the place was crowded. I saw a spot beside Axel but didn't want to sit there. Aapo called my name and waved me over to the crew's booth. They managed to squeeze me in. Even though an ass cheek hung over the seat and one crew member reeked of B.O., I was happier there than sitting beside Axel.

I agreed to Aapo's idea. "Sure, why not? I've seen the show a bunch of times now. I know the good parts to shoot."

"Bradley wants a bunch of footage of his hair," Aapo instructed me.

"I'm sure he does," I replied. Bradley had a great head of hair and he used it to the best of his ability. It was almost like an extension of himself. It seemed his hair could look sad when Bradley was unhappy, or electrically charged when Brad was hyper. Even women were insanely jealous of that freaking amazing hair.

Aapo handed me the video camera. "Thanks, Tammy," he grinned. "You're saving my butt, once again."

Ten minutes later I was in the front row of the audience. I saw Aapo had indeed been put to good use monitoring the crowd and he managed to get me up front and centre. "Remember the hair," he reminded me.

Like I said, I'm no videographer. My hand was unsteady, I was jostled by the concert attendees, I used the zoom button with wild abandon… but I managed to capture the band putting on a great show. All four members of The Noise saw I was videotaping them and they all tried to be the star of my cartridge.

Nobody behaved more outrageously than Bradley. Besides the shaking/rippling/convulsing/seducing antics of his hair, I filmed him doing some new and shocking moves. At one point he bent down to the screaming girls in the front row. As my zoom button zeroed in, it caught Bradley grab one girl around the neck and haul her in for a kiss. The camera distinctly showed his tongue sliding into her mouth.

Then there was this dance move he was trying out which apparently was going over quite well with the crowd. It involved a slow swivelling of his hips; a bit raunchy but you couldn't keep your eyes off him when he did it. Lately Bradley had been adding more dancing into his stage performance and now he could see for himself how well it was working for him.

Of course I caught his hair in action. At one point, I filmed his poor hair in agony as Bradley played air-guitar next to Tate, the lead guitarist. He did an about-face to move off but a knob on Tate's guitar caught his hair. It was a brief moment, but rather humorous, as Tate did his own about-face in the opposite direction and the guitar pulled Bradley backwards. They handled it well by just yanking Brad's hair off the guitar knob and not missing a beat.

Between songs, I filmed the audience cheering, fans crying, the crush at the front of the stage. My viewfinder happened upon Aapo and a member of the club's security. They were wrestling a struggling man away from the fifth row. As the band started another tune, my lens sought out the cause of the disturbance. There, among the cheering fans, were three people not watching the stage. A man, bleeding from his nose, was surrounded by two women. One was rubbing the man's head while the other pulled a sanitary pad from her purse, ripped it open and held it to the man's nostrils. He looked at it and slapped it away.

After the show, there was the usual party. I left the camera in my room but was ready to run back and get it, should anybody say the word. I didn't see Aapo yet, but noticed Bradley standing by a table laden with snacks. I sidled up next to him. He was in a bit of a pout.

"Chips. Cheesies. More fucking pretzels," he complained. "I can get fucking pretzels at the pub. Hey, you're the girl with the apple, aren't you?"

"Yeah, my name's Tammy," I replied, not adding, 'you prick, I've only been on the same tour bus with you for a month.'

"Tammy, huh? Well, tell me, you wouldn't happen to have any more of that health food, would you?"

I nodded. "It's just some fruits and vegetables. Mini-carrots. Some plums, bananas…oh, I got walnuts and pecans…."

"You got nuts too?" Bradley's eyes shone. He gave a derisive look at the food table. "Back home, ya know? I try to eat better than this crap. I don't mind junk food now and then, but every goddam night?"

"It's what the hotels think you want," I said. "If you want something out of the ordinary, you have to put that in your contract."

"Tell me, would a fuckin' mini-carrot be so out of the ordinary?"

Bradley griped.

"If you want, I can speak to the rest of the hotels along the tour," I suggested. Word was bound to get out, likely with enhanced-sound by Axel himself, that we had split up. Since I no longer felt the need to iron my ex-boyfriend's cowboy shirt with the delicate pearl buttons, or fetch him a coffee with four sugars, or sleep with him, Axel would declare me unnecessary weight on the tour.

The breakup was risky business as it would likely result in me getting sent home. Maybe I had enough money to eke out the remaining weeks of the tour but I certainly didn't have enough to get back to Toronto. Not unless I planned on thumbing a ride the whole way. I was hoping to make myself seem useful; it may buy me a few more days on the bus.

Bradley threw an arm around me. "If you could do that, I'd love you forever!"

"I'll get on it first thing tomorrow morning," I said, pulling a long strand of Bradley's hair out of my mouth.

"As for right now, ya think you can spare a little of your bounty?" Bradley asked. "Couple pieces of fruit, but some pecans for sure! Ya think?"

I ran back to my room and grabbed both bags of food. I also threw the video case over my shoulder. Seeing as how Bradley now deigned to talk to me, maybe I could show him some footage of the concert? I'd taken a quick look at what I'd shot - not great in general, but some good moments. Maybe too much hair though.

Upon re-entering the party, I stopped dead in my tracks. I had been gone all of four minutes. In that time, Bradley had managed to find a willing paramour and they were going at it on the couch. Vinnie sat next to the couple, oblivious to their heavy petting. Bradley glanced up and saw me staring.

"Oh, hey babe, you got the health food?" he asked, pushing away the mouth of Various Blonde #20 on this trip.

"It's just fruits and vegetables," I mumbled, looking away as I saw Bradley's hand kneading the woman's breast. He took it away long enough to point to the food table.

"Just leave it on the table," he said, his hand going back to the woman's boob. "Have no fear, I'm gonna get to it, soon as I'm done with Verna here."

"It's Roberta," came the groupie's muffled voice as she nuzzled his neck.

I backed up and put the bags on the table. Left holding the camera case, I decided it wasn't the right time to show it to Bradley. Maybe nobody else either…Vinnie was having his nightly squabble with his girlfriend, BiBi. Kevin and one of The Noise's girlfriends were looking through the latest issue of Bride Magazine. She seemed seriously interested in Kevin's opinions. The fourth member of Screw U, the new drummer named Benny, sat silently in the corner of the room. He was not a handsome man and very imposing in size. Once you got to know him, he was a pleasant fellow. That's if you could get past his scary outer persona and want to talk to him. By the end of the party, there was usually one drunk girl who would settle for him. Benny took what he could get.

Axel wasn't around but neither were a few other people, such as Aapo. I really didn't want to go back to my hotel room but I didn't know where else to go. I also didn't want to misplace the video camera.

Upon entering my suite, the first thing I smelled was smoke and I could see some form of flames flickering. I was about to scream "Fire!" when Axel's arm reached out and he pulled me into the room.

"What the hell, Axel!" I yelled. Stumbling into the suite, I could see there were about a hundred little tea candles lit. "Are you trying to burn down the place?"

"I'm trying to romance you back," Axel murmured, drawing me in for a big smooch. I shoved him off.

"So you lit a bunch of candles?" I asked cynically. "What else did you have in mind to win me back?"

"Uh…just the candles," he confirmed. "Oh, and this….," he said, trying to draw me back in for a kiss.

I reached my arms around his back, but only to flick on the switch located behind him. The room flooded with light. "You think setting the room on fire is romantic?" I spat out. "You know what's romantic? Not cheating on your girlfriend!"

"It won't happen again," the words easily tumbled out of his mouth.

"Did it happen before today?" I asked.

"No."

"Look me in the eye and tell me the truth," I ordered.

He looked me in the eye. "Yeah," he acknowledged.

"Look, Axel, I'm glad you took me on this tour, but it's not going to work out between us," I stated. Walking to the couch, I noticed it turned into a sofa bed. I pulled it out. "Bradley wants me to do some work for him tomorrow, so I need to get to bed."

"Alone?" he asked.

"Don't be dense, Axel!" I let out a sigh. "Yes, alone. But you can have the bed and I'll crash here tonight. You're the big rock star; you need a good sleep."

That seemed to assuage his feelings and he left to join the party. Poor Benny - last minute competition was on the way.

• • • • • • • • • •

Before leaving the hotel the next morning, I made a few phone calls. Instead of calling the upcoming hotels on the tour, I called The Noise's management company. Speaking on behalf of Bradley, I made it seem like a simple request - less junk, more nutrition. They reported they'd be happy to oblige. As Aapo liked to say, "Mission accomplished."

Speaking of Aapo, he joined us at the cafe before heading out for downtown Chicago. This was the biggest event of the tour - a two- night gig that, at last report, was almost sold out. We were digging into our bacon and eggs when a loud whoop came out of BiBi, Vinnie's girl. She'd been quietly reading the newspaper earlier and now she was standing in the aisle, waving it around.

"You guys are not going to believe this!" she screeched. "You made the paper!"

"It's not the first time," Bradley yawned.

"Beeb, sit down," Vinnie ordered.

BiBi brought the paper to Vinnie's face and then threw it onto the table. "Sorry, dork, that it wasn't your band," she said politely. Vinnie looked at the paper with disinterest at first and then he clutched it.

"Oh man! You can't buy publicity like this!" he yelped. "Brad! You see this?"

Bradley reached over to an empty table and took a newspaper off it. "What page?" he asked. "Is it a picture or just a story?"

BiBi looked at the paper in front of her boyfriend. "Page forty," she said. "First page of the Entertainment section."

Bradley flipped his hair away from the paper. This morning he seemed slightly hungover, a little under the weather. Suddenly his hair got some bouncy curl in it and he lifted his head in wonder. "Oh my God," he gasped. "Is this us or the Beatles?"

As the two newspapers were passed around, a strange enlightenment seemed to settle on The Noise. "We look like we're a mega super group," Bradley mused, then looked over at me. "You said we needed real publicity but how the hell did you manage this?" He kept shaking his head. I shrugged; I hadn't even seen the photo yet.

When it came into my hands, I was astonished at the picture. It showed the members of The Noise running pell mell for the bus, a horde of fans not far behind. I thought my running body should have been in the shot, but then I saw the bus door was open. I could make out the bottom of my legs. The photo was taken as I was urging the boys to get on the bus.

Reading the article, I could see the photographer had a fluke of good luck. He'd accompanied a staff reporter to file a story on the new statue of President Clinton being installed. His camera was at the ready when he heard the fans screaming. Though he was almost a football field's length away, his mighty zoom lens captured the scene as if he were steps from the action. It was a damn good photograph. I had a feeling that besides boosting The Noise's profile, this shot would put the photographer on the map.

"I like how your hair looks," BiBi told Bradley. She was always kissing up to Bradley. If he asked her to drop Vinnie and be his girlfriend, she'd do it in a heartbeat. "It's flying behind you like a scarf," she added.

I had to agree. Had Bradley been the first in line of the running group, his hair would have obliterated his bandmates' faces and the photo would have just been OK. With him last in line and his billowing hair mere feet from the fans, it added to the urgency of the photo.

"Hey, guys," Aapo announced, "we gotta get going. See you at the Arena."

Everybody started to make motions to leave. Bradley came to my table and picked up my bill. "Breakfast is on me," he said. "And before we leave, you buy as many of those newspapers as you can." He handed me twenty dollars.

I took the money and nodded. In a joking voice, though I really meant it, I said, "Don't leave without me!"

Once on the bus to the Arena in downtown Chicago, things got back to normal. We were heading straight for the sound check. I didn't want to go there in support of Axel but I didn't have anywhere else to go. I took the video camera with me as I set up camp in a seat in the auditorium. Usually I'd hang out in the dressing room but I no longer felt I had the right.

As I ran through some of the footage on the camera, I was surprised when Bradley sat down next to me. "What are you doing out here?" he asked. "Nobody watches a sound check. Why aren't you in the dressing room?"

May as well come clean now. "Well, Axel and I aren't really together anymore," I confessed. I was expecting some pity, maybe a bit of compassion, when Bradley grabbed the camera from me.

"Hey, is that my camera?" he asked.

"It's the one you gave Aapo to shoot some video of you guys," I said. "I ended up shooting it."

"Yeah, saw you….," Bradley muttered as he intently studied the playback.

"Brad!" one of the road crew hollered from the stage. "We're ready for The Noise soundcheck now."

Bradley glanced up and then back at the camera. "Coming!" he yelled back. He watched the playback for another few minutes. "Not bad, babe," he gave me faint praise. "But do you think my hair is getting too long?"

I took a deep breath and then said, "Maybe. There's another scene where your hair gets caught on a guitar. I'll show you that later."

"I remember that! Fuckin' Tate just rips my hair out!" The roadie called out to Brad again, saying they were only waiting on him. Bradley handed me the camera. "You go sit in our dressing room with this," he commanded. "I wanna watch it after we finish up the sound check."

Like a dutiful unpaid employee, I obeyed Bradley's orders. Waiting in the dressing room were a couple girlfriends. We said our "hey's" to each other and went back to doing our own thing. The groups on tour were close to their bandmates, always joking and spending time with each other. The girlfriends on the other hand - we acted like ships passing in the night. Who knew how long we'd last or who'd be replacing us tomorrow?

As soon as sound check was over, Bradley was the first to enter the dressing room. He bounded over to me and grabbed the camera. He fiddled around for a couple seconds before handing it back. "I don't have a clue how to operate that thing," he announced. "Can you rewind it and show me the whole tape?"

As he watched about sixty minutes of concert footage, the dressing room emptied. A roadie came into the room to warn us the tour bus was going to the hotel and not coming back until showtime.

"We'll make our way there later," Bradley shooed him away. Did he say 'we'? But I didn't get on the tour bus either.

The only part of the video that Bradley didn't like was when his hair got stuck. "Don't worry," I consoled him. "It all happened so fast, I'm sure none of the audience caught it."

"It's not the first time though," Brad mentioned. "Maybe we should stop doing that move on stage, but I like it. It's sexy."

"Could be your hair is too long?" I ventured, waiting for lightning to strike.

"I was thinking that myself," Bradley allowed. "Maybe I need a haircut?"

"It probably wouldn't hurt," I kept testing the water. "Just a couple inches, kind of clean it up."

"I know where there's scissors! Up on the stage," Bradley said. I expected him to tell me to fetch them immediately but he stood up and ran out of the room. "I'll be right back!" he said.

He returned with a giant pair of industrial scissors. Actually, they may be called shears at that point. Handing them over to me, he said, "Give me a haircut."

Now, I've even cut hair before, hanging out with drunken stoned friends who think they suddenly need a trim. And if there is one thing that I'm worse at than videotaping, it's haircutting. Still, the way he asked that I simply get to it…it made me believe in myself. I took the shears and started hacking.

Fifteen minutes later, Bradley had six inches missing from the bottom of his hair. Not a professional job by any stretch of the imagination, but since his hair was so accommodating, the different lengths all merged into one luscious hairdo. "Not bad, babe," Bradley admired himself in the dressing room mirror.

There was no broom so I took a piece of cardboard from a beer case and just scraped all the hair from the floor into a pile. I pushed the pile into a spot under a table, hoping the cleaners would appreciate my effort. There was enough hair to make a full-blown wig; it almost looked like a black cat was napping there.

We grabbed a cab to the new hotel and parted ways. He checked in while I found Axel's room. Knocking on the door a few times, he finally answered. Obviously he'd been napping and I woke him. "What do you want?" he asked in a grouchy fashion.

"I was going to see if I could sleep in your room," I said, trying to be as pleasant as possible. "Seeing as how you were the one to ask me to go on this trip."

"Are you going to sleep with me?" he sneered. I saw there was only one bed and no couch at all, just two armchairs. "And by sleep with me, I mean you'll also be fucking me."

"Didn't I mention we were absolutely through, Asshole?" I said as I turned to leave. That would be the last time I would speak to him. I returned to the lobby and approached the front desk. "Do you have a room for tonight?" I asked.

"Not really," the clerk gave me an apologetic look. "Just a fancy suite on the top floor." She told me the price and I blanched. Giggling, she whispered, "I'll let you in on a little secret….there's going to be a big party in the suite next to it…a certain rock band is in town…"

I took the luxury suite. Don't ask me why. I could have given in and screwed Axel for one more night's sleep. I could have slept in the tour bus. Maybe I could have found a cheaper place. I just didn't want to stray far from my 'family'. I didn't go out for supper with my eclectic bunch though. Suddenly all my funds fit into my change purse.

Returning with ice for the bathroom tap's fine water, I ran into Aapo. "You don't look ready for the concert," he noticed. "The bus is leaving in a few minutes."

"I'm not going," I said, then proceeded to burst into tears.

In a flash, Aapo was by my side. "Hey, hey, cookie," he consoled me. "I heard - you and Axel, totally kaput, huh?"

"That's not it," I sniffled. "I couldn't be happier about that. It's just… I'll probably be sent home now. Axel made sure I'm not registered as one of the band's guests so I had to get my own room. I can't afford it…."

Aapo patted my back. "Look, you've got the room for tonight so there's nothing we can do to change that," he noted. "But until the time comes for us to go home, you can bunk with me. Everybody in the crew gets their own room and I've got a big mattress. OK?" I nodded against his chest. Things were turning out swell - maybe I'd even get to bed him! "Now, you coming to the concert or not?"

"I'm not ready," I said, pointing to the pyjamas I'd already donned. "Maybe I'll take a walk later and swing by the Arena."

He left me in much better spirits. I went into my Presidential Suite to make myself presentable, mainly for Aapo. A long bath, lots of perfume, extra make-up and a slutty outfit. I looked like a veritable rock star myself.

By the time I reached The Arena, the air was cool and crisp, making me appreciate the warm leather jacket I had yet to return to Axel. It fit me better than it hung on his skinny frame. Instead of going through the front door and encountering ticket-takers who didn't know me from Cher, I headed to the back where I knew the stage entrance was located.

A throng of fans were crammed into the back lane. There must have been close to five hundred people. Some had autograph books and a few clutched newspapers in which I saw the recent photo of The Noise. Many held cameras at the ready. One girl near the back was sobbing. "I love Bradley so much! I would move to Canada just to breathe the same air as him!"

Her friend held up a mirror. "Look, your mascara is running," she pointed out. "The band has to come out this door. You don't want Bradley to see you like this." The crybaby grabbed the mirror and started scrubbing off the undesired look.

I stepped up to them. "Why didn't you guys just buy a ticket and go see the show?" I asked quite pleasantly.

"Who are you? The concert police?" the sniffling girl spat out.

The other woman gave me an apologetic look on her friend's behalf. "We couldn't get in," she explained. "It's sold out. Tomorrow night as well."

I smiled. "Ahhh, good for the boys!"

"What, you know them?" Miss Boo Hoo asked.

"You could say that," I replied smugly.

As I elbowed my way through the crowd, a persistent whisper seemed to follow me. "She knows the band…she knows The Noise." I wasn't about to turn around and make the pronouncement: "To be perfectly clear, I'm much more acquainted with Screw U."

Once I reached the first fans in the line, I saw Aapo manning the door, along with two hired security guards. He shoved a couple fans aside so that I could reach him. "Hey!!" yelled an irate guy. "Why does she get to be front of the line?"

"She's going inside," Aapo yelled back. "She's with the tour."

"Oh, darlin'!" shouted a woman in her forties. "Do me a favour and bring me a lock of Bradley's hair!"

"Oh, me too!" came a female voice from further back. "He's got the sexiest hair!"

I rolled my eyes at Aapo. "Crazy people," I whispered as he led me to the door. In a louder voice, I said, "I see you got help."

"You should see the front of the stage," Aapo replied. "Solid wall of security. I like ShyTown. Hey, you cleaned up good."

I pretended to blush as I squeezed by him to enter the venue. Before the door had even shut behind me, I could hear a new rumour passing down the lane. "She's with the band…she's with The Noise." I had to grin at the nonsense of some fans. But before I even took three steps, the smile fell off my face.

That lady's southern-accented voice sounded in my head. "Bring me a lock of Bradley's hair!" It was kind of weird but by coincidence, I knew where a lock of Bradley's hair could be located. Lots of locks even. Under a table in The Noise's dressing room! Unless the cleaning staff had been through…

Instead of going to the stage area as I'd originally planned, I sprinted to the dressing room. There was a roadie outside the door. He was standing on a chair and holding three guitar picks to an overhead lightbulb. He jumped when he saw me racing toward him.

"Yo! You almost made me fall off the chair!" he scolded me. "Nobody's allowed back here except the band." I was about to explain who I was when he climbed down. "Oh, wait, I know you," he said, looking me in the chest. "You're Axel's girlfriend." I just sort of shrugged. "Look, I gotta get these to the band. They're a new gimmick we're trying out."

"Guitar picks?" I questioned. "They been around…"

"Glow-in-the-dark guitar picks!" he corrected me. "They're going to start their encore in pitch blackness and hopefully, all you're going to see is the guitar picks moving. For the first ten seconds, that is, then we bring up the stage lights." He climbed back up on the chair and fanned the three picks against the bulb.

"That should look cool," I said in a monotone, trying to figure out how to get around his chair.

The roadie nodded. "I invented them myself. I just hope they have a big impact. Bradley said he wanted to be the band to give them a shot." Suddenly the roadie froze, like a bad cramp had caught him. I could hear The Noise giving their "Thank you (insert city name)! You've been great! We love you!" salutation. That meant they'd huddle just offstage for a couple minutes while the crowd clamoured for an encore.

"It's time," the roadie whispered. He jumped off the chair and turned to me. "Can you watch the dressing room for me?" I nodded as he ran off, holding the guitar picks like they were made of priceless ivory.

I didn't waste another second. Throwing the chair aside, I ran into the dressing room. The first thing I saw was a McDonald's coffee cup laying on the floor. I knew it had been there earlier today. Surely a halfassed cleaner would pick that up.

With a shaky breath, I looked under the table where I'd shoved the mound of hair. The row of make-up lights on the wall above lit the scene and I saw a pile that looked like it could fill a pillowcase. I had nothing in which to put the hair.

Through the walls of The Arena, I could hear The Noise begin the first of two encore songs. I ran around the dressing room, searching for a container of any sort, whether it be a baggie or a backpack. Nothing presented itself. The band began their last song.

Gathering my wits for a moment, I thought to myself, "What do you plan on doing with this hair?" Maybe for a second I thought I'd be a good Samaritan and deliver a lock to the fan outside. But the fact that I was next to broke, and the realization that fans might be willing to spend money on foolish things, made me go to Plan B. I was going to sell Bradley's hair.

Not wanting to hand tufts of it out of my pocket, my eyes scanned the room. There was a briefcase sitting on the couch. Brazenly, I clicked it open. Inside were various papers; contracts and the like, usual business things. Near the bottom I found a sheaf of stickers.

It was obvious these were promotional materials meant to be given away. Each page had a dozen square stickers, all with 'THE NOISE!' written in various colours on it. I'd never seen these stickers in circulation. I supposed the reason for it was because The Noise didn't have an exclamation mark after their name.

I thieved the stickers and slammed the briefcase shut just as I heard the guys coming down the hall. I spotted a Darlin' Donuts box under the couch and grabbed it. Opening it quickly to stuff the hair in, I gagged when I spotted a used condom in it. I flicked it onto the floor and shovelled the hair in as quickly as possible. I stood up as the band entered. Holding onto the donut box, I bent down to pick up the coffee cup on the floor.

"Just cleaning up in here," I said mildly. The band totally ignored me. I moseyed out of the area and ran into the crew's dressing room. As I thought, the room was empty since the crew were tending to postshow duties.

Though I had no idea how this would pan out - and it felt like I was flying by the seat of my pants - I hunkered down and quickly went to work. Ripping off a sticker, I'd grab a lock of Bradley's shorn hair and adhere it to the sticky side of the paper. I then loosely put it back onto the sheet and pulled off another sticker.

Within fifteen minutes, I'd gone through the donut box of hair. I grabbed a pen out of my purse and tried to think of a catchy name. From the sounds of it, The Noise were about five minutes from leaving. What to call this new enterprise? Nothing came to me, other than the sound of that woman's voice, telling me to bring…

Ah, fuck it. On the first sticker, around the THE NOISE! logo, I wrote "A Lock of Bradley's Hair." It wasn't original but it stated the obvious. And though my penmanship was nothing to brag about, I was ready to rock when The Noise left their dressing room.

• • • • • • • • • •

The Noise were in high spirits as they made their way to the exit door. It had been a good day, what with the newspaper photo and the sold-out shows. Tonight had been one of their best performances yet and they were laughing about the guitar picks.

"I couldn't even see my strings, but that pick was like a piece of hot lava in my hand!" Tate said.

"We should do a whole concert in the dark!" Bradley jokingly suggested. "We gotta tell Winston how good they worked."

"I didn't see anything," the drummer groused.

And nobody saw me as I followed them to the exit. I hung back as the door opened. The thick walls of The Arena didn't prepare The Noise for what was waiting on the other side.

"It's them!" "I see Bradley!" "Sign my t-shirt!" "Tate, sign my tits!" "Bradley, look this way!" The boys lost a little swagger as they allowed the security guards to surround them. In a huddle, they shuffled en masse to the waiting tour bus.

Even Aapo didn't see me as I stood in the open doorway. He was too busy blocking the fans as they reached out for Bradley's hair. I spied a rickety metal chair behind the stage door and pulled it toward me. I wedged it into the opening of the door, just so that it barely appeared open, and then faced the crowd. Everybody had their backs to me. I didn't know how to begin.

"Darlin'! Where you guys all staying tonight?" a voice rang out. It was THAT VOICE! My eyes roved the fans, looking for that fortyish-year-old woman. I spotted her jumping up and down to get a final look at Bradley as he boarded the bus. I made my way over to her.

"Hi, remember me?" I greeted her.

She barely glanced at me. "No, sorry," she said, looking back at the departing bus. "Should I?"

"I'm the girl on tour with...with The Noise," I said. Again, I was actually with Screw U who was touring with The Noise, but she didn't need to know precise details. "You yelled at me that you wanted a lock of Bradley's hair."

"Yeah, wouldn't that be nice," she deadpanned.

"Well, I have some if you're looking," I replied, then shuddered. It was a line I'd heard many drug dealers use.

"You didn't!" she said incredulously. "You got me a lock of Bradley's hair?"

I nodded. "It's what I do. I sell Bradley's hair." I showed her a sample. She read the writing on the sticker.

"And that's what you call your company?" she asked. "A Lock of Bradley's Hair?"

"Yup, thought you knew that by the way you called out to me," I lied through my teeth. "Well, I gotta get to work. You buying or what?"

"And it's for real?"

"Yeah, get it DNA checked if you want," I said. "But you know me; I'm with the band. This is legit Bradley's hair."

"How much?" she asked.

This was going too fast. I hadn't even considered the price. I plucked a figure out of thin air. "Twenty bucks," I said.

In seconds she was waving two tens at me. "I'll take the longest one you have!" As soon as I handed the sticker over, another fan witnessed the transaction.

"Hey, whaddaya selling there?"

"A Lock of Bradley's Hair," I answered loudly, causing a few heads to swivel my way. "Limited edition. Fresh today. Get 'em while they're hot."

"How much?"

"Twenty bucks."

"Will you take ten?"

I was tempted but wanted to see how this played out. "Sorry, that'll only buy you one hair. Twenty gets you a whole lock."

"Fine, give me a lock."

The crowd grew larger around me once it was clear The Noise wasn't returning for a lost wallet or anything. Nobody questioned the authenticity of the hair anymore; it was as if the whole crowd accepted that I was selling the real deal.

As I saw I was getting down to the last couple stickers, I started backing toward the stage door. "Alright everybody, I'm pretty much sold out," I shouted. Somebody tugged at my jacket and waved a couple tens in my face. "Please!" a voice begged. I pulled off my second-last sticker and gave it to the pitiful fan.

A glance behind me showed I was mere steps from the door. It was time to make a dash for it. I turned from the crowd and almost ran head-on into the "older" woman.

"Darlin', I just wanna thank you again for the hair," she gushed. "Did you smell it? It smells so clean and…happy…" Her throat welled up and she couldn't continue. I stepped around her, putting her between me and the crowd.

Turning back to her, I ripped off the last sticker. "It's me who should be thanking you," was all I said. I handed it to her and she gaped at me for a moment before bringing the lock of hair up to her nose.

Kicking the chair out of the way, I turned back to the approaching mass of people and yelled, "Sold out!" Slamming the door behind me, I ran through the Arena, right to the other end of the building. I left via the front doors, along with the departing staff.

I hailed a cab to get back to the hotel. It wouldn't have been far to walk but my purse was laden with twenties. I had three sheets of stickers. 12 stickers a page. 36 stickers but I gave one away so I sold 35. 35 at twenty bucks a pop....

You have got to be kidding. I did the math three times, although I knew I was pretty smart when it came to my multiplication tables. I had seven hundred smackers in my purse! Isn't that what Axel told me he was making per week on this tour? And here I made this in about twelve minutes.

Seven hundred bucks. Enough to see me through the tour, if I laid off the booze and drugs. Selling Bradley's hair was supposed to be a one-off thing but I instantly knew I was going to try this again.

CHAPTER V

Breakfast the next morning, 'round about noon, was a joyous affair. The Noise had their picture in the newspaper again, though it was nowhere as whimsical as the conga line photo. Today's paper offered a more sombre and sinister side of showbiz.

The shot showed the band as they were being hustled onto the tour bus. The drummer and the bass guitarist had grim looks on their faces. Tate's eyes looked wary. Bradley was looking back at the crowd but most of his face was hidden by his hair. Both edges of the frame had various arms straining to touch the rockstars.

"It's a cool shot," Tate commented. "Very dramatic, I will say."

"Any publicity is good," Bradley said. "But I don't like the way you can't see my face."

His statement put an idea into my head. On the tour bus, as we made our way to Milwaukee, I sat in a seat that enabled me to keep an eye on Bradley. He slept most of the way but as we neared our destination, I saw him stretch and then let out a loud, ten-second fart. BiBi, seated a few seats away, giggled and said, "That was cute, Brad."

Brad stood up, stretched once more and then moved to the rear of the bus. I saw him enter the commode. Acting nonchalant, as if the call of nature had just suddenly hit me, I picked up the newspaper and made the same walk to the bathroom. As I got to the door, I glanced at the locked handle.

"Oh? Someone's in here?" I asked of no-one in particular. I opened up the newspaper to the current photo of The Noise and waited.

Bradley was either doing a few lines or had to leave a number two as long minutes passed. Finally the door opened.

"Hey, it's you," I blocked his passage. "What a coincidence. I was just looking at your picture in the paper."

"Yeah, I seen it already," Brad said, waiting for me to move aside. "Excuse me, gonna get back to my nap."

"Sure, but it's too bad we can't really see your face that good, hey?" I asked, showing him the photo to make my point.

Bradley stopped to take another look. "That's what I thought too," he agreed.

Time for the pitch. "You know, I gave you a haircut, but that was just for the length," I said. "What you need to get is a better haircut. Something that will show off that... that handsome face a bit more."

Brad was instantly on board with the idea. "You might be right! You wanna give me another haircut?" he asked brightly. "We can do it right on the bus."

I desperately wanted to give him a haircut but I was no hair stylist. If I gave him one, especially on a moving bus, the newspaper photos would be showing Bradley as the newest media clown. No, Brad required a professional.

"We've got to get you to a hair salon," I said. "Let me set up an appointment."

"Wait, we got no time for shit like that," Brad cautioned me. "We don't have a day off 'til Monday. I guess we should do it then?"

"Leave it with me," I replied with confidence. Having taken care of business, I let him pass by. Obviously I couldn't follow him back; that would blow my cover. I walked into the latrine, only to discover Bradley had not been doing cocaine after all. The tiny cubicle reeked.

Once in Milwaukee, we pulled up to a decent hotel called The Astoria. It was in a section of town surrounded by pricey restaurants and elite boutiques. As the tour bus pulled to a stop, the driver opened the door. Sherman, the band's quiet, unobtrusive tour manager, picked up his briefcase (missing anything, Sherman?) and stepped off the bus.

Before the driver had a chance to shut the door, a guy jumped on. He stood stock still as he gaped at the bus's passengers. All we could see was his head as he gasped, "Is this The Noise?"

Winston, the guitar pick roadie, spoke up. "What gave you that idea? The big painted tour bus with The Noise written all over it?" He stood up, all five feet five of him. "Get off the bus, buddy."

The man quickly jumped out. Within what seemed less than a minute, about a hundred people surrounded us. Tate and the drummer were waving at the fans. "We're getting crowds wherever we go!" Stan yelled, then jumped as a fist pounded on the window.

"We get crowds in Canada too," Tate pointed out. "They're just more civilized."

I could see Sherman walking back with his head down. Everyone ignored the unassuming man until they saw the tour bus door magically open for him. "The rooms are ready," he informed us. "Just go up to the desk, give them your name and you'll get the key. Be back on the bus in an hour for sound check."

I got off the bus with the rest of the passengers. I wanted to make sure that people saw I WAS WITH THE BAND. But once in the hotel lobby, I hung back, away from my group. I loitered at a candy vending machine while everyone checked in.

Once they had dispersed to their rooms, I approached the front desk. "Hi, I'm with that group that just checked in," I said, acting blasé. "I'd like to get my room key as well."

"What name are you registered under?" the receptionist asked.

"Aapo....," I began, but couldn't for the life of me remember his last name.

"Is that a last name?" the girl asked.

"No, first name," I corrected her.

"And the last name?" she queried.

God dang, I know he told me....I recalled mentioning there was a film character with that name...from a show I liked....Costanza? Seinfeld? "Kramer!" I blurted out, as if I'd come up with the money-winning answer. "That's it....Kramer!"

"Here you are," she found the reservation. "Room 612." The key was handed over.

"May I have a spare key?" I asked. "For my boyfriend?" Maybe not yet but who knew what tonight would bring? A second key was given to me.

Depositing my suitcase in Room 612, I took a moment to change clothes. I needed to look the part of a rock group's entourage. The baggy sweats and Disneyland t-shirt I had worn on the bus did not make the grade. A little mousse in my hair, a lot of eyeliner on my eyes, and I was ready to hit the streets.

Instead of going to the sound check, I left the hotel and took a stroll down the avenue. Before I had walked a block, I came across two hair salons. The first was a beauty parlour called Lady Elegance. I glanced inside and saw three senior citizens, their hair tightly wound in perm curlers. A woman with a frightful shade of orange hair was on the phone while the other employee folded towels. The music of Celine Dion could barely be heard. Not the place I wanted.

From twenty feet away, I could tell Comb By Ya would be a perfect place to get Bradley's hair cut, if only he could take the time to come in personally. As soon as I got inside, I was greeted by a multi-pierced man with a purple mohawk. He asked if he could be of assistance.

"I guess I could use a haircut?" I said. It hadn't been part of the plan but what the hell. I had some time to kill and I did need a trim.

"You don't have an appointment?" he asked. I shook my head. He glanced down at a schedule. "Let's see...Shriva's four o'clock is a no-show...she might be able to take you...or you could see Dawn...Dawn's available." He jerked a thumb at Dawn...or was it Don? Seated in the customer's chair was a huge black man wearing a lemon yellow halter dress with big white polka dots. He had a full face of makeup going on and long, perfectly straight blonde hair.

The only other person not working must have been Shriva. She was a tiny thing with a head full of multi-coloured curls. She had the exact haircut I had in mind for Bradley. Acting nonchalant, I said, "It doesn't matter....I guess I'll take Shriva...."

Just then the front door opened and a young woman ran in, carrying a white poodle with pink bows attached to it. "Shriva, don't be mad! I know I'm late but you have to take me!" the woman pleaded. "My husband is guest of honour at this museum benefit. I've got to look stunning."

Shriva jumped to attention. "Of course, Mrs. Van Cliffe the Second," she smiled widely. "I was saving your appointment. I'm glad you could make it."

I turned to the receptionist. "Dawn will do."

Taking a seat in Dawn's open chair, I observed him sashay over on three-inch heels and pick up a black plastic cape to drape over my shoulders. He took a long moment to admire himself in the mirror and smooth down his tresses. Leaning forward and squinting, Dawn removed a spot of lipstick from his front tooth.

I waited impatiently for him to begin the mindless chatter in which stylists engage their customer. Dawn pumped on the hydraulic step of the chair so that I was at a comfortable height for him. "So how's it going?" he asked, studying my hair.

"Just fine," I replied. He fiddled with my hair. "I only want a trim," I said.

"No problem," he said, picking up a spray bottle. "So are you married?"

"Nope," I replied. Come on, move on, move on....

"Got kids?"

"Yeah, three of them," I answered. I had to take the bull by the horns here. "They're back in Canada while I'm out here working."

"Ohhh, that's so sad," Dawn cooed. He was missing the point.

"It's OK," I said, getting back to the important thing. "Their grandma is looking after them. They understand that my job takes me away from home."

"What kind of job you got?" Dawn absently asked as he took out a comb and started to de-tangle my wet hair. I looked away from my reflection in the mirror and up to Dawn's face to gauge his reaction.

"I'm...," and I paused for a moment. What was my job? Did I have one? I gave a generalized reply. "I'm on tour with a rock band called The Noise."

And I got a hair knot pulled out with extra force as Dawn gasped. "You're with The Noise? I love The Noise! I even got tickets for their show tonight!"

Thus the plan had commenced. After getting what Dawn called "a little clean-up" on my hair, I had almost a whole new look. Better than that, I'd convinced Dawn to show up at the hotel tonight. He was going to give Bradley's mane a makeover.

It wasn't difficult to make the deal; Dawn was in from the moment I brought it up. A big fan of The Noise, especially of the lead singer Brad, this was like a lottery win. He would get to meet his idol as well as massage and touch him all that he could, within the boundaries of getting a haircut. As soon as I paid for my services, Dawn was booking the rest of the day off to run home and change his look.

He came cheap too. All I had to promise him was A Lock of Bradley's Hair.

• • • • • • • • • •

Dawn showed up in the lobby and called my room, as planned. Entering the hotel's reception area, I didn't spot him at first. I knew he was around the place since he'd called me. My vision flitted across the dozen people in the area. My eyes passed over a blond babe with ultra-long legs and a striking figure. She was checking her flawless makeup in a compact mirror. I barely spared her a glance as I looked for Dawn, but had a brief thought, "She's gorgeous but she's got man-calves."

My head swung back to the blonde woman. Was that...? I took a couple tentative steps forward when the woman - Dawn - glanced up. "Oh, sugar, there you are!" Dawn squealed. "I was so scared you wouldn't show up! I thought maybe I'm dreaming and I'm not really going to meet The Noise's singer..."

"Sssh," I hushed her, I mean him. If I didn't know Dawn was actually a six foot six man in drag, his mewling might have sounded cute. "It's all set up. Wow, Dawn, I almost didn't recognize you there."

He stood up and did a little catwalk for me. The turn and pirouette were perfect; I could tell he'd had some modelling training. "You like?" he asked. "More important, do you think Bradley will like it? I wanted to look extra bomb when I met him."

"You have boobs....," I had to point out.

"Yeah, well, it's a special occasion, wouldn't you say?" he replied, striking a pose.

"It's just a haircut, ok Dawn?" I reminded him. "You're not going to the Oscars or anything afterward."

"I'm going to their concert!" she reminded me. "I would have worn boobs for that anyhow."

Since this conversation was going nowhere, I asked Dawn to follow me. We headed to the room I shared with Aapo. I'd seen my roadie friend for all of five minutes today, just before most of the tour headed for dinner. I let him know my stuff was in the room, reminding him of his offer to let me bunk with him. Everything seemed cool. And even though our hallway chat had been brief, I knew I'd see him later tonight. In the room that I planned to have wild, passionate love-making. But for now, it would be a hair salon.

Dawn was starting to hyperventilate on our approach to Room 612. Just before we got to the suite, I stopped.

"Look, Dawn, you have to get yourself together," I sounded gruff. "There's no sense getting all worked up right now. Bradley's not even in that room."

"WHAAAAAT?" Dawn roared, his heels screeching on the tiled floor as he turned his imposing frame to me. He stepped so close that I could see the tiny pinpricks of his chest hair growing back. "You're telling me Bradley's not even here?"

"Hey, settle....settle down, big boy...big ...lady...," I stepped back. "I'm going to go get him. I just want you to go in the room and get your stuff set up."

"Ohhh...," Dawn seemed to shrink a couple inches. "So I'm still going to meet him?" he asked, ever so politely.

"You're not just going to meet him, Dawn," I corrected him. "You're here to cut his hair, remember? " Dawn nodded. "OK, then I can't have you acting like a crazy fan."

"But I am a fan," he said. "And I'm crazy about Bradley."

"Well, Dawn, listen," I shrugged. "If you can't contain yourself, then I guess the deal is off. We have less than an hour before the bus leaves for the show. We need all that time to cut off a lot of hair."

He straightened up. "OK, let's do it," he simply said.

We walked the remaining steps to the door. Maybe Dawn's small mental episode had been for the best; he seemed to have recuperated for the time being. I opened the door. "You go on in and get set up. I'll be back in a few minutes with Brad. And remember, he's got to lose a LOT of hair."

•••••••••

The lead singer of The Noise was slow to answer my knock at his door. I'd met him earlier, just as they were wrapping up their sound-check, and told him I'd arranged a haircut from a stylist at one of the chicest salons in town. The next time he performed, I said, he'd have the best haircut in all of show business.

His vanity caused him to instantly dismiss plans to join the boys for dinner. Hanging onto Vinnie's arm, BiBi put on a sad face. "We'll miss you!" she called out.

How was I to explain the spectacle awaiting him back in Room 612?

I didn't. After my first loud knock, then a second nervous knock, and finally a panicked third rapping, a sleepy, dishevelled but delicious looking Brad opened the door.

"Oh, sorry, babe," he yawned, his odorous breath wafting my way. "Just grabbin' a nap before the haircut."

"Well, let's go," I said. "We don't have much time before the band gets back and you guys leave for the show."

"Let's go then, what are we waiting for?" He led the way to the elevator. Every time I was about to tell him about Dawn, I was interrupted. "So you make sure you tell her I still want it long, OK?" I'd nod and then try to say something. But no... "And I want to have my whole face framed by hair....And no colouring, no streaks, nothing like that...."

Before you knew it, Room 612 loomed in front of me. Bradley tapped three quick times. "Can I tell you quick about Dawn?" I rushed the words out.

"Is she a hair stylist?" he asked just as fast.

"Oh, there's a hair stylist in the room, but...,"

"But she's a fan, she's gonna go crazy, I gotta prepare myself... I know, I know," Brad said.

"Just have an open mind," I whispered, hearing heels clicking in our direction.

The door swung open and Dawn was face to face with his idol. The stylist inhaled a short gasp and froze on the spot.

"Yeah, I know, babe," Bradley broke the silence. "When I'm on stage, I look amazing but in person I'm even better." Dawn could barely nod his head in agreement. "But hey, you're not so bad yourself! Shall we get on with this?" Dawn turned and walked into the seating area of the suite. Bradley elbowed me in the side. "She's hot!" he said in a low tone. "I like tall black women."

Dawn had made good use of his time. Besides having redone his mascara and lipstick, I saw instruments of the hair trade laid out in an orderly fashion. As Brad took a seat, Dawn picked up the ubiquitous black cape and raised it momentarily in front of his face. He made eye contact with me and simply mouthed the words, 'Oh my God."

Flapping the cape once, he placed it over Bradley's shoulders and lovingly pinned it at the back. Dawn took a deep breath, which caused his squished together chest-made-to-look-like-boobs to heave. Bradley caught this in the mirror and gave that look I'd seen at many after-show parties. The one that said, "You will be mine tonight."

With a slight tremor in his hand, Dawn picked up a big brush and began to comb out Bradley's mane. The singer gazed at the stylist with growing lust. "You're real gentle, aren't ya?" he asked. "So did Tammy tell you what look I'm going for?"

"I'm..." Dawn began but stopped to have a slight cough. "I'm gonna take about two inches off the bottom. "

"Make that three," I amended.

"Frog in your throat?" Bradley asked.

Dawn coughed again. "Excuse me," he said, pausing to swallow a sip of bottled water. He turned back to his client and in a raspy low voice, continued, "But I really want to add layers to your hair." Bradley jumped out of his chair and whipped around. "Yes, Tammy," Dawn agreed. "I think three inches."

"Are you a man?" Brad asked, his voice incredulous.

"Sometimes," Dawn answered. "But not tonight."

"Holy shit, I thought you were a woman!" Bradley laughed. And kept laughing. At least he didn't seem mad. Dawn and I waited him out. With sniggers still emitting, he sat back down in his chair and arranged his cape. "Who'd have thought? In Milwaukee, of all places! OK, then, darlin', (causing Dawn to perk right up), get to work. Let's see what the Belle of Milwaukee can do."

• • • • • • • • • •

Bradley thought he was good looking before? The haircut that Dawn gave him begat an international sensation. Farrah Fawcett? Jennifer Anniston? Those hairdos were forgotten as everyone, men and women alike, bombarded hair salons for the Bradley Atwater look.

After pronouncing he was done, Dawn held up a large mirror he'd brought along. He held it in such a way that Bradley could see all angles.

The rock star persona dropped for a moment as all Bradley could say was "Wow....oh, wow oh, WOW!"

"You like?" Dawn asked, already knowing he approved. Forty minutes under the scissors and Bradley came out looking like every woman's fantasy.

Bradley stood up and took off the cape. I ran to grab it from him. He handed it off then faced Dawn. In one forceful stride, he took Dawn by the shoulders. Though he was still a head shorter, he looked deep into Dawn's eyes. "I'm so frickin' happy right now, I want to kiss you."

Dawn giggled in a manly manner. "Don't let me stop you."

Brad took a tiny step back, then leaned in again for a big hug. Stepping back once more, he said, "Man, those feel quite real." We all laughed and Brad continued. "Look, Dawn, you wanna come see our show tonight?"

"He's already going," I cut in. "He bought a ticket." I looked at all the hair lying on the floor. "But he might need a ride?"

Brad got the hint. "Hey, yeah! You wanna come with us? On the bus?"

"Are you for real?" Dawn went back to her former ways. "The Noise tour bus? With the rest of the guys?"

Brad nodded. "We leave in thirty minutes. Tammy? You coming?"

I shook my head in the negative. "Nah, I don't think so. Maybe later."

"Well, you make sure Dawn gets on that bus," he ordered. "I'll see YOU later," he said, cocking a finger at Dawn.

The moment he walked out, Dawn lost all control of his body. He swooned onto the couch, legs sprawled wide open. "Did that really just happen?" he asked.

"You get used to him after a few weeks," I said, looking around the hotel room for something I could use to pick up the hair. Spotting a truck magazine on Aapo's suitcase, I used it to gather all the hair into one place.

Dawn slowly rolled his head to look at me. "I should help," he said, "but I just want to lay here a moment and relive every second."

"Don't worry, I'll clean it all up," I said. "You just lie there."

Dawn did a good job. Piles and piles of lucrative locks awaited me.

• • • • • • • • • •

Seeing the hair stylist off made a person believe in miracles. Two hours ago Dawn was just an odd person toiling away in a hair salon. In two weeks, he would be a media sensation. Right now he was being treated as

Bradley's best friend, to the amusement of his bandmates.

BiBi, bless her heart, was trying to be friends. "Oh, I love your hair!" she trilled. "Is that your natural colour?"

Dawn adjusted the blond bangs. "It's a wig, dummy," he jokingly replied.

Vinnie, BiBi's boyfriend, laughed. "You're lucky, you can get away with calling her that."

"What are you trying to say, Vinnie?" BiBi asked.

"I dunno," he rather cowered. "Maybe sometimes you are dumb."

"And maybe I don't need to go to your show tonight," she retorted, then spotted me. "Maybe I'll just stay back at the hotel with Tammy."

"No, I'm going to the show," I cut in. "Just later. You're not dumb, Beeb. Vinnie, why would you say something like that?" Really, why utter the truth so loudly? Just think it, like the rest of us.

BiBi looked up at her man, her eyes batting. "Kiss me, Vinnie."

He gave her a kiss and then some. I don't know why BiBi didn't stop his hand from mashing her ass, what with it being so public. He was acting the rock star I-don't-give-a-damn illusion and BiBi....well, enough about her brains.

The upshot was that the tour bus left with everybody aboard, except me. I ran back up to the room I shared with Aapo. There was much to be done before I caught a cab to the concert venue.

The first thing I did was rip open the bag of tea candles I'd bought in a home-decor shop. There were a hundred in the package, and I set all of them in various places throughout the room. I had splurged on the candles guaranteed to smell like white wine. Then I set up my make-shift souvenir factory - pen, stickers, hair. I'd write A Lock of Bradley's Hair as clearly as possible on each THE NOISE! stickers. Then I would grab a pinch of hair and press it to the back of the sticker. Whatever adhered would be sold for twenty bucks.

Dawn had cut so much hair that I ran out of stickers before I ran out of follicles. Pulling the clean liner from the garbage bin, I stuffed the remaining hair into it and put the bag in my suitcase. My last few minutes were spent trying to make my new haircut look the way it did when I first walked out of the salon.

Digging out a pair of thigh-high boots to go with my de rigeur black mini-skirt, I found something squashed inside the footwear. I pulled out my long-lost backstage pass. Misplacing it had not presented any problems in the past; I was always in the company of somebody who could vouch for me. However, the little card stating I was officially with the band may finally serve a mightier purpose.

The cabbie drove me directly into the melee at the backstage door. Fans who were unable to get in were crowded thickly as I alighted from the taxi. A few people who spotted me, and more importantly saw my pass, instantly created a path for me. But it wasn't long before a woman didn't bother to look at my cleavage, where the big card nestled.

"Hey, back of the line!" she yelled as she blocked my passage.

"I'm with the band," I told her civilly.

"Like hell you are," she turned her back on me.

I was just about to tap her shoulder and make her look at my pass. I was stopped by a voice over to the left of me. "Hey! I saw that girl before!" he shouted. "She was on the tour bus! She was actually with the band!"

I looked over at the gangly gentleman who was verifying my existence and saw he was the kid who'd popped onto the bus unexpectedly. I'm glad his quick and abrupt removal didn't harbour a grudge. I raised my hand and gave him a slight salute.

The nasty woman turned back to me. "Ohhhh, I'm sorry! You know the band?" she asked in a totally different voice. I nodded as I moved past her.

"Yeah, I work for them," I said fairly loudly.

The fans were making way for me. Another woman tried to grab my elbow and I rudely brushed her off. Too near my purse of goodies. "What do you do for them?" she asked, impervious to my gesture. "Can you get me in to meet them?"

I shook my head and looked over at the backstage door. Nobody I knew was there! Now I was doubly glad I'd worn my pass. I whispered confidentially to the grabby girl, now unknowingly a pawn in my business venture. "I sell stuff to fans," I began.

"Like what?" she interrupted. "T-shirts? Posters?"

The crowd began closing in behind me so I rushed the rest of my delivery. "Nah, not that. I sell stuff for the true fans...personal effects.... like locks of Bradley's hair."

"No shit?" She was stupefied. "You got a lock of Bradley's hair on you?"

I nodded. I could make a quick sale right now but didn't want to catch the eye of the security guards at the back door. "Yeah, but I can't pull it out now," I said. "I'll be back after the show, same place we are right now. Look for me."

"Oh, I will!" the girl beamed. "Hey, how much?" she asked before being swallowed by the crowd.

"Twenty bucks!" I shouted as I made my way forward. And as I hoped, the murmuring began. I heard the magical words over and over, "She's with the band." And I hoped Grabby Girl would spread the rumour that there was special goods available after the show.

• • • • • • • • • •

It was a replay of the night before, only better and even more lucrative.

The security guards let me in with no hassle - that backstage pass having mystical powers. I made my way to the side of the stage and caught the last song. I could see the hair stylist, Dawn, standing right in the front; probably not the seat he'd originally bought. I was standing on the sidelines when The Noise came off. They knew there would be an encore and waited until the right moment to go back on.

The drummer beckoned to a roadie. After a brief conversation, the roadie nodded and then walked over to Bradley. "Stan wants the redhead with the camera," he said to Brad. "If that's ok with you."

"Yeah, not interested," Brad replied.

"Anybody you want me to message?" the roadie asked.

"Nah," Brad said, then saw me standing behind a big speaker. "Hey, Tammy! You made it, good! Yo, Marlowe!" he called to the retreating roadie. "Take Tammy with you! To that big black girl standing in the front row."

The roadie stopped in his tracks. "The real tall one? The one you can't miss?" Brad nodded, a big smile on his face. "Oh...I thought that was....oh, never mind," he reconsidered pissing off his employer.

Brad pulled me closer to him as the audience's chanting for an encore grew louder. "You make sure Dawn comes backstage after," he said close to my ear. This wasn't part of the plan, but I nodded. Brad went on. "But if I'm too busy to talk to her, you bring her to the party. Got that?" Boy, this really was putting a wrench into things, but again I nodded my assent.

Joining an ecstatic Dawn, I proved I was really with the tour as I expertly made our way backstage after the encore. We tried to get into The Noise's dressing room but Sherman, the road manager, blocked the door. "Sorry, girls," he meekly apologized. "There's no time for celebrations tonight. Strictly bandmates and press." He gave a sad face and shut the door.

We stood in the hallway, along with a number of other disappointed people. Dawn slumped against the wall. "Aw, that sucks!" he looked ready to cry. "I wanted to tell Bradley how much I enjoyed the show. And to thank him for the front row centre seat."

"You see how he worked that haircut tonight?" I laughed.

Dawn sighed. "He looked like an angel. He moved like the devil." He pushed off the wall and suddenly I was engulfed in a bear hug. "I love you, Tammy. You gave me a night I'll never forget."

The bystanders began staring. I delicately withdrew from his embrace. "Come on, Miss Milwaukee, stop it, we look like flagrant lesbian lovers." Dawn dropped his arms and started to get a pouty look again. "Oh, cheer up already. The night's not over yet. Bradley wants me to take you to the after-party."

The next bear hug almost killed me. But in the darkness of his locked arms, I did some quick thinking. It appeared I was saddled with Dawn for the next little while, but I still had some business to take care of. How do I make this work? Dawn suddenly let me go.

"I gotta get myself looking fresh!" he declared. "We gotta find the ladies room!"

I didn't want to miss The Noise's exit, so I suggested the closest one - next door in Screw U's dressing room. They had a couple groupies in there with them; I saw an overweight one sitting on Axel's lap as I walked in. Axel glanced up, saw it was me and shoved the girl from his knees.

Walking over to Axel, I helped the girl off the ground. With a grunt, I got her up and then placed her right back on Axel's lap. "You two make a nice couple," I told her.

Dawn waited for me while this took place. I rejoined him, ignoring Axel's comeback line. "You two make a nice couple," he sniped.

"The washroom's this way," I said.

"Come in with me," Dawn requested.

As we shared the washroom, I looked aside as he took a piss sitting down. The next few minutes were spent adding more eyeliner to his eyes. Taking out a compact, he began applying powder to reduce the shine on his face. It was time to outline a faint plan.

"Look, Dawn, you know I've seen the show a hundred times already," I exaggerated. "I don't need to see it every time. I came down tonight 'cuz I have some business to take care of. So after the band leaves, I do my thing, and then we go to the party. It won't take long."

"You're not going to ditch me, are you?" Dawn asked in a low growl.

"No! Actually, maybe you can help me," I said, an idea formulating. I was about to explain when I heard Screw U suddenly start packing up. A hard knock came on the washroom door.

"Bus is ready to go!" Tate's voice called.

"We're not going on it," I yelled back, then whispered to Dawn. "Just follow me, but don't talk to anybody." Dawn gave me a questioning look but did as I asked.

Lagging steps behind the departing bands, almost lurking in the background, Dawn witnessed the bands' exit method. First Screw U departed. Loud screams went up, anticipating The Noise, then dropped suddenly, almost disappointingly, when they saw it was Screw U. A few voices raised up again, supporters of the opening act, but Screw U safely and easily got to the tour bus.

The crowd turned back to the backstage door, hoping The Noise hadn't secretly escaped via another route. As soon as Stan, the drummer, opened the door, I saw two security guards appear. They stood side by side, acting as blockers for the band. The sound from the crowd was shrill - screams and whistles and near pandemonium. There were four more guards behind us in the tunnel. One of them shouted out, "We got your backs, guys! Just stay together, don't stop, just get to the bus."

Dawn whispered in my ear, "Oh, my God, this is so exciting! It's almost scary!"

"Ssshhh," I hushed, making him wait until the rear flank of the security brigade had passed us. The guards were so thrilled to be a part of this madness that they didn't even notice us. We followed a few steps behind and right up to the exit door. I stopped Dawn before he walked out. "We wait here a minute," I shouted over the din.

Watching the scene unfold, I could see various fans behaving erratically. One woman, who almost resembled me in looks and figure, burst into tears the moment Bradley walked by. I saw Stan spit out a wad of gum and two fans jump onto it like zombies onto brains. It was time to get my hair samples ready.

The guards had left the door unattended. There was no chair handy to prop it open, but I had that problem looked after. "Dawn, here's where you come in," I said. "I'm gonna go do my thing now. You stay here and when you hear me knock, you got to let me in. Got that?"

"Will it be a secret kind of knock?" he asked.

"No! Just a knock!" I replied. I didn't know if what I was doing was legal and I didn't want any trouble with the security guards. "And you let me in as fast as possible. Then we go to the party right after that."

Dawn took note of Plan A. There was no Plan B. I shut the door and waded into the foray. I went back to the spot where I saw Grabby Girl and sure enough, she was there, looking wildly about. She saw me and held up a fistful of twenties. We pushed through the crowd toward each other.

"You got the hair?" she asked before even reaching me. "I got a hundred bucks!"

"You want five locks of hair?" I asked.

She gasped. "I get whole locks? I thought I just got five hairs!"

Suppressing a giggle, I said, "Hey, you're dealing with the best."

In fifteen minutes, I sold fifty locks of Bradley's hair. The security guards were breaking up the crowd. I kept making sales, but managed to get closer to the stage door. Before I caught their attention, I finished selling my wares and banged on the door.

Dawn opened it so fast, I was still knocking and almost banged him on the nose. He really wanted to go to the after-party.

• • • • • • • • • •

I stayed at the party just long enough to see Aapo arrive. The roadies always arrived late, unless we had another gig at the same venue the next night. There was equipment to be loaded onto the truck, cords to be wrapped, work to be done. As soon as my room-mate roadie walked in, I started to stretch and yawn.

"Whew! Long day!" I walked over to Dawn and gave him a hug. "It was great to meet you, Dawn, but I've got to get to bed. We'll keep in touch, ok?" I sauntered over to the door and just called out, "Good night everybody!"

Aapo was standing in the entrance. "Going to the room?" he asked. I nodded, a little smile on my face. "Well, I won't be far behind," he said. "I'm beat."

Yeah, sure...But I played along. "OK, see you later." I went up to Room 612. Taking out my lighter, I lit the hundred tea candles. From my suitcase, I pulled out a bottle of wine and laid it in a bucket of ice. Checking my hair and make-up one more time, I then put on a slinky nightie and turned down the bed.

I waited on the couch for Aapo's imminent arrival. I tried out various languorous poses that Aapo would find me in when he walked through the door. After twenty minutes of this, I quit and grabbed my purse to sort out all the twenty dollar bills.

I knew I'd pull this little scam again. Tonight I'd made enough to completely pay my Mom back the thousand bucks she'd given me. But she didn't say it was a loan so I knew I wouldn't be paying her a cent. My three children's futures danced around in my brain and I decided to think about it some more... but not tonight. I hid my money and went back to the couch.

Aapo took so long that I fell asleep. I woke up to "....the fuck?! It smells like cat piss in here!"

I sniffed and he was right; the room reeked. "It's the candles, I guess," I admitted. "They're supposed to smell like white wine."

Aapo began to blow them out and I joined him, noticing the candles had almost burned themselves down completely. Good thing Aapo showed up when he did. "There's so many!" he laughed. "You must like candles!"

Oh, Aapo, you silly goose, you obviously don't get it. I slunk over to the bottle of wine. "Can I fix you a drink?" I purred.

"Oh God no," he shook his head. "I have to get up in four hours. I shouldn't have stayed out so long."

I glanced at the clock and saw it was almost four in the morning. "Oh, I didn't know it was so late! I thought you said you were beat?"

"Ah, you know how it is," he said. "Got talking to the guys..." He looked at the bed and then at me. "So you're taking the bed then?" He didn't catch my wanton look as he walked to the couch and pulled off the cushions. "Oh, good, a sofa bed," he said.

He began to arrange the couch while I jumped quickly into the bed.

I called over to him in a singsong voice, "Aapo, you don't have to sleep on that lumpy thing...you can always jump in with me...."

With no shame, he dropped his jeans and pulled off his sweatshirt. "You're sweet, Tammy," he said. Not gorgeous or sexy or hot...I was sweet. "I appreciate the offer. But all I need is some prick on the tour to see us in bed and then rumours start up. "

"Who cares about rumours?" I asked. Especially if they were true.

"I sure do!" Aapo exclaimed. "What if Trinity hears them?"

"And Trinity is?"

"My girl back home in Toronto," he replied. "She wanted to come but only the bands got to bring girlfriends."

"Oh. You have a girlfriend?" Why didn't he tell me during our few talks? Maybe because it was always about me and never about Aapo.

"Fiancee, actually," Aapo beamed. "We're getting married in a couple months."

"And you're pretty faithful, aren't you?" I asked, giving it one last try.

"Have you seen me with anybody yet on this tour?" he replied, getting into the sack.

"No, I haven't," I agreed. And accepted it. He wouldn't be with anyone, including me. "You're a good man, Aapo. Women appreciate loyalty."

"Thanks for understanding, Tammy," Aapo murmured, already falling asleep. "Thanks for not trying to jump my bones."

He had no idea how close I came.

· · · · · · · · ·

The last week of the tour was spent in the state of New York, with our final show right in New York City. There were two days off and I spent the first day fretting over what I could use to attach the leftover hair. I was all out of THE NOISE! stickers. On the second day, I went over to a print shop and for a whopping twenty bucks, I got a whole slew of new stickers made. I even enhanced them, adding A Lock of Bradley's Hair to the print on the sticker. No more messy handwriting! Things were starting to look professional.

The day of the first New York concert, I prepped the new stickers. I no longer used a full lock of hair because I was conserving... maybe I should have put 'A Sprig of Bradley's Hair' instead. Or 'A Wisp'. Still, the customer was getting at least ten hairs. And I had lots more product to sell. The tour was about to end; may as well make hay before making for home.

There were five shows that final week, and I shilled my wares every night. Though each session was a different town, a different crowd, a different stage door entrance...the one constant was the fans. They loved The Noise and if they couldn't get to touch Bradley, owning a piece of him was the next best thing. I did not hurt for business.

To add to my success, Bradley's new 'do was making headlines. Photos began appearing in newspapers, YouTube had videos and in less than a week, beauty salons were reporting the Bradley Atwater hair trend.

The last show was pretty much perfect. Bradley gave me his video camera again and told me to just focus on him. Every now and then I'd quickly shoot a couple seconds of the other band members. You could see them being conscientious musicians, giving the audience their money's worth. I was going to miss the excitement, though I guess it was time to get back home to my kids.

We partied the night away. Everybody got shit-faced and we were a motley crew when we all assembled on the tour bus after lunch. Some sat in their seats with hats pulled low over their eyes, others had headphones on, some moaned. Vinnie came on with a garbage can he'd thieved from the hotel. He kept it on his lap, ready to heave any moment. Still the bus did not move.

"What are we waiting for?" Bradley yelled at the driver, who pointed outside. The road manager, Sherman, was on his cellphone, pacing back and forth. "Honk the horn or something. Let him know we wanna get going," Brad ordered.

It wasn't necessary, as Sherman knocked on the bus's door. The driver opened it and Sherman got on. The bus began to pull away, but Sherman put a hand on the driver's shoulder. "Just hold on a moment," he said in his usual quiet manner. "We have something to discuss."

"Let's talk about getting home," Tate suggested.

Sherman ignored him. "I've just been on the phone with your record label," he announced. "Rap City is doing a 45-date tour. They need an opener and want to know if you guys are interested."

Now, The Noise was a headline act...in Canada. Taking it on the road to the US had been taking a chance, which fortunately worked out quite well. Going back to being an opener would usually be a bad idea except.... Rap City was HUGE. The Stones would probably agree to open for them.

The entire bus went deadly quiet as every person stared at Sherman. Sherman waited patiently for an answer. Finally, Tate spoke up, "You said Rap City, right?"

Sherman nodded and then held up his giant cell phone. "I really should give them an answer since...."

The rest of his reply was drowned out as the four members of The Noise began to hoot and holler. There were high fives and chest bumps; hangovers seemed to fall by the wayside. Bradley grabbed Sherman, who passively let himself get put into a headlock. "You little Jewish Canadian princess," Brad said, knuckling him in the forehead. "You get on that phone this minute and you tell them a big fat yes!"

As Brad skipped back to his seat, he passed me. I smiled up at him and said, "Congratulations." He just beamed at me, messed up the top of my hair and kept going to his seat.

Sherman was about to step off the bus again when he turned back. "Oh, I almost forgot, The Noise is going to be the second act before Rap City goes on. You guys are going to have your own opener." At this, the four members of Screw U sat up. For one screwball moment, how I wished I were still Axel's girlfriend. How I wished I could continue on this magical mystery tour. It felt like I was finally fully alive, just when the time came to go home and renew my humdrum life.

Seeing the interest from Screw U, Sherman almost crumbled. "Ah, maybe I shouldn't have said anything just now," he squirmed. "Thing is, Rap City gets approval of all the acts. They never even heard of Screw U." Axel snorted at that comment. "They got this novelty act, an all-girl band, signed up."

"Don't tell me," Axel groaned. "Hissy Fit?"

Sherman nodded. "Their song 'I Wanna Be on Top' is number one on the charts right now."

On the day-long ride home, the bus oddly became two separate camps. The Noise sat at the back, already making plans, discussing a set list, loudly enjoying their good fortune. Meanwhile, at the front, Screw U sat in sullen solitude. Vinnie and BiBi were in the rear of this group, and BiBi kept stealing glances back at Bradley. I knew she was going to make her move soon. For one thing, she'd gone to the washroom and passed Brad maybe seven times already. Though she lingered, nobody asked her to join the party.

In the middle section, I sat alone. Opposite me, a couple roadies played some kind of handheld video game. I wished Aapo could have sat with me, but his job was to drive the equipment truck. In our last week, I'd grown closer to Aapo. Knowing I couldn't have him for a lover, I settled for just being friends. And as a friend, Aapo was highly rated. There was no b.s. with him - he was an old-fashioned square and I loved that about him.

Crossing the border took almost as long as the journey from Ohio to Michigan. The whole group had to disembark while the bus was searched. They ran our identification through their computers and one by one, they let us back outside. Approaching the bus, we could see our open suitcases laying by the luggage bin. We were apparently expected to repack it ourselves.

Finally everybody was on board except The Noise. Thirty minutes later, all four bandmates ran to the bus. The driver whooshed open the door and they jumped on. "Was there a problem?" Sherman asked. "They wouldn't let me stay with you guys."

Tate cocked a thumb at Stan, the drummer. "Fucker started sweating so much, the guards got suspicious."

"I thought they was going to check up our fuckin' ass!" Stan shuddered. "You see the way they turned our wallets inside out?"

"What the fuck you carry a photo of Mariah Carey for?" Tate asked.

The Noise made their way to the rear again as the bus started up, but Bradley plopped down beside me. I was pleasantly surprised. Ever since the infamous haircut, I had barely spoken to him. I did see him a couple times coming out of Aapo's (and my) room, munching on one of my bananas or having outright stolen a can of grapefruit juice. He knew they were from my supplies, and he'd lift the banana and mumble a "Thanks". I cut him some slack since I was secretly raking in the dough from his hair.

"So, my little health food nut," Bradley opened. "Where you going?"

"Home," was my simple reply.

"You gotta go home?" Bradley asked. I nodded yes. "Why? You still love him?"

I gave him a look of shock. "Who? Aapo? No! He has a girlfriend!" I defended his honour.

Bradley looked confused. "Aapo? I know he has a girlfriend," he said. "I'm talking about Axel."

"Axel!?" I repeated, maybe a bit too loudly as Axel turned to look at me, thinking maybe I'd called him. He did a double-take when he saw Bradley sitting beside me. "No, me and Axel are done. Kaput. Finito."

"Then why not stay with us?" Bradley suggested.

I gawked at him. He had no idea how much I wanted to continue this lifestyle. A different hotel every night, all the fried food you could eat, the great potential of bedbugs and S.T.D.'s. I didn't want it to end. However, I didn't want to be taken for a fool. I was nobody's girlfriend and I wasn't going to come along as unpaid labour.

"Oh, man, I'd love to go back on tour with you guys, but...I got to make a living, right? So I guess I have to get back to Toronto and find a real job." I gave him a rather sad smile. "But this tour was amazing, so thanks for the memories."

"Maybe you got me wrong," Brad furrowed his brow. "We already talked to Sherman, he said we can hire you. You've even got a job title - Assistant Road Manager."

"What!" I gasped. This was out of left field. I asked the obvious question, "Why me?"

"You got skills, Tammy," Bradley explained seriously. "We saw the way you got Axel's costumes so perfect. You kept me healthy on this tour. You got us better snacks. And you found Dawn. who gave me the haircut." I didn't want to ask about him and Dawn; I had a feeling something fetishy went down and that Bradley was the smitten one now. "Anyhow, what's waiting for you back in Toronto?" he asked, standing up.

I looked up at him. "Just...you know...family."

"We all have family, babe," he said. "So? You in?"

"Are you kidding?" I laughed. "I'm SO in!"

"Sherman!" Brad yelled at the road manager. "Ya got yourself an assistant road manager! Go ahead and put Tammy on the payroll."

Axel's head whipped around and caught my ear to ear grin. BiBi took her shot and called after Bradley, "I'd love to go on tour again! Does anybody need me?" A pause while nobody responded. With a desperate edge to her voice, she continued, "For anything?"

I had a job! I couldn't ever remember working for money before, unless you counted the dollar Mom would give me to do the odd chore. The idea of "working" didn't appeal to me but how hard a job would it be? Driving around the US of A, hanging out with a cool rock band?

You bet I was thrilled. Not even Axel's continuos dirty looks could diminish my mega-watt smile. Before reaching the city limits, and maybe to rub it in, I stood up and made my way to the back to join The Noise. I belonged to them now, didn't I?

Little did I know it would be for the next fifteen years.

CHAPTER VI

Pretty much fifteen years to the day, to be precise. On the road to all corners of the globe, seeing the sights, living wild and fancy free. All this while grandmother Kitty Canseco held down the fort back in Toronto, raising my kids from toddlers to teens.

It all began when my first tour with The Noise came to an end and they invited me to be their assistant road manager. With nary a second's hesitation, I agreed. Discussing it with my mother had never crossed my mind.

Walking into the front door of my house (actually my mother owned it), I was met by three terribly excited children. They immediately wanted to know what I'd gotten them. "Uh...A Lock of Bradley's Hair?" I said, pulling out three samples. Not an ounce of gratitude was shown.

"Eww...you want us to touch that?" Tatum asked.

I stood up and put them into a little drawer in the hallway table. "You hang onto this," I advised them. "One day they may be worth something."

The next hour was spent looking at kindergarten drawings and listening to their school tales. Sadie was barely four and she had a boyfriend. Tatum had become best friends with a kid named Scarletta but tomorrow she was switching to Bethany. My oldest child, Rain, looked a little thin, in my opinion.

"Geez, Mom, what have you been feeding him?" I asked. "Has he lost weight?"

"Normal healthy food," she replied. "He's fine."

"Well, give him a burger and fries, for Pete's sake," I squeezed his ribs.

We then dug into a late supper of salad and lasagna; I wondered why I never ordered lasagna when I was on tour. It was so good, I ate three helpings. Screw the salad. After our meal, the kids wanted me to watch some silly Disney movie.

"Isn't it bedtime yet?" I asked.

"I thought they could stay up a bit later, since they haven't seen you in so long," Mom said. "You weren't planning on going out, were you?"

"No, but I want to talk to you about something," I muttered.

"I'll be here when the movie's over," she said, gathering up the dishes. So while Mom puttered about in the kitchen, I endured The Little Mermaid with my children. To be honest, it was a pretty decent flick. I just wish I didn't have pressing matters on my mind, such as how to dump these three precious darlings onto my mother again.

Movie over, it was bath and bedtime. I rushed things, not doing tasks the way Grandma Kitty did them. I didn't towel them off briskly, I didn't dry their hair, I made them pick out their own pyjamas. "Everybody's got their own style," I said, thinking that was good parental advice. So I added some more. "Go with the flow."

Before the cries of "Bedtime story!" got too fierce, I promised them another Disney movie tomorrow night instead. That seemed to be a good bargain so I shut off their lights and bid them good night. I could smell coffee brewing, so with nerves of jello, I walked into the clean kitchen.

"Sorry I didn't help you with the dishes," I apologized.

Kitty laughed. "Oh, don't be sorry! Like when have you ever helped me with the dishes?" That was true; I was pretty lazy around the house. Or Mom was just too quick to do everything. "So, Tammy, how was the tour? I mean, really, now that the kids are in bed, you can tell me...how was it?"

"Well," I began, "it didn't take long before me and Axel broke up...."

"Oh, baby!" Mom reached out to stroke my arm. I pulled back.

"Oh, God, don't worry about that!" I laughed. "He was such a dick, I was so glad to be rid of him."

"Yet you got to stay on the tour?" she asked incredulously. I nodded, as amazed as her.

"Yup! I did all sorts of jobs for the lead singer of The Noise...you know, the headline act? Anyhow, I guess he appreciated it... I mean, nobody made me get off the bus," I replied.

"And did you enjoy yourself?" Mom continued the inquiry.

"Oh, Mom, it was so much fun, I can't wait to go back!" Ooops. I slipped and she caught it immediately.

"Go back?" she repeated. "Why would you do that? Especially if you're not with that Axel anymore?"

I plunged in. "Mom, they offered me a job. Assistant road manager. I think I'm finally finding myself a career."

"What an exotic choice," she said, not looking unhappy. "Well, we'll cross that bridge when the time comes. You just returned from a trip so you should be home for a few weeks, I'd imagine.... "

"A few days," I interrupted her, before she got her hopes up. "That's how it goes in this business. We were on the way home and Rap City called, offered them a big show. It starts in less than a week."

"And you have to go on the road again with them?" she asked. I nodded sadly.

"That's what assistant road managers do," I said.

Kitty began to get a miserable look on her face. "So you want to leave your kids with me again? How long will you be gone? The twins have a piano recital in two weeks; you're going to miss that. Rain has hockey tryouts coming up."

"Mom! I'll do what I can while I'm here, ok?" Suddenly I really wanted to convince my mother that this job was important to me. I grabbed my purse and opened up a secret zipper, where I'd kept all my "hair earnings". I pulled out a wad and began to count it off. "Look, I...I got paid while I was on tour," I stretched the truth. "I meant to send this home, some money to take care of the kids, you know. School clothes, school supplies..."

"I can manage," Kitty said, though she eyed the dough with obvious interest. "How much do you have there?"

"About five hundred dollars," I said. Probably a tenth of what I made. "And Mom, I want you to take this. Maybe I won't have money next time to give you, but I have it today. Take it or... I'll just spend it on myself."

Kitty plucked it from my fingers.

• • • • • • • • •

That first tour with The Noise had been a blast. The second tour, but my first one as a paid employee, was just as interesting. Circumstances had changed; I was unable to go out nightly and sell A Lock of Bradley's Hair. Instead I was kept busy taking care of my boys. That's not to say I was out of business though.

I reunited with The Noise at the back of The El Durango club. The tour bus was taking up most of the tiny back alley and I immediately saw an old face standing there, talking to the bus driver. Aapo had been hired back on tour. "Aapo!" I cried in delight. "I didn't know I'd see you so soon! I thought you were getting married?"

"Still gotta work," he replied. "The wedding is like a week after I get back."

"Cutting it close, huh?" I asked. "She doesn't need your help or anything?"

"Nah," he replied. "Her and her mom and her sisters...they're planning the whole thing. I just gotta show up."

I changed the subject. "Have you seen any of the band? This is my first day on the job."

"I heard," said Aapo. "Assistant road manager, huh? First time we had one of those on tour. Boys are getting big."

"So have you seen them?"

"Yeah," Aapo confirmed. "They're in the dressing room, cleaning up from last night. That was some party!"

I knew the band had played one last show before leaving Toronto. I had no interest in catching it; I'd seen the show a bunch of times before and would likely see it forty-five more times in the next couple months. As soon as I saw the members of The Noise, I could tell the partying had been severe. Everybody looked hung-over.

"Hi guys!" I said brightly. "Reporting for duty! Anybody know what I'm supposed to do?"

Tate glanced up from the guitar case that was on his lap. "Sherman will tell you what to do. He should be at the bus."

"I didn't see him," I replied.

Bradley was sitting in a chair, his head between his legs, his long hair almost draping the ground. It looked like he was due for another haircut. He glanced up, a green pallor to his face.

"Here's your first job," he said in a weak voice. "Go find me a bucket or a pail or something and bring it on the bus. I know I'm gonna yak."

Stan, the drummer, picked up a backpack and a set of sticks and dragged himself to the door of the dressing room. "I'm done in here. I'm getting on the bus. And I'm not picking up the condoms in the john; they're not mine." He left the room.

Mickey, the bass guitarist, approached me. He was the mildest guy in The Noise rock band, probably because he was the only married guy. "My wife is coming on this tour," he informed me. I simply nodded. "I got a job for you down the road." I now lifted my eyebrows. "Shayna has a big crush on the singer of Rap City," he confided. "I mean, BIG crush."

"Well, so do about a million other women," I replied. "Me included."

"But those million other women aren't Shayna," he worried. Sure, his wife was gorgeous; even most ugly rock stars had model-type babes, but she wasn't exactly charming or personable. "And once we get to our first city, Shayna will be around him almost every single day. Maybe you can keep an eye on her?"

"Mick, think about it," I warded off his anxiety attack. "Scott Mc-Dowd is a mega-star. Every city we get to, he's got radio and newspaper interviews, he's got public appearances, sound checks...the guy is going to be super busy." Mickey seemed to perk up somewhat. "And it's going to be the same with you guys. You're opening for the biggest band in the world! You don't think you guys are going to get the royal treatment as well?"

With a boyish grin (he was quite young to be married, in my opinion), Mickey said, "We got a lot of that on the last tour. I didn't mind the attention!"

"And Shayna will be with you every step of the way," I said. "With her big rock star husband."

With a little more swag, Mickey threw a bottle of whiskey into his knapsack. "Thanks, Tabby," he mispronounced my name. We'd barely spoken on the first tour. "Don't tell Shayna we had this little talk, OK?"

"I won't say a word to her," I promised. I hoped I literally wouldn't have to speak to her at all on this trip. Shayna, the only wife on the last road trip, had been mean and catty. Even BiBi, who could probably find Hitler's good points, avoided the witch.

"OK, see you on the bus," he said. "And do me a favour?" I waited for my next assignment. "Clean up those condoms?" He walked out.

Left alone, I made a quick search for something to hold Bradley's vomit. There was nothing available and I didn't want to miss the bus. Upending a plant that was dying anyhow, I emptied the container. That would have to do for now.

As I ran out the back door of the club, I could see a taxi parked behind the bus. Sherman, the official road manager, was opening up the rear door of the cab. The driver was unloading multiple suitcases.

"First time we ever beat Sherman to the bus," Tate observed.

"And when did Sherman ever own pink luggage?" Mickey asked. "You think he might be gay?"

That question was barely uttered before we had an answer. Sherman, the short, quiet mole of a man, reached his hand into the taxi. The band, the roadies and I watched as first some long painted fingernails appeared. Then a shapely foot wearing high-heeled booties rested itself on the ground. Finally the whole body emerged.

As one, we all gasped, "BiBi!"

She turned a big smile on us. "Hi, y'all!" and then inexplicably, "Hi, Bradley! It looks like I'm going to be seeing a lot of you guys again!"

No explanation given. Nothing like "I'm Sherman's girlfriend," or "I was so crazy to be with Bradley again that I seduced The Noise's road manager and now I'm pretending to be his girlfriend." Nope, she just sent us a toothy smile as we all picked our jaws off the ground.

Brad began to stagger forward from the bus but he wasn't aiming to give BiBi a welcome back gesture. He took a couple steps in my direction and, while I held onto the plant container, he proceeded to vomit into it.

• • • • • • • • •

In a nutshell, that is what my employment as assistant road manager amounted to - babysitting a foursome of overgrown boys.

In the fifteen years I was with them, I got to know each one quite well. There was, of course, Bradley, the singer and acknowledged leader of the group. Then you had the lead guitarist, Tate, a star in his own right. Stan was the drummer and Mickey the bass player.

Out of all four, Bradley was my favourite, though I can't say why. Maybe it's because most of my energies were spent on keeping him happy, sane and sober. Through the next decade, as The Noise got to be world-famous, Bradley stretched his exotic tastes in friends and drugs. He discovered opium in China, kush on the outskirts of an army base in Iran, heroin in a groupie's New York hotel room. It wasn't long before I smartened up and bought a whole supply of cheap disposable puke pails.

Though I considered myself attractive, and was basically single throughout our entire working relationship, Bradley never made a move on me. I never made one on him either. We had this brother/sister love/hate relationship going on. There was an unbalanced respect between us for each other's job - when all was said and done, Bradley was an incredible musician. But he could also be a huge cretin with his demanding ways, his narcissistic attitude and his assumption that we should all scrape and bow before him. His fellow bandmates told me he was like that before they even had their first gig, playing at a high school prom.

Suggest an adventure? A new experience? Bradley was always up for something to heighten his feeling for life. I guess being a well-known working rock star wasn't enough. He wanted to try racing cars, he wanted to explore the deep sea in a shark cage, he wanted to go spelunking. When he had time off, he was allowed to do that. When he was on tour, all he wanted to experience was sex, drugs and rock n' roll. Add liquor to that combo and that was life with Bradley. Besides the shows, there were always appearances and interviews of some sort. The record label expected The Noise to arrive somewhat on-time but definitely looking presentable. That's where my job came in.

The other three guys in The Noise were much less time-consuming. The drummer, Stan, seemed capable of doing everything on his own, from waking up on time to getting his own food. The only thing he didn't bother to do was meet girls the old-fashioned way. He'd simply wait until he did a show, and then tell a roadie what girl(s) interested him. The roadie would go off to the victim and say the drummer would like to see her backstage. Stan tried to get me to take on this task one night. I said I'd try, but upon approaching the screaming fan waiting for the encore, I felt like a pimp. Later I told Stan the girl wasn't interested and to never ask me to do that again. But after the tenth time, it became easier.

Mickey was such a worry-wart, I tended to be completely business-like with him. His main expectation of me was to keep quiet around his bitchy wife and I was happy to oblige. I actually didn't like Mickey very much, simply because of his double-standards. He expected his spouse Shayna to stay loyal to him, yet Mickey seemed to have a problem keeping his pecker in his pants. He wasn't really into groupies though; Bradley and Tate had first dibs on them anyhow. No, Mickey seemed to enjoy secretly bedding the hotel staff or the waitress at Knockers or the concert venue's cleaning ladies. He knew I knew - that was usually the reason he was late getting on the bus. If his actions would have affected anybody but Shayna, I might really have had a problem with his behaviour.

Tate, the lead guitarist, was the secret to The Noise's success. Tate had collected the musicians, had developed their sound and wrote the songs. Even though Bradley was the person the fans sought out the most and the media dwelled upon, he was just the eye candy in the store window. Tate was the brains and the whole band deferred to his ideas. Back home, Tate had a successful girlfriend who was one of Canada's top models. Pia was forever jetting from Italy to the Caribbean for photo shoots. Tate did pretty well, for a guy whose looks I'd rate as a generous four and a half.

Those were the boys I came to know very well over fifteen years. They became big rock stars but I can't say I continued to be impressed by them. When you're throwing out Mickey's used rubbers or washing skid marks out of Bradley's underwear, their celebrity status tended to lose some of its shine.

• • • • • • • • • •

As grungy as some of my work was, the perks kept me coming back for more. In between giving Bradley his third wake-up call, making sure Stan's latest groupie left without stealing anything, grabbing the newspapers for Tate ... there were daily highlights. The constant subterfuge of escaping adoring fans, the dressing room's jumbo shrimp I'd snuck onto the rider as Bradley's request, meeting other famous show biz celebs. One time Celine Dion came backstage. I never even liked her before but I became starstruck.

Chicago, Illinois, did not disappoint when it came to memorable moments. After a long bus trip, we reached a hotel that was decent, but not quite what I expected. For some reason, I thought Rap City would enjoy nicer digs, seeing as how they were so well-known. This hotel had nothing but a desk clerk for security.

After lugging in leftover detritus from the tour bus, I was the last of the road crew to check in. The desk clerk decided to get a little flirtatious with me.

"Wow, so you travel with a rock band, huh?" he marvelled.

"Yup," I replied.

"A cute young thing like you," he winked. "I wonder what you could possibly be doing?"

"Assistant road manager," I announced like I was Secret Service. I then flipped open a wallet that I'd found on the washroom floor of the bus. The photo inside read Bradley Atwater. "Do you have my room key?"

The smirk fell off the clerk's face. "Yeah, sure, Room 321, top floor," he said, handing me a plastic card. "Your whole group is on the third floor."

I took the key. "Thanks. Is Rap City on that floor as well?"

The desk clerk did a double take and then barked out a short laugh. "Did you say Rap City?" I nodded. "Ha! Like they'd stay here!"

"Well, we're...The Noise is opening for them," I explained. "I just thought the whole tour would be staying at the same hotels. So no Hissy Fit?"

"I won't have one if you won't have one," he replied.

"No, I mean...oh, never mind," I said. I took the elevator up the three floors and dumped my luggage and bag of bus-stuff onto the bed. I quickly left and began roaming the halls of the third floor, looking for Bradley's room. I could tell I was close when the smell of marijuana assaulted my nostrils. Like a bloodhound, I followed the trail to the suspect hotel room.

Timidly knocking, praying it wasn't actually some hip hop gangster on the lam, I was happy when Tate opened the door. I could see Bradley at the room's window, studying the parking lot out front.

"Hey, Tate, is this your room?" I asked.

His lungs compressed with smoke, he shook his head and squeaked out, "Brad's."

Bradley held his hand out for the joint. "Want a hit, Tammy?"

"No thanks," I said. "Hey! We just got here and already you're smoking weed? You didn't sneak that across the border, did you?" I heard a toilet flush and then glanced at the bathroom door. "Oh. You have a connection in Chicago?"

Brad resumed looking out the window. "You'd think there would be fans outside," he mused. "Even when things are kept a secret, somebody always finds out. There's not one person out there."

"Sherman wanted to start things off low-key," I explained. "You probably won't see any of your fans until we get to the Dome."

"Not our fans," Tate explained. "The Rap City fans."

"Yeah, that's what I came to tell you," I said. "Rap City is not staying here."

Bradley wheeled around, his buzz instantly killed. "What!? We're not at the same hotel as Rap City!?"

"It seems all three bands are staying at different hotels," I explained. I had no idea why it worked like that; I was new to this business. "I guess they want you all to get along...they don't want your fans getting mixed up with the Hissy Fit fans...."

"Like there's going to be any fans left for us," Bradley groused. "I'm not worried about Hissy Shit, but Rap City? That's who everybody's coming to see."

I had no idea Bradley would take it so hard. He yanked the blinds closed and then slapped at them when he realized his hair had caught in the slats. He turned and glared at me, like it was my fault. Backing out of the room, I quickly said, "Sound check is at noon. Breakfast at ten."

I didn't return to my room. After a day of junk food meals, the guys would want a decent breakfast. I needed to find a restaurant and make a reservation.

The next morning, all of us seated around a big table in the back room of a Benny's Restaurant, I observed the group while I ate a foreign substance called grits. Sherman was trying to eat, conduct telephone business and be an amusing dining partner to BiBi, seated by his side. But every time Sherm had to speak on the phone, his attention firmly on business, BiBi's eyes and constant dreamy smile would wander over to Bradley.

I followed her gaze and saw the object of her desire. Bradley had doused a mile-high plate of pancakes with syrup. He reached his hand out to the centre of the table and grabbed a couple napkins out of the holder. His hair acted almost like a magnet as it swayed forward with

Brad, but then found the plate and immediately stuck to all the syrup on it. Brad didn't seem to notice until BiBi pointed it out.

"Oh, Bradley, your beautiful hair...," she moaned, pointing. Bradley looked down at his hair, the ends of it laying in and around the sticky pancakes.

"Oh, fuck!" he yelled. His eyes met mine. "Get me something to clean my hair," he commanded.

I left my grits and got a dishcloth from the kitchen. Wetting it, I started to try and rub out the syrup from Bradley's hair. BiBi watched the scene, looking like she could cry. "You know, Bradley, maybe it's time for another haircut," I suggested. "Your hair grows like wildfire."

"Nobody's cutting my hair," Bradley replied, definitely in a sour disposition. "Who is ever going to cut it again like Dawn did?"

"So what are you going to do?" I asked, not in the mood for his behaviour. "Never cut your hair again?"

"It still looks alright though, doesn't it?" Brad suddenly looked concerned.

"It looks great, Brad!" BiBi added her two cents.

"Yeah, sure, it still looks good," I admitted. "It's just getting a bit long." A thought hit me and I stepped back. "Soak it some more when we get to the Dome," I told Brad. "I'll see you guys on the bus in thirty minutes. I've got to make a phone call."

I actually needed to make two phone calls. One to directory assistance to get the listing for Comb By Ya, and the second call was to the salon itself. Glory be! In the three weeks since I'd last seen Dawn, he still worked at the salon. I explained the situation with Bradley's hair and asked if he'd consider meeting us somewhere on our US tour. I told him we'd be in Chicago tonight, followed by a show in Rockport. Then in four days we'd be performing in...

"Tammy, honey, darling...just tell me where you are right now," Dawn interrupted.

"Right now? Headed to sound check at The Dome," I replied. "Then back to this little hotel we're staying at in Chicago. Called the Regal Inn."

"I'm on my way," Dawn replied. "I don't know what time I'll get there but you keep a candle in the window, ya hear?"

• • • • • • • • •

The next morning , I was a mess. I'd stayed up half the night awaiting Dawn's arrival. I kept flitting down to the lobby, awkwardly sitting in one of their two lobby armchairs. The only people I saw were Sherman and BiBi, returning arm-in-arm from their dinner date. At 3 AM, I called it quits. Mentally blowing out the candle, I crawled into bed.

Shortly after six the next morning, I began knocking on the band member's doors. "Wake up, wake up, we got that morning TV show to do, " I told each door. After sound check yesterday, the guys had the rest of the day off. Sherman had asked them to behave and go to bed early. I gave them five minutes and then, like a snooze alarm, went back to the doors. "Wake up, let's go, bus leaves in half an hour!" At this point, three members of The Noise grunted they had heard me.

Not Bradley. He opened his door with a beatific smile on his face. "Hey, Tammy, thanks, I'll be down soon. We grabbing breakfast first?"

"No, the studio said they'd...," and I stopped short. Bradley had cut his hair! I knew the boys were excited to have time off; I'd heard talk about catching a professional sports game or going to a strip joint. Obviously Bradley chose a beauty parlour instead. "Oh, you got your hair cut!" I said. "Oh, damn! I mean, it looks nice, I mean wow, it actually looks like you found somebody to recreate the original cut, but... ah, shit, I was going to surprise you. I called Dawn, asked him to come out, and he said he would but he hasn't shown up yet. And now you already got your hair cut!"

A low voice rumbled from behind the door. "Hey, sugar!" I stopped babbling and stepped into the room. Dawn was forcing a girdle over his man parts. "Guess who was the first person I ran into when I got here?" Bradley looked in the mirror and swung his hair from side to side. "So we just got to it, didn't we?" Brad's eyes met Dawn's in the mirror and they shared a giggle. I didn't know why and I didn't want to know, so I just smiled stupidly.

"Bus leaves soon, be on it." I said. Dawn approached me and I was about to reach out for a hug when he turned his back on me, presenting a bra that was unhooked.

"Do me up," Dawn said. "You coming back to the hotel after?" I grunted in the affirmative as I stretched the two bra parts together. "K, good, I got something I want to give you."

Unless it was an STD, I couldn't wait to see what this big black brawny man, dressed in a purple miniskirt and wearing three-inch wedge heels, had for me.

• • • • • • • • •

The TV morning show went off without a hitch. The 'green room', where we waited for our cue, was filled with bagels, croissants, cheeses, spreads. After an interview in which Bradley almost charmed the pants off the middle-aged female host, the band played a song from their up-coming album. It wasn't 'She's Gonna Get It', which had been a number-one hit in Canada for a couple weeks already. The next single was due to drop any day and the band decided to play that one instead.

'Too Good 4 Me' would eventually become The Noise's anthem song. It had a catchy riff and all sorts of neat musical twists. Today, the slow start (perfect for young romantics to slow dance) offered Bradley the chance to grind against the mike stand, look expressively into the cameras, and let his hair mysteriously shield half his face. Then the song shifted gears and ripped into a full-on rock n' roll saga. Bradley went into madman mode, pulling off creative dance moves, whipping his hair to and fro. Stan offered up a new trick with his drumsticks. Mickey's bass notes were integral to the refrain and he delivered them reverently. Tate played guitar licks with a pained grimace on his face. It didn't do much for his attractiveness but it added intensity to the number.

We were back at the hotel by ten AM. Elated by the morning's success, it had left us oddly exhausted. The Noise had another interview that afternoon at the WKIX radio station. Although Sherman suggested we all meet for lunch, the boys declined the idea.

"This is our first show tonight," Bradley said. "I got jet lag or something. I need to get some sleep." Though we travelled by bus and were still in the same time zone, nobody corrected him. He looked at me. "Make sure I'm up by one."

I headed to my room to find Dawn. He wasn't there and since I'd left my sole room key with him, I had no access to my suite. On the way down to the lobby to get a new passkey, I passed by Bradley's room. He was just putting out a container of wine bottles. "These are stinkin' up the place," he whispered.

"Hey," I whispered back, then wondered why the low tones. It was mid-morning after all. "Hey," I said in a louder voice. "Have you seen Dawn?"

"Sssh!" Brad hushed me and opened the door wider. There, on the bed, lay Dawn in his gorgeous dress, full makeup, wig slightly askew. He was sound asleep, lightly snoring. "Isn't that the cutest thing you ever saw?" Brad acted like Dawn was some newborn baby.

"Oh, there he is, " I made the obvious discovery. "Shit, he has my room key...and we made plans."

Bradley pulled a key off his table. "This must be your's," he said, handing it over. Yawning, he gently pushed me out of the room. "And wake us up at one."

It wasn't until later in the evening when I finally got to spend time with my new friend Dawn. Of course I was required to tag along to the radio interview; the only time I was needed was when Stan wanted a glass of water to down his Tylenols. Once we got back to the hotel, Sherman told us we had a few hours to ourselves before the bus left for the show. Dawn showed up at my room around six.

"I was wondering when I'd get to see you!" I enthused. My eyes were on a huge Frederick's of Hollywood bag. "What's that you got?"

"I come bearing gifts," Dawn teased. "Not from Frederick's though. Look inside."

I took the bag and noticed it was light. Inside I saw bright pink material. As I pulled it out, I wondered if it was a silk peignoir. It turned out to be a humungous pair of Dawn's panties. She plucked them from my fingers.

"Those are mine," he said. "I just used them in place of tissue paper. You know - to hide the real goodies."

There was another bag inside. I shook it - light as a feather. Opening it up gently, I peeked inside, screamed, then threw it aside. "What is that?" I yelled. "Some kind of animal?"

"Somebody's head," he said ominously, laughing as my eyes widened. "Somebody's head of HAIR!"

"From your shop?" I asked a bit peevishly. I didn't want to seem ungrateful, but what kind of present was this?

"Noooo..., from Bradley's haircut last night," Dawn corrected me.

I played dumb. "What an odd gift," I said. "Why would you give me

Bradley's hair?" Dawn gave me a steely look. "No, really," I continued. "I don't get it."

"You did me a good one a few weeks back," Dawn said. I raised an eyebrow so he elaborated. "That haircut I gave Bradley? Sugar, I've gotten so much attention over that, I got appointments lined up into the next year. I'm the Queen Bee of Milwaukee right now."

"Can you believe all the press a simple hairdo can get?" I asked. "I'm glad it's working out for you, Dawn, but I still don't know why you're giving me...hair. What should I do with it?"

Dawn pursed his luscious lips at me. "You know what to do," he murmured. I shrugged my shoulders, still acting naive. "OK, Miss Tammy, I'm going to make a confession. Do you remember the last time we were together, the night of the show, when you made me guard the stage door? So you could get back in?" I nodded. "So sue me, but I was curious. I thought you'd be back in a couple minutes, but you were gone longer."

"Not that long," I said defensively. I prided myself on conducting a brisk business - in and out as fast as possible before I got arrested. "But go on."

"So I was wearing a necklace that night with big baubles, right?" I didn't remember details, but I kind of recalled everything from the waist up being big baubles, so I nodded. "I took it off and stuck it in the door and went out to see what you was up to. You didn't see me, but I saw you. Saw you selling Bradley's hair!" I hung my head in shame as she went on. "And I realized - here I had given Bradley a haircut and I didn't even keep a lock of my own, like we planned! So I gave a girl twenty bucks to get me one. Then I ran back to the stage door and acted like I never left."

"OK, you busted me," I muttered. "I guess you're going to tell Brad?"

"No way!" he slapped my shoulder. "What you're doing is so radical! I love it! But I thought you might need more product?" He pointed at the bag.

I sifted through the soft tufts of hair. "Here's the thing, Dawn," I sighed. "I only did it for a couple weeks. Just to make some extra cash, you know? But man, it was a money tree!"

"So why stop?" Dawn asked.

"Actually, I considered doing it again on this tour, but... I think my job might get in the way," I explained. "As assistant road manager, I just have to always BE there. In case somebody needs me for something."

Dawn sat down. "Hhmm, you said it was pretty lucrative?"

"Yup. Like a thousand a night."

"Get out of town!" Dawn roared in disbelief. "For that kind of dough, let me help you! I'll go out and sell them! Whaddaya say? Fifty fifty?"

It didn't take me long to deduce that fifty per cent of any profit was better than the no profit I'd planned on earning from A Lock of Bradley's Hair this tour. I went to my suitcase and unzipped the compartment where I'd stashed my collection of Hair stickers. "That's a deal!" I announced. "Here's all the stickers. We have a couple hours before we leave. Let's make up a whole bunch."

Dawn edged toward the door. "Aww, sorry, hun, I just stopped by for a minute," he apologized. "Bradley likes my make-up. He wants me to do his face before the show tonight. But you make up those pretty samples and I'll sell my little ass off."

Little ass, my ass, I thought cattily as I went to work on the new locks. But he was a doll for bringing me this fresh batch of long silky money-making tresses.

• • • • • • • • • •

On the way to Chicago, all The Noise could talk about was holding their own against Rap City. The Noise weren't dumb; at least, Tate wasn't. He pointed out the obvious - we were big in our country, but we lived in Canada. And though their last hit, 'She's Gonna Get It', had cracked the charts in the USA, it was their only American hit so far. Everybody was coming to see Rap City; The Noise was just an appetizer.

"We're going to have to play hard, guys," Tate admonished. "I want us to make some kind of an impression."

"I want us to sell some t-shirts!" Stan threw in. Tate gave him a withering expression but I secretly sided with Stan. I wanted to sell a bunch of Bradley's hair.

"I mean it," Tate warned. "It's our first show. Make it a good one."

What the boys weren't prepared for was Hissy Fit. It may be possible the girls had the same talk on their tour bus because they came on with a fury. On any other night, Hissy Fit could have been a fabulous headliner on their own but tonight they were the first of three bands to play. You wouldn't have known; if I were there as an audience member, I could have walked out after their act very musically satisfied.

Backstage, instead of hanging out in their dressing rooms, The Noise stood in the wings. Not one man spoke as they watched Hissy Fit belt out their encore. What with their shapely bodies wearing next to nothing, their hair big and teased, their dance moves too sexy for words...they had the audience under their spell. After their set, the girls ran off.

The singer, the one with the big burgundy hair that looked like a dark cloud over her head, slowed as she passed Tate. "Hope they don't ask for another encore!" she laughed. "We got nothing else in our repertoire!"

The keyboardist came up behind her and bragged, "Listen to the crowd! You guys better keep them going or else tomorrow, you'll be opening up for us." Giggling, she ran after the other four female members of Hissy Fit as they made their way to the dressing room.

Tate turned to the rest of The Noise and jerked his head. "Back to the dressing room," he said. I followed at a distance, just to let them know I was near if they needed me. Tate slammed the dressing room door shut before I could enter, but I put my ear against it. I couldn't hear much. Tate was doing most of the talking, and I heard the word "bitches" a lot.

Sherman came down the hall and saw me standing there. He splayed his right hand open, fingers wide. That meant five minutes. I knocked on the door and gave them their five minute warning. Turning around to give Sherman the thumbs up, I saw Dawn there instead.

In a girlish voice, Dawn knocked again and said, "Braaad? I want to check your make-up one last time." In a quiet voice, he hoarsely whispered to me, "And I've got the locks in here." He lifted up a bedazzled purse. I peeked in as the door swung open, and we both jumped back guiltily.

Bradley stood there. "How do I look?" he asked in a squeaky voice. Had he asked me, I would have told him he looked scared to death.

"Oh, honey, sit down, let me fix your eyes," Dawn pushed him into a chair in front of a mirror. "You look pale, but that's ok. Pale works on you. But let's make your cheeks stand out a bit more then." Dawn pulled out a brush, did a bit of that, a swoosh of this. "Now just a little guy-liner, and you're good to go."

The rest of the boys were spiking their hair, or tying scarves around their heads. Stan was playing a beat on a couple of aluminum take-out containers. "Let's go, guys, showtime," I said. They seemed to be daw-dling, very unlike them. It was like they were waiting on something. "Let's go," I repeated. "You can hear the crowd. They're cheering for you."

That wasn't it. It wasn't until Tate said, "Fuck it. Let's go for broke or we go home."

The boys ran out screaming, like they were taking the field for a foot-ball game. I didn't want to follow them; I was actually afraid. Dawn was so silent himself, I'd almost forgotten he was still in the room.

"So?" I heaved a big sigh. "Shall we go watch a train wreck?"

• • • • • • • • •

My boys, my fighters, my champions! They were so worried that His-sy Fit would overshadow them, they forgot that even on a normal day they were a great band. But that first show, they reached heights I'd not seen up to that point. And by the end of the night, I'm sure it was Rap City wondering where they'd find themselves on the line-up.

As for my business enterprise with Dawn? A total bust. He avoided me at the raucous party after the concert. I don't know where he spent the night, though I had every intention of telling him, "I invited you out, you can stay in my room." I was starting to wonder if I'd been robbed when he came down to the hotel's cafe.

"I'll have two coffees, one black, one with three sugars and three creams," Dawn ordered.

"Hey, Dawn!" I called to him from behind my newspaper. "Got a min-ute?"

He came over, his body language showing abject shame. "I'm a fail-ure," he said, giving me the most puppy dog-eyed look I'd ever seen. "I could only sell ten of them."

"Well....it's not your fault," I said. "They weren't the headline act..."

"It wasn't that!" Dawn cried out. "You left with the band, you saw! The fans were crazy for them! I don't know...I tried...but it was hard. Some people were afraid of me, I think, though I don't know why. 'Cuz I'm tall?" He pulled out a hundred dollars. "Anyhow, I'm a lousy sales man. Here's your cut. I got the rest of the hair in my bag upstairs."

I gave a weak laugh. "Yeah, and I've got about three hundred more samples in my suitcase. Oh well, it was fun while it lasted." The counter clerk placed Dawn's two coffees by the cash register.

"I'll see you on the bus," Dawn said. "Bradley asked me to come along for a few more days, do his hair and makeup...ya know, until he knows how to do it correctly himself."

"Alright, I'll catch you later," I said. Dawn picked up the coffees and then stood stock-still. He swung his bald pate at me, his eyes wild. He was my friend, but I didn't know him all that well. He could still look like a crazed murderer.

"Unless...we go another route," he said, almost sounding like a robot, until he ran back to me. "eBay! We sell it on eBay! Oh my God, sugar, this way we reach out to millions of fans, not just the hundred standing by the stage door. Or there's other places on the internet! Fan clubs and music sites and....and..." He put the coffees down and held his hands out for me to see. "Look, I'm shaking, I'm so psyched. This is a good thing, Tammy. You sit with me on the bus and we're going to talk this through."

"Uhhhh....okay...," I gave a shaky assent. I knew nothing about eBay, let alone computers. I didn't know how I felt about this idea. It wasn't until Dawn was about to leave the cafe that his business knowledge gave me some needed confidence.

"Hey!" Dawn said to the bored counter clerk. "I just had a business meeting. Give me a receipt for these coffees."

Dawn's obvious desire for financial accounting made me think of my own bank account. As usual, there was nothing in it. This job was my first real job as an adult. However, I wasn't the rock star. I wasn't even the road manager. I was basically another roadie, getting paid little more than minimum wage. Worse than that, I would only be paid when The Noise was on the road.

To top it all off, I did tell my mother I would try to send money home. If I didn't do that, Mother might not let Tammy out to play anymore.

•••••••••

Fifteen years later, A Lock of Bradley's Hair didn't make me rich, but it kept me alive. I stayed on with The Noise, never rising above assistant road manager. Maybe I could have risen above that rank if Sherman hadn't also stayed on as their road manager. BiBi was always in the picture as well, having married Sherman five years after they started dating. Awkwardly, Bradley was their best man. He showed up completely stoned for their wedding and BiBi said it was sweet that he even made it.

In the first couple years of my employment, I would go back home to Toronto between gigs. I'd be happy to see my three children, but it wasn't long before I'd be waiting for the phone to ring. One day this band's record label called me - Taste was going on tour for a month and could I come along as an assistant road manager? Taste had opened up for The Noise and obviously appreciated what I did for my boys. It wasn't long before I was back on the road with a new band, cleaning up their vomit and running to the store for cigs.

I had just come off tour with Taste, our last gig taking place in Los Angeles. I had a week to relax before I started another road trip with The Noise. Their first gig was taking place in San Diego, with Hissy Fit as their opener. In the two years since I'd last seen the female group, apparently their drummer and Stan, The Noise's drummer, had started up a volatile relationship. Having them both on the same bill would make the tour interesting.

The thought of flying home for a quick visit entered my mind. The idea of lazing on a beach and just having time to myself appealed to me more. I spent a couple days doing absolutely nothing in LA and then called up Dawn.

"Hey, you coming out to see any of this tour?" I asked him. "We're not going anywhere near Milwaukee."

"Oh, sugar, I don't know," Dawn moaned. "I want to, and Bradley called....he wants me to as well..."

"He's probably due for a haircut," I laughed.

"Oh, no, I gave him one last week," he said.

"You saw him last week?" I asked. I knew they were friends, but...

"Yeah, he agreed to do the photo shoot for my new make-up line," Dawn replied. "And he badly needed a hair cut. I have a big package to send you. Anyways, so I'm about to launch the line, I have three celebrity haircuts to plan, the album cover shoot for... "

"So you can't make it?" I whined.

"Let's see," Dawn said, as I heard pages riffling. "I have a couple things I can switch around...I can take Thursday and Friday off, but I can't be there for the show on Saturday."

"Then just come out for a mini vacation," I suggested. "A couple days in San Diego, you surprise Brad when he checks into the hotel, and we get you back on a plane Friday night, early Saturday morning....Come on! We can have some girl time."

"Hhhm, OK, I'll come. But I'll be showing up as Dawn, the MAN. I'm too busy to get all dolled up," Dawn said. "But when Bradley arrives, I'll be alllll woman for him!"

I swallowed. "You do whatever works. OK, I'll see you in San Diego. We'll be at the Skyway Inn, right downtown."

I arrived Tuesday night and spent the evening alone. I walked along the docks and admired this particular plot of America. On Wednesday, Dawn arrived early. More strolling, this time in the vibrant downtown core of San Diego. After a delicious dinner in a seafood restaurant, our meal having been caught before our eyes, we headed back to the hotel.

"Let's digest our dinner and then maybe we could go nightclub-bing?" Dawn suggested.

"Sure," I replied. "You gonna change?" By this I meant gender.

"Nah, saving it for Bradley," Dawn answered. "But I am going to put on some Man MakeUp." That was his new line coming out - Man Make-Up. When word got out that Brad was using make-up, a small trickle of laughter started. Bradley nipped it in the bud by giving some interview where he condoned it by calling it a special make-up, made for use by men. Dawn told me, at that point, that was a total fabrication. NovaStar Blemish Stick and NovaStar Eye Liner in Very Black were his go-to products back then.

Suddenly other rock stars wanted this special make-up. Soon drag queens and performance artists and stock brokers on fetish nights demanded the product. Dawn was besieged with orders and terrified of getting sued by NovaStar. "So I came up with my own product," Dawn explained. "Basically, it's still NovaStar make-up, but I've found a way to mush it all up, add my secret ingredient, and then reform it, put it in my packaging and voila! Man MakeUp!"

"And the secret ingredient is...?"

"Secret!" Dawn answered. I didn't pursue it further.

Before we went out dancing, my business partner and I spent some time putting together more Bradley's Hair locks. To be more accurate, Dawn handed me the box of newly cut hair and then sat on the toilet for a good hour while I plastered a pinch of follicles to each sticker.

On Thursday, Dawn informed me I was not to wake him up for any reason. He wanted to get as much beauty sleep as he could. We'd stayed out until four in the morning, having met up with a fun bunch and partying at their upscale home, so I didn't mind sleeping in. Once Dawn finally awoke, just in time for an early dinner, I had the rest of the sticker samples completed.

"I'm out of stickers!" I said. "I can't wait to see Brad; he must look like he's in the military! You gave him quite the haircut. I have about two thousand samples here." I lifted up a small pharmacy bag that had recently held a big box of aspirin. "This is all the hair that I have left."

"Two thousand, huh? That's a lot," Dawn considered. "I'll put it up on eBay and say we only have ten."

"But we have two thousand," I corrected him.

"But we say we have ten," I was informed. "That way, people think they're getting a real special item. Only ten for sale! New strategy. When I sell a hundred, then I adjust the number to nine for sale."

"Is that legal?" I wondered.

"It's business," Dawn said. "Now you're sure Bradley's coming in tonight?"

"The whole band is coming," I replied. "I was just down in the lobby getting them checked in."

"Then I'm getting ready," Dawn said. "Oh! I have an idea! I know how I'm going to surprise Brad!"

So that's how Dawn came to be hiding in Bradley's room when he arrived in San Diego. And due to bad timing, I also happened to be there. It wasn't pretty.

I was in my suite, anticipating the arrival of The Noise, when the hotel phone rang. Dawn was calling from Bradley's room. "Go in the bathroom and get me my shaver," he said. "I'm showing a lot of cleavage and I don't want any chest stubble."

"I'll be right up," I replied, smiling. What a weird and wonderful life I was living. My mind flitted to my children; more to the fact that I was glad not to be making my hit n' miss mac n' cheese or reading another brain-numbing children's story.

Chest stubble or not, Dawn looked like a runway model; tall, beautiful, striking...if a little wide in the shoulders. He was wearing long fake lashes and a wig so cute, I wanted to rip it off his head and pet it. His dress had a long slit up the side, showing shapely legs made even longer by his four-inch stilettos. "Can you just run that over my chest area?" Dawn asked.

"I don't know if I can reach," I replied. "Let's go in the bathroom," I suggested. We walked into the john but it was obvious Dawn had just had a good smelly bowel movement. "On second thought, you sit on the bed and I'll do it."

Out of nowhere, the sound of people arriving on our floor caused us to freeze. Dawn whispered, "Listen to their accents," he said. "They're not from around here. That's a Canadian accent."

I sprinted to the door and eased it open. Bradley's room was at the end of the hall. I could see a bunch of people, but the only one I could see clearly was Tate, unlocking his door and having a laugh with Sherman and BiBi. I shut the door. "They're here!" I quietly screeched. "I have to get out of here!"

"No!" Dawn said. "You'll blow my surprise. Quick! We have to hide!"

My eyes darted around the room. I could easily hide in the washroom but no thank you. I heard Bradley's voice say, "We'll see you in a bit then. Maybe we'll join you for dinner." I didn't want to do this, but I dived behind the armchair in the corner. In the reflection of the large wall mirror, I could see Dawn position himself to be hidden behind the door when it opened.

What should have been a simple prank had to go and turn into major drama.

The door opened, completely shielding Dawn. I saw Bradley walk in and then he held the door while a second person walked into the room. It was at this point that I knew trouble had arrived in the persona of a gorgeous girl, probably a real runway model. Tall, slim, fabulously dressed, she was also black.

Trouble walked in as Brad shut the door. Dawn sprang out, shouting "Surprise!" but he missed his target; he ended up shouting it into the girl's face. "Whoa! What the fuck? You're not Bradley!"

The girl took a couple frightened steps back. "Bradley!" she shrieked. "Call security! There's a crazy fan in here!"

Brad looked stunned to see his hairstylist. "Dawn! What are you doing here? I thought you didn't have time."

"I made time," Dawn said pointedly. "But I can see you have a new friend…"

"Girlfriend," the model corrected him.

"La di da," Dawn smirked at her.

"Well, actually, we've only been going out for a couple weeks," Bradley said. "She's not officially my girlfriend. But…well…she's coming on tour for a week until she has to fly off to Italy. She's a model, you know."

"But of course, " Dawn replied, then looked the model up and down scathingly. "Really? You're a model? I haven't seen your picture anywhere."

The girl shook her long mane. "Almost a supermodel," she bragged and then gave Dawn the same once-over. "And you must play tackle for some second-rate football team."

"I'm a lady, through and through," Dawn said through gritted teeth. "Be grateful for that; otherwise you and me might just be gettin' into it." She turned to Bradley. "Enjoy your time with Miss Anorexia Nervosa here. See you never again."

The model flounced the rest of the way into the room and deposited herself in the armchair I was hiding behind. Bradley grabbed at Dawn's arm. "Dawn!" he pleaded. "If I knew you were going to be here, I'd have come alone. You know that."

Dawn sadly shook his wigged head of hair. "I thought I meant more to you than that," he said. "How easily one can be replaced." In a louder voice, to the model, he snarled, "You hear that, bitch? One can be replaced!" He yanked open the door and walked out into the hallway. Before the door had a chance to completely close, Dawn re-opened it. "Tammy?" he called. "You coming?"

Did Trouble ever let out a scream when I stepped out from behind the chair where she sat. Bradley gaped at me as, red-faced with embarrassment, I ran out of the room. Being caught was never fun.

•••••••••

Dawn was supposed to be with Bradley. I intended to enjoy the evening to myself before the big tour began. Instead, Dawn and I had an all-night business meeting.

Heading back to my suite, Dawn was almost apoplectic with anger. "I should have done it! I should have just given her a beat-down. I could've taken her."

"Easily," I agreed. "I mean, you're six and a half feet in heels, you've got way more muscles, you outweigh her by a couple hundred pounds. Plus, you're a man."

"True, true, but tonight I was a lady, don't you think?" Dawn asked. "I mean, she was asking for a fight and I just walked away."

I didn't think Miss Trouble was looking to get into an actual brawl... maybe more of a shriekfest, but I let it slide. "You were pretty hard on Bradley though," I had to say.

Dawn stuck his nose up in the air. "Bradley and I are through! I'm never speaking to him again!"

I took a big gulp before asking the burning question, but I had to know. "Dawn, what exactly is it between you two?"

Dawn looked pitifully sad as he replied, "We have a bond. The two of us...we're different from the rest of the world. Brad and I, we understand each other! And just because I can't be on the tour this time, he brings along a miniature version of me."

I unlocked the door to my hotel room. "Come on, Dawn, you know Brad, he's a big rock star. So he brings along a groupie..."

"I know, how cheap!" Dawn cried out. "Well, like I said, I'm done with him! That business we have with his hair? You can have it."

"No, Dawn!" I wailed. "I need you!" He had no idea. While I was very adept at the factory-work part of the job (affixing hair to stickers, mailing them out to the customer list Dawn emailed me), I had no idea how to work eBay or any of the other computer sites.

"You don't need me," Dawn returned. "You can run the company alone. It's not difficult. Now what are we going to do tonight? It's still early. Let's go out and get drunk, go dancing, do something to get Brad off my mind."

"I know!" I said, as if I'd just come up with a brilliant idea. "How about you show me how to run a computer?" Dawn blinked at me. "Just the sites to run A Lock of Bradley's Hair."

"It's so easy," Dawn insisted.

I winced. "I doubt it," I replied. "But if you can show me how to work it, let's say within two hours, then drinks are on me tonight."

We went to the business room in the hotel where they supplied a computer and a printer. Shooing Sherman off the computer, Dawn became an army drill sergeant as he taught me how to work the business end of A Lock of Bradley's Hair. He didn't suffer my errors mildly; before long I avoided his wrath by not making mistakes. Lo and behold, it was so much easier than I'd imagined.

"I don't know what I was so scared of to begin with," I marvelled. "You just basically follow the computer's commands."

"And look, we still have thirty minutes left," Dawn said, glancing at the clock. "Let's print up the contact files and then I want to show you something."

As the printer did its job, Dawn switched programs on the computer. "Look, here's the website for ManMakeUp," he bragged. "Wow, check out how many hits I've gotten already! The site's only been up a week!"

The website, though selling make-up, was decidedly manly. No splashy colours, no quirky fonts. The only problem? "Geez, too bad Bradley is the main model! Are you going to have to re-do it?"

The printer finished its task as Dawn cleared the computer history. "Nope, I'm going to ride Bradley's coattails all I can. If he wants these pictures off the website, he can tell me himself. Until then, I'm not going to love him...I'm going to use him. Do you have a problem with that?"

I considered my hoard of Bradley's hair. "No, I guess that's business, right? Now how about those drinks?"

"I'm going back up to the room first and fixing my makeup," Dawn said. "We're going dancing and I'm gonna find myself a live one!"

Drinks didn't cost me much. After the first round, a couple cowboys took a liking to us. We danced and necked with our partners and did a lot of laughing.

The night ended when we had to part ways at four in the morning. Dawn had decided to catch a red-eye flight back to Milwaukee. He was going to run back to the hotel room and grab his stuff; I was going to hook up with Dylan. As the four of us waited for a taxi, Dawn shivered and his date put his arms around Dawn's bare, shimmery sparkle-dusted shoulders. Nuzzling his neck, his date whispered, "Come on, sweet thing, come back to my place."

Dawn twisted around and pressed his body up close to his date, giving him a deep kiss. "There, something to remember me by," he purred.

"Oh God, who can forget a hot dame like you," the guy panted. The cab pulled up and Dawn disentangled from the gent and faced me.

"Though I hate his guts, you take care of Bradley, you hear?" Dawn said. "And promise me we'll stay in touch."

I nodded. "I will and I will." And then, "Good-bye, kind sir," I said as Dawn bent his body into the taxi. Dawn's date had a rueful smile on his face that disappeared when his body gave an involuntary shudder and he staggered backwards. I turned back to Dawn, "What? You didn't tell him?"

He sadly mouthed, "I forgot" as the door shut and the cab pulled away. I laughed nervously. Too bad the cowboys didn't find it that funny. Since my date suddenly demanded I prove I had a vagina, I immediately lost interest in him.

My taxi to the hotel probably arrived fifteen minutes after Dawn's, but I still missed him. He'd packed up and left, leaving nothing but his false eyelashes sitting on the sink like a pair of exotic insects.

• • • • • • • • • •

That tour would change, if not my life, at least my address. I fell in love with San Diego. So did the guys from The Noise. On the last tour, I heard a lot of talk about moving to the USA. The only thing holding them back was the anticipated scorn from their fellow countrymen. Another famous Canadian leaves to seek their fortune in the US. That was the key word - fortune.

On this trip, the guys were barely in town three days before Tate had a solution, as well as a realtor. "Guys, we keep our primary residence in Canada," he explained. "But we can all have a second home, can't we? We're big fucking rock stars, are we not?"

Bradley spoke up. "I already have a second house. That cottage in The Muskokas."

"Oh, right, the one you never go to," Tate recalled. "So then own a third home! I say we get a place here in San Diego, and base ourselves out of here for awhile."

Mickey was all for the plan. "Have to live somewhere, don't we? And we're always in the States these days anyhow. Save us having to cross that miserable border every time we have to come here."

Stan gave his vote. "Tell your realtor guy to find me something in the half-mil range. I'm all for this idea. Now I can live closer to Nina. Toronto to Los Angeles was a head-ache. San Diego to Los Angeles? Hell, I can drive that."

Nina was Hissy Fit's drummer. A fiery petite redhead, prone to cursing and acting like a typical diva, she drove Stan crazy. She lived to please only herself and her much-publicized antics made Stan wild with jealousy. It seemed every man wanted her, but she chose Stan to be her official boyfriend. That was enough to make him put up with her constant philandering.

I never did get to know Nina, other than to stay out of her way, but she did account for A Lock of Bradley's Hair forming a subsidiary company. We were barely into the tour when Nina and Stan had a blowout that was witnessed by about forty people. The Noise had just come offstage and headed for their dressing room. I tagged along to fulfill my obligations - hand Bradley a cold Coors, light Mickey's cigarette, take the sweaty towel Stan used to wipe his face. He had about a dozen specially-monogrammed towels he used onstage, made by an adoring fan. She also made Tate a dozen do-rags, which he tossed to me in disgust. "Use these to clean Brad's puke," he suggested. He had a point - Bradley liked to experiment when he partied, even though his gut continuously let him know it was a bad idea.

I'd just managed to squeeze into the packed dressing room, filled with groupies, management executives, contest winners, people who knew someone who got them in. Suddenly a roar went up from a guy by the washroom door. I was surprised to see it came from Stan, who stood glaring into the space, a drumstick hanging limply in each hand. "What the fuck?!" was what I'd heard him say.

A voice drifted out, quite calmly saying, "There was no privacy in my dressing room. You guys were on stage and this room was empty... "

Stan dropped the sticks and reached into the stall. He pulled out a man who had his leather pants draped around his ankles. "Hey, hey, cool it, man," the guy said, his erection quite impressive. "Nina's an old friend.... "

Stan threw him up against the wall. "Nobody fucks my girlfriend!" A few people in the crowd tittered and Stan again banged him against the wall as he added, "...in my dressing room!"

Nina came out, bare-chested but doing up the zipper on her red mini-skirt. "Stan! Stop it!" she screeched. "This is Flavio! He gave me my first break in this business!"

Holding Flavio up with both hands, Stan turned his head over his shoulder and said, "So this is how you continue to pay him? With pussy?"

"Oh, you're a pig!" Nina screamed. In a flash, she picked up one of Stan's drumsticks and darted forward with it, holding it aloft like a dagger. Nobody moved, nobody spoke as she drove the pointed end of the stick into Stan's eye. Stan immediately dropped Flavio from his grip as he threw both hands over the blood spurting from his face.

"My eye! My eye!" he cried, followed by, "You bitch! You bitch!"

It was only then that the crowd sprung into action. People took photographs, the media called in 'live on the scene' reports, a couple groupies threw up into the bowl of chips. Only the rest of The Noise and I ran to check on Stan. Sherman was already on the phone to 911.

"Dude, it's not as bad as you think," Tate tried to reassure a crying Stan.

"How can you say that?" I asked. "What with the drumstick still stuck in his eye?"

Tate gave me a look that made me shut up. "The ambulance is on its way, buddy," he said. "Just hang in there."

"Get the stick outta my fuckin' eye," Stan moaned.

Bradley looked ready to pull his usual vomitus routine. "You just let the paramedics take care of that," he said. "That's their....you know... area of expertise."

"Take it out!" Stan yelled. "Take it out!"

"Stan, take it easy… Listen, I hear the sirens," Tate said. "Can you hear the sirens?"

Everybody pretended they could hear sirens; even Stan stopped moaning and was still. We weren't expecting him to suddenly reach out with both hands and pull out the drumstick. It withdrew cleanly, but with a sick slurpy sound. Bradley immediately turned around and puked into the same chip bowl as the groupies. They both seemed thrilled that Bradley would join them.

"Jesus Christ!" Mickey jumped out of the way, banging into Nina.

"I'm out of here," he said.

"Me too," Nina decided.

Flavio was pulling up his pants. "Wait for me," he said, though nobody listened. He made a quick exit.

Tate backed away from the blood spurting from the drummer's eye. "You fucking idiot, I said don't do that! Oh fuck, what a mess." He turned to Sherman. "Fuck man! Did you call an ambulance yet?"

"They're on the way!" Sherman yelled. "There's a lot of traffic because of...you know...the concert."

"Well, he's gonna lose an eye if they don't get here soon!" Tate yelled back, then turned to Stan. "Why the fuck you still going out with that bitch, man?"

Stan looked up at me. "Does it look bad?" he groaned.

"Uhhhh….," I didn't know how to answer. Do I pick 'Oh God it looks like you may die!' or do I just go with a simple 'Yes'? Instead I chose, "It's hard to say; there's so much blood."

"Does it look bad?" Stan repeated.

I was still holding his sweaty towel so I knelt down and gingerly dabbed at the area surrounding the wound. "Maybe if I clean off some of the blood, I can see better what it looks like." I calmed my fear by telling myself it was only blood; I'd seen worse in the piles of Bradley's vomit I'd clean up. Once I swear I saw an undigested goldfish.

Sure enough, it wasn't as bad as it looked. After clearing away most of the blood with the moist towel, I could see the ragged hole in his eyeball, which was still pumping out a river of blood. "Wow," I said, "whoever thought an eyeball could hold so much blood!" I held up the bloody towel. "I guess you should be putting pressure on it."

Stan was about to take the towel from my hands when the paramedics rushed in. I stepped aside, almost losing my footing as the drumstick slash weapon rolled under my boot. I reached down and picked it up, ready to hand it over to any official who asked for it.

One of the paramedics reached Stan and before he even looked at the wound, he shouted over the din, "Can everybody leave the room, please! We have a stretcher coming in and we need some space!" Nobody moved, and the paramedic yelled his order a second time. "If you have no business here, please leave!" He glanced at his partner, who was looking at Stan. "How's he look?"

"Looks like he's going to lose an eye," the partner replied.

I took that as my cue to leave.

· · · · · · · · ·

As it turned out, Stan lost his right eye. The incident made the head-lines, of course. How could it not, what with the eyewitnesses and the reporters. Nina got off with a warning, her and Stan reunited for a couple more months, and both bands only got bigger. For some reason, even Flavio got some kind of a recording deal.

I kept that bloody towel, as well as the attempted murder weapon. Stan wore a drab medical eye patch while he was in the hospital. We celebrated when he came out and he discarded the eye patch for a new one. I picked the discarded eye patch out of the kitchen garbage, wiped the bit of guacamole from it and added it to my collection of weird stuff. The first patch he wore was not to his liking; he feared it made him look like a pirate. Within days he'd exchanged it for one more fitting to a rock star's lifestyle - purple, with a snake coming out of a skull embroidered onto it. Pretty soon he became like Elton John with the various eyeglasses; Stan had about a hundred styles of eyepatches. I also managed to snag that first plain black one, left discarded on a bathroom counter when he exchanged it for his new look.

At first I thought I was collecting mementoes to remind me of that shocking event. Then one day I looked at my collection and suspected I might be going a little overboard with it. I was going to throw away the boring black eyepatch but for a lark, decided to offer it up on eBay. I had photographs of him wearing it from a couple newspapers and could also supply a certificate of authenticity. I gave it a week and hoped it would be worth the effort.

One week later, I was a thousand dollars richer. That money was in-stantly wired home to my mother to spend on the kids. I urged her to buy them toys and candy and take them to the mall and let them pick out anything they wanted. It had been three months since I'd last seen them and probably six months since I'd last given any money to Kitty. She would tell me it wasn't necessary, but she never refused it. Sending that money home felt so good. It seemed to lift a lot of guilt off my shoulders.

So good that I started to seek out other things I could sell. I went years and years picking up odds and ends without The Noise getting any wiser. Scribbled notes, guitar picks, earrings, anything I could authenticate and attribute to The Noise. Selling this eclectic assortment of mundane stuff to zealous fans helped to supplement my intermittent salary as assistant road manager.

It was hysterical what fans coveted. It could be the fork Bradley used in a diner to Tate's broken guitar strings. Deciding on a price was difficult so I just went with what felt right, what I might be willing to pay if I were a diehard fan.

And when I sold big-ticket items, such as the six hundred bucks for Bradley's worn out electric toothbrush that played the Spiderman theme song, that income went to Kitty. It made my conscience feel so much better.

CHAPTER VII

Volumes could be written about my fifteen years as an assistant road manager, yet the decade and a half seemed to pass far too quickly. The party felt like it had just begun when I was asked to leave.

Here's how it went down - The Noise were doing a round of summer concerts throughout Canada. One show a week, often sharing the bill with a dozen other acts. Sometimes they were the headliners, often not. The Noise were still cranking out records, though achieving a number one hit now seemed almost impossible. Their fame had peaked about five years ago, but they still had their loyal fans.

When we left on this tour, I noticed Bradley brought along a new girl-friend. Trisha was a lovely thing; pert and vibrant and ever so devoted to her besotted twenty-year older boyfriend. She couldn't do enough for him. I didn't mind. Bradley took up a lot of my energies so I let her have her fun. She'd probably be gone before the tour was over. Brad went through a different girlfriend every new moon.

Speaking of girlfriends, at this point only Brad was single. Stan still continued to have me garner love-mates for him from the crowd - I had that task down to a fine art - but he got married to his long-time (long-suffering?) girlfriend five years ago. And he no longer lived in San Diego; Stan was the first to move back to Canada and lived in Winnipeg. Mickey had divorced that horrid woman I'd first met and went on to marry two more horrid women. I had a feeling his third marriage was on the rocks as well but that was Mickey - always looking to get hurt. He now lived in New

York. Bradley lived wherever he felt like - I couldn't even say for certain he used any of the homes he owned. Tate was the only one who kept his California home, but he rented it out. Still married to the supermodel, his wife foresaw the future for aging women and quit the business to take on a role as a talk show host for Boom TV in Toronto. Since she was currently bringing in more dough than her lead guitarist husband, and since he was still over the moon about her, Tate was content to move back to Toronto.

I still lived in San Diego. With my kids? No, but I did once fly the whole bunch out to visit me. My apartment, small to begin with, became crazy with three young teens and all their baggage. Oh, and my mother who had fifty ideas about what they should do on this trip. I know San Diego had a famous zoo, but did she know the cost of taking five people? I had different plans - getting the twins' upper ears pierced, taking Rain to a band rehearsal. What with Kitty wrecking my cappuccino maker and the twins trying on all my make-up and Rain screwing up my TV's recording schedule...well, I never had them back again. I stuck with making my twice-yearly trips home.

Of course I was judged an unfit mother by some and I didn't bother to defend myself. I had an inkling all along that motherhood was not my calling. With firm conviction, I was able to declare that they were being raised in a sound and healthy home, away from toxic contaminants such as myself.

I digress. On this trip, everything was as per normal. I administered to the needs of The Noise, while still managing to find bits and pieces of sellable goods. I will admit that maybe I no longer dressed to kill. Sure I travelled with a rock band, but my duties really didn't call for me to wear more than jeans or sweats with some logo'd t-shirt. I would smile to myself upon seeing Trisha's get-ups, reminiscent of my earlier years. The short skirts, the fishnet stockings, the low-cut tank tops. The style that never went out of fashion.

We were pulling into Halifax about midway through the trip. As we neared the hotel, Bradley pulled himself out of his three-hour smooch fest to say, "Tammy, would you get me my duffel from the overhead?"

Even though it was right above him, I did as I was told. I lifted the door to the compartment and saw Bradley's army-green duffel bag wedged inside. I tugged at it but it was stuck tight. The moment it sprung clear, I noticed the falling bag had quite a bit of weight to it. As I tried to catch it, my peripheral vision caught sight of Brad and Trisha right below the duffel, their tongues exploring each other's mouths. As the bag tumbled out, I bent over the oblivious couple to protect them. The corner of the duffel, what felt like whiskey bottles, struck my neck and upper back.

I collapsed to the floor, the bag on top of me. I saw Brad look over his seat. "Thanks," he said. "Could you pass it over?"

BiBi, seven months pregnant, stood up and glared. "Jesus Christ, Bradley, can't you see she's hurt?" This was her third child with Sherman, but the first time I'd ever seen her cross with Bradley. Pregnancy may have been affecting her.

"I'll get your bag for you, Bradley," Trisha said. She slid over her lover's lap and picked the bag off me.

"Owww...," I moaned.

"Get up, Tammy," Brad ordered. "You're ok. We're almost at the hotel."

I tried to stand. "Owwww!" I said louder. BiBi was instantly by my side.

"Where does it hurt?" she asked.

"Owww, my back, I think...or my neck ... owww. "

BiBi looked over at Sherman. "We better get her to the hospital," she decreed.

Of course we had to go to the hotel first. BiBi helped me into a bus seat and I waited for twenty minutes while Sherman checked them in and the luggage was unloaded. Stan walked up to me. "Can you make sure the new drumsticks get to my room? They're in a box, it's written 'new drumsticks' right on it."

I gave him a withering look. "Does it look like I can do anything right now?"

Trisha, picking up the litter on the bus, said, "Don't worry, Stan, I'll cover it."

Finally the bus emptied and we got directions to the closest hospital. Turned out I had a dislocated shoulder from the duffel bag, a couple broken ribs from hitting an arm rest as I fell and various aches, pains and bruises. Nothing a couple days of bed rest and an arm sling couldn't cure. BiBi, bless her heart, became my nurse. Shame on me for the years of secret scorn I'd felt for her! As we waited for hours in the hospital, we got to reminiscing about how long we'd known each other. I did the math and discovered this was my fifteenth year with The Noise.

"We should throw some kind of party for that," BiBi said. "It's been a long time since we celebrated anything."

"There's still parties after the shows," I said. BiBi threw back her head and laughed.

""If you can call them parties," she scoffed. "So much talking about the good old days when they used to make hit records. Trying to still look virile for those stupid groupies and instead they all look pathetic."

My disbelief at her heretic remarks almost made me forget my discomfort. "BiBi, I can't believe you said that, but man, you're dead on. That's how I see it too. There's times I don't even feel like going to the parties."

"So let's make a real party," she said. "Celebrate your fifteen years with the band."

In the end, we decided to just present a big cake at the party for the last show on tour. BiBi ordered it in advance from a fancy bakery in Victoria, where the final gig would take place. How I wish I'd gotten to know her better earlier in our lives...or maybe she'd matured in the many years since I'd first met her, but by then I was too lazy to give it a chance. On this trip, she became my new best friend. By coincidence, Aapo was along on this tour, but our friendship had cooled. That was a good thing. For a couple years, Aapo toured with The Noise and as our friendship cemented, so did the secret yearning I had for him. Then he hooked up with a different band after that and I didn't see him at all, allowing my desire to burn out. His accommodating replacement helped matters.

For me, Halifax was a washout. I laid in my hotel room bed while the boys played two nights in a row. I worried about how The Noise was getting along without me to make sure their flies were zipped up before going onstage. "Don't worry, " BiBi said, bringing me some fresh-caught seafood. "Trisha is taking up the slack."

"Yeah, for Bradley, but what about the rest of the guys?" I wondered.

"Oh, she seems to be making everybody happy," BiBi replied.

I was relieved that things were under control. As we left Halifax and headed to Moncton, I lay back in my bus seat. BiBi had found some pillows and made my chair almost like a hospital bed. As I watched Trisha picking up rolling pop cans and spraying air freshener into the wash-room, I appreciated her efforts. And seeing as how I was still in an arm sling, I let her toil away through the Moncton show as well.

We had a long road trip after that into Hamilton. That was a skip and a jump to Toronto, so I made a quick trip home. Rain had finished his first year of university and the girls were about to start their first year. What was to be a joyous reunion - who knew when we'd all be in the same city again? - turned into a dour time. The kids had something to talk to me about, something I never saw coming.

"Grandma Kitty seems sick," Tatum began.

"Whaddaya mean, 'sick'?" I asked. "She told me she sees a doctor. I never heard of anything."

Sadie continued. "Mom, it's like she's getting senile or something. She turns the stove on and then goes for a nap. Or just last week, she goes to the corner store and somehow ends up sleeping in a park?"

Rain nodded. "That had us scared. Took us four hours to find her."

"You know we love her to death, but we're worried," Tatum said earnestly. "Come September, none of us kids will be here. Grandma Kitty will be all alone. What are we going to do about her? Is there somebody who can come live with her?"

As it transpired, we found a couple senior's homes and got Kitty on the waiting list. Through Rain's contacts at his medical school, he found some fairly cheap help to come and look in on Kitty. He even found a couple to live in the big house rent-free, but they left before two weeks had passed, claiming my mother was not the charming old lady they were led to believe.

It was during the show in Hamilton where I realized I was still not in top physical condition. My ribs still ached, I couldn't carry anything heavy and my bruised back was slow in healing. Speedy Gonzales I was not. There were no complaints, thanks to Trisha's unasked-for help. I couldn't thank her enough.

I got better as we neared the end of this road trip, though I wasn't yet one hundred per cent. Even though the boys weren't very solicitous as to my well-being, I looked forward to their last concert. In the past, the after-party for the final show would have been a blow-out. These days, it was more like a relief. They could get off the road and back to their cushy homes, making the odd MegaMusic appearance or lending a hand as a celebrity judge on "Canada's Rock Star Search". However, at this party, I was going to publicly pat myself on the back for having stuck with this band for fifteen years.

Finally the tour came to its last gig in Victoria. The after-party was in full swing; Mickey and another guitarist in his 60's from the opening act were showing each other different riffs on their bass guitars. Tate was having a quiet conversation with a group of suits while Stan sat on a stool, surrounded on either side by a fairly attentive pair of women. They appeared to be a mother and her daughter; Stan cautiously played his hand in the hope of landing this fantasy hookup. Bradley sat on the couch, his feet up on the coffee table. His girlfriend Trisha, unbelievably still on the tour, had unlaced his boots and was massaging his feet. A couple members from another band The Noise had befriended were also hanging out in the suite, picking at the snacks on the food table.

I walked to the door and peeked into the hallway. BiBi was due to show up any moment with the cake; I wanted her to hurry before it reached midnight. I was afraid the boys were ready to hit the sack. I had just barely closed the door when there came a knock. With a big smile, I shouted out to the general assembly, "Hey, guys, got a little surprise for you."

I swung the door open and in walked Sherman. The guys all laughed. "Oh, wow, Sherman!" yelled Stan. "Like we haven't seen him enough all summer!"

"Where's BiBi?" I asked him.

He shrugged. "I dunno, she had to go down to the hotel's kitchen for some reason. She should be here any minute." He turned his attention to the boys in the room. "You think you've seen enough of me already?" he teased. "Then I guess you don't want to get back on the road with the Legends of Rock tour?"

Brad looked up from his foot massage. "Legends of Rock? That's been going on for a couple weeks already," he commented. "And besides, none of those bands are real legends, unless you count Hard Knocks."

"Yes, Hard Knocks, the headliners," Sherman said mysteriously. "The same band that just got busted for possession of cocaine...much cocaine... at the border. They're off the tour."

Tate stepped away from his group of men, Stan used his female bookends to haul himself off the stool and Mickey stopped playing that depressing chord. Bradley stood up slowly and held up a cautionary hand. "So you're telling us that we've been asked to replace Hard Knocks? As the headline act? Cuz the rest of the acts...Rainbow Arc and The Hogan Family, shit like that...we're not that calibre. I'm not going to be dumped in with them."

Sherman looked like the cat who swallowed the canary, nay, a freaking pigeon, he was so smug. "Your name, top of the bill. You guys want to talk about it or what? I got to call them back. They're desperate."

Tate said, "Desperate? Maybe you can get us nicer hotels than we got on this tour?"

Sherman spread his arms wide. "Guys, why do you think I'm here? That's a done deal already."

"So when would we leave?" Mickey asked. "I have to prepare the old lady back home. She hates me being on the road all the time. This should be good for a month of nagging."

"Well, like Brad said, the tour is already booked," Sherman explained. "They've had to cancel the Niagara Falls shows on both sides of the border, as well as the one in Toronto. They want to know if we can make the Casino Kato show. That's next Friday, less than a week."

"That sounds good to me," Mickey said.

"Ohhh, Casino Kato!" Trisha's voice came from the couch where she was folding Bradley's poncho. "I've never been to a casino!"

Sherman looked at her and then said apologetically, "Sorry, doll, we're all travelling on one big bus. No wives or girlfriends, just the bands and (he pointed at himself and me) essential road crew." He turned back to the boys. "It's going to be a lot of work," Sherman warned. "It's not just weekend shows. You're looking at a lot of travel. The schedule looks like there's about five shows a week, all different cities."

Stan snuck a peek behind him at his two groupies. Assured they couldn't see his actions, he cupped his penis area. "I'm up for five shows a week...ha ha...ya know what I mean."

Tate looked at Bradley. "Would be a good way to keep flogging TNT Time," Tate said. TNT Time, their latest album, or was it a CD at this point, had not been doing very well. The songs on it were quite terrific but the album title made me think of scones.

Bradley dramatically flung his hair to the left and then looked at his bandmates. He zeroed in on Stan. "You got that STD of your's under control?" he asked, saying it loudly on purpose. The ladies heard that remark and shared a horrified look. Stan simply nodded. "Well, then, I say let's get back on the road."

The boys let loose their pent-up excitement. Stan leaned forward and gave the mother a big kiss. She immediately withdrew a tissue out of her pocket and wiped her lips. Mickey tried to high-five his guitar pal, who gave him a dejected limp hand. Tate grabbed the reporters, telling them they had an exclusive. Bradley picked up his tiny girlfriend and swung her around in a big circle.

In the joyous noise, I thought I heard a knock at the door. I reopened it and saw BiBi standing there with a gigantic cake. She went all out. It was emblazoned with miniature guitars and microphones and speakers, as well as a little toy bus with a tiny lady in front. The writing on the cake simply said Happy 15th Anniversary!

"What's going on?" BiBi asked. "I had to knock twice, almost dropped the cake."

"We're going back on tour," I replied. "Like, immediately."

"Ok, let's put this cake down. It's heavy," BiBi said, resting it on top of her pregnant baby bump. "Get ready for your big speech."

"Guys!" I called out over the unaccustomed noise. "Here's the surprise I was telling you about!" I almost had everybody's attention. Tate was still busy talking to the reporters. Bradley held Trisha's crying face in both his hands and he seemed to be speaking to her quite seriously. I amped up my voice. "Guys! Tate and Bradley! I want to celebrate something here so can I PLEASE have your attention!"

Everybody finally turned to me as I brandished a knife. Bradley let go of Trisha and looked over at the table. "What? It's just a fuckin' cake." He reached back to Trisha so I quickly spoke up.

"Bradley, it's not just a cake, it's an anniversary cake!" I said with glee.

Mickey shuddered. "Eww, I've seen a few of those."

"Someone has a wedding anniversary?" a reporter asked.

"No!" I shouted. "We're celebrating fifteen years since I signed on with The Noise. Fifteen years I've been the assistant road manager to you bunch of slobs," I joked.

"That long, huh?" Bradley asked. "Wow, you're getting old."

He was in a peculiar mood; it almost seemed like he was picking on me. He wasn't going to break the party atmosphere I was trying so hard to conjure up. "Speech! Speech!" BiBi reminded me.

I pulled out a couple pieces of paper. I'd worked hard on the heartfelt message I wanted to deliver. I cleared my throat and then began. "To the members of The Noise. When I first met you fifteen years ago, I went on tour with Screw U....."

"Oh! The tour!" Sherman interrupted my speech. "I have to go make that call!" He ran out of the room.

"Where did you say your first show with the Legends would be?" a nosy reporter asked Tate.

"Casino Kato," Tate replied, always looking for more press. He turned to Bradley. "You know, I bet I can get my wife to do a segment on us for her TV show."

"Connections," Brad said. "That's what it's all about."

"Can we cut the cake already?" Mickey whined. "I'm beat, I wanna go to bed."

I handed the knife over to BiBi, rather than using it on the party poopers. "Fine then," I groused. "I'm kind of glad I ended my speech at Screw U."

"Lighten up, Tammy," Bradley said. "You've been a real drag this whole trip."

I was insulted. "No, I haven't!" I denied. "I was injured. Geez, give me some slack!"

BiBi cut the cake into squares and placed them onto plates. "Come and get some!" she called out. The reporters came over, but the band had resumed their own private activities. I ended up personally delivering everyone in the room a slice of cake.

Remembering the bottle of champagne, I pulled it out of the fridge where it was chilling. With the corkscrew in hand, I walked up to Bradley. "Would you mind opening this?" I asked. "I can't do it. My shoulder is still sore."

"Babe, opening champagne bottles? That should be one of your priority jobs," Bradley teased, a bit scathingly. He popped the cork and handed it over. I filled a glass for him, one for Trisha since it would have been rude not to, and one for myself. We all threw our drinks back.

"Brad, how many plastic pails do you think we've been....," I tried to reminisce.

"Oh, really, you want to bring that up?" Brad said dismissively. He completely turned his back on me. I walked to Mickey. Another glass went to him and his friend.

After downing our glasses, I made another attempt. "Mickey, when we met, that first wife of your's terrified me! I was...."

Mickey crushed his plastic glass in his hand. "Ah! You can call that my nightcap!" he said, clapping his friend hard on the shoulder. "You look us up if you can, though I have no idea where we'll be. Give me your number." I was totally ignored.

Moving on to Stan, I poured a small tumbler as well for his lady guests. We toasted my anniversary and then I began to speak. "Stan, remember that bloody eye patch the hospital sent you home in? You're not going to believe this, I still have.... "

"Oh, fuck, the new eye patches I ordered!" Stan griped. "Tammy, you get in touch with House of Leather and have them shipped to me the minute they're done."

By this time, the mother groupie was planting kisses on Stan's neck, rubbing her chest against the sagging skin of his muscular arms. She no longer seemed to have a problem with his medical issues. Her daughter didn't know me from Adam so she turned around and began snapping some cellphone photos. She thought she was being discreet. Discreet? I wrote the book on cell phone camera discretion. How do you think I could authenticate so many items?

Tate was my last prospect. With the rest of the champagne, I poured a glass for him and the two reporters. "Cheers," Tate said, downing his glass. He looked at me. "Was there something else?"

I opened my mouth and then clamped it shut, just shaking my head. I went to sit on the couch next to Bradley and Trisha but they rudely stood up and immediately moved off to the opposite end of the suite. I was so happy to see Aapo walk in, I actually made a big production out of it.

"Aapo, my long time buddy! Come sit with me! Have a piece of cake!" I called out with forced cheer. "We're celebrating! It's a party!"

Aapo looked around the room. "No music? Good, that's a party I like.

I'm sick of music."

Bradley punched him in the arm. "Don't talk like that. I want you back on tour."

Aapo looked thrilled. "Back on tour? Already?" Brad did a little happy dance. Aapo joined him "Oh, man, that's great! I can't stand to be at home. Me and the wife...not so good..." My slightly inebriated heart soared. Maybe there was still a smidgen of a chance I could make Aapo mine! At least for one frigging night.

"I wish I had some champagne left to offer you, Aapo," I apologized.

"Oh, no, I can't drink," Aapo said. "I just came back for a set of keys. We're not done loading the truck yet. I will take a piece of cake though!" He read the words on his large helping. "Whose anniversary?" he asked.

"Mine," I answered. "Fifteen years with The Noise."

"Happy anniversary," Aapo said courteously. "And Brad, dude, thanks for the job!"

Aapo's exit seemed to start a mass exodus. Stan announced he was going down to the front lobby; they were going to hail a cab for the daughter. I guess Mommy was staying overnight. The suits walked out with the reporters; I heard one of the suits asking if there were any strip joints around, and one of the reporters offering to take them. Tate declared he had to call his wife before she conked out.

"Ah, you're pussy-whipped!" Bradley teased him.

"Yeah, well maybe there's a little more that goes on in that call than you know," Tate teased back, fairly skipping out of the room. "See ya guys in the morning!"

Good ol' BiBi tried to stick it out but as soon as Tate left, she said, "Sherman just texted me. For crying out loud, I've got a gigantic belly but he wants me to get back to the room right away. What can I say, business always makes him horny."

That left Bradley, Trisha and myself. Three's a crowd? Elephant in the room? A rose between two thorns? All those cliches seemed to rain down as I digested the situation. Yeah, maybe time to take my cake and leave.

Trisha and Bradley sat entwined on the couch watching me clean up the food table. May as well take the chips and the mixed nuts as well. I walked to the door, looked over at the couple and said, "Well, night, you two."

As I turned back to the door, out of the corner of my eye I saw Trisha nudge Bradley with her elbow. A sixth sense told me the nudge had something to do with me as a dark foreboding snuffed out my champagne high. Bradley spoke up in an odd high-pitched tone. "Tammy, hang on just a minute."

I stood by the door and looked over at the pair on the couch. Trisha stood up. "Maybe I should leave you two alone," she suggested. She leaned in and gave Bradley a small kiss. "Strength, baby," she whispered. What the hell kind of see-ya-later was that?

Trisha slid by me as she left the suite, making sure not to touch me or make eye contact. I shut the door after her and then looked over at Brad, who was checking himself out in the mirror. "Do you think my hair's getting thin in the back?" he asked me.

"I don't know. Why don't you ask Trisha?" was my comeback. I shouldn't bite the hand that feeds me, but he'd been pretty much a bastard the whole night.

"Yeah, Trisha, that's what I want to talk to you about," he remembered.

I relaxed a little. Bradley just probably wanted to bend my ear with his romantic woes. Did I think they were a good match? Did she cramp his style? Who had the best hair? The usual issues that bothered the insecure singer. "What? You and Trisha?" I asked, leading him into the conversation.

"No, YOU and Trisha," Brad answered, confusing me somewhat. The blinking of my eyes must have conveyed my bewilderment. "I think it's time for you to trade jobs," Brad explained.

I laughed and said, "What? She becomes assistant road manager and I become your girlfriend?"

Brad didn't laugh. "No, more like she becomes assistant road manager and you don't."

"But...but...," was all I could think of to say. Finally I added, "...but why?"

Brad shrugged insolently. "You know, you're injured..."

"I'm almost all better!" I jumped in.

"And you've been with us a long time," Brad continued. "I mean, fifteen years? I never realized it'd been so long. It's time for some new blood, new faces."

"And you think Trisha's face is going to be able to clean up your puke,

Brad?" I shot back. "Clean up the ashtrays Mickey fills up? Or his disgusting condoms?"

"She's been doing a pretty good job of it this whole tour," Brad pointed out. "Anyhow, there's no point in talking about it. I've made up my mind."

"Brad! You can't just boot me out of a job like this!" I sputtered. "After all the time I put into taking care of you guys. Jesus, I was like your mother! And now you're firing me?"

"Tammy, you're right, you're right, you've been good to us," Brad acknowledged. I stopped snivelling, glad he was seeing it my way. "We should keep you in the organization. I'm going to talk to Sherman, see if he can find you a job somewhere."

His reply left me speechless. As I tried not to break down crying, Brad walked over to the food table. "You took all the cake? Ah, that's ok, I didn't really want any. But happy anniversary, Tammy. See if you can find Trisha for me."

As far as I was concerned, I was off the clock. He could find her himself. I hustled to my hotel room, laid the cake down and then burst into tears. Some celebration.

When it comes to throwing a party, tonight's was definitely a bust.

• • • • • • • • • •

When the time came to say good-bye the next morning, the boys all gave me a quick hug and wished me well. Even Bradley acted like he hadn't stabbed me in the back. The only person who seemed to be responsive to my sad frame of mind was BiBi. I gave her a tight squeeze as I muffled a few sobs into her scented neck. You'd think we'd been good friends for the past fifteen years rather than the fifteen days it had been.

"Hush, hush, now," BiBi patted my back, at the same time adroitly moving me aside as Trisha passed with somebody's suitcase. "It's all gonna work out, you'll see. And don't you worry about Bradley. I'll keep an eye on him for you."

That was enough to stop the waterworks. I pulled back from her embrace and sputtered, "Bradley? Bradley? Why the hell would I give a royal FUCK about him? BiBi, he's the one who screwed me over!"

We both looked over at the front of the bus, where Brad had Trisha in a PG-rated kiss. They broke apart and Bradley handed his duffel bag to her as she boarded the bus. BiBi scrunched up her nose. "I didn't think she'd last this long," she muttered. With a tortured smile, she said, "Looks like Brad's in love. I guess we should all be happy."

I wasn't happy. Didn't look like BiBi was either. Something clicked in my tear-laden brain and I pulled my new friend away from the group. "Look, Beeb, I'm going to tell you something, but it's a big secret," I warned.

"A secret? I love secrets!" BiBi squealed.

"But you can't tell anybody, not even Sherman," I demanded.

"No problem," BiBi concurred. "There's lots I don't tell Sherman."

So in the scant moments I had left before the bus departed, I told BiBi about my sideline business. She listened with some amusement. "So I need you to try and find me some stuff I could sell. Any t-shirts they don't use, guitar picks, any notes or letters..."

"And people buy this stuff?" BiBi asked. I nodded. "Wow, I could be like a spy collecting intel!" She giggled. "Oh, why not? It'd be a cool way to stay in touch too."

"Yeah, and it's a cool way to earn some money 'til I find a job," I bitched.

"Let me talk to Sherman," BiBi offered. "Maybe he can find you a job with the record label. I mean, after fifteen years? They owe you something."

This time, when the bus pulled away for the airport, I wasn't one of the passengers. I waved good-bye on the sideline, but all my waving was directed at BiBi. As it rounded the corner, I dejectedly walked back into the hotel lobby. The man behind the counter was talking to a member of the cleaning staff. He did a double-take when he saw me.

"Oh, maybe you can help us!" the clerk said. "You're with the band, right? I saw you with them."

"Yeah, what's up?" I asked.

The clerk nodded at the cleaning lady. "You tell her," he said.

The cleaner faced me, standing tall, all four foot nine of her. Her accent was thick but I could follow her complaint. "OK, so I go into one room - Room 501 - and it looks like nobody left! All the clothes still there, all this cake in the fridge... "

"Yeah, yeah, that's my room," I cut in. "I didn't leave yet."

"I thought you'd have left with everybody else," the clerk stated. I didn't care for his assumption.

"Well, I didn't," I retorted. "I stayed behind. I have things to do."

The cleaning woman wasn't done with me yet. "Listen, lady, I don't care if you don't leave. But then I go to next room and it has used condoms on the floor..."

I nodded as if this was an old problem. "Yes, yes, that would be Mickey's room." Again the mental gear turned in my head. "Look, that's part of my job, to go into the boys' hotel rooms after they leave. I look for lost... ah....belts and...uh....credit cards...," My story sounded good. "Cameras, cell phones, underwear, anything they might have left behind. And to clean up after the pigs. What can I say? They're rock stars."

They seemed to accept my explanation. The clerk asked me if I had keys to their rooms and I bluffed that one out as well. "Is OK I come back in an hour?" the cleaner asked me.

"Hour would be fine," I agreed.

And in that one hour, I had a pair of g-string underwear left behind by Stan and a prescription bottle of medication for Mickey. I left the condoms behind, but I did throw them in the trash. By this point, handling them was like picking up a candy bar wrapper. Tate's room didn't yield much of interest, but I did take a doodle of a heart with his wife's name inside of it. The drawn arrow piercing it strongly resembled a penis. Bradley's room was where I scored best. A garbage can gave up a stub of eyeliner (ManMakeUp the brand), on the bathroom counter was an ivory-handled hair brush and on the desk were three scrunched up pieces of paper. I smoothed them out to discover they were legal papers regarding his skipped DNA testing. Seemed Brad was suspected of having a love child. Again.

I didn't bother cleaning my own hotel room. I just packed up my summer's worth of touring gear and caught the next plane home...to San Diego.

Maybe I didn't have a job anymore but I was still in business.

• • • • • • • • •

BiBi must have berated Sherman all day because by the time I landed in San Diego, there was a message for me to call him.

"Hey, there, Tammy, how you been?" Sherman opened.

"What, since I saw you this morning?" I asked. "Fine, I guess. Just got home."

"Look, I hear you may be in need of work?" he asked, not giving me time to answer. "I've been talking to the record label and they have a couple job openings, if you're interested."

"Tell me more," I said.

Sherman was succinct. "This one may be up your alley," he began. "Steady work, steady paycheque. In their San Diego warehouse. Not bad, hey?" he bragged.

It didn't appeal to me. "What's the other job?" I asked. Please let it be assistant road manager...I didn't care what band it was. That's all I knew how to do.

"This one isn't officially open yet...but I happen to know it will be next week...only problem is, it's strictly commission," Sherman warned.

"Back on the road selling t-shirts and caps and shit?" I asked, in a hopeful manner.

"Not really," he hedged. "Blast Records manages a few bands, right? One of them is Twisted. You know them, the country-western group?"

I did know them. "Yeah, I toured with them once."

Sherman continued. "So this girl started up a fan club and it got quite popular. Now it turns out she's getting married to the singer from Twisted - funny world, eh? And he doesn't want her doing that anymore. It was turning a profit for the label so now Blast Records wants to make it an official fan site."

"I could do that kind of job from home," I mused.

Sherman put a quick stop to my consideration of the job. "Look, I'm telling you, Tammy, unless Twisted ever hits it real big, you're not going to make more than a couple hundred a week. The warehouse is probably triple that."

I took the warehouse job. And it wasn't actually in San Diego but in some dinky suburb that took two hours to reach each day by public transit. I lasted the whole week, just so I could collect a paycheque, but the hours spent lifting crates of CD's and loading trucks was not the job I'd envisioned. My shoulders and back ached from the mindless work. Before Friday was through, I put in a panic call to Sherman.

"Hey, is that fan club job still open?" I almost begged. There was an ominous silence on the other end. "Oh, no!" I wailed.

"We're on the verge of hiring this girl, Eliza," Sherman said. "But she drove a hard bargain. She didn't want one band, she wanted three. The record label said why not? We never had our own official record label fan club before. And the one for Twisted gave us a decent kick-back in sales... so we're about to agree to her terms."

"Which are?"

"She gets five per cent profit for every sale."

"Five per cent?!" I shouted. He could tell I thought that a mere pittance.

"Hey, we started off offering her one per cent," Sherman admitted.

"What if I agreed to her deal?" I asked. There was a momentary silence.

"Well, at least you're acquainted with one of the bands," he noted. Like being on one tour with Twisted ten years ago amounted to a lasting friendship... "And BiBi would be ever so pleased with me..." I waited with bated breath. "OK, poor Eliza will hate us, but you've got the job."

"Oh, thank you, Sherman!" I cried. "So who are the bands?"

"Twisted, of course. This up and coming band called Starburst and the other one you might remember? The Noise?"

• • • • • • • • • •

I lasted less than two more months in San Diego. Had I stuck with the warehouse job, I might have lasted longer. As it was, I could see why Eliza had demanded three acts. Twisted's t-shirt sales, at five per cent profit, was netting me about a c-note every week. At the rate I was going, I could live in a flophouse but I sure wouldn't be sending any money home soon.

Being the de facto president of The Noise's fan club brought in the same amount of money. They were the biggest band Blast Records managed, but fans didn't know they could find an official club to join. The label wanted me to offer everything from scarves to wristbands to freaking sticker sheets, all with The Noise logo.

The third band, Starburst? I highly doubt Eliza chose them for her repertoire; Blast likely dumped this difficult group into the mix. The band wanted their fan club to sell bongs and rolling papers and pipes. Geez, didn't they know what shipping cost? They had a hit on the radio at the moment, "Fire Down Below", which was a mixture of rap and reggae. It wasn't a bad song, but not my taste. Their fan club needed a push; I just wished I was a fan.

My days were numbered when I knew I couldn't pay another month's rent. I told the landlord to use my deposit as I guess I had to leave. I waited for him to offer it to me rent-free for a while. Instead, he asked me how soon he could start showing it.

As I looked in the newspapers and on the computer sites for a cheap place to live, I came to realize that I actually had been living almost rent-free. I hadn't changed apartments since the day I moved to San Diego and in those years, my rent had gone up less than ten per cent. Crummy basement apartments with no windows and shared laundry facilities were going for the same cost as the top floor of the seaside house I had rented. I didn't want to take such a drastic step downward, literally and figuratively.

With my bank account drained and spending more time looking for a place to live than earning a living, I decided to grovel. I didn't have a lot of friends; in this business you'd have a great pal on tour, you'd promise to stay in touch when it was over, and you just never did. BiBi was the only one who actually tried to maintain a connection.

She'd recently mailed me a package of things she'd secreted from their hotel suites and dressing rooms. I planned on thanking her and to ask her nicely to stop sending me cigarette butts. She went to a lot of work sorting out what butts belonged to whom, but I couldn't even bear to look at them. I'd cleaned out so many overflowing ashtrays in my life, the look of each baggie-d cigarette butt made me gag. I would tell BiBi she shouldn't be damaging her unborn child's life by touching them, and then I'd ask if maybe I could sleep on the couch for a few days.

I placed the call, only to reach a house in a state of pandemonium. Sherman answered, out of breath. "Doctor Goldstein?" he asked.

"Hey, Sherman, it's me, Tammy," I replied in a light mood. "Can I talk to BiBi?"

"Afraid not, Tammy," he said. "We're just getting in the car now, going to the hospital. BiBi's started labour. We're going to have a baby!"

"Well, yeah, for the third time," I reminded him. "You can't put her on for just a second?" Then I instantly reconsidered. Would they really want a houseguest at the same time they're bringing home a new child? How about if I promised to stay out of their way? I doubted it. "No, never mind, Sherman. Just tell her I said good luck. Go have your baby."

The phone disconnected. Now I had no options left but a women's shelter. How could I work from there? I plopped onto the couch and used the remote to turn on the TV. I'd just zone out for awhile; maybe a brilliant idea would come to me.

A re-run of Law and Order was playing and I instantly knew I'd seen this episode. I watched it a few minutes, wondering why I remembered it, when a scene came on just before the commercial break. A simple shot of the two lead detectives walking up the pathway to a house. I had the same reaction as the first time I'd seen this episode - "Hey, that looks like my house."

By that I meant my mother's home back in Toronto. The one that sat vacant while my kids were away at universities and Kitty was in a senior's home. We had all urged my mother to put it on the market; the sale would go a long way to paying Kitty's room and board at these places. I was the most vocal supporter of this idea as there was no way I could afford to keep her in these retirement joints. However, Kitty refused. She insisted there be a home for her grandchildren as long as they needed it. No mention made of me.

Now I was glad I hadn't tried to convince the kids to secretly sell the dwelling. That big old house with nobody living there...the whole place to myself, with ample room to set up a decent office. I could wake up when I chose, go to bed when I wanted and have nobody to report to other than myself. It would be just like the old days when I lived with Mom, except this time Mom would be living away from home.

There was no other solution. San Diego was breathtaking and had been my home for years, but it was time to leave. I pulled out a large carry-on bag, the essential one I'd take on the airplane to safekeep it. It didn't contain much of a personal nature; rather, it was my collection of trash that I kept selling. I briefly considered dumping it but the sale of Bradley's hairbrush last week had netted me enough to pay my cell phone bill.

The TV clicked off. I knew the power had not gone out. The cable company had sent a couple notices reminding me my payment was past due. I planned to pay it eventually, maybe after the third notice? Instead they stuck to their threats of cutting off my television. I was relieved they'd given me just enough time to catch half of that Law and Order episode.

It had been the sign I needed. I don't know why I didn't originally think of my Toronto domicile. Suddenly I was excited to move back to my childhood home.

Except this time I'd be the Lady of the Manor.

CHAPTER VIII

Getting into my childhood home wasn't as easy as I'd thought it would be. For one thing, my long-held house key no longer opened the front door. After trying the back door and the windows, I had no choice but to break in. As I reached through the broken pane of glass in the rear door, I snagged my sweater on a shard.

I can't live in a house I can't lock up, I thought. Looking around the place, I tried to locate a set of keys but couldn't find any. Deciding to call my son, I picked up the house phone, but it was dead. I had to use my cell phone to make the call.

"Hey, Rain Man!" I greeted my eldest child. "I'm in Toronto!"

"Oh, no!" Rain moaned. "We weren't expecting you! The girls and I all left a week ago. We wanted to get settled in before school started up."

The realization that all of my children were attending universities suddenly hit me like a wrecking ball. Sure, I'd bragged about their earnest studies and their accomplishments, but I'd never considered how these schools got their money. My kids had part-time jobs but if it were me, that income would have been spent on weed and mascara. I didn't see how they could afford it.

My more pressing problem came to the fore. "Rain, I couldn't get into the house," I complained. "The key I had doesn't seem to work."

"Yeah, there was a break-in the first week Grandma Kitty was in a home," Rain explained. "I'm so glad she wasn't still living in the house. That could have given her a heart attack."

"So you changed the locks?" I asked.

"Yeah, the crooks took all the spare keys, so we don't leave them hanging by the door anymore," Rain said. "Every lock is changed."

"The house phone seems broken too."

"No, we shut it off," Rain corrected me. "If nobody is there, why do we need a phone? Tatum and Sadie have their cells, so do I."

"Oh, shit, my cell is still hooked up to California, every call I make they're going to charge me for roaming, long distance...," I worried.

Rain cut in. "Well, how long are you in town for?"

"I think to stay," I answered.

"Oh, Mom, that's awesome!" Rain exclaimed. "The girls and I felt so bad - there's nobody to go visit Grandma. Now you can go see her every day if you wanted!"

That was not what I wanted at all, but apparently I'd have to pay her a visit very soon. Rain said she held the spare key to the house; the siblings had the others. After bidding him a loving goodbye, I called Tatum and then Sadie. Just like their brother, the twins thought this move back home would bring me closer to Kitty.

"You haven't seen her for so long!" Tatum warned me. "She's aged like twenty years since you last saw her."

"Is she sick?" I asked.

"She sees a doctor," Tatum said. "Besides the usual getting-old stuff, nothing to worry about. I think she just got lonely after we all left for school."

"Well, I'll pop in and check on her," I replied. Get my key at the same time too, I thought.

"Don't just POP in," Tatum chided me. "Try to do some bonding."

Sadie had the same advice. "Mom, now's the time to get to know Grandma again. When you left us, she said you were still a brat. A kid trying to raise a bunch of kids. But Mom, now you've grown up and you should appreciate her. Before it's too late."

"Oh, don't get dramatic, Sadie!" I said. "I never had a problem with my mother. We just didn't see eye-to-eye on how kids should be raised. And of course I appreciate her! Hell, she was more of a mom to you than I was this past fifteen years."

"You think?" Sadie replied cheekily. "But don't beat yourself up over it. We still love you."

After hanging up with her, I walked around the big old house, getting homesick for my children. Here I was, finally back home, but with no last chance to become Mother Tammy. My grown kids weren't here; they were all miles away building their own independence. Seeking challenges, facing reality. The sad truth was, I just wanted to come home with my tail between my legs and have somebody tuck me into bed for a month or two, catering to my needs.

I guess I wanted my mother.

• • • • • • • • • •

Vista Shores didn't have Katherine Canseco registered; I belatedly realized she'd been relocated to a different place halfway across town. I called Better Days Ahead Retirement Centre and asked what time visiting hours were. When I was told I could drop by anytime if I were a family member, I said, "Yeah, I'm her daughter. Katherine Canseco is my mom." I took down directions on how to get there by bus, since I still couldn't find the keys to Mom's old Town Car. Beast of a vehicle, especially for Toronto's traffic jams, but it would have to do. I was hoping Mom had those keys as well.

I was just about to call the phone company next to reconnect the home line, when my cell phone chirped. I debated answering; probably some lame fan club business. Need to ship 40 t-shirts to a concert in Albany for Starburst, need 20 Twisted baseball caps for a radio station promo in Charlottetown. Probably a whole ten bucks of commission awaiting me with that call. The roaming charge alone would eat that up. Still, it could be somebody important, so I answered.

"May I speak to Tammy Canseco, please?" said a rather chilly voice.

"Speaking," I replied.

"I'm glad you answered," the lady replied a bit haughtily. "We tried to reach you a couple times last week but we couldn't get through."

"Yeah, my phone was disconnected," I admitted to the stranger. "Who's this?"

"I'm the administrator at Better Days Ahead Retirement Centre," came the answer.

"Oh, hey, hi!" I said, trying to infuse some warmth into the conversation. "I'm planning on dropping by there today."

"Oh, I suggest you do," came her ominous reply. "And when you leave, we'd like you to take Mrs. Canseco with you."

I laughed. "What do you mean? Like take her out for ice cream or something? Sure, I can do that."

"What I mean is, we don't want her here anymore," the administrator said. "She is far and beyond the care we can give her."

I sucked in my breath. "So she is sick?"

"Sick? She's a pain in the ass, is what she is," the lady shockingly replied. "She's self-centred, she's demanding, she's constantly undermining every ....."

"Wait, wait," I interrupted. "Are you sure we're talking about the right woman? Katherine Canseco? Because that doesn't sound like my mom at all." Actually, it sounded more like me.

"Katherine Canseco," the lady confirmed "And we have it here on her form that you, Tammy Canseco, are her daughter. We want her removed. Immediately."

Damn. When did my my simple dignified mother turn into such a bad-ass?

• • • • • • • • •

The taxi deposited my mother and I in front of our house. The cabbie waited while I emptied his car of my mother's earthly belongings. The trunk was tightly packed, the front seat held plants and the back seat had smothered us with plastic bags. Kitty stood on the sidewalk, gleaming at the sight of her old home.

As I toted her belongings to the front door, I said to Kitty, "I don't have a key to get in. Rain said you had one?"

Kitty surveyed the bags and suitcases surrounding our entrance. It looked like we were about to have a yard sale. "Did you remember packing it?"

"No, I just emptied drawers into bags," I replied. "I didn't sort through anything."

"Then it's got to be in one of the bags," Kitty said. I emptied bags, all thirty of them, but found no key.

"If it's not in a bag, then it wasn't in a drawer," I decided. "Think, Mom, where could you have put it?"

"Maybe I left it in a pocket?" she suggested. Thus her three suitcases were emptied, her jackets and pants pockets all searched. It was a futile attempt.

"Ah, I'll just break in again," I decided. First day I've seen my mom in a long time and I'm showing her at my finest.

"Oh, hold on, dear," Kitty said. "We haven't checked my purse."

Sure enough, she opened the little envelope-purse she carried under her arm. In full view was a keychain, with a large photo of my three smiling children. I shook my head but kept mum; sure we'd just wasted thirty minutes of our lives on this key search, but I didn't want to get angry and make this day any worse than it already was.

"You're sure you're not suffering from dementia, are you?" I teased. "And how come I don't have that picture of my kids?"

As I re-packed the suitcases and hauled them into the living room, Kitty walked around the house, touching photos on the fireplace mantel, fingering the curtains, caressing the stove. I heard the cupboard doors opening.

"I'd make you a tea if we had milk," she called out. "Would you take it with that fake creamer? I have no idea why we'd have some of that in my cupboard."

"Sure, let's have a cup of tea," I said. She busied herself while I found a spot for her plants. The last one went onto the dining room table when Kitty walked in, balancing the two cups of tea.

For the first time, I took a long hard look at her. When I showed up in her room, Kitty was sleeping, but it wasn't long before she was awake and preparing for her departure. From our hasty retreat, we were in the taxi and now home. As my eyes wandered over her frame, I deduced that she may have lost thirty pounds in the last couple years. On a thin frame to begin with, that kind of weight loss is quite noticeable.

Other than that, her joyous mood seemed to override any health issues. She was grinning ear to ear with hearty cheer. "Here you go," Kitty said, placing my tea cup down with a tremulous hand. "So I was thinking that I'd take my old bedroom back, but I notice you slept in it last night."

"No, you can have it," I replied. "I'll just take my shit out."

"Language," my mother said reflexively, before going back on subject. "If you like, Tammy, you can have that room. I'll take one of the twin's. Then they can bunk together when they come home."

"Don't go making any long-range plans, Mom," I said. "We're going to start looking for another home first thing tomorrow."

Kitty had been about to take a sip of tea but froze with it midway to her mouth. She gave me a wounded look. "But I thought you were moving back to Toronto!"

"I am," I replied.

"Where are you going to live?" she asked, cup still hanging in the air.

"Uhhh...here, at home," I stuttered. "That is, if it's ok with you?" I added, just to appear polite.

Kitty took her sip of tea with a soft smile. "Of course it's ok," she beamed. "You're my daughter. And I'm your mother. So we'll both live in the house together. It'll be just like old times."

Between a rock and a hard place. That's where I had to live. What could I do? Kick my mother out of her own home just so I could live there by myself? My mom had no apparent illnesses that could force me to place her somewhere. In the beginning, Rain had used fancy medical jargon to get her placed quickly into a home when the reality was - no family member lived close enough to watch over her. Now that I was living in Kitty's house, I had no choice but to allow her to live there as well.

The main thing is that I was living rent-free. Maybe the meagre income I earned from the Blast Records Fan Club would pay for my latte habit, but I needed to sell some fan stuff fast, if only to help mom pay the phone bill.

"Hey, I want to ask you something about the kids' schools," I broached a subject that had started to eat at me. "I wasn't here to sign any papers and nobody told me anything but...isn't school expensive?"

Kitty nodded. "You have no idea."

"So how are we affording it?" I asked. "I mean, I know they all have part-time jobs but still...they have their own bills as well."

"You certainly helped pay for a lot of it," Kitty told me.

"Say what?" I gave a short bark of a laugh. I'd long ago gotten used to the idea of my kids just hopefully finishing high school. That would be farther than I'd gotten.

"You used to send money home," she reminded me. "Every month or so. A couple hundred here, couple there. One time you gave me a thousand dollars."

"I know, I know," I said, "but that was for food for the kids!"

"Did they starve to death?" she asked. "No, I put it into RESP's...."

"R E Who P's?" Remember, my formative adult years were in the US.

"A fund for children's education," Kitty informed me. "I did it with the first dollar you gave me. And you know, I think I've taught you often enough about compound interest...."

I put my hands over my ears. "Aaagh, I know, I know!" I moaned.

"So there's enough in there to cover some of their expenses, but not everything," Kitty shrugged. "They each had to take out a student loan. But once they graduate and get a good job, they'll be able to pay it off in no time."

I felt sick to my stomach. "In the meantime, I guess I should try to help them out," I decided. "Just right now, I'm flat broke."

"Don't go worrying about it, Tammy," my mom patted my arm with her liver-spotted hand. "We'll manage. The government will help us."

Why did she always say that?

•••••••••

"'It'll be just like old times?'" Hardly!

The good times lasted until the next week. By then I'd had seven full days of being back home and getting reacquainted with my mom. Kitty had her week to acclimate to life back in the place she felt happiest. Then why didn't she seem beholden to me? And if it was to be like old times, why did it seem like I was doing all the work?

I realize it had been fifteen years since I had been home for any length of time. And when I did come to visit, I barely paid attention to my mother. All I wanted to do was hang out and play with my kids. Maybe I wasn't the world's greatest mom, but I sure could be fun! What other mother took their sixteen-year old twins for a tattoo on their birthday? I hadn't really noticed age creeping up on Kitty; now I could see she was showing her almost eighty years. What had made her turn so old? Surely raising three kids into your late seventies couldn't have been that difficult.

For the tenth time in two days, Kitty whined, "Come on, Tammy, let's go out and do something."

I glanced up from my computer, where I was trying to dump a load of Extra Small t-shirts. Nobody ever bought that size; I was annoyed at the record label for ordering them. "We went out yesterday," I growled. "I have work to do. I do have a job, you know."

"We went out to the pharmacy to fill my prescription," Kitty declared. "That's not what I call going out. Let's have some fun."

"Go watch TV," I suggested. "Isn't there a game show on you like?"

"Since when did I ever watch game shows?" Kitty asked. "Or even much TV?"

"I have to go get stamps and send out a package," I said, my eyes darting to the wrapped baseball cap of Bradley's that BiBi sent me. It didn't take long for me to get a hundred bucks for that. The first real money I'd made since I arrived and it would have to be spent wisely. The Blast Records Fan Club did a mediocre business with the three bands I oversaw, but my sideline enterprise was sinking fast. The Noise still had their loyal fans but it was nothing like the old days. "How about I drop you off at a movie?" I asked.

Kitty harrumphed. "Just like watching TV. Boring!"

I had a deja vu of my son Rain saying that when I suggested we go clothes shopping when he started school. "Then I'm afraid you'll have to stay home," I told my mom. "Especially if you're going to behave like a child."

"You're not my mother," Kitty pouted. "I can do what I want."

"Fine, Mom, do whatever you want, just quit bugging me, please," I said firmly. "I'm going to the post office. I'll be back in twenty minutes or so."

The line-up to mail my package was interminable and it was an hour before I got back home. I was surprised to see the ironing board set up in the living room and thought, "Good, Kitty found something constructive to do." I called out for her but there was no answer. Searching throughout the house, a little nervously because I didn't want to find her dead of a heart attack, I was relieved to find her gone.

Maybe she went for a walk, I thought, as I eyed the board and a couple blouses littering my work space. She could have tidied up after herself! I figured I'd have to do that myself and angrily picked up the iron to return it to the cupboard. At the same time I grasped the iron, I saw it was still plugged into the wall. The searing pain in my palm told me the iron had been left on. As I ran my hand under cold water, I couldn't wait for Kitty to get back. She was going to get a piece of my mind.

It was a couple hours later when I wrapped up my work for the day. I thought Kitty should be home by now but decided not to worry too much. Maybe she took long walks. Maybe she did go to a movie. I took a leisurely bath.

After my nap, I made supper, enough for both Kitty and I. Now I was starting to worry. It was beginning to get dark and Kitty had yet to return or even call home. She didn't take her cell phone and I had no idea where she would go. What were her hobbies? Her habits? I barely knew anything about this woman I called Mom.

By midnight, I was in a panic. I wondered if I should call Rain or the twins, but I didn't need them worrying. Not yet anyway. Finally I decided the best course of action would be to call the police. I was debating whether this was an emergency or not; would it be appropriate to dial 911 or find an alternate number, when the house phone rang. I scrambled to answer it.

"Hello?" I gasped.

"Oh, Tammy, I'm glad you're home," Kitty answered sweetly. "I was wondering if you could come and get me?"

"Where are you?" I bellowed. "I was freaking out!"

"Oh, I'm sorry, I meant to be home by now," she replied. "But I guess I got on the wrong bus."

"So where are you?" I repeated.

"I'm not sure," Kitty said. I heard her speak to somebody else. "Excuse me, where am I right now?"

"Who you talking to?" I asked.

"This nice brown boy," she replied, while I gasped in horror at her remark. "He's with all his friends and I asked him if I could use his phone. They're a very fashionable bunch, quite stylish with their matching bandanas...."

"Mom! Quit talking!" I cut in. "I'm coming to get you! Give me an address!"

"Well, I got off the bus because I saw a pay phone, but when I got to it, the phone was missing," Kitty said. Not a good sign, I thought. Definitely not the finest part of town. "So I came to this plaza because I saw the boys here, though I don't know why...there's nothing open....."

"Oh, Mom, stop talking!" I pleaded. "Just ask one of those guys to give me an intersection and I'll be right there. Don't go anywhere except... back to that phone booth. Shut the door and don't speak to anybody else, please, I'm begging you."

As I got the cross-streets, I almost decided to make the call to 911. Kitty had somehow managed to find herself in the worst possible part of town, well-known for violent gangs and nightly shootings. As I told her I'd be there fast as lightning, I heard her thank the cell-phone owner and offer to pay him a quarter for the use of his phone.

Yup, Kitty, that's it...pull out your change purse. May as well pull out your wallet too; I'm sure the gangstas would want to see that next.

• • • • • • • • • •

According to Kitty - when I spoke to her at breakfast the next morning - the gang were perfect gentlemen. They escorted her back to the phone booth and refused her offer of money. They even chided her for being out alone so late at night, in such a bad neighbourhood. "I was lucky to run into them," she concluded.

"I can't believe you ended up there!" I said. "Where'd you go yesterday? You were gone the whole day!" I'd tried to get this information out of her last night, but when I pulled up to the deserted phone booth, I could see she was barely standing. I detected some motion by the side of the plaza, but didn't even turn my head, let alone make eye contact. I pulled the car as close to the booth as possible and ordered my mother to get in. She was asleep before I'd even finished buckling her seat belt.

Once we got home, I woke her up. "Let's go, wake up, let's get you inside," I said. She said something that was pure gobbledygook and then walked straight from the car and up to her bed. I looked in on her, sleeping with her blouse and skirt and pantyhose on still. I could put her nightgown on her but I figured - if she could hang with the homies, she was tough enough to sleep in her clothes.

"I had a nice day," Kitty said, cutting the crust off her toast. "The best day I've had in ages."

"Even though you got lost and I had to come rescue you?" I asked. Kitty nodded blissfully. "So I'm asking you, where...did...you...go?"

"I went out and had some fun, but I'm beat," Kitty replied. "My outing seemed to take a lot out of me. Maybe I'll go back to bed for awhile."

Even though I didn't get my answer, all was forgiven since Kitty slept until suppertime and then went right back to bed afterwards. I had a productive day with my fan club business, I enjoyed a night of popcorn, M&M's and reality TV and best of all, I did not have to look after my mother. I didn't have to fetch her sweater from upstairs, didn't have to fix her Metamucil, and I didn't have to answer any questions about "what's on the agenda for tomorrow."

The short respite ended the morning Kitty woke up after her day of rest. "So what's on the agenda today?" she asked for a change.

"Today?" I replied. "Let's see...today is a Thursday, making it a work-day. I guess I will earn a living. What's on your agenda?"

"You don't want to do something?" Kitty asked. She was beginning to sound like a broken record.

"Mom! I have to work!" I repeated.

"Then maybe I'll just go out," she decided.

"No. NO! You're not going out by yourself again," I said. "I think may-be you're getting too old to go off galavanting alone. We'll do something together on the weekend, I promise."

That remark seemed to hold her for a couple days. Friday night she was giving me the eye, but I ignored it. There was nothing I much felt like doing and I really couldn't afford to be taking in a theatrical play or a musical concert. On Saturday, I told Kitty to cool her jets; I had a surprise outing for her on Sunday that I thought she'd enjoy.

Waking her up early, I suggested she dress warmly. We drove down-town but traffic was already heavy. "Where are we going, Tammy?" my mother asked.

"You'll see," I teased.

"Why are there so many people? Where are they all going? Why aren't we moving?" Kitty fretted.

I sighed. "I guess this is as close as we're going to get. I'm going to find a place to park."

After securing the car about fifteen blocks from my destination, Kitty and I walked to a Tim Horton's coffee shop. The line-up was out the door. As we waited, Kitty said, "My hands are getting cold."

"Where's your gloves?" I asked.

"I forgot them in the car," Kitty replied.

Lending her mine, I eventually got a couple hot chocolates and started walking again with Kitty. "We should be almost there," I said. "You can tell by how thick the crowd is."

"You still haven't told me where we're going," Kitty said from behind me.

"Come on, catch up!" I enthused. "We're going to the Santa Claus parade!"

My mother stopped short. "That's why we're here?" I nodded, awaiting her delight and appreciation. Instead, "Do you know how many times I've seen this parade with you? And your kids?"

"Oh. I thought you'd like it," I said, somewhat hurt. "I know I would. I haven't seen this parade in about thirty years!"

"It still has the same ending," Kitty supplied the spoiler-alert. "Big guy in a red suit. Ho ho ho, the end."

"Do you want to go back home then?" I asked.

"No!" Kitty yelled, causing a couple with their baby in some kind of knapsack to glance behind them. "I don't want to go home! There's nothing to do there! Let's go to this damned parade already."

Again the couple looked back at Kitty and then shared a look that read 'Crazy lady'. The seniors home may have possibly been right - my mother was not in her right mind these days. We reached a spot that seemed as good as the rest, except my mother couldn't see over the people in front of her. After listening to her kvetch about this for a few minutes, and not wanting to ruin everybody else's fun, I looked around for a solution. There was a tall brick fence behind me; already a couple dads were lifting their youngsters to seat them there. I turned to Mom and did the same thing.

"Well, I guess I can see a little better," Kitty allowed, as I rubbed my aching shoulder. But the moment Santa approached, Kitty demanded I take her down. "I wanted to come down an hour ago," she said. "Didn't you feel my boot kicking your back? That stone was cold on my derriere...I may have gotten piles."

"Lovely," I muttered. As Santa passed me, waving to the people on the opposite side of the street, I made a wish on him. "Please Santa, all I want for Christmas is life to be easier with my mom."

Now I know Santa must be fake, because my wish was not granted whatsoever. Instead, my mother seemed to find ways to make my life miserable. Nothing I did pleased her; not my grilled cheese sandwiches or the way I washed her clothes or the style in which I cut her toenails. After one more of her pitiful complaints, I blew up at her.

"Jesus Christ, Better Days was right about you!" I yelled. "You are a pain in the neck, Kitty CASINO," I said scathingly. The moment I said this, I stopped talking. We both just stared at each other as if I'd struck gold. "Hey...wait....I bet you'd like to go to a casino, wouldn't you?"

A small, timid nod came back at me. "I would like that very much," Kitty said meekly.

"Hhm, I've never been to a casino," I remarked. "I guess I could take you, though I'm not a big fan of gambling. But if you really want to go... "

"Very much," she said again. "Tonight?"

"Whoa, that's soon," I said, suddenly scared. Going to a casino meant I'd be forced to spend money. To gamble away my minimal income and forever be lost in debt and addiction. I knew personally of a famous musician who lost everything due to baccarat. And there was one tour with a poker-loving opening band named ScudMissile. I know our drummer Stan lost a lot of money every night playing cards with those guys. Next tour he was back into banging groupies with a vengeance. And didn't BiBi tell me her brother was in trouble with online gambling? "How about we go tomorrow?" I offered.

The old lady instantly agreed. I don't know why she looked so happy. Didn't she know that her daughter was about to cross over to the dark side?

CHAPTER IX

Next morning, as I groggily walked into the kitchen to make coffee, I almost had a heart attack when I spotted a figure sitting in the darkened living room. It was Kitty, already dressed and coiffed and ready to go.

"Whoa, Mom, it's not even 7 AM," I shouted. "You scared the hell out of me, sitting there. And you look ready to go out....where you going?" I didn't trust her going any farther than the corner store.

"To the casino," she replied.

I gave her the three-second dead stare. "The casino, you say. At seven in the morning? Who in their right mind would go to a casino that bloody early? I said we'd go at seven, but obviously I meant at night. Go back to bed."

"Bed is boring," Kitty replied. I steeled for more childish babble but instead she said, "I'll just wait until seven this evening then."

"Good, 'cuz that's when we'll leave," I settled it. "I have a ton of office work to do before that, so if you need me, ring your bell." The bell was simply that - a bell I'd bought her so she could ring it if she really needed me. Why the bell? One night she felt ill and feebly called out for me. I couldn't hear her over the jungle noises on the Survivor TV show I was watching and Kitty had a messy accident in her bed. Not wanting to deal with such a disgusting situation again, I bought the bell so she could use it in case of emergency. Now her needing crackers for her tomato soup constituted a 911 ring.

The Blast Records Fan Club got a day's work out of me like they'd never seen before. I hope they noticed I logged on at 7:12 AM and stayed on until 6:27 PM. Usually I don't devote so much time to this pitiful joke of a job, but today I was bound and determined to make some real income. I wanted a way to justify throwing away money later tonight.

Instead of the booming sales I'd imagined, I was looking at an order for a dozen t-shirts for a baseball team who also wanted to be known as The Noise. The next email was asking if we could supply any party favours from Twisted. I hoped cheap cowboy hats were to their liking; we didn't supply decorations or paper plates for crying out loud.

These two cheesy orders were followed by a request for a big refund. As usual, from a sale of Starburst t-shirts. This one was from a store in Detroit who wanted their money back from fifty shirts I'd recently sent them. Same old problem - shit quality for the price paid. Starburst, a reggae-hip-hop whatever group, insisted that their t-shirts be crafted at a factory in Jamaica. They urged that these workers be paid American wages. So far the record label had agreed to all this. Once these standard issue t-shirts were made, the cost to ship them to the big warehouse in San Diego was atrocious. The t-shirts sold for $20 to the retailer, but were worth maybe 5. One wash and the shape was gone. That was the stuff of my business life.

It was hit and miss all day with the fan club sales. Starburst had their one big song and was now becoming a one-hit wonder. The Noise hadn't played live since the Legends tour - word had it that Tate and Bradley had a falling out - so their popularity was at an all-time low. Twisted accounted for the bulk of my work as they were finally hitting it big in America. Thanks to a late-afternoon sale of thirty t-shirts to a new (unauthorized but welcomed) fan club did I figure I came out in the black for the day.

All that tiring work, staring at the computer for hours on end...without Kitty yakking at me or annoying me or harassing me. Still her behaviour managed to get on my nerves. She didn't move all day; just sat in the living room with her bag at her feet. "Mom, watch TV or something," I urged.

"No thanks," she replied. "I'm saving my eyesight for the machines."

"Well, you're just sitting there," I remarked.

"I'm not bothering you, am I?" she asked. "Because I'm not doing anything to bother you. I'm just waiting."

"I know," I said. "It bothers me."

Even though I said we would leave at 7 PM, I just couldn't bear to see her being so docile. Afraid that she would anger me and I'd change my mind about going to the damn casino. I slammed my computer shut at half past six and told Kitty we could leave now if she wanted. She attempted to stand up but had obviously been sitting for too many hours. I hauled her out of the easy chair and we got into the Town Car.

Kitty tried to buckle herself in before I could help. After poking the seat belt connector near the receptor about six times, I finally took it from her and buckled her in. "So where's the nearest casino?" I asked.

"That would be FiveStar Racetrack," Kitty replied. "It's the only place to go in Toronto."

"Racetrack? Like in horses?" I asked. "I thought we were going to a casino?"

"It's a racetrack and a casino," Kitty answered. "You'll see."

I set the vintage GPS to FiveStar Racetrack and noticed it would still take about thirty minutes to get there. "Let's grab a quick sandwich first," I suggested. "McDonald's or something. I'm starving."

I should have ordered a feast. What with being the twelfth car in the drive-thru line-up, complete with an hysterical woman disputing her bill and Toronto's notorious rush hour traffic (3 PM - 8 PM on a good day), it took ninety minutes to reach FiveStar Racetrack. And then what felt like another thirty minutes to find parking in the oversized lot and make the trek to the front doors. Signs everywhere screamed in bright letters - Live life to the max!

The long walk in the cold air had me worried. I didn't want to be giving Kitty a piggyback ride. I noticed a shuttle bus picking up a couple people at the far end of the lot. "Mom," I said, then, "Mom! Kitty!" She was already twenty paces ahead of me. She stopped and turned. "Do you want to wait for the shuttle bus?" I asked her.

"Come on," she said. "We'll be there before it even gets here."

I had to run to keep up with her. "Slow down, woman! You're going to make me spill my coffee."

"Drink up," Kitty commanded. "You won't be able to take that in with you."

"I can't take my coffee in?" I whined. "Why not?"

"You just can't," Kitty said. "But don't worry, they give you free coffee when you're in there."

"Free coffee?!" I gasped. "Really? Free?" Throughout my life, I flirted with various addictions, never really committing to any. I drank, I took cocaine, I smoked weed, I played video games. The one thing I did get hooked on and still craved on a daily basis was my cup of java. And if cash-strapped Tammy had to go to a casino, at least the free coffee would take some of the sting out.

An ambulance was parked at the entrance to FiveStar Casino. I slowed down to watch the action, always eager to witness drama in the making. Two attendants were wheeling out a man on a stretcher, an oxygen mask attached to his face. The man looked to be in his nineties.

"Look, Mom," I whispered. "Guess he couldn't take the excitement."

Kitty barely paid the scene a second glance. "Happens all the time," she said.

"Poor guy," I muttered. "Maybe he...." But Kitty was already at the door, holding it open for me. I picked up the pace.

As we entered, I prepared for the flames of hell to come licking at my feet. Security guards manned the posts at both the entrance and exit to the gaming room. One guard was busy checking the ID of a gambler so I got into line behind him. Kitty just barrelled on past all of us. The guard beckoned me to pass on through. "Good luck!" he wished us.

Suddenly I was in the FiveStar Casino and was unprepared for the thrill that ran through my body. Was it the sounds or the bright flashing machines or the sense of what the night could bring? I didn't know where to look or what to do so I just stood in one spot, drinking in the vision.

"Come on, let's go sign you up," Kitty said.

"Sign me up?" I asked.

"You need a Player's Card," she informed me. "Some people don't use one, but they give you money to play if you sign up for a card."

"They'll give me money?" I repeated. Geez, free coffee, free money....I suspected they were trying to suck me in to a life of depravity. "Fine, let's sign me up."

In no time, I had a Player's Card as well as ten bucks to spend. "Now let's go gamble!" Kitty urged, heading over to a bank of machines. "I'll show you how."

There were four different slot machines in a row. The two end seats, Cats and Golden Goddess, were taken. I saw my mom stand in front of a game I thought was called Kitty Litter. "Is this your favourite game?" I asked. "Kitty Litter? Why? Because it has your name?"

"It's Kitty Glitter," she said. "And it's ok, but I prefer the one next to it, Noah's Ark. Let's play these two; they're empty and they're next to each other."

The games were what is known as penny machines. If you really wanted to conserve money, you could play one single cent. I inserted the ticket I was given by the casino, and saw my ten dollars show up under 'credits'. Kitty inserted a twenty dollar bill into Noah's Ark. "OK, let's make a bet," she said.

I looked at the buttons and then made a one cent bet. "You don't want to play one cent," Kitty frowned at me. "That's a waste of time. You'll never win anything." I watched her place a bet - thirty cents. Neither one of us won anything on our first spin. "Make another bet," Kitty said, "but make it higher."

I matched her bet of thirty cents and still won nothing. Even though I wasn't even playing with my own money, I felt a small stirring of nervous discontent. Already I had wasted over thirty cents. 'Wasted' was the word that seemed to stick in my conscience. After we both made a couple more thirty cent bets, Kitty had a win. It gave her fifteen cents.

"So you bet thirty, you got three giraffes in a row, and you won back half your money?" I asked. "You won, but you really still didn't make your money back on that bet, did you?"

"I got some of it back," Kitty replied.

"I'm going to lower my bet," I said. I decided to play a nickel and boom! I won my nickel back with three A's in a row. I preferred that to a constant decrease of my free funds. "I won five cents!" I crowed to Kitty, but she had started speaking to the man playing the Cats machine. He was about the same age as her.

Looking about the place, I took in the general crowd in my vicinity. What the hell? Was there some kind of senior citizen's convention in town? Even though I was in my late thirties, I was probably the youngest woman in the place. There were enough wheelchairs, walkers and canes to open up a metal scrapyard. This can't be normal, I thought, as I went back to my gambling.

Loudly, with a pleasing sound, three diamond-encrusted cat dishes sprang onto my screen, followed by another noise that signified my machine did a special trick of some sort. "Oh, you got the bonus!" Kitty trilled.

"What's the bonus?" I asked. "Is that good?"

"Just watch," Kitty said.

That first bonus was what made me come to enjoy gambling. Kitty Glitter's bonus offered fifteen free games, with extra things going on that just made it almost unbearably exciting. By the end of it, I'd won four dollars!

"Oh, that was amazing! I won money!" I shouted, causing heads to turn.

"How much?" asked the woman on my right, playing Golden Goddess. I noticed she was betting ninety cents.

"Four dollars!" I said with an ear-to-ear grin. The woman didn't even respond; she just returned to spending her rent money. "Do the other machines have bonuses?" I asked Kitty.

"Yes," Kitty said. "Not all of them give fifteen games. Some more, some less. No matter what, it's a thrill to get them."

"Yeah, I agree, it is," I beamed. "And I won four bucks, so that's enough of this game. Shall we move on?"

Kitty looked at her machine. "No, I'm going to play this one a bit more," she said.

The man next to her let out a whoop as his machine paid out eighty dollars. He turned his big beaming Slavic face to us and in a thick accent, said, "I love the sluts!" He cashed out and cleared his seat. I immediately sat down in his vacated chair.

"Was he talking about us?" I asked incredulously. Kitty ignored my question as she blocked the 'bill insert' slot of my game.

"You don't want to play that machine," Kitty warned. "That man cleaned it out."

"What, is it like an ATM machine?" I asked. "It only holds so much money?"

"I just think that it's probably gone cold," Kitty said mysteriously.

I watched Kitty for a couple minutes. Her twenty was already down to five dollars. I began to play the Cats machine and wondered if Kitty was right. Within minutes, my free money was used up. No winnings, no bonuses. I turned to watch Kitty play and saw she was down to a few pennies. She cashed out and received a ticket for nine cents.

"Now we can move on?" I asked.

Instead, Kitty pulled out another twenty dollar bill. "I'm staying put," she informed me. "This machine hasn't paid me anything yet. It's due."

"You think that's how it works?" I asked. Kitty didn't reply. I watched her lose thirty more cents but then, on her next spin, she won some money. "Oh, you won a dollar! Good for you."

"That's not the kind of money I'm talking about," Kitty muttered. "I'm still waiting for that bonus. Come on, you doves...I need five of you. "

"Are you playing that machine?" came a voice from behind me. I turned around and at first saw nobody, but then looked down. There was a lady standing there, what you would call a "little person". She was about my age but we had more than a difference in height. She was maybe four feet tops, all toned muscle shown off in a tank top revealing ample cleavage. Her bleached blonde hair was clearly aided by extensions, as were her lashes. Kohl-rimmed eyes, collagen-enhanced lips, gel-tipped nails... she was like an oversized Barbie doll.

I stepped aside. "Knock yourself out," I said.

"Did that at the card tables," she replied. "Lost twelve hundred bucks."

I gasped. That was currently more than I made per month! "Wow..." I began, but then didn't know what else to add. "Wow, you must be rich?" "Wow, can you afford that?" "Wow, are you crazy to spend that much?" So I just left it at 'Wow'.

"Yeah, that's how I feel," the little lady said as she hitched herself onto the stool. "So now I'll just play sensibly until it's time to go home." She inserted a hundred dollar bill into the slot. She turned to my mom. "Hey, do you know what the maximum is you can play on this?" she asked.

Kitty looked over at her sidekick's machine. "I think it's two dollars and fifty cents," she replied, pointing to some print on the face of the machine. "My eyesight is not what it once was but I think that says two fifty."

The woman looked and then made the bet. Immediately she won six bucks. "Woo hoo!" I said to her.

The woman stretched her head up to look at me. "Got a long way to go before I get my twelve hun back," she spat out, her hand slamming the re-spin button.

I nodded like I completely understood but I just didn't like the vibe of this little person. I wasn't being racist or whatever you'd call it in this case. It was this woman's quiet sense of desperation that was making me feel queasy. I prodded Kitty on the shoulder. "If you want to stay here, that's fine by me but I'm going to take a walk around, ok?" Kitty just nodded as she racked up another dollar win. "How about I meet you in an hour?" Kitty nodded again. "Mom? Kitty? It'd be good to have a meeting place, don't you think? I mean, you're not just going to play Noah's Ark all night, are you?"

Kitty didn't even glance up at me. Her face was maybe six inches from the screen on the slot machine. "You saw that big drum when we came in?" she asked. "I'll meet you there."

I glanced at my watch. "OK, it's nine o'clock now...I'll see you at ten, ok?" I waited for her response but instead Kitty just switched her bet to fifty cents. "Whoa, you know you just played half a buck?" Her eyesight must really be on the wane, I thought.

"I know," Kitty replied. "Sometimes you have to change it up a bit to get the machine's attention."

"Well, don't go crazy," I admonished her.

She immediately placed a bet for a quarter. It paid off fifty cents. "See what I mean?" she said. I did some quick math and still didn't see how she came out ahead but what the hell, let the old biddy have her nickel and dime fun.

"Ok, I'm going then," I repeated. I had thirty bucks burning a hole in my pocket.

The place was jammed with gambling aficionados, most of whom wanted to play the penny machines. Time was slipping by so I ended up on a couple two cent machines. My money seemed to go too fast, so I went in search of another penny machine. I found one and immediately on the first spin, I received the bonus. There was no denying the tingle that hit me head to toe - a free spin for a total of eight games. I sat back and let the magic begin. It wasn't until the last spin that I finally won a dime.

"Ten cents? That's it?" I said aloud. In disgust, I cashed out. I found myself in front of a bank of machines that were playing very short clips of I Love Lucy. All the machines were based on the show. It cost a quarter to play but I'd always been a fan of the show so I decided to splurge. After two bucks, I didn't get a bonus but I did win three dollars back. I was so excited and so taken with the nostalgic game that I played another four dollars in no time.

I was glad I'd looked at my watch and saw it was almost ten o'clock. I didn't want to keep losing at I Love Lucy but the lure of the game was strong. I cashed out and went to go find my mother but I was all turned around. I was lost in the casino, though not in any kind of panic. And in my search for the big drum, I spotted many other games where I wanted to try my luck.

Suddenly the barrel was in front of me. Kitty was digging in her purse, probably looking for her decade-old cell phone to call me. "Hey, Mom!" I said. "I'm here."

Sure enough, Kitty pulled out her phone, brought it right up to her nose and pressed a button. "You're late, " she said, looking at the phone's screen. "It's past ten."

"Only by five minutes," I replied. "Sorry. I got lost."

"I have to get back to my game," Kitty said. "I have somebody watching my seat. How are you doing?"

"I'm not ahead of the game, if that's what you mean," I said. "But I'm not down much."

"I'll see you later then," Kitty said. "I'm going back to Lucky Fountain. It's been doing pretty good for me."

Don't ask me why, but I was relieved when she said that. As I wandered about, I saw senior citizen gamblers making outrageous bets. I felt anxious for these complete strangers; I didn't want to be feeling that way about my mother as well. "OK, let's meet in an hour again," I suggested. "Back here at the barrel."

"Don't be late this time," Kitty shot back. She turned and did the fastest walk I ever saw an old lady make. Totally the opposite stride from when I took her to the grocery store. If the Lucky Fountain game had been on the third floor, I'm sure Kitty would have run up the stairs rather than wait for an elevator. I couldn't believe the change in her physicality.

I had a cash-out voucher for sixty cents, as well as twenty dollars still in my pocket. Off I went to play some more games. Even though I almost orgasmed over a few more bonuses and I managed a couple small wins, my money was going down fast. With five bucks left to play, I stuck to the penny machines. Still my luck sucked and before you knew it, I pressed the button for my final nickel bet on the Gone Fishin' game and came up empty.

There was more money in my wallet and I also had my debit card on me. However, I told myself that if I'd gone out to a movie, with popcorn and a drink, that would have cost me about thirty bucks. Maybe a restaurant dinner with a glass of wine would also have set me back thirty dollars. So a night on the town, on my tight budget...thirty bucks seemed acceptable. But not one cent more. This wasn't a shopping spree! I certainly wasn't seeing value for my money spent.

I slowly found my way back to the barrel and at eleven, I saw Kitty scurry up, right on time. "Still at Lucky Fountain?" I asked.

"No, I moved on to Chieftans, though I don't know why," Kitty said. "It's never liked me. Now I want to see if I can find a Mayan Sun game that nobody's playing...."

"I was thinking we could leave now," I said. "I tried gambling, it was fun, but I lost all my money. So I guess that's when it's time to go."

"I can lend you some," Kitty offered.

"No!" I said. Accepting the loan would be succumbing to the temptation to gamble more. Or I could take the money and just throw it into the wind.

After making the suggestion, Kitty reached for the shoulder strap on her purse. She slapped at each shoulder and reached around her body before she realized her purse was missing. "Oh, no, Tammy! My purse!" she cried, a panicked look appearing on her wizened old face. "I left it at the last machine! The Chieftans one! We have to go back to get it!" She spun around in a circle, looking at all the gaming slots.

"I don't know where Chieftans is," I wailed. "Oh, Mom!" But before I could even begin to berate her, she took off at a fast shuffle straight ahead. I almost lost her as she made a sharp left turn into another mass of machines, her black-clad sweater ensemble meshing with everybody else's fashion attire.

I spotted the majestic head-dressed chief and heard its loud music before I noticed Kitty had already arrived. There was a security guard there, holding her purse. I ran up to them. "Oh, I'm so glad you found her purse!" I exclaimed. "I hope everything is all there."

The guard politely turned to my mom. "You understand that we have to make sure this purse belongs to you?" My mother nodded. "You have photo identification in here?"

"I have my driver's license," Kitty confirmed. I accidentally let forth a snort of laughter; it was just the quick image of my mother actually still trying to drive.

"Can you get it for me?" the man asked, completely ignoring me but being quite tender with my mom.

"Certainly," Kitty said as she took the purse from him. She opened it up and dug deep for a simple little plastic card holder. She opened it up to show her face on the driver's license. For good measure, she also held up her Players Card, which read Katherine Canseco.

The guard gave her identification a quick look. "Great, that's all I needed to see," he affirmed. "You have a good night, ladies."

"Thank you ever so much!" Kitty called after him.

"You got lucky, Mom," I said.

She turned to me with sparkling eyes. "I did! We should stay and gamble a bit more. Maybe that's a sign that my luck has changed."

I let her play for just five dollars more. Within a couple minutes, we were headed for the parking lot.

· · · · · · · · · ·

Bliss. That's the only way to describe the following day with Kitty. She slept until noon, she made her own ham sandwich and she calmly watched a long movie on television the whole afternoon. For supper, I made something different in the kitchen. It wasn't quite the success I'd hoped for but Kitty still ate it without complaint. She did drink three large glasses of water.

On Sunday, Kitty wanted to reminisce about our trip to FiveStar Racetrack. "Was that really your first time at a casino, Tammy?" she asked. "You? Who's been all around the world and back?"

"It's true," I said. "I've been to a lot of strange places, believe me, but we just never got around to playing casinos." I almost did, I recalled, but had been replaced in my roadie job.

"But how about when you weren't doing a show? Did you go there for some time off?" Kitty continued.

"No, if they weren't playing, they were either partying with a bunch of others, or they were on the bus going to their next gig," I explained. "Nobody had any interest in casinos."

Kitty let forth a little knowing grunt. "Oh, they'll get interested when they get older."

"Yeah, what was with all those old people at FiveStar?" I asked. "Was there some kind of convention or something? I mean, it was just packed with senior citizens!" Honestly, I was still confounded by the sight.

"Maybe because we went on a Friday night?" she replied. "But the casino has always been busy when I've been there. Didn't you have fun?" she said wistfully.

"Yeah, I guess," I said grudgingly. "I mean, I lost my thirty bucks in two hours but still...all that action! I don't know how to explain it....It was like, when I was young and there was a special event to celebrate, you would take me to Chuckie Cheese, remember? That was my favourite place in the world. It's like a Chuckie Cheese for grownups!"

"I think of it as a Disneyland for adults," Kitty corrected me. "That seat is your ride and those machines are pure entertainment."

"I don't remember Disneyland," I said.

"I took your kids," Kitty replied. "So maybe you'd like to go back there one day?"

"To Disneyland?"

"To the casino," Kitty suggested.

"Oh, I don't know, Mom, I don't know if it's really my thing," I said, scrunching up my face. "But I did enjoy our outing! We should maybe go to a museum or take a ceramics class...., shit like that...."

"Watch your language," Kitty responded automatically, her face seeming to age before my eyes.

"I'll look at the internet and find some fun things to do, ok?" I continued.

"The casino was a fun thing to do," Kitty countered.

"We'll go again one day, I promise, but surely there can be better ways to spend thirty bucks in no time at all," I ended the subject.

Next day at dinner, I presented her with a list of ideas for us to do. Three hours spent poring over every senior club offer and discount and deal I could find. Narrowing it down to about a dozen choices (hopefully one per month?), I presented my findings to Kitty.

"Ta dum!" I opened. "Check out all the cool stuff old folks can do in this city! See the list that I made. Take a look at it, tell me what you think. I printed them out in large font; I know that helps you."

Kitty dourly took the list and laid it next to her plate of chili. "Is this spicy?" she asked me in a petulant voice.

A pang of guilt struck me as I recalled the handful of red pepper flakes I'd used. "Just try it," I said. "I made it all the time when The Noise were making their album in France and we had that beach house. The guys loved it. So look at the first idea, Mom. Doesn't that look like fun? Let me know 'cuz I have to book it by tomorrow."

And even though my idea had no appeal to my mother, I booked it anyway. There was an online coupon to use that got me a two-for-the-price-of-one deal. I was never one for coupons; that was my mother's hobby. She wasn't into it in an "extreme" way; but in the past, she would keep, maintain and use coupons on a regular basis. Saving fifty cents on paper towels pleased her to no end; it was rather a shock to see her squandering more than that in one single spin of the slots.

On the Thursday of that week, we attended a matinee performance of a play, The Seagull, by Anton Chekhov. It was held in the fancy Royal Leon Theatre and included a pre-show tea. After driving around the block trying to locate fairly cheap parking, I finally found a place. Kitty had resumed her old lady walk, where she made stepping off a curb look like she was descending Mount Everest.

"Mom, can you toddle a bit faster?" I called out to Kitty, half a block behind me. "We're going to miss the tea!" Tea and crudites, whatever that meant. All I know is that I skipped lunch for this.

I waited at a perfectly good walk signal for my mother to catch up. "You should have dropped me off at the theatre and then parked the car," Kitty commented.

"Oh, right," I sarcastically agreed. "And when I come back and I can't find you? Would you remember to call me? If you even remembered your cell phone? Do you have it with you?"

"No, I didn't think I needed it," Kitty replied. "I knew I was just going to be with you."

"And that's why you're making this long walk with me," I stated. "I can't trust you by yourself anymore."

Kitty didn't reply. She knew she'd been naughty this week. I woke up one morning to the smoke alarms going off - Kitty had fried up some bacon at an ungodly hour and then went back to bed, leaving the frying pan still cooking on the hot element. That same day, she ran herself a bath and then got involved in a crossword puzzle. The drip of water falling onto my laptop was what alerted me to the upstairs flood. I didn't want to face it yet, but it looked like my mom was getting some kind of illness.

My growling stomach appreciated that we made it to The Royal Leon Theatre in time for the end of the tea. In the large foyer, a couple stations had been set up. One held styrofoam cups and an assortment of five teas you could choose, with a large steaming canister of hot water. The second station held an assortment of sandwiches already going stale, as well as the leftover pickings of tarts and scones. I tried to fill up my saucer-sized plate with as much as it could handle, which probably amounted to half a normal sandwich and two tarts.

Kitty chose one triangular shaped sandwich and a scone. There was no available seating so we placed our cups of tea on a windowsill and ate our food as we stood. Kitty lifted up the top layer of bread on her sandwich. "I knew this was missing something!" she declared. "Look, just cucumbers, no meat." She took a bite of her scone instead and then made soft spitting sounds. "Oh my, that's dry. Did you take one of those?"

I shook my head and ended up giving her one of my butter tarts. I was just about to go and refill my saucer when I saw the caterers run in and wheel the food carts out of the room. Another set of white-aproned workers sped around picking up any litter left behind. The doors to the theatre opened to the non-tea drinking public.

"What do we do now?" Kitty asked. "Take our seats?"

"I guess," I replied. "At least we can sit down."

It was thirty minutes until curtain. Kitty and I engaged in people-watching, maybe the one thing we always had in common. It used to be a lot more fun when Kitty had better eyesight. Now it was reduced to "Mom, check out this lady in the mink coat...too afraid to leave it in coat check, I bet." Kitty squinted to see who I was talking about, forcing me to raise my hand and point. "That one!"

"Tammy, it's impolite to point," Kitty said, pulling my arm down. "Oh look, I think a bear just walked in!" she yelled, raising her own pointing finger.

I swivelled my head in disbelief, and then huffed. "That's not a bear! Geez, you need a new prescription for those glasses. That's the woman's husband. He's got himself a big fur coat too."

"Oh. Well, you can obviously see why I made that mistake then," Kitty said.

I bit back my sarcastic reply in the nick of time. Let it slide, Tammy, let it go…I'd noticed lately that my rapport with my mother was deteriorating. My temper and her suddenly feeble state of mind didn't go hand in hand. I wanted to come off as, if not loving, at least her child. And I did love her! It was just that she was becoming more and more infuriating. My patience was having a hard time finding its way home.

Just as the announcement came for everyone to take their seats, Kitty decided she had to use the washroom. "It was that cup of tea," she explained. "It just went right through me."

"We have to hurry," I urged. That word apparently had left her memory as we laboured out of the seats and over the legs of the theatre-goers. "Excuse me, sorry, hurry, mom, I'm sorry, excuse me… " Until we finally made it to the steps. An usher sprinted up and bade us to return to our seats.

"Tell that to my bladder," my mother rudely said. She managed to go down the stairs with a little more speed as the usher fairly dragged her out.

"You're going to have to miss the curtain," the usher said as he shooed us through the door that led back to the lobby. "You'll have ten minutes before we open them again for latecomers."

We made it back, just as the last late arrival was being quietly led into the theatre. The same usher gave us a sour look when he saw us race up. "Please hurry!" he loudly whispered. "The actors are about to go back on stage!"

As soon as we got back into the theatre, the usher shut the door behind us. My mother clutched my arm. "Oh, is it ever dark in here!" she exclaimed, far too loudly for a quiet room. As the thespians returned to the stage, the usher tried to take us silently back to our seats, but Kitty's eyesight was poor at high noon, never mind Act I, Scene 2. "I'm sorry, was that your kneecap?" she spoke over the actor's opening lines. "Hang on, hang on, I think your purse strap is wrapped around my ankle," she said to a woman so dark, all I could see was a white knit hat floating above a white shawl.

All the sssh's! and the "Quiet!"'s embarrassed me. When we finally found our seats and began watching the play, Kitty prodded me in the ribs. "When do we get to see this seagull?" she asked. "Do you think it will be a real one? Probably fake, right? I don't think you can train a seagull." More hushing from people around us. Two minutes later, "I'm not quite following the story. What is that man moaning about?"

The man next to me tapped my knee. "Please," he almost begged. "These seats cost a fortune. Could you tell your mother to quiet down?"

"I got a two for one deal," I bragged, before turning to my mother. "Mom, you can't talk during the performance! I'll explain everything in the intermission."

"I'll probably be using the bathroom during intermission," Kitty responded. "I'm still feeling the effects of that chili you made." A couple in the row ahead of us turned in unison and sssh'd the both of us. "Sorry," Kitty apologized. "We'll stop talking. Enjoy the show."

I tried to get some pleasure from the long-winded play I'd chosen. To be frank, it wasn't my cup of tea and probably not my mother's either. However, I'd been so eager to prove that we could have fun somewhere other than a casino that I snapped up the first grown-up hoity-toity event I could find. To make the play even less enjoyable, Kitty kept squirming next to me. At one point, I quickly whispered, "Are you alright?" She cupped her hand to her ear and I said, "Are you OK?" Again the couple in front looked around. Sheesh, give me a break, we'd been silent for almost a half-hour already!

Once intermission was announced, Kitty sprang up from her chair. "I have to use the washroom!" she announced loud and clear. I stood up as well but she pushed me down. "I don't need your help, Tammy, I know where it is."

"You sure?" I asked, but she was already moving down the aisle. I settled back to read the program I'd been given, but kept one eye on the door to the lobby. As soon as I spotted my mother, I planned on hooting and hollering to get her attention. So what? It was intermission, I was allowed to speak.

The announcement came on for everyone to get back to their seats as the performance was about to begin again. I stood up and looked all around the room, thinking Kitty had snuck in and was sitting in somebody else's seat. My next plan of action was to run down the stairs, past all the people returning to their seats, and bolt into the lobby. I ran into the washroom and stopped dead in my tracks at the sight before me.

Kitty stood there, calm as rain, drying her panties in the hand dryer of the fancy Royal Leon Theatre. "Oh, no, Mom, you had an accident?"

"Not a bad one," Kitty said. "But I didn't want to keep wearing them if they're dirty."

"I guess there was a line-up when you got to the washroom," I snarled. "Why can't people let an old lady cut to the front?"

"Oh, they did," Kitty reassured me. "Just in the nick of time, too. I almost had a BIG accident right before I went in."

"Just throw them out," I said. "The play is about to start again."

"I'm not throwing them out! Not after I gave them such a good wash," Kitty replied.

"Ugh, don't tell me you washed your panties in the sink?" I asked.

"Where else would I wash them?" she countered.

I took her underwear and stuffed them into my purse. "Let's just get back to our seats."

The usher made a face like he was going to cry as he took the doorstops away from the massive entry doors. "I should have known," he said, as if he was joking but I knew he meant it.

This time it was me pulling Kitty up the stairs. She asked me to wait a moment before we traversed over the many sets of knees before us. Huffing and puffing, her eyes widened in alarm as the house lights went down. Bent over, using people's heads and shoulders to aid her progress, she finally joined me in our set of seats.

Three minutes later my mother began to make a noise that sounded like the growl of a bear. Even though every person around me snuck a look, nobody seemed to be quite bothered enough to complain. Kitty kept up with the guttural snore as she slept soundly, her head on her chest.

So yeah, I got to watch the rest of the play, which I really did not like. Add to that the fact that I paid almost a hundred bucks just so Kitty could have a nap and do her laundry in one of Toronto's elite theatres. Seriously, as far as outings go? This one was a fail.

• • • • • • • • • •

If at first you don't succeed, be an idiot and go for round two. As a bonus for getting rid of all the Extra Small t-shirts, Blast Records sent me a gift certificate to a local nail salon. I had a feeling good ol' BiBi, Sherman's pampered wife, was still looking out for her redneck friend. I planned to re-gift them to the twins but instead I wasted them on another failed outing.

"Come on, Mom," I pleaded. "It'll be a girl's day out! We'll go for a nice lunch, get our nails done, maybe go for a coffee after...."

"Sounds like stuff we can just as easily do at home," Kitty replied in a snit. In the past, it took a lot to ruffle Kitty's feathers. She was grace under pressure, the rock you could lean on, the proud matriarch of the Canseco clan. These days? A fucking pain in my ass. If she wasn't leaving every light on in the house, she was cranking up the furnace to ninety degrees. She was walking the house at all hours and I was sleeping fitfully, fearing she'd head out the front door. I had half a mind to lock her into her bedroom at night.

"I'm sure we could, Mom, but it's not costing me much, so don't worry about it," I said. Come to think about it, she hadn't mentioned anything about the price of the outing. Maybe it was just me; obsessing about how much money I had in my bank account. In the past, I never had much moola but I always managed to get by. Suddenly I had three kids in university and an elderly mother and a shitty job. Yeah, now I was worried about my finances. "I'm using a gift certificate, I have a buy one, get one free coupon for this new restaurant and we'll go to any place you want for a coffee. That'll make for a full day." And then hopefully, like a baby, she'll sleep the whole night through.

It started off so promising. I managed to find a triple space open in front of the restaurant, enough to just slide the big Town Car in with ease. Upon entering A Taste of Africa, we encountered a family of four sitting around a table. Two men jumped up and immediately went into the kitchen. One woman scurried behind the counter while the other lady picked up a couple menus.

"Hello, and welcome to A Taste of Africa," the waitress greeted us in an exotic accent. "My name is Yenee...."

"Oh my goodness," my mother interrupted. "Say that again? Or better yet, do you have a nickname?" Becoming obnoxious seemed to be another new trait Kitty was developing.

"My family calls me Banchayehu," Yenee replied, as my mother snickered. "It means 'I See Life Through Your Eyes.' When we came to Canada, I was the only one who could speak some English language. I still translate everything for them." She gestured towards the counter, where the older woman smiled and waved at us. "Here are your menus. Just let me know when you're ready to order." She walked two steps away and sat down at the next table.

Kitty and I opened our menus. Next to print I could barely make out, listing meals with ingredients I didn't recognize, were the photographs of the dishes. Everything looked brown or creamed and just the worst kind of advertising. Kitty held the menu right up to her face. "What kind of place did you take me to?" I heard her ask.

I lifted my own menu and spoke. "It's an Ethiopian restaurant. I may have been all over the world, but I've never been to Ethiopia. I wanted to try their cuisine."

"When I hear the word 'cuisine', these pictures don't spring to mind," Kitty said, laying the menu down and pointing to a mess of what looked like creamed brown beans. "I have no idea what to try."

As I stared at the menu, the waitress stood up. "Are you ready to order?"

"Uh...not really," I said. "I have a two-for-one coupon, by the way." The waitress didn't even ask to see it; I'm sure she was just happy to have somebody come into the deserted joint. "Maybe you can help us? Why don't you bring us two of your most popular meals?"

The waitress walked into the kitchen, followed by her mother. There ensued a rather boisterous argument about what was their most popular dish. Kitty smacked her lips loudly. "I could sure use a glass of water," she commented, then called out, "Hello? Some water?"

"Mom, she'll be out in a minute," I said. "I'll ask for some water when she gets here."

It wasn't long before both mother and daughter arrived with the meal as well as the utensils. They quickly deposited the food onto our table and joined the two men who had come out of the kitchen. They all sat at the table next to us, watching...staring...

In turn, Kitty and I stared down at our plates. "What the hell is this?" my mother asked. For her to use a cuss word, she must have been bamboozled.

I had no idea what I was served nor any idea on how to eat it. Along with three rows of various brown-shaded strips of slop was some kind of grey bread. Adding the sole bit of colour on my plate was what appeared to be a purple beet ball. I didn't know if I was to use the bread for dipping or eat the mush with a spoon. Kitty's plate was not much better, but it had some foods I could recognize. Large chunks of raw carrots, giant wedges of onions and lots of what looked like rolled up fajitas.

With a bright cheery albeit fake smile on my face, I chirped, "It's good for the soul to try different things! Let's dig in!"

Kitty ignored everything except a piece of onion she nibbled on. She did try a piece of the bread but spit it out into her napkin. When I offered her part of my dish, she reared back as if it were LSD. With the family sitting right next door, I felt compelled to try everything on my plate. I didn't want to be rude; poor Ethiopia already had their share of troubles. Mom could get away with not eating and be forgiven because she was an old lady. I was a mature woman who should know better than to order too much food. Didn't I realize there were children starving in Africa, as my mother used to say?

After gagging on the mush and tearing the bread up into dust, after saying things like "Why did I have to eat such a late breakfast?" and "I guess I'm not as hungry as I thought I was," I finally felt I could call for the bill. The contents on my plate were sufficiently maneuvered so as to appear I'd eaten something. I was so happy to leave that barren restaurant, I over-tipped. And Kitty never did get her glass of water.

"I may never have been to Ethiopia either," Kitty stated, "but I sure do feel like an African kid right now."

"What do you mean?" I asked.

Kitty glared at me. "Because I'm starving!"

• • • • • • • • •

Next stop, the nail salon. I sat back in the chair next to my mother, prepared to be pampered. An Indian woman laid a basin of warm soapy water on the floor and in a faint British accent, told me to soak my bare feet in it. Another Indian woman put a similar basin by Kitty's feet.

"Please put your feet in the water, Ma'am," the lady said.

Kitty raised her feet, the toes misshapen with arthritis, and dropped them into the basin. Water slopped over the edge as the Indian woman jumped out of the way. My technician left my side and ran to get towels.

"Go easy, Mom," I whispered.

"Wasn't my fault," she whispered back. "I couldn't see that pail of water."

As the women cleaned, our toes soaked. My lady came back to me and raised one foot out of the water. She towelled it off and prepared to give me my pedicure. Kitty's lady did the same but as soon as my mother's dried foot revealed itself, I saw the two women exchange a glance.

"Your nails are so long," Kitty's lady commented. "They look very thick as well."

"Her nails grow like weeds," I remarked. "I cut them every two weeks."

The two nail salon employees went to work. My pedicure took no time at all while Kitty's lady laboured over each nail. "Ow!" she yelled as a clipped toenail struck her cheek. It had not been the first time. She looked over at her pal. "It's like being in artillery gunfire."

My technician and I laughed. "Welcome to my world," I said.

"Really, Tammy?" my mom dampened the mood. "It's not enough the Indians have to make fun of my messed-up feet, but you have to join them?"

"I will tell you in all honesty, Ma'am, but you should see a doctor about these feet," her technician said, standing up. "I am talking about the toenails. I will be right back." She walked over to a desk and rummaged through the bottom drawer, returning with a face shield and safety glasses. "Now maybe I can finish this job."

By the time I had my nails done, Kitty's lady had completed her right foot. "I'm tired of this," Kitty complained. "Leave the left foot. Tammy can finish that at home."

Her technician was only too happy to comply. "Let's do your manicure though," she faintly insisted. "What colour polish would you like?"

"Black," said my mother.

"Mom! Why would you pick black?" I cried out. "Don't give her black!"

"I'm feeling black," Kitty replied.

"Black is a popular colour these days," the technician told me.

"Just give her a clear polish," I ordered. "If she feels like black tomorrow, I'll do that too, when I chop off her left foot." I turned to my mom and gave a fake laugh, just to show her I was kind of kidding.

The Indian women didn't get a huge tip. Actually, they didn't get any. I could see Kitty watching me carefully to ensure no money passed. Since I felt I'd already hurt her feelings somewhat, I didn't want to endanger the rest of our planned trip.

"So now it's coffee time," I reminded her. "Your choice, I don't care what you pick, my GPS will find it. Where do you want to go for coffee?"

As I buckled her into her car seat, she gave me her choice. "Home."

• • • • • • • • • •

"There's a whole box of mail for your mother here," said the person calling from Better Days Ahead Retirement Home.

"Why would you still be getting her mail?" I asked.

"I don't know," she answered. "Did you put in a change of address when you moved her from here?"

"No," I responded.

"Then how are we to know where she went?" the lady gently berated me. "We know she didn't die.... "

"How would you know if she died?" I asked. "Do you get some kind of official notice?"

"Of course not," the woman scoffed. "We just have a lot of residents who read the newspaper obituaries. So what are we to do with this mail?"

Kitty had an optometrist appointment that afternoon, so I made arrangements to drop by Better Days after that. I neglected to tell my mother about this pit stop and was thus unprepared for her wail of anguish as I turned into the driveway of the senior's home.

"You're taking me back!?" cried Kitty, as she began to weep. I pulled to the side before I even reached the parking lot. In the past few days, my mother had begun having crying jags that had more of an effect on me than I cared to admit. I could put up with her rudeness, her complaining, her slipping mental capacity....but I just couldn't stand to see my mom in tears.

"Mom, please, don't cry!" I begged, taking her in my arms. "We're here...."

"I'll try to be better, Tammy!" Mom interjected. "I won't cook anymore, I won't iron, I'll stay in my room....." She was breaking my heart.

"Mom! We're just here to get your mail!" I said. "Why would you even think I'd bring you back?"

"Why? Because I'm nothing but an old bag of trouble," Kitty replied. "You're still young and single, but now you're saddled with looking after your broken-down mother."

I stroked her thinning head of silver hair. "I don't look at it that way," I declared. "For one thing, I'm not so young anymore." I tried a little laugh, just to lighten the situation, but it backfired as Kitty began to weep even more. "Mom, please stop. You've been crying so much lately, maybe we need to see a doctor."

Kitty sniffled as she tried to stop. "I don't need a doctor. I know what the problem is. I'm just so tired of life."

Her comment unsettled me. She sat back in her seat and stared ahead rigidly. I drove into the lot and parked the car. "Why don't you come in?" I suggested. "Maybe you'll see somebody you know."

"No, thank you," Kitty replied. "They thought of me as a big problem."

"I know!" I exclaimed. "Imagine that!"

Leaving my mother, I went into the retirement centre and walked up to the reception desk. "Hi, there's supposed to be a box of mail here for me to pick up?" were my opening words.

"Yes, I spoke to you," the receptionist replied, looking around her tiny cubicle. She called into the office off to the side. "Marta! Where's the box of mail for Kitty Casino?" In my emotional state, I was about to tell this woman that I thought her nickname for my mother was tasteless and derogatory. Before I could say anything, she yelled out, "Never mind! Found it!" She lifted a big baggie of bingo dabbers and under that was a shoebox with 'Kitty Casino' written on the side. As she handed it over, the first thing I could see were pieces of junk mail from assorted casinos. I let my comment die on my lips.

Returning to the car, I found my mother asleep. She woke up enough to enter the house and go straight to her bed. It wasn't until I'd prepared a late dinner that she joined me in the kitchen. As we sat down to eat the chicken nuggets and rice, I pointed to the box in the middle of the table. "There's your mail," I said.

Kitty dragged the box towards her and then spotted the first piece of casino mail. It was like receiving a letter from her soldier son away fighting the war. She caressed the paper, smoothed it out and read every word. We didn't speak much, but at least she wasn't crying.

After dinner, I said, "Tomorrow you have a doctor's appointment, first thing in the morning. How about I run you a shower?" Lately Kitty had a hard time lifting up the spout to make the shower come on. She claimed it had gotten stiff, but it gave me no problem.

As Kitty showered, I began to clean the table. My eyes fell on the pile of casino mail my mother had received. Right on top was one from Casino Kato. I had a momentary pang of anger as I recalled my missed opportunity to accompany The Noise on that gig. I picked up the flyer to take a gander at what this casino was all about. The first thing I saw was the list of concerts being held there.

I saw Neil Sedaka and Dwight Yoakam had played there already this month. Both well-known but neither quite to my taste. My eyes travelled to the next date on the calendar, just three days away. Playing that night was Living Large. No way! Living Large was still together?

As I'd mentioned, The Noise was my bread and butter for fifteen years, but I would occasionally hire myself out to other bands for short road trips. One act was Living Large, a kind of electro-pop band that had a huge hit - Give It Up - when I worked for them. As it turned out, that became their only hit, but it had been so catchy, it was still being used for commercial jingles today.

Now, I'm also not a big fan of electro-pop but there was a hidden agenda as to why I'd like to see this band again. It wasn't like the six weeks with them had been marked with wonderful memories but I did have quite the intense fling with the keyboardist in the band. Listen, I never claimed to be an angel, but after Axel, I tried to stay away from musicians. I just found them a little too flaky and a little too lax in monogamy. Ninety per cent were bona fide divas. I tended towards the occasional roadie affairs or the one-night stand with some cute news reporter or hired hand.

Ulysses pursued me from the moment I stepped onto their tour bus. I ignored his flagrant come-ons and humorous attempts to get to know me better. After three days of this, he gave me a day of the silent treatment. For some reason, I ached to hear his voice, even if it was to call me 'Sweet Cheeks'. The next day, he acted like everything was normal... too normal. It seemed he accepted we were going to be just friends. So that night at the after-party, I came on to him like a tornado in a trailer park. In my mind, he didn't know what hit him. In retrospect, I probably played right into his hands.

The time we had together was great though. I don't know if we fell in love, but we told each other our deepest secrets, we spent every non-working moment together and we screwed like bunnies. He completely dropped the rock star persona when he was around me and it became common knowledge that Ulysses and Tammy were a couple. At least on this tour, because that's how long it lasted.

When the tour ended and the bus dropped us all off in Tampa, Florida (their home base, not mine...from there I'd have to find my own way home - to San Diego), I stood by the luggage bay while Ulysses dug his big duffel bag out. He slung it over his shoulder and beckoned me to come in close. Wrapping one arm around me, he planted a luscious kiss on my lips. "Sweet Cheeks, you were amazing," he murmured, looking deep into my eyes. Then he kissed my forehead and said, "I'll see you around."

I didn't take it too hard. That was show business. But damn! They were still touring? I looked again at the flyer and saw a little chili pepper symbol next to their name. What could that mean, I wondered, as I questioned its significance. At the bottom of the flyer, I was astounded to see that it meant Kitty could get two free tickets to see this show! As I scanned the flyer, I saw she could also go see The Orillia Philharmonic Society for free...or The Nylons ... even The Bills and Brendas Barbershop Quartet! Kitty could see four shows for free with a guest, but the only one that I really wanted to attend was Living Large. Something in me yearned to see Ulysses again.

Seeing the number to call to book a ticket, hoping I wasn't too late, I picked up the phone and dialled Casino Kato. I didn't know I needed Kitty's Players Card number, but I knew where she kept it - hanging like a medal around the large mirror on her dresser. I ran to my mom's bedroom and recited the number into the phone. Within two minutes, I had two free tickets to go see Living Large.

I couldn't wait to tell my mom, but I wanted to draw it out. As she reclined in bed, a book in her lap, magnifying glass in her hand, I walked in with her clean laundry and began to put it away. "So I've been looking for a place to go for our next outing," I said.

Kitty's shoulders slumped. "Tammy, if there's something you want to do, go ahead. You don't have to include me all the time."

"I thought you'd like to go out and do stuff," I said.

"It depends on what kind of stuff," Kitty replied. "I'm telling you right now - I have no intention of taking a ceramics class."

"How about a ballroom dance class?"

Kitty gave me the evil eye. "Oh, please, you didn't....One person steps on my toes and you'll have me in the hospital."

"Don't worry, I didn't," I quickly said. "But how about a concert?"

"What kind?" Kitty asked, her interest barely rising. "Symphony? Good for a nap. Or is it a piano recital? I bet...."

Again I cut her off. "No, Mom, it's kind of like rock and roll...."

"And you thought 'Ohhh, Mom would enjoy this!' Is that right?" Kitty asked me sarcastically. "I'm already half-deaf, a rock concert should make me completely deaf."

I pretended to pout. "Oh, darn, 'cuz I already went and got the tickets. It's in three days."

"Let me be clear," Kitty said firmly. "I am not going to any rock and roll concert."

"Please?" I begged.

"No. Now leave me alone, I'm going to bed," Kitty dismissed me. She reached over and clicked off her bedside lamp, as if for punctuation.

I walked slowly to the door. "Alright then," I dragged it out. "I guess I'll just have to get somebody else to go with me. I wonder who in the world I can find to accompany me to Casino Kato?"

Kitty's bedside lamp clicked back on. "I'll go with you," she squeaked out, her smile making her seem twenty years younger in the lamplight. "Hail, hail, rock n' roll!"

CHAPTER X

Living Large's concert was in the evening at Casino Kato and as I sat before my computer, trying to drum up business, I debated with my mother as to the best time to leave.

"MapQuest says Kato is almost two hours away," I said. "I didn't know it was so far."

"That's nothing compared to when the seniors took the bus," Kitty said. "It takes three hours since we have to stop and pick up people along the way."

"Well, consider it's Friday night rush hour, which is worse than any other night," I said. "It'll probably take about four hours to get up there. I don't want to be late for this concert."

"May I offer a suggestion?" Kitty said tentatively. "Maybe we could leave early and have a supper when we get there? Did you see the coupon I had when you looked at the flyer?"

"Coupon?" I asked, my mother having said one of my new favourite words.

"Yes, for two people to dine for free," Kitty answered.

"Free?" I again repeated Kitty's words. "Nothing is for free! You mean one is free if you buy the second meal, right?"

"No, Tammy," Kitty spoke slowly, as if speaking to a brainless child. "Two people eat for free."

"OK, but it's probably like a hot dog and a bag of chips," I decided.

"They actually have some nice restaurants there," Kitty said. "You'll see. I like to go to the buffet."

I gawked. "A BUFFET? A free fucking buffet?"

My mother winced. "Tammy, please, your language...."

"This I've got to see," I said, slamming my computer shut. "What's Casino Kato trying to be? A mini Las Vegas? I'm hungry now, so I'm going to wait until we get up there and then I'm going to eat like a pig. Do you want to leave in an hour?"

"I'm ready any time you are," Kitty replied. She had pulled the same thing she did last time we went to a casino. Primped and ready to go at the crack of dawn, waiting like a good dog at the front door for the sound of her master's footsteps.

The drive to Kato was a bit of a trek. Kitty entertained me all the way with tales of trips she'd taken on a special casino bus. "When I lived at Vista Shores, one of the stops for the Kato bus was at the mall across from us. As long as the home knew where we were, we could go up to Kato whenever we wanted."

"Did you go often?" I asked.

"Not as often as some others," Kitty replied. "Maybe every second day."

"Wow! That must have been expensive!" I gasped. "How much to take the bus?"

"Only five dollars," Kitty answered. "But they give you cookies and water and a candy."

"That's not too bad, five dollars," I acquiesced .

"And when you get off the bus, they give you fifteen dollars," Kitty added. "To spend on food or to gamble."

"Wait, let me get this straight....Casino Kato pays you to go up there to gamble?" I asked in disbelief. Kitty nodded. "Six hours round trip on a bus. I don't know if I could handle it, but I guess you seniors have time to kill, don't you? Spend time sleeping on the bus or sleeping in your bed, it makes no difference."

"The destination makes a world of difference," Kitty said, sounding like the Dalai Lama.

At first Casino Kato didn't seem like a gambling mecca. I thought I'd arrived at some Native Canadian heritage site. Drums, feathers, indigenous dancers and art installations...so much to admire! I accidentally parked in the hotel parking lot rather than the casino lot, but Kitty said we could still enter the casino that way. Upon entering the hotel lobby, my breath was taken away by the splendour of it all. How I wished we were staying there.

Stomach growling, I suggested we think about eating fairly soon. "Oh, Tammy, we just got here!" Kitty whined. "Can't we gamble for just a few minutes?"

"Fine, let's say thirty minutes?" I suggested.

"How about an hour?" Kitty countered.

"Tops," I ended the discussion. "Maybe I'll gamble with you. It's not too busy, we can probably find a couple machines next to each other."

We hadn't walked more than ten steps into the casino when Kitty spotted a machine she wanted to play. Though there was an empty seat next to her, I didn't put money into the slot. It was a two-cent machine and I had decided I had an affinity for the one-cent slots. Kitty played a few bets; I noticed forty cents was her favourite amount to bet, though she'd switch it up every few spins. I saw her go down to a two cent bet, followed by a dollar bet. It finally paid out five dollars and Kitty cashed out.

"I made my money back, and then some," Kitty said. "I know you want your penny machines so let's go find you one."

It didn't take long and she played Crystal Fountain while I played a cartoonish game that kept making me laugh aloud with its graphics and sound effects. Planet Moola it was called, and it had cows in spaceships that moo-ed quite comically. I played a couple dollars with my usual five cent bet, until I hit the bonus. A man seated on the opposite side of me said, "I put forty bucks into that game and never got the bonus. You should make out pretty good."

At the end of my seven free spins, I'd won back over three dollars. That was good enough for me on this machine, so I cashed out and watched Kitty for a bit. She was having no luck whatsoever. "Let's try a different game," Kitty said, taking out what was left of her twenty dollar bill.

"Let's play one near the buffet restaurant," I said as my empty stomach grumbled.

"Oh, there's lots of good machines there!" Kitty said, taking off at a fast trot. "I'll find us a row of penny machines."

The bank of machines was in full view of the Stay Awhile Restaurant, where the buffet was located. Already there was a long line-up forming.

"Mom, is there always so many people here to eat? Look at how many there are in line!"

"Your rock and roll band must be popular," Kitty declared. "There's only a line-up if it's a good act."

"Well, I'm starving and we don't want to miss the show," I replied. "Maybe I can get in line and you play a machine where I can see you?"

"We could do that," Kitty agreed, already jogging off to the last remaining chair at the bank of machines.

Before Kitty could get to the seat, two other women also made for that solo gaming spot. It was like a game of musical chairs as the two new gals, one elderly and petite, the second chunky and half her age, both plopped their arses down. "I was here first!" they cried in unison.

A scuffle ensued as both women tried to push the other off the chair. A crowd immediately gathered to watch the drama. Of course I was there as well, watching with mouth agape. In less than a minute, the screeching brought a couple of security guards running. By now, the older woman had been pushed off but was standing and hugging the machine. The younger one had staked claim to the chair and was trying to insert her player's card into the machine over the senior's shoulder.

"Ladies! Ladies! Break it up!" one of the guards shouted.

"I was here first!" they both yelled.

"Any witnesses?" the same guard asked, looking around. The entire set of onlookers shrugged. "Then there's only one way to settle this. Ladies, I'm going to ask both of you to step away from the machine."

Neither woman moved; they simply stared at the guard as if he was out of his mind. "Then who gets the machine?" the senior gambler asked. "Why doesn't she leave and I get to stay here?"

"Why don't you fuck off and I stay here?" the younger one retorted.

"Ladies, there's plenty of slot machines here," the other guard stepped in. "Now you will both have to step away or we're going to escort you out of the casino."

I guess they save those magic words for a last resort. As if there were a spring in the chair, the younger woman bounced off in a flash. The older lady peeled herself off the machine and picked her cane up off the floor. I didn't miss the slight threatening gesture she made with it toward the younger woman.

They barely cleared the game when Kitty pounced onto the empty chair. She looked up at me with gleaming eyes enlarged by her heavy-duty prescription glasses. "I bet this machine is going to be lucky!" she crowed.

"OK, you play here where I can see you and I'll get in line. Keep an eye on me; I'll be waving when I get near the front," I commanded. Kitty simply nodded as she inserted her players card into Lucky Leopards. "Mom, did you hear me?"

"Yes, Tammy," she responded. "Now go get in line. I'm getting hungry and it's almost time for me to take my pills."

Yes, her mysterious pills, for the illnesses she kept under wraps. I often asked her what the pills were for and her only answer was "For my continued good health, of course." I'd ask her what ailed her, that she had to take so many pills. She'd reply, "Just chalk them up to getting old. Worry about your own health."

Just as I began to walk away, giving my mom a pat on the shoulder for luck, I noticed she was playing at a nickel slot. I stopped. "Whoa, Mom, that's a five-cent machine!" I reported. "Are you sure you want to play this one?" I looked around the casino and saw all the machines near the restaurant were being played.

"I'm staying," Kitty said. "I know it's going to pay out."

I patted her shoulder again and went to take my place at the end of the food line. As I watched Kitty play, my mind began to work out her bet. I knew she didn't care for the amount I liked to play - five cents. But with that very moderate bet, I still had a decent chance of winning something at the penny machines. If I only bet one penny, all the symbols would have to line up correctly, left to right, on one line only. My five cent bet got me three lines across, as well as a couple lines going at an angle...all sorts of fun things.

But the nickel machine? If I played my normal way on that, my bet would be twenty-five cents. Kitty played 40 cents usually on the penny machines...I kept trying to do the math, and though I prayed I was wrong, it seemed like she was spending two bucks every spin. I almost wanted to get out of line to warn her.

Suddenly I saw Kitty pull out her player's card and stand up. She looked around the casino, everywhere but at me. I was waving but I didn't want to shout out her name. She started to walk around to the other side of the slot machines, where I couldn't see her. Glancing around, I saw that maybe forty more people had joined the line behind me. The couple in front of me had noticed me waving.

"Was that your mother?" the gentleman asked.

"Yeah, she's old and doesn't listen," I complained. "Now she's gone wandering off...," I stopped blathering when I realized the couple were probably the same age as Kitty. "I'm in line for the two of us, but I better go get her."

"We'll hold your space," the man said, no offence taken. He turned to the punk era-dressed foursome behind me. "You hear that, kids? We're going to save this lady her place in line."

"Sure," said one with his hair gelled into spikes, though one seemed to have been neglected and was wrecking the whole 'do. "Plenty of meatballs to go around," he said, adding more to my suspicion of this casino buffet with the comforting name.

I squeezed under the rope and ran to find my mom. I passed her machine and saw her purse still wedged against the adjoining slot. I pulled it out and kept going. As I turned the corner, I immediately spotted Kitty on the end machine.

"Mom!" I cried out. "Why'd you leave the machine?"

"It was taking all my money," she said, not appearing fazed by the fact. "I heard the lady leaving this one so I switched machines."

"Well, I can't see you from the line-up," I pouted.

"I can see you," Kitty said, and demonstrated. "I just look around the corner."

I saw that she would be able to see me once I approached the front of the line-up. Rather than make matters worse, I said, "OK, I got a nice couple holding my place in line. Please, Mom, keep an eye on me! I'm starving!" I grabbed my stomach for emphasis and noticed I had her purse in my hand. "Oh, and once again, you forgot your purse. I'm going to hang onto it."

As promised, my spot in line was reserved and I noticed it had moved up significantly. As we edged closer to the front, I tried to see what kind of food they offered, but I was so ravenous, I was beyond caring about the quality. Kitty, true to her word, kept glancing over. She even stood up a time or two, peering myopically at the line-up until she spotted the waving, dancing spectacle of her daughter. Short of fitting her with a binocular-strength prescription for her eyeglasses, I didn't know what else to do about her vision.

Kitty didn't worry me further when I approached the head of the lineup. She appeared at my elbow. "I managed to win back some of my money," she grinned. "Figured I'd better quit while I was ahead."

Her two statements didn't quite gel in my mind, but I didn't bother to dwell on it as we reached the casino worker. She took my mother's player's card and I fished her ID out of her purse, as well as the offer that two could dine for free. That piece of paper I handed over rather suspiciously, waiting for the catch.

The worker immediately allowed us through, passing a receipt to a server that said our meal was paid. That lady asked us to wait a moment while she found us a table, or would we prefer a booth? Kitty chose a booth and within two minutes, we had a seat. I didn't even bother to sit; I just waited while Kitty took off her jacket and then stated, "I'm going to see what they have to offer. Don't forget where we're sitting."

Five minutes later, I found Kitty still mulling over the salad choices. There was nothing on her plate but a tea biscuit, a rolled up piece of ham and two different varieties of a single pickle. "I'm trying to decide between a leaf salad or a pasta salad," my mom said as she saw me approach.

"Who cares? Take them both!" I almost shouted. "Did you see what they have? Oh my God, I've died and gone to heaven. I'm going back for everything. It all looks so good!"

Plate after plate I devoured of the most delicious food I've ever eaten. Each bite was a revelation and an homage to the chef's prowess. There were ribs, but these were Southern Comfort-infused Hoisin-marinated Grade A Alberta Beef Ribs. Nothing overpowering - a faint taste of mild whiskey, a subtle hint of hoisin. Chicken? Sure, every buffet has chicken. But baked, almond-encrusted lemon butterflied breast of chicken?

For some reason, I even took food that I normally didn't eat. Never a fan of mashed potatoes and definitely tired of pizza, I chose these very items at the buffet. They made me a convert. I knew I had to save room for dessert and almost cried when I saw their array. Had I known it would have been as pretty as a magazine spread, as plentiful as a Roman feast, I would not have had my third or fourth plate of food. My all-time top three favourites were represented - the nanaimo bar, the apple crumble, the cheesecake - but many of my runner-ups also appeared. Black Forest cake, pies of all sorts, mousse for miles, even a giant round metal station overflowing with artery-clogging chocolate decadence. What the hell - you only live once, so I dove in.

I could barely make a dent in my second dessert plate. I looked at Kitty's tiny saucer holding a small date square alongside a cat-dish sized bowl of rice pudding. "Why'd you take so little?" I asked her.

"There's only so much a stomach can hold," Kitty said. "By the way, did you notice how some people here are dressed? It's almost like they're in costumes."

"That's just their style," I explained. "They're probably here to see Living Large. The band - at least when I knew them - used to attract kind of a weird following."

"I don't like it," Kitty said. "It's scary. Dog collars and army boots up to the knees. And maybe it's my eyes, but just awful haircuts."

"Well, get used to it," I warned. "You're going to see a lot of them at the show."

Kitty tried to hide it but I could see her face momentarily crumble. It suddenly dawned on me that I was taking an eighty year old to a rock concert. The music would be loud and the crowd could get physical. I wanted to see the show, just to satisfy my curiosity about my ex-lover. Why was I dragging Kitty along? Only because I didn't want to sit by myself.

Either my conscience was tugging at me or the buffet food was having a negative effect. Since I was a new fan of the Stay Awhile Restaurant, I dared not hold them to blame. I was being an inconsiderate daughter. Just as I was about to let my mom off the hook, a voice boomed out.

"Holy shit! Tammy! Is that you?"

At first, oddly, I felt like cowering when I heard my name called. It was as if I were ashamed to be seen at a casino...almost like I was caught surfing porn on my computer or discovered in a crack house. Then I straightened up - I was just in a hotel restaurant, by all appearances. Nobody could tell I was even considering gambling. I looked around to see who recognized me.

A huge bear of a man came running at me, his arms outstretched. I stood, if only to block him from careening into my mother. Something about his crazy mane of hair struck a chord with me and I tentatively opened my arms. He reached me and swept me up, enveloping me in a hug that blocked all light from my vision. "Tammy, I thought it was you!" the man said as he put me down.

I took a couple steps back and looked way up at the giant. Then it hit me who he was - the road manager of the opening act when I toured with Living Large the one time. He was thinner back then, though still as tall. I recalled he taught me how to cook up his famous hang-over remedy, and that I'd even considered having a fling with him before Living Large's keyboardist caught my attention. "Yeah! Hi!" I laughed. "So nice to see you again! It's Cory, right?"

"Kerry," the man corrected me. "So what brings you to Casino Kato? The slots?"

"No!" I strongly denied, then laughed as if he'd made a joke. "I'm here to see the concert. How about you?"

"Me? I'm working for the band," Kerry replied. "Remember, when we met? I was road manager for that piece-of-shit band Techno Drive?" I nodded my head, the memory of that lame act racing back to me. "You worked for Living Large, right? So when Large got another tour, their road manager still wasn't sober...I mean available. They asked if I would be interested. Man, I was never so glad to switch jobs."

"That must have been ten years ago," I commented. "You've been with Living Large all that time?"

He nodded. "Yeah, they've had their ups and downs, but what band doesn't? It pretty much went downhill when Spencer left...their original singer? The new guy is ok but...aahhh...I don't know. Maybe their sound is not so popular anymore. But they still get a lot of gigs, lot of smaller venues for sure, but this place is nice, hey?"

"Oh, I agree!" I said. I wanted to tell the world.

"So what are you up to?" Kerry asked, glancing at my mother. "Do you want to come upstairs? We got a big suite where everybody is hanging out before the show."

"Would that be ok?" I asked shyly. An invisible foot kicked my ass... of course it would be ok. I've seen it happen often. It's never really a party, but if the venue is in the same building as the one the band is sleeping at, usually a hospitality suite is provided. I've seen the rooms full of press, groupies, friends and drug dealers.

"For sure!" he yelled, sealing the deal. "And you can watch the concert from backstage too, if ya want."

That idea appealed to me in a spectacular way. "For sure!" I yelped back, but then looked at my mother, who sat there with no expression whatsoever on her face. I'd deal with that problem later.

"OK, then, come on up to Room 505," Kerry said. "Anytime between now and showtime." He grabbed me in another clinch. I was so stuffed with food that it made the hug uncomfortable.

As he ambled away, Kitty said, "He seemed like a nice man. Did you date him?"

"Worked with him," I replied. "Hey, Mom, we have a little dilemma here. That guy invited me to hang out with him before the show."

"Oh, that was nice of him," Kitty said politely.

"Yeah, well, that's not all," I continued. "He also said I could watch the concert from backstage. You know that makes a show a hundred times better, right?"

"Was I invited?" Kitty asked.

"Uh...wow, no," I replied. "Sorry, mom, I didn't even think to ask."

"So you want me to miss the concert?" she asked. I nodded my head in shameful assent. "And here I was about to go into the ladies room and rip up my blouse, just so I could fit in. Aww, and now I won't be able to bang my head either."

"It's not that type of music," I began and then looked at her. "Wait, you're joking, aren't you?"

"I don't want to hurt your feelings, Tammy, and I know how much you want to see this concert, but actually," and Kitty took a deep breath, "you can thank that man from the bottom of my heart that I don't have to partake in this strange event."

"But I'm going to be gone for hours," I warned. "HOURS. How are you going to pass the time?"

The biggest smile came over Kitty's face - a pure feline grin. "Oh, I'm sure I'll find a way."

• • • • • • • • • •

The night at Casino Kato was the most fun I'd had since my arrival back in Toronto. Even before I left San Diego, I hadn't enjoyed a night out like tonight.

Kitty had promised me she would call just before 9 PM. If necessary, I would meet up with her but if she was fine and dandy, I would meet her after the show at the Aladdin machine, a bright tall gaming console that was easy to spot.

Tentatively, with my nerves on edge, I parlayed my way down the hallway of the fifth floor of the Kato Hotel. The walls were adorned with First Nation paintings, the rugs were luxurious, the very paint on the walls seeming to be made of cream. How I wished I ran the Casino Kato Fan Club rather than Blast Record's. Arriving in front of Room 505, I fluffed up my hair, tucked my T-shirt into my skin-tight jeans (funny how in a couple months home I'd already gained ten pounds. The pants weren't meant to be skin-tight), and adopted an attitude that said I belonged at the party.

After my firm 'shave and a haircut, two bits' knock, the door was opened by a woman in her early twenties. Though she was a definite knockout and looked downright sexy in her quazi-Nazi get-up, one couldn't help but notice her piercings. She was tattooed pretty extensively as well, but the piercings took away her beauty and replaced it with freak-show appeal. A quick count revealed maybe twelve on her face alone.

"Can I hawp you?" the girl asked almost inaudibly, as a big round silver ball stuck to her tongue clicked off the back of her front teeth.

"Yeah, hi, I'm an old friend of Kerry's....," I began, before a man slid up behind Miss Pierce. Oh my Lord, it was my old boyfriend, Ulysses! I simply gawked, a dopey look taking over my face, as Ulysses slid his arms around the front of Miss Pierce.

"Hey, Babe," he growled, not talking to me. "Who you hanging out with here?" He gave me a fleeting glance as he tried to drag Miss Pierce back to the party.

"Some girl who says she knows Kerry," she replied.

"Come on in then," Ulysses said to me. God damn! He didn't seem to recognize me but I wasn't overly concerned. Upon a quick appraisal, the past ten years weren't kind to my old beau. He was showing his four decades of hard living, but was still trying to cram his thickening body into spandex and leather.

Kerry, on the other hand, looked almost delicious in his Mr. Big N'

Tall jeans and Mark's Work Wearhouse plaid shirt. He spotted me immediately as I walked into the hospitality suite and again came lumbering toward me, arms spread wide for another hug. "Tammy!" he shouted. "You made it!"

I was flattered that it meant that much to him and was doubly-rewarded when Ulysses did a double-take upon hearing my name. "Did you say Tammy?" he asked Kerry. Kerry ignored the keyboardist while he picked me up like I weighed less than a supermodel. I prepared for the spin and Kerry didn't disappoint as he went for three laps. With each turn, I could see Ulysses trying to catch a better glance of me. "Your name is Tammy?" I heard once. The next time was just a questioning look but the third spin I heard, "I used to know a Tammy."

Kerry dropped me back down to earth but didn't even acknowledge Ulysses as he hustled me over to a corner of the room. Three more roadies sat there, one of whom I'd worked with a number of times over the years. The other two were strangers but we all either worked for, or knew, the same musicians. Before thirty minutes was up, our gossip and tales of life on the road had us feeling like lifelong friends.

The members of Living Large and their entourage occupied the rest of the suite. Some invisible dividing line seemed to keep the rock stars from the working stiffs. Still, Ulysses kept looking at me and was just about to cross the room when the door opened and a couple members of the press entered.

"Excuse me, Tammy, I have to attend to business," Kerry said. He cracked open another beer and handed it to me. "I'll try to be as quick as I can." I appreciated the effort he went to in order to make me feel at home. He walked over to the reporter, had a couple words and then announced, "OK, boys, we're going to take some photos in a few minutes. We just need Nigel to give a quick interview first."

One bandmate groaned. I vaguely remembered him as the guitarist, a very talented one. He could play any stringed instrument. He was also very intelligent, to the point that I was afraid to speak to him. I couldn't remember his name, but he griped, "Why Nigel all the time? Just because he's the singer?" I also had to wonder about that, as Ulysses was the person who attracted the eye. Not only was he handsome, but he played the keyboard like he was having a ball. His enthusiasm was contagious with the audience. Nigel, the singer? Bland, motionless, pasty-skinned, large-toothed, an Adam's apple the size of a doorknob...but with the voice of Elvis and Prince combined.

"No," Kerry set the matter straight, "it's because he's the one who's sleeping with a Kardashian and you're not."

I couldn't help it; I swivelled my head to my band of new roadie friends, my face swathed in disbelief. All three nodded, their faces reading 'Yeah, can you believe it?' As I turned back to the scene, I was startled to see Ulysses standing right in front of me.

He stared deeply into my eyes. "It is you!" he said, his breath reeking of garlic. "You remember me, don't you?"

"Of course I do!" I said. "Though you didn't remember who I was when I was at the door."

"Sorry, I didn't really look at you," he said. "But I remember you now! We had a thing, didn't we?"

"Are you asking me if we did?" I countered.

"No, I know we did," he replied. "It was pretty good too, wasn't it?"

"Yeah, we got along great."

He put on a questioning look. "Whatever happened to us?"

"The tour ended," I said.

"Oh, yeah!" Ulysses recalled. Made perfect sense to him. He looked around the room. I surmised he was looking for his girlfriend, Miss Pierce. He glanced at Kerry. "So you with Kerry now? Is that the story?" he asked in a low voice.

"No, I just ran into him earlier," I admitted. "How about you and that woman I saw you with? Is that your girlfriend?"

"What woman?" he asked, suddenly coming in even closer, putting on a move.

"Who do you think?" I asked. "Eva Braun or whatever her name is."

"Oh, Virtue? She's just a friend," he said. I raised an eyebrow, so he elaborated. "Well, a friend with benefits, if you know what I mean. We can always use friends like that, can't we?"

I kept backing up, trying to get away from his breath. At the exact moment I banged into the wall - just as Ulysses was about to press his body into mine - Kerry called out, "Time for a few quick photos, guys. Let's go! It's almost showtime!" Ulysses gave me a look that he perhaps thought made him look sexual, if you find Bela Lugosi sexy. I gawked at him, my mind blaring one thought - what did I ever see in him?

Even while I watched the concert backstage, my eyes rarely strayed from Ulysses. I kept trying to find some redeeming factor to make me appreciate the time we had together. His energy no longer looked youthful and fresh; now it appeared forced and like he may hurt himself. He wasn't the sole reason why they stank up the stage. The singer raised boring to new levels and the rest of the band put on their usual lacklustre performance.

By the end of the show, I was in a happy mood. Thrilled the show was over as I'd never liked their music. Satisfied I didn't pay anything to see them. And very pleased that I could now think about my affair with Ulysses and no longer be left with the feeling that he may have been the one that got away.

Kerry passed me with some towels in one arm and a cigarette and lighter in the other hand. "Don't go away, Tammy," he said. "There's going to be a party after, back up in the suite. You're coming, right?"

"Sure," I said, staying rooted until I remembered something. "Oh, my mom!" I yelled. "I gotta go check on her! How about I meet you up there?"

Kerry stopped and got a worried look on his face. "You're not gonna bail on me, are you?"

"No, no!" I replied. Was he kidding? I was finally alive tonight, out and about, in the land of the living. Damn right I was going to a party!

• • • • • • • • • •

The throng of concert-goers packed the exits as I tried to make my way back into the casino. A bunch of people headed into the parking lot, but about the same number headed for the slots. Instantly the room was filled and I worried about locating my mother in this monster crowd.

Rather brusquely, I pushed my way through the Living Large weirdoes and past walkers and wheelchairs until the Aladdin machine came into sight. I scanned the people standing by it, looking for my mother, cursing her usual dark attire. As I walked up to the game, relief flooded through me as I saw Kitty sitting on a chair, actually playing Aladdin. There were five people watching her progress.

I paused briefly at the edge of the crowd. A man glanced over at me and said, "She's doing pretty good, won two mini-jackpots since I been standing here."

My eyes popped wide and I squealed, "Really?" then hustled over to my mom. "Mom! You won two jackpots!?"

She nodded. "Mini jackpots," she confirmed.

"Well, still...I like the word jackpot," I said. "How much does a mini one pay?"

"The first was fifty and the second one was thirty dollars," she replied. "I want to win the big jackpot though."

I glanced up at the graphics at the top of the Aladdin machine. An LED sign claimed the big jackpot was currently at five thousand dollars. "Just make sure you don't spend five thousand dollars trying to win it," I warned, just as a bunch of bells and whistles went off.

"Look at that," Kitty laughed. "I just won twenty bucks." Then she suddenly stiffened and slowly turned to look at me, a ghastly look on her face.

"Mom!" I whispered loudly. "What's the matter?"

"The concert is over?" she asked incongruously. "So now we have to go home?"

"Actually, I was going to ask you if we could stay a bit longer," I began tenderly, concerned she may be having a medical issue. "That guy...."

But before I finished my sentence, Kitty immediately perked up, the radiant smile returning to her face, her hands flying back to the machine. She stroked an image of Aladdin on the screen. "You go have fun, Tammy!" she urged. "I'm staying right here with my guy." She pressed the Spin button. "Come on, big jackpot!" she yelled. She was rewarded with a fifty cent win. Someone in the crowd gave a weak cheer but Kitty went right back to making another bet.

"So ok, how about we connect in a couple hours?" I suggested. Kitty simply nodded. "Mom, we need to make sure we keep in touch. Can you call me on your cell phone?" Again I was rewarded with the nod as she peered at the spinning wheels.

A lady with a coffee cart wandered by and Kitty glanced up. "I'll take a coffee," she called out and then looked at me. "What are you still doing here?" she asked. "I'll call you in two hours."

I squeezed her shoulder, wished her luck and eventually found my way back to the hotel lobby. About to leap onto a waiting elevator, I wondered about my appearance. I glanced around the stunning lobby, looking for a public washroom. Signage led me to one just around the corner from the elevator.

I stepped into a washroom fit for a Queen, never mind a First Nation Chief. Words cannot describe the opulence assigned to this latrine. As I glanced into the rock-framed mirror, I was glad I took this opportunity to fix myself up. A complete make-over took about ten minutes, leaving me feeling much more prepared to take on a room filled with young tarts and groupies. A small part of me was hoping that Kerry would still find me attractive with all the new talent showing up for this party.

As the elevator door opened on the fifth floor, I nervously stepped out and immediately saw Kerry exiting his hotel suite. He instinctively glanced over at the elevator and spotted me.

"Good timing!" he announced, as he held out his arm in an old-fashioned manner. "Could I escort m'lady to this evening's soiree?" he asked in a bad French? British? accent. I laughed at his gesture and took his arm. Little did he know how much it meant to me; I was now able to enter the party looking like I had every right to be there. After all, I was showing up on the arm of Living Large's road manager.... NOT as a single lady hoping to get laid by a member of the band, or at least one of their crew. That was never my intent, but tell that to the dirty minds at the party.

It's possible I had a better time at this party than the ones I attended when I was road managing The Noise. For one thing, I was kept busy just having fun and being fussed over by Kerry. He fetched me a beer, made me a plate of food, kept me company. His eyesight needed attention perhaps, as there were plenty of beautiful babes in the room, but he apparently didn't see them. The point is, I wasn't doing what I used to do at these after-parties, which was keep an eye on Bradley and his appetite for destruction, make sure there were no under-age bimbos who could get the boys in trouble, run interference when security was called...the list was endless. Having a good time was often an elusive task to accomplish.

Ulysses was in the hospitality suite as well. Miss Pierce hovered over him, staking her claim. The singer, Nigel, completely blended in with the cream-coloured paint on the walls. He had two women, one white, one Asian, fiercely competing for his attention. One had her tongue in his ear while the other woman was massaging his upper thigh. I knew the scenario, knew the outcome - those ladies would end up sharing the singer at the same time later tonight. I searched for the guitarist, knowing I'd find him just as I did - off in a corner with a couple other musical geniuses. The guitarist was showing them some kind of synthesizer. As for the drummer? That was an electronic gizmo safely stored back on the tour bus.

I paid absolutely no attention to Ulysses; I couldn't believe how dead my feelings were toward him. However, I couldn't help but notice my long-ago boyfriend often looking at me. Maybe he was using mental telepathy, but every time his face happened to cross my vision, he let me know he was checking me out. My eyes showed zero feeling, they just skipped over him like he was simply the room's hair dryer.

Kerry was a perfect gentleman - rarely leaving my side and then apologizing if he had to attend to some quick duty. I sat with the rest of the roadies again and we had a million laughs, especially when some of the girls tried to make moves on them. As I sat next to Kerry, a spandexed woman with a multi-hued mohawk hairdo came over and sat on the arm of his chair. Her next move was to start running her hands through Kerry's hair and make purring sounds. Kerry's eyes widened and his reaction was to lift me off my seat and place me on his lap. The groupie got the hint and walked off. I remained on Kerry's lap.

Some time later, we were enjoying the fact that one of the roadies put AC/DC on for music, replacing the Living Large's last album that had played thrice already. Kerry said something over the noise and I bent my head closer to his mouth, asking him to repeat what he'd just said.

"Your ass is buzzing my leg," he replied. I jumped off him.

"Oh, I'm sorry!" I said. "Am I too heavy?"

"No," he laughed. "Something in your pants is buzzing."

I gave him a questioning look and then remembered my cell phone squeezed into my back pocket. "Oh, my phone! Oh, my Mom!!" I pried the phone out of my pocket and saw three missed calls. I quickly glanced at the time and was relieved to see it was barely two hours since I'd last seen Kitty. She was calling me right on time - being such a good little mother tonight!

I called her back and she answered immediately. "Hey, Mom, it's Tammy," I said.

"Tammy? Is that you?" she asked. All I could hear was a cacophony of sound from her end. "I can't hear you over that loud music."

"Speak up, Mom, I can't hear you over those machines," I replied. "Are you OK? Having fun?"

"Are you having a good time?" Kitty asked. This conversation was going nowhere. I gestured to Kerry that I was going to take the call into the hallway outside the suite. He nodded that he understood.

I exited the suite and was rewarded with a quieter zone. I re-entered my conversation. "I'm having a great time," I assured Kitty, speaking loudly. "Are you OK?"

"Why wouldn't I be?" she asked. "I'm winning big tonight!"

"Really?" I asked. "Did you hit the big jackpot?"

"No, I finally left Aladdin," she admitted. "He was stealing all my money. But I just won sixty bucks on The Wizard of Oz."

I glanced at my watch. It was already one in the morning and I didn't want to keep the old lady up all night. We still had a long car ride home. Still...."Mom, would it be alright if I could stay another hour?" I asked.

"Oh, by all means!" she trilled. "This is your night, Tammy. I'm just along for the ride. You take as much time as you like."

"Let's connect in an hour," I suggested.

She replied with a "Yippee! I just won fifteen dollars!"

"Mom, talk to you in an hour, ok?" I repeated. "You call me or I'll call you."

The phone disconnected. I was going to call her back but decided to just let the dice roll. I'd find her later, I'm sure, but for now I just wanted to get back to the party.

I was about to knock on the door when it opened and Ulysses appeared. I mumbled "Excuse me" as I tried to slide past him. Instead, he grabbed me by the shoulders and pushed me back into the hallway, letting the door shut behind him.

"I was worried you left the party," Ulysses cooed.

"Worried?" I echoed. "Why would you be worried?"

"Well, you know...we leave this place in the morning, who knows when I'll get to see you again?"

"And who cares?" I asked.

"Come on, we had some pretty good times together," he murmured, backing me to the far wall. "Let's go to my room," he suggested. "I have something from the old days I wanna show ya."

"You do?" I asked, mildly curious as to what it could be. A photo? A memento? And then I was angered by my naiveness as he pressed his body into mine. He meant his pecker. I pushed him off as the sound of a Rolling Stones song suddenly seemed to pound into my head. Honky Tonk Women. I don't know if it empowered me but I let Ulysses have a piece of my mind.

"Get off me!" I said, pushing him again to create a larger gap. "You think you can just have any woman you want? Because why? Because you're a rock star? Let me tell you - your road manager Kerry has way more class than you can ever hope for. I wish I'd hooked up with him ten years ago instead of a cliche like you. Man, I don't know what I ever saw in you but believe me, whatever it was, it's so gone."

Ulysses had a defiant look, like what I was saying wasn't going to hurt his feelings. It only served to disgust me more and I made an about-face to head back into the party. Though the door was open and I could hear Stones music, it felt like I walked into a wall. It turned out to be Kerry's upper frame. I looked up at him in astonishment.

"Just coming to check up on you," Kerry said. "Little concerned you were skipping out on me." He responded to the embarrassment on my face. "Yeah, got here just at the right part...about me having class and all..."

At this point, Ulysses rudely shoved Kerry aside as he made his way back to the party. Kerry just shook his head and then, in a similar fashion to what I'd experienced earlier, took me by the shoulders and propelled me back into the hallway. It didn't feel so icky this time.

"Maybe I should get going," I said. "I don't think I'm welcome at the party anymore."

"I was thinking of leaving too," Kerry said. "It's getting to the weird hour. Groupies getting desperate, the boys getting drunker. That's usually when I make my exit."

We both stood there awkwardly a moment, with Kerry's hands still on my shoulders. Suddenly he leaned in for a kiss and it took me by delicious surprise. It wasn't a long or a passionate kiss, but I gave it an A+ for tenderness and feeling.

As our lips came apart, our eyes opened and we looked at one another. Kerry chuckled. "Oh, wow, this is harder than I thought," he muttered.

"What is?" I asked.

"Trying to get back into the swing of things," he replied. "I'm single right now, but I was in a long-term relationship for quite awhile. We broke up last year but I never felt ready to meet anybody. That is, until I saw you tonight."

"That's sweet," I said, making it short so he'd continue.

"We busted up cuz I was on the road all the time. So I'm not looking for any long-term deal," Kerry stated. "I just know that right now....I'd like to ask if you want to come to my room?"

"Sure," I agreed, and since I knew he caught the tail end of my conversation with Ulysses, I put him at ease by adding, "I like your style, Kerry. You've got class. But maybe you heard that before?"

• • • • • • • • • •

I was quietly shutting the door to Kerry's suite. It had been over an hour since I'd spoken to Kitty and it was time to check on her. I'm sure I could have stayed in Kerry's room and gone for round two, but the single bout was hugely satisfying. If I'd known he had such lovemaking skills, the affair with Ulysses would never have happened.

As I waited for the elevator, I called Kitty. She said I could take more time if I wanted, but I assured her I was coming to get her. As we were deciding where to meet up, the elevator doors opened. I met the embarrassed gaze of Living Large's guitarist. Miss Pierce was on her knees, her face attached to his pelvis.

"A little help here?" he asked.

I stepped into the elevator, pressed L for Lobby and held up my hand, indicating I was on a call. As I spoke to Kitty, arranging to meet her at a machine called Wolf Run, I glanced down at Miss Pierce. It appeared the ball she wore on her pierced tongue had somehow gotten into the little hole at the end of the zipper on the guitarist's jeans. She was struggling to remove it.

As the elevator hit the ground floor, I stepped out. I was about to walk away but my old road manager skills came back. I held the door open and faced the two drunken people. "Look, you have three options. You go back up to Floor Five and get Ulysses to help you out." They both recoiled at this option. "Second choice, dude, you slide out of those jeans and Miss Pierce, you get to wear them on your face all night." The guitarist immediately tried to slither out of his pants but Miss Pierce whinnied in pain. "Third option, just take the piercing out of your mouth." I released the doors and they slid shut. I wished I'd only given them the first option but that would have been catty.

The casino was nearly empty when I walked back inside. It didn't take too long to find Kitty as she played a two-cent machine. Her face was, as usual, scant millimetres from the screen. "Move back," I said as I approached. "You'll go blind sitting that close." I sat in the empty seat next to her.

"Are you going to play some?" Kitty asked.

"Nah, I was thinking we should get going," I replied.

"Were you drinking?" she asked out of the blue. "I smell alcohol on you."

"I had a couple beers," I confessed. "But that was over an hour ago."

"Maybe you shouldn't be driving just yet," Kitty warned. "Remember how I was telling you about the bus trips out here? Well, if you ever wanted to take one with me, you'd need a player's card. We should go sign you up for one."

I agreed to this and we made our way to the desk. The whole process took less than three minutes and when the casino worker handed me my new card, she also gave me a voucher for ten dollars. "What's this?" I asked.

"New members get ten dollars free slot play when they sign up," I was informed. "But you have to use it within the next twenty-four hours."

Behind me, Kitty giggled. "Some people could go through that ten dollars in one spin."

I was grateful for the free money. As I happily went to play penny machines, Kitty tagged along, playing whatever was nearby. That ten dollars, what with my occasional forty cent wins and, once, four dollars, lasted me over an hour. By this time it was close to four in the morning. As the Tigress machine ate my last nickel, I announced we were hitting the road.

Kitty put up no resistance. I sensed she was getting tired - she'd been gambling for about twelve hours. My suspicions were confirmed once we got into the Town Car. As I clicked on her seatbelt, Kitty asked for the blanket that laid on the back seat. I handed it to her and watched as she wadded it up and used it as a pillow. Before I'd even gotten out of the parking lot, my mother was fast asleep.

Once I got onto the highway, things went smoothly for the next hour. After that, though I was not yet home, I began having catnaps. The only problem with that was I was still driving. Finally, I cranked my window open and turned the car radio on full-blast. "Sorry, Mom," I said, though she slept on.

It was almost 6:00 AM when we got home. I jumped out of the Town Car, feeling like an old version of myself - coming home at dawn, screwed and partied-out. That is, until I remembered I had to haul my mother out of the car. Her slight figure seemed to weigh a ton as I draped her arm around my shoulder and helped her inside. I still stuck to the old vision of myself - but this time it was of me helping a drunken Bradley to his hotel room. Any version would do - other than the one awaiting me when I woke up. Back to being a penny-pinching babysitter to an old lady, while struggling to make ends meet on a low-end job. Single, lonely and uninspired.

That would be when I woke up though! Right now I was going to hit the hay and relive every moment of this amazing night, from the scrumptious buffet meal to finding myself getting laid by a really decent guy. Never mind the free ten dollars.

Yeah, tonight I liked the casino. Maybe I'd consider taking Kitty back there, though I doubted such a magical evening could ever happen again. I was just happy it even happened.

CHAPTER XI

It didn't take a rocket scientist to discover Kitty only wanted to go to the casino. The daughter of one? It took a touch longer.

I was feeling down in the dumps and searching for something to amuse me. I was considering a movie, perhaps a nice dinner out. The only thing stopping me was my wariness about leaving Kitty at home. She'd resorted to doing foolish acts, like when she peed the bed and tried to wash the bedding. The amount of soap she used helped to wash the floors of the entire main floor. Yesterday she watched a cooking program on TV and learned how to make an easy-to-prepare smoothie. I ran downstairs when I heard the racket at midnight and discovered she'd left the metal spoon in the blender.

Today I snapped at her while I was perusing the computer, looking for free things that might interest me. Her crime was simply being in the same room as me.

"For Pete's sake, Tammy," Mom reprimanded me. "You've been on edge for days now. I know something is bothering you. You can tell me, you know."

I knew I couldn't tell her the entire reason, so I skipped around the truth. "I'm just bored! I have no life! The bands I'm representing are doing shitty, I have no boyfriend, I never have any fun anymore..."

"I know where we could have tons of fun!" Kitty chirped. "And all it will cost you is five dollars."

"What's five bucks gonna get us?" I grumpily retorted.

"Remember that bus I told you about?" she merrily asked back.

The five-dollar bus ride to Casino Kato, which we took weekly for the next month. Our first trip was great fun - for the piddly five dollar bill that I handed over at the beginning of my ride, I was given a bottle of water, a mint and a packet of crackers. The bus ride took almost three hours and just as I was falling asleep, we pulled up to the casino. Upon disembarking, we went straight to the cashier. She ran our player's card through a machine and handed us fifteen dollars each.

That fifteen dollars, what with the five-cent bets I was making, lasted me most of the day. Just as my stomach growled, Kitty informed me we should visit the buffet, as she had another coupon. Back to Stay Awhile? She had me at "coupon". Another memorable meal, another full belly and back to the slots. Maybe I spent five of my own dollars at the end of our five-hour stay. I also drank about six cups of the delicious coffee they offered for free.

Back on the bus, just as we started rolling, the hostess came around with a smile and an open purse. My mother dug into her change bag and pulled out a couple loonies. "Time to tip the hostess," she explained. I added two dollars.

It was another three hour ride home. About thirty minutes into the journey back, I woke up a sleeping Kitty. "I have to use the washroom," I whispered.

"You can't," she whispered back.

"What do you mean, 'I can't'?" I asked. "I have to go."

"They don't like you to use the washrooms on the bus," Kitty explained. "You have to ask first, she'll follow you with cleaning spray and towels, and then you have to clean up after you use the washroom."

"You're joking, right?"

"Did you see anybody use the washroom on the way up here?" she asked. I couldn't recall anybody walking the aisle so I shook my head. "And you won't see anybody else using it on the way home either. It's too embarrassing."

I settled back into my seat and groused. "Jeez, I want my tip back then." As soon as the bus finally pulled into its last stop, I bolted out. Kitty apparently knew this hostess quite well from prior trips as they bid each other a fond adieu. I was about to piss my pants.

We got into the car and I drove about a hundred metres to a McDon-
alds. I barely shoved the car into 'Park' before running in to use their facilities. Once I felt back to normal, I left the restaurant and got back into
the car. "Well, that was fun," I said to my mom. "We ate well and I barely
spent anything. How'd you do?"

"I came home with money," Kitty replied.

"Good! We'll have to do this again sometime."

'Sometime', in this case, meant one week later. I wasn't really in the
mood to go to a casino again, especially one that required a six-hour
round trip. However, Kitty caught me in a weak moment, bellyaching
about the lack of work one second and in the next, whining about having
to fix another uninspired meal.

"Tomorrow we can go to Kato and I'll buy you the buffet," she tried
to entice me. Believe me, that buffet was a deal-sealer. "That is, if you're
not busy."

"Let's see, I spent all day on the computer and I sold one t-shirt and
two posters," I replayed my work day. "I worked so freaking hard that you
know what? I think I deserve a day off."

Kitty was so thrilled, she dove into the mushroom omelette without
complaint. "I'll call the bus company just as soon as we finish dinner!"
And just to show me how super pleased she was, she gushed out some
faint praise. "I swear, this omelette is even better than the one you made
last night!"

The next trip to Kato was on a completely different level than the week
before. To begin with, as we boarded the bus, the hostess gave my large
cup of coffee a very dirty look. It was a different lady than before. As soon
as we'd picked up our final passenger ninety minutes later, she went into
a long spiel about how we were not to use the washrooms. She then proceeded to hand us all a water bottle.

As soon as the bus landed at Casino Kato, all the occupants got off
and every single one headed for the washrooms. Then we next saw most
of our bus-mates at the cashier, snapping up the free fifteen dollars. From
there I saw a few head off to the buffet. I turned to my mom. "Too bad we
used you your coupon last time," I said. "I don't like the idea of you buying me an expensive lunch, just so you could come to the casino."

"I think I should have enough points for a free meal," she said. "We should check on that."

"Points?" I repeated. "Free meal?"

"Let's ask somebody," she said, leading the way to the sign-up desk. "Wait up," I told Speedy Gonzales as she race-walked ahead of me. The little old lady who had slept most of the way up, her dentures hanging halfway out her mouth, was nowhere to be seen. "If I lose you, you're hard to find in your little black ensemble. You're like a magic trick - you just melt into the background."

Once at the info booth, the points system was explained to us. Based on how much you spent at one time at one machine, you were rewarded with points. These points enabled you to get free slot play or free meals, even a free hotel room. Kitty was eligible for everything they had going. The man helping us laughed out loud, "You could have free meals for a month with all the points you have!"

"You hear that, Tammy?" Kitty asked. "We could come to Kato every day!"

I rolled my eyes. "Yeah, if I wanted to eat six thousand calories a day." I handed the man my player's card. "Can you tell me if I have any points?"

He ran it through the machine and I swear he handed it back with disdain. "You have zero points."

"Zero? But I've played the slots here before," I said, confused.

"Yes, you may play the slots," he said, in a condescending tone, "but you don't put very much money into them."

I wanted to defend myself against his true statement, but couldn't think of an argument. Sorry?

Kitty pulled me away. "Let's go gamble for an hour and then meet at the buffet," she commanded, fully taking charge.

"Why don't we try another restaurant?" I suggested. "They have so many here."

This turned into a bit of an argument. Kitty didn't like change and I didn't like regularity. Finally I got my way and we agreed to meet at the steakhouse on the premises.

An hour later, I was waiting for Kitty. Ten minutes after our agreed-upon time, she ambled up. "Sorry, I was in a bonus, couldn't get away on time." We were immediately seated by a very attentive, yet unobtrusive waiter.

"At least you got a bonus!" I snapped. "I've spent almost all the free money they gave us in an hour, and I haven't even gotten a bonus."

"Maybe you aren't spending enough on your bets?" Kitty suggested. "Or you aren't spending enough time at the machine."

"God, you make it sound like I'm dating it," I said. "I'm ordering a steak - medium rare - and I hope they do it right."

"I'm sure they will," Kitty said. "This is Kato."

She was right. When it came to class and luxury, Kato couldn't fail. My steak was only the best BY FAR from any steak I've ever eaten. Kitty, who admitted her steak was also divine, complained that she couldn't pick out some watermelon or have a side bowl of chili or a slice of pizza. "That's because we're not at a buffet, Mom," I said. "Obviously different circumstances."

"I don't even think I can get my rice pudding," Kitty said, almost shocked. "From now on, we only go to the buffet." As wondrous as my steak was, I didn't mind her proclamation.

After I'd spent thirty of my own dollars, I went to find Kitty. The bus was due to leave in an hour and I wanted to firm up plans on meeting her. She was supposed to be at the row of Duck Stamp machines. Though her purse was on the seat, Kitty was nowhere to be seen. All the other chairs were occupied, so I asked the people on either side if they'd seen Kitty. Both said her purse was there when they arrived; they assumed it was meant to "hold" her seat. I knew she would never leave her purse behind - it was filled with her important ID, photos of her grandkids, medication. Even her phone was in there, as I discovered when I tried to call her.

"I'm taking this," I declared. "I'm her daughter." One of the gamblers frowned at me. I waved up to the ceiling. "I'm sure there are cameras everywhere," I said, lifting the purse. "Hello, I'm taking my mother's bag."

I made ever-widening circles around the Duck Stamp machines, looking for Kitty. It seemed half the patrons wore black and when sitting down, almost everybody looked short. As for gray hair? That would account for nearly everyone. I couldn't find my mother.

At one point, I almost walked past her. An unusual smell wafted into my face and I glanced around for its origin. I spotted Kitty with her face pressed up against the glass of the Kilimanjaro game she was playing. I plopped into the empty seat next to her.

"Look, Tammy! I won eight hundred games!" she laughed. "I still have over five hundred left to play out."

I stared at her game. "Oh my God, you do have that many free spins!" I gasped. I glanced at her winnings. "Whoa, you said it played over three hundred games already?" Kitty nodded. "And you've won only seven dollars?" I glanced at her wager. "On a forty cent bet?"

Kitty nodded at all my questions. "All it takes is one nice spin for me to win big," she reminded me. "Are you going to play Cave King? You like that game."

"I like the cartoon graphics," I stated. "And no, I spent my limit already."

"We have forty minutes still, before we leave for the bus," Kitty said, looking at her vintage watch. "I can lend you money."

"No, I'm good," I said. "That's what I decided to spend and I spent it. The fun is over. Don't you have a limit?"

"I guess," Kitty murmured, her eyes glued to the game. "When the bank machine says I've reached my maximum for the day."

I don't know how much I liked that answer; my bank gave me five hundred a day from the machine. Before I could ask her, that disgusting smell hit me again. "Ugh, do you smell that?" I asked. Kitty nodded, her hand stroking two of the mountain-range images that appeared. "What do you think it is? I can't believe there's a smell like that at Kato."

"I think it's me," she whispered.

I lowered my voice as well, since people were sitting beside us. "You? What happened? Did you have an accident?"

Again Kitty nodded. "It's this game! I never won so many free games. Just before I hit the bonus, I was thinking of quitting it and going to the ladies room. But then the three mountains came up and I won forty-five games. Then the three mountains kept coming up and the games kept adding up and I couldn't leave...."

"Listen, I'm going to watch your machine," I said. "You go clean up. The bus leaves soon and you can't get on smelling like that."

Kitty got off her chair and looked around for her purse. I realized I had it slung over my shoulder, the one that wasn't holding my own purse. I held it out to her.

"Why do you have it?" she asked.

"You left it on the Duck Stamps chair," I stated. "I hate that purse. And I don't want you going out wearing black clothing anymore either."

"You have a problem with my clothes?"

A man wearing a shirt that said DUN RITE AUTO BODY, looking like he came straight from under the hood to the casino, stood at my shoulder. "Hey, are you going to play Cave King?" he asked.

I got off the seat. "No, go ahead, I'm watching this machine for my mom," I said. The smell again rose up and I strongly said, "I'll see you when you're all finished, Mom." She ambled off and I was about to slide into her seat when I saw the faintest puddle of urine in the centre. I made an awkward recovery as my butt barely missed sitting down, and decided to stand behind the chair.

Twice the bonus came up again, adding another ninety games to her total. I started to worry about missing the bus. Kitty returned, sneaking up on me like some kind of ninja. Before I could squawk out a warning, she slid right back into her chair.

"There's still three hundred games?" she asked, confused. "I was gone so long! The bus leaves in twenty minutes."

"I know!" I whined. "Why would you play a game like this when it was almost time to go?"

"I got on at three, the bus leaves at five-thirty," Kitty replied. "How was I to know I'd get so lucky?"

At the end of her near-thousand spins, (with a grand total win of twenty-six dollars) we still had to get her ticket cashed out and grab her jacket from the coat check. Even though she wore seven layers at all times, she always had to check the outer one. I was almost causing her to take flight as I pulled her quickly out the front doors of Casino Kato. We boarded the bus just as the hostess came running up.

"I already have you paged," she said. She turned to the crowd and said something to them in Chinese and got a couple laughs. She said a few more words and everybody started to giggle and point at the two sole white women. Not that we were the only white people on the bus; there was also one Jewish man.

As for the ride home, it was almost bearable if I kept my hands over my mouth and nose. "Mom, you didn't have another accident, did you?" I asked at one point.

"I don't think so," Kitty replied. "And I did clean up as best as I could."

I inwardly made plans to cover the seat of our Town Car when we got back. Neither the Kato slot chair nor the bus seat escaped the clutches of my mom's bladder, but my main ride was going to get some respect.

The trip going back to Toronto was not pleasant. Even though I couldn't use the badly-needed bus washroom, sitting next to Kitty felt like I sat in the john the whole trip home.

• • • • • • • • •

It wasn't two days before Kitty started asking me if I was bored. Asking her why she thought that, she pointed to my computer screen. I was again playing Spider Solitaire, an online card game that was threatening to take over my life if I allowed it. I shut the laptop.

"Maybe I'll make supper," I declared. "Feel like bacon and eggs?"

Kitty ignored the question. "You know, there's lots of men on the bus ride to Kato," she noted.

"I noticed," I said. "They're all old and they're all Chinese."

"You're displaying racism," Kitty said sternly.

"Yup. And ageism," I agreed. "So it's bacon and eggs then?"

"Did you notice how, the last time we ate at the Stay Awhile Buffet, they served breakfast food as well as lunch food?" Kitty mused. "And it was already mid-afternoon! Remember, you promised we'd go to the buffet next time..."

I interrupted. "Woman, listen, if you're hinting that you want to go back to Kato, it's not going to happen anytime soon."

Kitty gave me a look of pure horror and then seemed to shrivel in size as she whimpered, "Why not?"

I looked at her incredulously. "What happened on our last trip to Kato?" I asked.

"I won a thousand spins on Kilimanjaro," she replied instantly.

Sighing, I said, "I'm talking about you having an accident in public."

"Oh, that!" she said. "Don't worry about that, it wasn't the first time."

"Really? Don't you think you should do something about it?" I asked.

"Like what?" Kitty replied. "Tammy, I'm getting old. These things happen. What can I do?"

"Gee, I don't know," I said sarcastically. "Maybe wear a diaper?"

Kitty made for the door. "I don't have to listen to this kind of talk.

You're just being mean."

"Mom, come back!" I said. "Don't be so insulted! Old people wear diapers, don't you know?"

"Of course I know," she retorted. "I've seen them in the old age places I was locked up in. I'm sure those diapers are specially made for hospitals and seniors' homes."

"Haven't you been to a drugstore lately?" I asked. "They have a giant area reserved for adult diapers. Big, small, male, female....."

"Oh, this I'd have to see," Kitty retorted.

A plan started to hatch, a possible solution to getting a few things cleared up. "I'll make you a deal," I said. "I'll go back to Kato with you once you accomplish three things. Number one, we get you adult diapers and you will wear one at all times when we go to a casino.... "

"I hope we find one that fits," Kitty muttered. "I have a small waist but an Italian bottom. What's number two?"

"Your clothes," I stated. "I want to see you in anything other than black pants and black blazers. We're going shopping and you're going to buy some clothes with colour."

"My, I haven't been shopping in years," Kitty muttered. "What's the last thing I have to do?"'

"Lose the purse," I commanded. "That should be no problem, you lose it every time we go out. Find a different way to carry your shit but I don't want to see you using a purse anymore. So that's it. My three demands. Think you can handle it?"

"Can we make time for shopping tomorrow?" Kitty asked.

"Sure," I said. Kitty stood up. "Hey, where you going? You're not mad, are you?"

Kitty paused in the doorway. "We're busy tomorrow but the next day is free. I'm going to reserve a couple seats on the casino bus."

•••••••••

At 9 AM, we left the house and decided to take a walk to the commercial area near our residence. Today Kitty was in full-on old-age mode, walking four tiny steps to my one stride. I had to wait at every street corner for her to catch up. Within thirty minutes, we were at the local pharmacy. I steered my mother directly to the adult diaper aisle.

Suffice to say it was like the heavens had opened for Kitty. She stared in awe at the copious amounts of assorted diapers that lined the shelves. As she looked down the aisle, she was delighted to find two other old ladies (as well as a youngish man) scanning the items.

"Oh, Tammy, I never knew!' she whispered in awe. "This is unbelievable! The answer to my prayers!"

"Adult diapers?" I asked. "Maybe if you told your doctor..." I let it go at that, not wanting to start a fight. That was another bone of contention with us - Kitty being so secretive about her state of health and the myriad of pills she took. I was not allowed to come into the room for her doctor appointments and my advice as to her well-being went unheeded.

"I need to find the right product," Kitty muttered, pulling down a box to study it up close.

An elderly voice piped up. "You won't like those," a rake-thin woman said. She had a cart laden with diet soft drinks and two cases of water. "Those are just like wearing giant menstrual pads. They'd be more for her," she said, gesturing at me. "I think what you want is a diaper that's just like wearing panties."

"I like the sound of that!" Kitty enthused. "Where are those?"

As Mom and her newfound friend wandered off down the aisle, I sped around the store looking for aspirin. I wasn't gone five minutes before I returned to my mother's side. In that span, Kitty had managed to open up four boxes. I arrived at the same time as a frowning store clerk.

"Sorry," I immediately said. "She's old. She's senile. She doesn't know what she's doing."

The clerk came forward and started stuffing the diapers back into their correct box. "Please ask her not to open the merchandise. We can re-tape it but now it has to go on the clearance shelf." He stalked off to find the tape.

"Good cover story," Kitty complimented me. "Maybe we should wait a few minutes, see if they go on sale. Did you see how expensive they are?"

"Let's just grab a box and scram," I said. "Did you find anything you like?"

Kitty pointed to an open box on the floor and I picked it up. She paid for her purchases, graciously offering to cover the aspirin. And so she should, I thought.

"Where to next?" I asked. "It's a bit of a walk to the mall, but we can shop in the stores along the street."

"What's wrong with Goodwill?" Kitty asked, already heading in that direction. It was in the same plaza as the pharmacy. "I've been shopping there exclusively for years. I like the selection. Come on."

She had more energy than when we'd left the house and I didn't want to waste it visiting a dozen different boutiques. I agreed to the thrift store. The first sight to greet me was a rack of t-shirts. A vintage The Noise shirt, in mint condition, was selling for $1.99. I scooped it up. Directly behind it was another find - an old Bob Marley and the Wailers shirt. Though it was ragged, barely usable for anything more than a dust cloth, I grabbed it. The price-markers at Goodwill weren't stupid to mark it at $9.99.

I spent ten minutes digging through all the t-shirts in the store but nothing else enticed me. I was just about to look for Kitty when I saw her approach. She handed me a large Goodwill bag. "I'm ready to go," she announced.

"Already?" I said. "It seems like we just got here. You need to buy new clothes, Mom. What's in here? A blanket?" I hefted the light bag.

"It's my new outfit for when we go to the casino," Kitty replied. "That's all you asked for. Some clothes with colour, so you could find me easier."

"That's true, but....," But what? Did I want her to pick out a whole season's worth of clothes with one Goodwill visit? And she did have my wishes in mind when she bought whatever clothes were in the bag. "OK, just let me pay for my t-shirts."

I approached the cashier, where I saw my mother's purse on the counter. I picked it up and gave her a mock glare. She plucked it from my hands. "Oh, that silly purse!" Kitty laughed up at me. "Soon as we get home, it's going into storage. I got something else, you'll see."

We were home before noon. Kitty loaded the washing machine with her purchases and made sure to put the right amount of soap into the washer. She made herself a tuna sandwich for lunch. I hated tuna, wouldn't touch it, but Kitty loved the stuff. The only way she got it was if she bought and made it herself. Another trip to the laundry room to transfer her clothes into the dryer. While she watched a game show, I did her dishes and microwaved myself a pizza pop.

Kitty passed the kitchen on her final trip from the laundry room. "That was a long walk we had today," Kitty said. "I'm tired. I'm going up to bed.

I need to rest up for Kato tomorrow."

"It's not even two o'clock!" I said to my mother's retreating back. I felt defeated somehow. For months I tried to figure out how to deal with mother-issues that were driving me insane. I finally lay down the law and in two short hours Kitty makes the changes that were guaranteed to please me. So why did I feel so let down?

Next time I made demands, I was upping the ante.

• • • • • • • • • •

I predicted Kitty would be ready and waiting by the front door when I came down the next morning. I had set the alarm early so I could look at the computer and try to sneak in a little work-time. Surely, with the time difference, I could sell some fan-wear to China.

"Don't you want a bite to eat before we leave?" Kitty asked.

"Noooo," I groaned, looking at a news item Blast Records had forwarded to me, complete with a shocking news photo. It appeared Starburst were expanding from their known ganja use. The picture showed a member suffering from an ecstasy overdose and being attended to by paramedics. In the email's subject line, Sherman had simply written "I HATE THESE GUYS". I sensed trouble brewing.

"It's a long bus ride," Kitty reminded me.

"No shit," I replied, avoiding the look I knew she had on her face when I cursed. "I'm saving myself for the buffet."

I boarded the bus with a small coffee and made sure to use the coffee shop's washroom before we left. Things were moving briskly - all the old folks were nimble when it was time to GO to the slots. Everybody boarded quickly and just as the last batch of gamblers got seated, our hostess went into her welcoming speech.

"That's odd," my mom said. "She started in Chinese. Usually she does the English version first."

We weren't forgotten. In a speech that took a third of the time in English, we were welcomed aboard, reminded of the fifteen dollars that awaited us upon our arrival and told not to use the fully-functioning washrooms. Then she began another speech, again in Chinese.

"This is new," Kitty said. "She's giving another speech."

Our hostess's speech caused a stir among the Asian crowd. People started muttering and shouting out, I think, questions. The hostess simply continued and when she finished, everybody who understood her words let out a collective groan. Kitty and I, as well as the old Jewish man, looked at each other with dread. We were next.

In a nutshell, here is what our hostess said. "The bus to Casino Kato is changing the way we operate. From now on, the bus will not run every day but only on Monday, Wednesday and Saturday. It will no longer cost five dollars, now it will be thirty dollars. And there will no longer be fifteen dollars when you get off the bus. This change takes place as of tomorrow. Thank you."

The Jewish man spoke up. "Why can't we get fifteen dollars still?"

The hostess said, "The casino felt that too many people were just spending that money and none of their own. They're trying to get more serious gamblers up there." The Jewish man hung his head in shame.

Even though she was almost describing me as well, I was pissed off. Thirty dollars! With no reward for the long bus ride to get there? I fumed my thoughts at Kitty.

"Tammy, I can see Kato's point. I've seen it happen all the time," Kitty said. "Seniors just want to get out and say they did something with their day. They'll pack a lunch and sit in the rotunda the whole five hours and keep the fifteen dollars as if they earned it. Or they might sit at a slot machine and play silly one cent bets all afternoon. That's not why they built a casino."

"So what if some old people want to get out?" I asked. "As long as they're still healthy, why deny them? Now what are they going to do? I think Kato is being mean."

"There's other casinos," Kitty said. "Bus rides that take the same amount of time. When I was at Rolls Royce Living, they had a bus that went every day to Niagara Falls. That trip seemed to go fast. We should go there one day."

Before I could answer, the bus began to brake sharply. I glanced out the driver's window and thought we were going to rear-end the Smart-Car in front of us. Thankfully the SmartCar veered onto the shoulder and we stopped a couple feet from an eighteen-wheeler. There we sat parked for five minutes.

"Must be an accident," Kitty said, just as our tour bus began to inch forward. "Oh, there we go, we're moving again." The words were barely out of her mouth when the bus again braked. We sat there for another twenty minutes. Kitty yawned.

"Go to sleep, Mom," I advised. "This may take awhile."

Ninety minutes later, the bus gave a great lurch and started to move. Kitty jolted awake. "Are we here?" she asked.

"No, we just got moving from the accident," I said. "I think some people were hurt. There were a lot of ambulances and fire trucks."

"We should be at the casino by now!" Kitty cried out, looking at her watch.

"According to the hostess, we're going to be two hours late," I groused.

"Two hours!" Kitty whined. "That leaves us with no time to gamble."

"The hostess said she's trying to arrange for a later time for us to leave," I tried to give her hope.

"That never works," Kitty replied. "Somebody always has a spouse waiting or a seniors' home to report to." Kitty swung her head to look towards the back of the bus. "And I really have to use the washroom."

"Tell me about it," I agreed.

We both sat there a moment when Kitty bolted up. "Oh, wait! I can go to the washroom." I looked at her in horror as a satisfied look came over her. "What a nifty invention!" she said, before settling back to sleep. I remembered her adult nappy and must confess, I felt vaguely jealous.

We hit Kato at 2 PM, two hours late. The hostess had gone seat to seat, asking us if we could stay longer. I agreed. Behind me the two Chinese ladies had a heated debate, leading the hostess to make a call. She didn't talk to anybody else as she went onto the intercom.

"Hello, everybody, we will be at Casino Kato in two minutes. Please have your player's card ready to be swiped so you can get your fifteen dollars. Sorry we can not stay later. We have two ladies who have to make their bus connection back to The Better Living Centre." Just so the rest of us would know who to blame; it wasn't the bus line's fault.

The grumbling voices were loud as the smiling rep from Kato boarded our bus. People rudely jostled to be the first ones off the bus, Kitty and I among them. I had a bladder about to burst and Kitty had slots on the brain.

Once we were finished in the ladies room, Kitty sped off ahead of me to the cashier. I joined her in the line-up to get the last fifteen dollars Kato would ever give me. "Now let's go eat," I suggested. "I'm so hungry I'm nauseous."

"Must we?" Kitty pouted. "We just got here and it's already almost time to leave."

"We have three hours," I pointed out. "Can't we just eat quick? Remember, I promised you the buffet the next time we came to Kato?"

"How about I promise you the buffet the NEXT time we come here?" Kitty offered.

"Mom, I don't care how good the food is, there's no way I'm spending thirty bucks to come up here again," I retorted.

"Fine, then, a quick bite to eat," Kitty said. "Heaven forbid you pass up anything if it's free." She turned her back to me and sped-walked to the buffet. I ran to keep up and almost plowed into her when she stopped short.

"What's this, a new game?" she said. She got right up close to the machine and peered at the graphics. "It looks like a cowboy game. I like those."

"You can come back to it, after we eat," I reassured her. I looked up at the game's name and read it aloud. "The Good, the Bad and the Money." Kitty giggled at the play on words and gave it a loving pat as she left it.

At the buffet, I could sense my mother's urgency. Rather than taking in the sights and then carefully choosing the best tea biscuit or the choicest slab of salmon, Kitty asked me to fill a plate for her and take it back to the table. Once I left her to eat, I went back and got my own meal, part 1. As I returned to my seat, Kitty was just handing her empty plate to the waitress.

"Could you get me a glass of milk?" she asked the waitress. "I can only take my pills with milk." The waitress nodded; she'd heard this statement before. To me, Kitty said, "And Tammy, can you get me a small dish of rice pudding and a piece of watermelon?"

I did as she asked and was finally allowed to enjoy my meal. Kitty ate her dessert in record time but waited for me to finish my plate of mainly meat. "Oh man!" I exclaimed. "That pork chop was so good! You should try one, it's like the best thing I've ever had here."

"Are you about ready to go now?" Kitty asked.

I stared at her in disbelief. "I know this is supposed to be quick," I said, "and I ate this plate as fast as I could. You're lucky I didn't choke to death. But I haven't had any salads or fruits, never mind the desserts."

Kitty took her last pill out of the sandwich baggie she kept them in. This one was always the biggest of them all and speaking of choking to death, I felt Kitty ran a daily risk when she swallowed this behemoth pill.

"I wish you'd find a way to chop that in half," I said. "What the hell is that one for anyhow?"

"Sustenance," she replied. "Look, I don't feel like wasting time here. I'm done eating."

"Mom, go back for more," I said. "You barely had anything. You're going to get hungry in two hours."

"I'm satisfied," Kitty brushed off my concern. "How about I meet you back at that new game? The cowboy one?"

I agreed and watched as Kitty sprang up and made a quick exit. I was left to enjoy a quiet meal to myself, complete with four more plates of food. One dish alone held just those inch-thick barbecued pork chops. A fine cup of coffee without having to engage in conversation was the perfect ending to my last visit at my favourite restaurant in the world.

Maybe I was too long in the buffet as Kitty wasn't anywhere near The Good, The Bad and the Money machine. I looked at my watch and saw we now only had two hours before the bus left. I wanted to find Kitty quick and get to spending my free money. I started my search and rescue method and though she was extremely close, I almost missed her.

Walking over to the next bank of machines, I glanced at the chairs. Though three out of the four held black-clothing clad people, that wasn't my mother's style today. The fourth person was a guy, so that ruled him out. However, standing next to the row of machines was Kitty. Her ensemble - the new clothes she'd bought - were so bright that she almost resembled a slot machine.

I encountered the get-up when I came down the stairs this morning. Bleary-eyed, I looked at the armchair and thought Kitty had taken down the floral living room drapes and piled them on the chair. Then I saw the little feet poking out at the bottom and realized it was my mom.

"Those your new clothes?" I asked. "They're...well, they're bright." I could have used the word 'loud' or 'garish' but 'bright' seemed safer.

"You said you wanted colour, you wanted to be able to spot me," she said. "I got two outfits. The other has yellow pants and the blouse is yellow with white suns on it." The clothes today had pink as the major colour - hot pink pants and a pink blouse with parrots and flowers on it. When I finally saw the other blouse, I never did have the heart to tell her the white suns were actually skulls and crossbones.

As we were about to leave the house, Kitty presented her "purse" to me. "Look at what I found," she said, so damned pleased with herself. "It's a fisherman's vest, but look at all the pockets!" She put it on over her blouse and demonstrated. "See, these little pockets can hold my ID and my player's card. These pockets hold kleenex and my pills. This zippered pocket holds my money. And see this big pocket? It's big enough to hold a couple diapers."

She threw on the vest over her blouse as we headed to the front door. I stopped and gave her a shrewd look. "You know, that vest is just not working...." Kitty immediately got a saddened look, like maybe her fashion taste had left her. "I mean, I like the idea of it, everything is on your person but...well....I think the diaper being in plain sight is what is bugging me."

"It doesn't quite fit in the pocket," Kitty explained.

"Maybe...how about....," and without asking, I went and stripped the vest off my mom. Next, off came the blouse. I wasn't worried about embarrassing her; I knew she had another couple layers of clothing on still. I put the vest back on her and then covered that with the blouse. "How does that feel? Does it feel too tight?"

Kitty glanced briefly in the hallway mirror and then walked to the door. "It feels like we're going to miss the bus. Let's go. Don't forget your purse."

Now, back at Kato, I had to laugh as I found my mother. "Remember when we went to FiveStar?" I asked. "I was playing that game that doesn't pay out bonuses? What was it called?"

"Aloha Delights," Kitty replied.

"Yeah, that's it, you remind me of that game," I said.

"My blouse?" she asked, seeming pleased.

My hands sketched her from top to bottom. "Just...the whole thing. So what's the plan? The bus leaves in two hours."

"Let's meet at the exit fifteen minutes before it departs, " Kitty said.

"Not one minute sooner." She didn't even wait for my answer as she took off.

I had my free fifteen dollars and within an hour, it was pretty much gone. I couldn't get lucky for trying. I spotted Kitty and sat at an empty chair next to her. The voucher I inserted into the Sheepload of Cash machine had less than a dollar on it. That went quick. In seventeen spins, I won a dime back. When that was gone, I slouched in my chair.

"Do you need some money, Tammy?" Kitty asked me, not taking her eyes off her game.

"No, Mother," I said. "I don't need money. I haven't spent my own money yet. It's just weird today. I can't catch a break. You think it's because I'm playing with Kato's money and not my own?"

"I don't know," Kitty said. "Try putting some of your own money in."

I pulled out a five dollar bill and inserted it. On my second spin, I won fifty cents, enough to cause me to perk up. On my fifth spin, I was awarded the bonus, which won me three dollars. "Now how can that be?" I asked. "I didn't win anything for the past two hours and now that I'm spending my own cash....? Do you think that's possible? That the machine somehow knows which money came from Kato and....?"

"Who knows how it works?" Kitty said. "When the seniors' homes planned weekend outings here, nobody ever won. But if we came on weekdays, somebody always won big. I think they tighten the machines on weekends."

"Tighten them? How would they do that?"

"They have their ways," Kitty said mysteriously.

I took my eight-dollar voucher and started playing Lucky Llamas. In no time, I was crossing behind Kitty, who was still playing the same game. "No luck at Lucky Llamas?" she asked.

"They should call it Unlucky Llamas, " I said, sliding into a chair near her. "I'll play SnapDragon for awhile." I inserted the player's card and the voucher and started punching my usual buttons to make my five-cent bet. I was keeping half an eye on Kitty, half an eye on my game, when suddenly I noticed my credits were nearly gone. "Hey!! What happened to my money!" I yelled.

Kitty pulled out her player's card and came to my machine. I was staring at it dumbly. "Oh, you're not playing five cents, that's why," she said.

"I always play five cents," I strongly contested. "The machine says I'm playing eighty cent bets? I think a button is stuck or something."

Kitty pointed to the buttons I'd pressed. "Not all machines start at one cent, even though they might be penny machines. This one has a minimum bet of forty cents. I guess you were pressing the second button, which is an eighty cent bet."

I nearly vomited to think I had played so recklessly. The pork chops I'd eaten earlier suddenly could be tasted again at the back of my throat. I cashed out of that machine immediately, vowing never to look at another Snapdragon as long as I lived. Pulling out another five dollar bill, I played the game right next to Kitty. I played my five cent bet, making double-sure it was only five cents. Three 8's in a row and I won back my nickel.

But with another two spins... my money was gone. "What!?" I shrieked. "What's going on?!"

Kitty leaned over. "What happened now?"

I gestured to the machine. "I put my money in, I pressed the bet, and then I just hit re-spin a couple times and suddenly my money's disappeared."

KItty pointed to the big blue button. "You hit this button?" she asked. I nodded. "On most machines, this is a re-spin button. But on some machines, it's a maximum bet button." She almost laid her face on the button to read it. "Yup, this is a maximum bet button."

Now I was mad. Though I hadn't spent my limit yet and there was still time before the bus left, I'd had enough of the casino. I just wanted to go home.

I waited while Kitty played to the final minutes and then cashed out. As we exited the casino to look for the bus, I was astounded to see how the weather had turned. Dark storm clouds raced across the sky and the wind was approaching gale force. The hostess was at the foot of the bus, waving at us to get on board.

As we neared, I glanced at my watch. "We're still early; it's not five-thirty yet," I faintly admonished the hostess.

"Bad storm in Toronto," she replied. "We have to get going."

I was made to feel guilty as we stepped onto the bus, but then I saw only a couple others already seated. I watched our hostess, hoping she'd give the same treatment to her Asian customers. I was in a surly mood and not feeling up to the three-hour ride back.

Three hours if you don't encounter a torrential downpour that has cars pulled to the shoulder and other vehicles travelling about five miles per hour. Tonight we didn't pull into the last stop (our's) until almost eleven o'clock at night. Double the time to get home.

And while on the ride back, even though I didn't partake of any of Kato's excellent coffee for the last part of my visit, I had to use the washroom. After seeing one Asian person after another use the facilities at the back of the bus, I finally said, "Fuck this," and stood up. I made my way to the smelly bathroom and did my business.

Upon opening the door, who was waiting for me? The hostess with the bottle of cleaning spray.

•••••••••

Didn't I say I'd never go back to Kato? Then how did I find myself on another interminable bus ride going up there? Mildly put, it was the lesser of two evils.

It had been two weeks since our last visit. Kitty had been fairly back to normal for the first couple days, and then I had three days of her being extremely well-behaved. Rather than enjoy it, I had to go and say, "If you're being extra nice just because you want me to take you to Kato again, you can forget it." So she did. Rather than revert to normal (irritating, grating, troublesome), she turned hellacious.

I tried to handle this unknown entity for a week. Finally, after finding her dish of macaroni and cheese in the garbage, bowl and all, I snapped. "Mom! What is with you?! I don't ever remember you acting this way."

"Maybe you should ask the chefs at Kato how to make a proper macaroni and cheese?" she asked.

"And maybe you should see if there's any retirement homes up near Kato, if you want to go there so bad," I yelled. "Sixty bucks for the two of us to go up there? I told you, forget it. Get over it."

"Tammy, PLEASE," she begged. "I'll pay your way."

"Mom, you need your money for your old age," I said, lowering my voice. "I can't let you pay for me and I refuse to pay that much. OK? Can we let it go?"

Mom stayed in bed for two days. She wouldn't eat. She wouldn't come down to watch TV. Frankly, I was getting concerned. "Mom, maybe we should take you to the doctor," I said, delivering her a cup of tea.

"I'm not sick," she said. "But I'm tired of staying in bed. I called Kato. I'm going there tomorrow."

"Oh, no you're not!" I shouted.

"Who's going to stop me?" she glared at me. "I have my vest packed and I'm going."

"Mom... I'm worried," I confessed. "What if you get lost? Or something happens?"

"I'd be ok if you came with me, Tammy," Mom said quietly. "Again, my offer stands. I'll completely pay your way. I don't mind, really, I want to pay it. I'd feel better if you were there."

I huffed. "Oh, fine then! I'll come with you."

Kitty breathed a sigh of relief as she pulled her cell phone out from under the blankets. "Oh, thank goodness," she said. "Now I don't have to cancel the two seats I booked."

• • • • • • • • • •

Three hours exactly to get there, three hours exactly to get home. I took exactly twenty dollars cash, as well as a few coins for tipping. I chose my machines wisely, making sure I was only playing five cents at a time. When it came time to eat, at the midway point, I had lost half my money. At this rate, my twenty should last the day.

The buffet was its usual five-star self, and I knew this was definitely the final time I'd be enjoying it. I made sure to wrap up a nanaimo bar in three napkins and stash it in my purse. I wish I could have done the same with the salt-and-pepper spicy shrimps in black bean sauce but I was afraid of leakage. The other thing that secretly found its way into my purse was Kitty's baggie of pills.

Kitty had laid her medication on the table as soon as we'd settled down with our first plate of food. She realized she needed the washroom, which was a fair distance away. During the fifteen minutes she was gone, I stared at that baggie. When I spotted Kitty returning, my hand instinctively grabbed the pills and I shoved them in my purse. When Kitty couldn't find them, I played dumb and said I thought she had taken them to the washroom. Kitty finally gave up the search. Good, because now it became my search - to find out what kind of medication my mother was taking and why.

Back at the slots, I chose a game called Whales of Cash. Usually I'd play up to two dollars in total at a game. If it hadn't performed to my expectations (a couple good wins or better), then I'd leave. I was down to my eighteenth spin, thinking I'd give it one last spin and then cash out and move on.

Once again, I had an eerie thought. "Can these machines read my mind?" My last spin brought up a strange screen - one filled with dancing whales, marred by a single iceberg. Bells and whistles started going off and the WIN graphic on the machine started flashing. I watched as my credits piled up and was startled to hear a voice.

"Wow, you don't see that often, what'd you win?"

I turned to see a man drinking a beer and squinting at the numbers. "I'm not sure," I said. "It hasn't shown me the final figure."

"You only bet a nickel?" someone else asked. I hadn't realized I'd drawn a crowd.

"Yeah, I'm just here to have fun," I said, shrugging off my bet.

"You should have bet more," the same guy said. "You probably would have won a couple thousand bucks."

"Well, I'm not here to make a living," I threw out. I didn't feel the need to defend my wager. The final figure rang up. "Wow! Thirty dollars!" I said. I almost added it was my biggest win yet but felt I would be mocked.

"Ya know, if you would have played the maximum, you would have won close to five thousand dollars," said a short buxom blonde, wearing last millennium's denim mini-skirt. She pointed to a prize chart on the machine that verified her knowledge. "You probably would have gotten your picture taken and shown in the newsletter. That would be neat."

I didn't know if I wanted to have my likeness displayed, advertising the fact that I threw money away at casinos. Before I could reply, a man with a big build and an army crewcut threw his fat thumb onto the screen of my game.

"Look at this," he said to the six people behind me. "She's only playing five cents!" He almost came across as a bully.

I uttered what was to become my mantra. "Hey, I'm putting three kids through university. You think I can afford to bet large?" That seemed to do the trick. Everybody oohed and aahed, seeming to agree that yeah, I was lucky I was able to spend even a nickel. I got the feeling I was forgiven.

As we got off the bus and headed for our car, I asked the usual question. "So? Did you win? Or did you lose it all?"

Kitty answered with her usual, "I did ok. As long as I come home with some money, I consider it a good day."

I had a good day as well. That thirty dollars I'd won quickly disintegrated; I barely won more than ten cents after that. (Did it read on my Player's card that the low-baller won big, so don't award her any more cash?) But I also was coming home with money. I brought twenty and was bringing home half. All in all, a good day of dining and gambling cost me ten bucks. I'd do it again, if only for the thirty dollar tariff to get up there. I know I didn't pay it, but it just broke my heart to have my mother pay for me. She noticed too, when she handed over a fifty and a ten to pay our fare. Maybe it was my groan of anguish that gave it away.

I think Kitty Casino understood that was our last bus ride to Casino Kato. As some party pooper once said, all good things must come to an end.

CHAPTER XII

Tammy Canseco is the world's worst daughter. There should be a billboard in downtown Toronto proclaiming the fact. I deserved the humiliating punishment. Instead I was dealt the silent treatment from my mother.

Kitty was scheduled for a doctor's appointment. I'd been awaiting this day, knowing my plan was about to be put into action. I double-checked to make sure I had Kitty's baggie of pills in my purse before we drove across town to her doctor.

"I wish you'd find a doctor closer to home," I griped.

"I like Dr. Mack," Kitty said. "He's been my doctor for the past thirty years. I'm keeping him."

I couldn't wait to meet this Dr. Mack. I groaned inwardly while Kitty dragged herself out of the car. She'd been pulling the old lady act lately, walking slowly, acting like every curb was a mountain to climb. Her behaviour only made me out to be the bad guy - the family member who refused to lend a hand. Impatiently I kept getting ahead of her. I entered the doctor's office, greeted the receptionist and looked behind me to see Kitty struggling to open the door. I gestured for her to use the revolving door and she moved over to them. Feebly, she tried to push them forward. I was just about to go help when the receptionist moved past me to assist my mother.

We didn't have to wait much more than an hour before they called Kitty's name. She didn't seem to mind but I kept glancing at my watch and sighing aloud. Kitty was in for perhaps thirty minutes. I kept an eye on the room she had entered and caught a glimpse of the doctor as he came out. I jumped up.

"Excuse me, are you Dr. Mack?" I asked. He paused and said he was. "Then could I have two minutes of your time? You just saw my mother Kit...Katherine Canseco?"

"Certainly, come into my office," the doctor said. I followed him in and quickly sat in the chair opposite his desk. "Is there something you wish to discuss?"

I pulled the baggie of pills out of my pocket. "I need to find out what these pills are for," I said in a voice stronger than I'd intended. "My mother is very secretive. I don't know if she's sick or has some disease...I don't know anything. She won't tell me."

The doctor gave me an apologetic look. "You know I can't discuss my patient's health with you. There are confidentiality laws."

"But she's my mother!" I cried. "Surely you can tell me if she's sick. I mean, yeah, she's in the early stages of dementia...."

"What gives you that idea?" he asked.

"Well, she's so forgetful sometimes!" I said, though a small part of my brain reminded me she could remember where her favourite slot machines were. "She forgets she's baking muffins, she can't remember where she leaves her purse...."

"I came home yesterday and realized I'd left the iron on all day," Dr. Mack said. "It's all part of getting old - you get forgetful." I looked carefully at the doctor and saw he was probably due to retire any day now. "I can tell you, your mother does not have dementia."

"Then she must have...I don't know, what do you call it?...when you're up and you're down?" I was grasping at straws. "Manic-depressive! Or bipolar! Is she that? Or does she have an antisocial disorder?"

Dr. Mack had a bemused smile. "My, my, are we talking about the same woman? Katherine is a dear."

"Says who?" I said. "She's driving me crazy. Something's wrong with her." I placed the baggie of pills on his desk. Opening the bag, I let the pills fall out. "What are you prescribing her?" I demanded.

The doctor picked up a blue tablet. "Well, it's no secret Katherine has arthritis. This is the daily pill she takes for that, for which she has a prescription." He put it down and then picked up two identical brown pills. "These are vitamin D pills," he said. "For her bones. I didn't prescribe them, but I did suggest she take them." He picked up a tiny blue pill. "This is an aspirin. She said she takes one daily for her heart." The next pill he picked up was large and orange. He brought it to his face - I thought he was going to ingest it but he simply smelled it. "Yup, this is a Vitamin C pill." The next pill, a long one, he declared as a multivitamin.

"How do you know?" I asked. "You barely looked at it."

He held it out to me. "It says Women OneADay right on it." So it did.

I picked up a giant pill. "This is the one I don't like. What is it?"

The doctor picked it up, turned it over and over and smelled it. "I'm not sure what this is," Dr. Mack said. "I don't recognize the odour or the maker. Maybe we should ask Mrs. Canseco?"

"Oh, no!" I said. "My mom would have..." Just then the door opened.

"There you are!" my mother said. "I was wondering where you went and then I heard your voice..." Her eyes came across the baggie and her pills strewn across the doctor's immaculate desk. "How did my pills get there?" she asked.

"OK, OK," I immediately jumped on the defensive. "I brought them here. I wanted to find out what's wrong with you."

"You stole my pills?" Kitty asked in a shocked voice.

"Not really stole them," I corrected her. "You lost them, I found them and I thought I'd ask the doctor what they were."

The doctor held out the large pill. "What's this one?"

Kitty brought her face close to his hand to see which one he held. "That's my bee's pollen pill. I take it for energy and vitality." She looked hard at me. "For sustenance."

"Sorry, mom, I just wanted to see what's making you sick," I apologized.

"I'm not sick!" Kitty said vehemently. "I told you before, I'm bored! Sorry if you can't stand to be around a boring old lady."

"Mom, you're twisting it all around," I said. "Doctor, please don't tell me that bored old people act this way."

"When I'm bored, I like to go to movies," Dr. Mack said.

"I like to go to casinos," Kitty replied.

"Maybe you should go to them more often," the bad doctor suggested.

"Oh, for God's sake...," I said, disappointed in how this meeting was going. Scooping up the pills, I thanked the doctor for his time and got Kitty into the car.

"So now where do you want to go?" I asked. "Home? Somewhere to eat?"

Kitty sat straight in her seat. She refused to make eye contact with me. "I know you took those pills, Tammy. I don't like people going behind my back like that."

"I told you in the doctor's office, I'm sorry," I said. "But I was worried. I thought you were sick." In a slightly sarcastic voice, I added, "And I'm sorry I didn't understand that being bored gave you such terrible symptoms. So where are we going? Home?"

"I say we follow the doctor's orders," Kitty said with what looked like a triumphant smile. "You can take me to FiveStar Casino."

•••••••••

We made three trips to FiveStar Casino in one week. I wished I'd gotten a second doctor's opinion. I didn't appreciate losing my twenty every time, but really - how often does one walk out of a casino a winner? Five per cent of the gamblers?

The first trip, we ended up spending eight hours at the casino. I stretched out my cash by taking long walks from one end of the place to the other, just observing the action. On a Monday afternoon, the place wasn't overly busy. If I saw a machine sitting empty and I wanted to play it, I could outrun any senior citizen vying for the same game. I kept bumping into Kitty before our pre-arranged meeting times. She was playing her usual forty-cent bets. The day was made even more pleasant when we discovered Kitty had a multitude of points here as well. We dined at their buffet, which was actually pretty good.

We cashed out when we figured rush hour traffic would be finished. I asked my mom, "You still have money? I lost all of mine an hour ago."

"I'm leaving with money," Kitty said, her usual answer. "I know you won't ask for money, but you can, Tammy. We could call it a loan."

"Mom, seriously, have you read the signs they post everywhere?" I asked. "Know your limit. Mine is staying at twenty dollars."

The next day was Tuesday. Work-wise, nothing much was shaking. I received a decent order for Starburst t-shirts. Every time there was even a hint of scandal, sales went up. 'Rocketed' would be an ill choice of word, but forty t-shirts was a godsend to my dwindling bank account. My error was that, after completing the transaction in under five minutes, I decided to celebrate with a game of Spider Solitaire.

Kitty wandered into my work area and saw me goofing off. "Slow day?" she asked.

I shrugged, not wanting to discuss Starburst's recent publicity due to a drug called ecstasy. She still talks about the time she found "hashish" in my laundry. "You never know what the day will bring," I tossed off. My cell phone vibrated on the table and rather than disrupt my card game, I looked at the e-mail message via my phone.

It wasn't important, so I tossed it back onto the table. "It sure is amazing how you can do your work on the cell phone," Kitty commented. "You don't even need a computer these days."

"I'd hate to play solitaire on my cell phone," I said, my eyes glued to the screen.

"Shouldn't you actually be working?" Kitty asked.

I lost my game so I switched it off and went to my e-mail site. Kitty puttered around me while I tried to look busy. After thirty minutes, Kitty went up to her bedroom and came downstairs dressed in her casino ensemble.

"I'm not going to the casino," I said immediately.

"I didn't ask you," she said, sitting down in her chair near the front door.

"You're in your casino clothes," I noted.

"I'm thinking I might take the bus to FiveStar," she said. "I had such a nice time there yesterday. And if I go, don't make supper for me. I'll eat at the buffet again."

"Don't try to woo me with buffet food," I warned. "We were just there yesterday."

"I know that," Kitty said. "I'm not senile. But I still don't feel up to par so maybe the doctor was right. I should go back to the casino."

"Yeah, I love his prescription," I said sarcastically. "Take two doses of a casino and you'll feel all better. Mom, I have work to do. It is a workday, you know."

"So stay home and work on the computer," she said. "Or you can take your phone and work off that at the casino. Either way, I'm going. The bus comes in twenty minutes and I need time to walk there." The bus stop was at the end of our short street - it would take a normal person two minutes to reach it - but I didn't argue the point.

I brusquely shut the computer down and threw my cell phone into my purse. "Can't forget that!" I said. "My lifeline to the world!" I opened my wallet to make sure I had a twenty. I had a faint feeling of anger at being forced to spend money foolishly again but a wee devil spirit whispered, "but maybe you'll win this time!"

Walking into FiveStar at 10 AM felt downright sinful. I avoided eye contact with the ever-so-welcoming security guards as I slunk into the brightly lit casino. Kitty flew ahead of me and I shouted out, "See you in two hours! At the drum!" FiveStar had an area where you could swipe your card through a machine and a ticket would fly out. You then deposited the ticket into a big drum, enabling you to enter the daily draw. Just another way to further infuse your gambling experience. And if you had extra cash to blow, there was a lottery kiosk just outside the entrance to the casino.

I settled in at a Queen of the Wild slot machine and took my time to read the machine's payout and what I needed for the bonus. Just three of the overly sexy lady in the barely-there animal hide clothing to come up. Even though two came up often, the woman cracking a whip to increase the excitement, I couldn't land the bonus. I bitched slightly to the lady next to me. In her nurse's outfit, she seemed a sympathetic ear.

"I've put sixty bucks in this machine," she rudely gestured at the Kronos game she was playing. "I got one bonus and it didn't even cover my bet." I saw she was playing two bucks a spin. She glanced at her watch and then quickly hit the cash-out button. "Shit, I'm late for work. I just wanted one decent win...." She scrambled off, literally running out of the casino.

Instantly there was a commotion at a row of machines nearby. I cashed out and put on an innocent act as I wandered over to the kerfluffle. The only thing I could see were five or six security guards in a circle. The chairs at the five machines had been moved aside. I edged myself into the small crowd of onlookers and saw a man down on the ground. He wasn't moving. Always attracted to what life had to offer, I inched closer. A guard put his hand on my shoulder.

"Please move aside," he urged. "We have emergency personnel on the way."

I moved aside, but I didn't leave. I stared at the man on the floor, until the rug started making me dizzy. FiveStar Casino uses this rug that is overwhelming with its concentric circles; I guess designed to increase the visual overload that comprises every gambling hub. Within moments, more casino staff came running with a stretcher, followed by a couple actual paramedics.

Once the emergency personnel were bent over the man, assessing him, the security guards went back to crowd control. I don't know if it's a stipulation that every security person working a casino has to have the highest of manners and politeness, but even in a scary situation like this, they were civil and even-tempered.

"Please move along, folks," they kept saying, while their hands gently guided us along the aisle. "There's nothing to see here." I begged to differ but a woman guard was pushing me off toward the five-cent slots. I veered away from her and moved myself away, but I kept my head turned toward the action. With the help of two guards, the paramedics hoisted the limp man onto the gurney. They didn't waste time as they sped him out of the casino.

I couldn't wait to tell Kitty but I couldn't find her as I searched the casino. At noon, as I was heading for the big drum, I saw Kitty playing a machine very close to it. I quickened my pace when I saw she was on a dollar machine.

"Mom!" I said, running faster than the paramedics earlier. I grabbed her hand before she could press the button. "For God's sake, you're on a dollar machine! Didn't you realize?!"

Kitty bypassed me by reaching for a metal arm attached to the side of the drab slot machine. For being an expensive game to play, it had black and white as its primary colours. In fact, the game was called Black and White. The arm allowed her to make a more physical effort at placing a bet.

"I just wanted to make sure I saw you," Kitty said, watching her spin come up with nothing..

"Couldn't you see that this is a dollar machine?" I repeated. I glanced at her credits and saw she had over two hundred dollars sitting in the machine.

Kitty pressed the cash-out button. "I was barely playing it anyways," she said. "Just one line, the lowest amount they allow...."

"Which is a dollar."

"It's ok, Tammy," my mother said, tucking her player's card in one pocket and her cash voucher into another. "I won two jackpots already! A fifty dollar one and then just two spins later, I won sixty! So who cares if I lost twenty to this machine?"

"Twenty!" I yelled. That was my entire limit. "Geez, how long were you waiting?"

"Oh, not long," Kitty replied. She dismissed my concerns with a youthful shake of her permed grey hair. "You did say noon. I'm hungry. Can we go eat?"

That idea appealed to me. I'd seen a restaurant there before with the most tantalizing smells emanating from it. It was an open kitchen and all the diners were visible to the rest of the casino. Today a line-up had formed before they'd even opened. As we approached the Poplars Restaurant, I suggested we eat there instead of the buffet.

"They only serve soup, it appears," Kitty said, looking at the customers slurping bowls of steaming noodle soup, pure enjoyment on their faces.

"It's Vietnamese soup," I educated Kitty. "It's called pho. I've eaten it often. So good and it's totally healthy. You'll love it."

"Can I get rice pudding after?" Kitty asked.

"Probably," I said. "But maybe not."

"And look at the line-up," Kitty observed. "I'm very hungry. And I was looking forward to rice pudding again. They do it very nicely here. How about I promise you Poplars next time?"

All these deals we were making lately...where somehow Kitty seemed to come out the victor. Sure, maybe she wouldn't get rice pudding but she still got to go to the casino. We made our way to the restaurant that had the buffet. If Kitty wasn't with me, I'd never have found it. The eatery was tucked into a corner of the casino and I couldn't even find the name of the place. And just like yesterday, there were only a couple other customers inside. Still, the food was as good as ever.

Kitty sat down with a sliver of salmon, a razor-thin slice of ham, a couple melon balls and a scoop of wild rice. She dug in with gusto. "I can't believe how lucky I've been this morning! How about you, Tammy? Are you winning?"

"I've barely played," I said. "I've been mainly looking for you. I saw something so terrible!"

Kitty stopped eating and looked at me with concern. "Where? Here? At the casino?"

I nodded. "I think a man might have died! He was down on the ground and he wasn't moving and the paramedics were called and man! Did they get him out of here fast!"

Now Kitty nodded. "They don't want things like that spooking the gamblers."

I smirked. "I'm sure it's because he needed medical attention."

"Oh, he was probably dead," Kitty calmly said. "It happens all the time here."

"Live life to the max," I intoned, repeating the advertising phrase often used for the casino. I didn't say it in the usual happy-faced way.

"Did you get much work done?" Kitty asked.

"Oh, shoot! I totally forgot!" I said. I pulled my cell phone out of my purse and pressed the e-mail icon. Sure enough, business awaited me. I got a second plateful of food, this time concentrating on assorted salads. While I ate, I checked my messages. On my third plate, this time just a smattering of all the foods I'd liked in the previous two, I replied to a few customers.

Kitty was trying to finish her pudding. I hadn't even gotten to desserts yet and could sense her impatience. "Why don't you get out of here?" I asked. "I'll take care of the tip."

"I can wait," Kitty said.

"Nah, I have some orders to place," I replied. "Starburst stuff."

"That regular band?" Kitty asked, pulling out her player's card as she made ready to exit.

"Reggae band, and yeah," I said. "They got themselves in a speck of trouble. Somebody might go to jail, somebody's still in the hospital but hey...it's all good. Free publicity which generates into sales."

"Ooooh, what a harsh industry," Kitty frowned.

"Money makes the world go 'round," I said, a foolish comment though it got an appreciative nod from a passing waitress. I felt like an important bigshot, waving my mother off as I remained at the table conducting business while I drank two cups of coffee and enjoyed a dinner plate of desserts. I was probably there an hour, placing orders for t-shirts and rolling papers. On rolling papers, I only made twenty cents apiece, but on t-shirts, I was averaging a couple bucks each. Today was so good, I left the waitress an extra fifty cents on top of my usual two-dollar tip.

Back on the casino floor, I found Kitty playing Golden Goddess. I walked up just as she won the bonus. Kitty gasped. "Isn't that just the most beautiful sight you've ever seen?" she exclaimed as nine roses appeared and blossomed. "This whole game has the most gorgeous angels and winged horses but those roses....," Kitty gently rubbed the screen with her arthritic fingers.

That gesture used to embarrass me. Since my first visit to a casino however, I've seen multitudes of people caressing images on the screen. I've also seen people punch the screen, knock on the screen, shake it. Once I saw a man yell at a machine, start to walk away and then return to spit at it.

Her bonus paid off quite nicely. We made plans to meet at three, back at the drum. I had it in my mind we'd leave by then, barely beating rush hour. When Kitty didn't show up at the appointed hour, I tried to call her. On the fourth try, she answered.

"You're late," I said, in lieu of 'hello'. "I'm at the drum. Where are you?"

"I'm still at Golden Goddess," my mom said. "Trying to win my money back."

• • • • • • • • • •

We beat rush hour traffic home, but only because we left at ten o'clock that night. By then I'd long blown my twenty, had completely taken care of business, deleted a whack of old unnecessary emails from my cell phone and worked up another appetite.

Kitty approached the drum machine right at ten. "Are you ready to go?" she asked. "I've had enough. I'm just going to cash out my vouchers. I'll be right back."

Instead of waiting, I followed her. I don't think she was aware of me behind her as I watched her insert a voucher for eight cents and one for two cents. A dime rattled down the chute and she scooped it out. Turning, she saw me standing there.

"So you cashed in all your vouchers?" I asked. "Coming home with money?"

Kitty pushed past me. "Yes, I'm leaving with something. I didn't blow it all. Let's use the washroom before we leave."

I followed. "I saw what you cashed in. Ten cents."

"That's right," Kitty agreed. "I like when I can say I'm coming home with money."

"But Mom, I saw you after lunch; you had over two hundred dollars," I said.

"Well, Tammy, we've been here all day," Kitty remarked. "Sometimes you win, most times you lose. As long as you have fun, right?"

I was just shocked that my mom could lose two hundred dollars. I don't know what she started with but the idea of gambling that much floored me. I still didn't have that hunger...or addiction. A plexiglass box on the wall caught my attention. It was filled with cash-out vouchers. I looked at a few and they ranged from one cent to one that said thirty cents.

"Mom, look at this," I said. "Instead of standing in line at those cash-out machines, you can just throw your voucher in here. It goes to the employees who take care of the washrooms."

Kitty walked up to the box and squinted at the vouchers. "Aawww, if you add them all up, it probably doesn't equal five dollars. And that box is stuffed."

"Let's make a deal," I said. "No more cashing in vouchers for just a few pennies, OK? Give it to the needy."

Without a second thought, Kitty slid her dime into the opening of the voucher box.

•••••••••

Kitty spent Wednesday sleeping the entire day away. Aahhh, the rewards of being old. I conducted my business, which had picked up since Starburst's singer had the overdose and the guitarist was in jail on a charge of trafficking. I silently thanked them for their stupidity. When Kitty showed up Thursday morning, coughing and sniffling, she was again dressed for the casino.

With some anger, I admit, I forbid her to leave the house when she was feeling ill. As well, since it was clearly a workday by most people's calendars, I was travelling only between my computer and the coffee pot today.

Kitty didn't put up too much of a fight. "Maybe tomorrow?"

"Another workday," was my prompt response.

"You did work off your cell phone the other day," she reminded me.

"I know and I hope to do it again," I replied. "But I need access to my files (a mini filing box) and I have international calls to make. I'm using the home phone for that."

Kitty sniffled and rubbed her sore throat. "How about Saturday?" she kept at me. "It's not a workday."

"Fine already!" I snapped. "We'll go back to the damn casino on Saturday. That is, if you're feeling ok."

"I'll be better by then," Kitty assured me.

Come Saturday, Kitty was even sicker. Her cold had progressed to the point that she was continuously blowing her nose in between hacking up a lung. And for a frail little thing, her sneezes could sway the leaves on our houseplants. I told my mother she must be crazy to think I'd take her anywhere.

So call her a lunatic, because by 7 PM, we were back in our old Town Car, making the trek to FiveStar Casino. I just couldn't take her haranguing me any longer. I didn't dare escape the house to go shopping or catch a flick, concerned that Kitty would try to make a break on her own for the casino. Instead, I stayed cooped up in the house with my contagious virus-spewing mother. But just after a supper of canned chicken soup, good for the soul as well as a cold, Kitty made her final plea.

"Tammy, I can't explain why I want to go, only that you promised me you'd take me Saturday and today is Saturday," she explained, dumping her bowl in the sink.

"How about I promise you we'll go next Saturday?" I compromised.

"I'd call that a broken promise," Kitty said. "How about we make this deal? I won't bother you for a week if you take me tonight."

"Two weeks," I counter-offered, wishing I'd said a month. Kitty paused and then, with a big sigh, agreed. "And you promised me Poplars Restaurant!" I remembered. "Their Vietnamese soup!"

"We just had supper," Kitty said. "And it was soup, so who wants it twice in the same day? And your soup had too much salt in it."

"It was from the can," I said. "I didn't add anything to it."

"Next time you should try making home-made soup," Kitty replied, just as two mighty sneezes came my way. "Now let's go. You've kept me waiting all day."

So much for her keeping her promise about me getting my hit of pho at Poplars. As for the chicken soup theory? Go to hell, best-selling books. My soul felt like crap.

• • • • • • • • •

Making the half-hour drive to the casino, we listened to a talk-show program on the car radio. Kitty enjoyed them and it saved me from having to make conversation that could quickly take a bad turn. The topic today went something like this - a man died without a will. His new wife got everything. Five years later, his kids discovered the will amongst his scrapbooks collection of matchcovers. The thirty-year old son, a heavy smoker, was pulling matches out of the scrapbooks for years until he turned a page and there it was. Now they were trying to retrieve what inheritance was left from the new wife/widow. Lawyers were involved and if the case went on any longer, the only winners would be the law firm.

As we pulled into the casino lot, I shut off the radio. "You have a will, don't you, Mom?" Just making conversation.

"Of course I do," Kitty said. "At the first home I went to, they made sure all the residents had a will."

"Oh, good," I replied, edging into a parking space. The lot was jammed full with cars. "Where do you keep it? In your safety deposit box?" I knew she had one of those - she'd had one since I was a little girl. I recently saw the annual bill from the bank arrive.

"You'll know when the time comes," Kitty answered. I was just unbuckling her seatbelt when she said that. It froze me as the absurdity of it went through my head slowly. "Come on!" Kitty urged me, "I can feel Swords of Honour calling my name tonight." Last time at FiveStar, she watched me lose a couple bucks on it. I only played it because two of the swashbucklers in the game reminded me of ex-lovers. One with the look on his face and the other by the clothes he wore.

"Uh....when the time comes might be too late, Mom," I said uneasily. "You should really tell me where you keep it." I unbuckled her completely.

"You'll know when the time comes!" Kitty repeated forcefully. "Why must you be so morbid when I just want to have some fun while I'm still alive? You're mad because we ended up coming here after all, aren't you?

And now you want to ruin my night?"

"No, Mom, geez, we were just listening to that radio show so I thought I'd ask a simple question!" I was trying to make amends. Kitty wanted no part of it. She pulled herself out of the car and tried to hustle off to the casino. I got out, locked the car and caught up with her a minute later.

"You go ahead, Tammy, I don't need your help," Mom said. She stopped dead in her tracks. I gently took her arm.

"Come on, Mom, let's just go inside," I said. She didn't budge when I started walking again. This time I put my arm around her shoulder and tried to force her to walk into the casino.

"I don't want to be with you right now!" Mom said, digging her heels into the cement. "Leave me alone. I'll see you in two hours like usual. Maybe I'll be happy then."

"Oh, don't cause a scene!" I said. "Let's go! Now!" This time I got behind her and almost tried lifting her. She flung out her arm and grabbed at a signpost. I tugged and she yelled at me to let her go, so I did. She didn't exactly fall down completely, just onto one knee. I reached out and yanked her back up by the shoulder pads on her blouse and Lord forgive me, I had the strongest compulsion to just give her a single slap to the face. I think my arm had even started to rise - I know I can still sense how my hand had stiffened into a ping pong paddle - when an inner voice froze me physically.

"So this is how you want your fifteen minutes of fame?" that voice said. I glanced around, seeing video cameras mounted everywhere. Images and snippets of news reports flashed in my mind, of mothers beating their children in parking lots and of nannies mishandling their charges. I was sure this would be a new low for the TV stations bound to get a hold of the vicious footage.

Stepping back three giant steps, I said ominously. "Go have your fun. I'll see you in two hours at the drum." She walked past me and I sketched a good-bye wave at her, mainly for the camera's sake. I went back to the car, fighting the desire to start it and drive off the closest cliff. I was ashamed at myself, as well as sick of being the sole caregiver to my cantankerous mother. Where was the Katherine Canseco that I remembered? This Kitty Casino was not a person I'd have willingly chosen for a housemate. But I was stuck with her.

And I knew I'd be hunting her down in two hours, checking in to see that she was still alive and able to mentally kick me to death. Until then, I'd stay in the car and have myself a long overdue cry.

•••••••••

I was in FiveStar Casino long before our scheduled meet time, red puffy eyes and all. I'd decided to drown my sorrows at any penny machine I could find but they all seemed taken. The crowd on a weekend night was huge. I saw a bridal party come in, all the dames looking stunning, ready for a night of fun. I tailed them for a moment, watching them as they tried to find a bank of machines they could all play. Luck wasn't with them. Geez, I couldn't find a single machine; I highly doubted they'd find five in a row. A gallant man spotted them and gave up his chair. The one wearing an I'm the Bride headpiece sat down while her maids gathered to watch. The chivalrous man began chatting up one of them.

I saw a machine open up and though it wasn't one of my favourites, Meteor Storm was ready and waiting. I'd played it before, enjoying the crackling sounds it made when a meteor showed up, as well as the alarm sounds the SOS tower emitted. However, the three towers needed for a bonus were near impossible to achieve.

I settled in, deposited my twenty and glanced at the time. Twenty minutes were more than enough to lose two bucks and go meet Kitty. Meteor Storm had a different agenda. I saw the previous bettor had been playing eighty cent bets. On my first spin, I was awarded with forty cents. It still pleased me to win, but now I'd seen bigger prizes. Having more money than what I started with was nice, though.

And it never went below twenty. The bonuses came up again and again. I'd think, "Two more spins and I'll leave. I've won enough." And the three towers would shoot up and I'd win more money. At one point, I got two bonuses within the original bonus. I was loving this machine, especially since it had doubled my money.

With a quick glance at my cell phone, I saw it was time to meet Kitty. I sincerely did not want to leave my new best friend but knew that if I wasn't there to meet my mom, she'd wait approximately sixty seconds and then wander off. Reluctantly, I cashed out. Looking around to make sure nobody was watching, I reached out my hand to lovingly pat the image of the tower on the game. A voice startled me. "You giving up that game?" It was one of the bridesmaids from the bachelorette party. I guess they'd had to split up if they wanted any casino action.

"Yeah, it's all your's," I said. "It's paying out pretty good too."

She flopped down and I lingered a brief moment. I saw her make a buck-twenty bet and get nothing. She slid me a look. "I'll take your word for it," she said. I skipped off, not wanting to be held responsible for any losses she may incur.

At the drum, no Kitty. I knew I was barely a minute late so I doubted she'd shown up. Still, I asked a security guard who was standing by the drum, "Hey, did you happen to see an old lady around here?"

"I did," he said. "About a hundred in the last five minutes." He smiled to show he was joking. I laughed politely.

"No, seriously," I replied.

He nodded. "Yeah, seriously. Is there a problem?"

I shook my head and commenced to wait. For a couple minutes, fond memories of Meteor Storm played through my mind, and the thrill I'd received when I won the biggest prize on getting five of a kind. The machine played a haunting strumming music that kept singing in my brain. After ten minutes, my fond memories were turning to dust. I could have still been playing that game! Instead I was waiting on Kitty.

Eventually I saw her walking down the hall towards me. To my horror, she stopped at an empty five-cent machine to study it. I swear, if she'd put in any money, I would have walked out and left her on her own. Instead, she ambled away and continued to the drum.

"There you are!" she said. "I thought we were meeting at Poplars!"

"Why would we meet there?" I asked. "We never meet there."

"I remember we were talking about Poplars and getting some soup," she said, before reaching into her vest and pulling out some tissue. She coughed for a moment.

"I sure hope you're using those hand sanitizers they have all over the place," I warned. I appreciated the casino's worry about germs and I'd even seen somebody once use the sanitizer. "You don't want to get everybody sick."

"I feel better now that we got here," Kitty said, before coughing again into her wad of tissues. "Shall I see you in two hours then?"

"At the drum! The drum!" I said to her retreating back. She didn't go far, just back to the game I'd seen her study. I didn't like that; I knew it was a five-cent machine. I went to her side. "I don't want you playing the five cent machines, Mom," I admonished her.

She looked up at me with eyes that were bloodshot and leaking. "Is this your money or my money, Tammy? And do you think I have the energy to walk around looking for an empty machine to play? There's too many people, everybody's being rude and greedy."

I'd noticed that too. When I was at Kato, I didn't see a lot of people younger than me. A few, but not many. At FiveStar, during the week, it was mostly seniors. But on a weekend? Half the crowd were old people and the other half were people who had no time for the elderly. Even though I had more money in my pocket that when I'd entered, I felt a mutual dislike for the weekend crowd.

I headed back to my game. In one second, I was saddened to see the bridesmaid still on it. In the next moment I was elated that one of her fellow celebrants showed up and whispered something in her ear that caused the bettor to quickly cash out. I ran over and stood behind the chair, waiting for the gal to get out of there. She spotted me.

"You can have it back," she said. "Thanks, I made some money on it."

With a smile, I settled back into the chair and what the hell, I gave the meteor storm tower emblem a little rub for good luck. Inserting my forty dollar plus voucher into the machine, I awaited more riches to befall me. I played my usual two buck limit, without so much as a five cent win. As it was so benevolent to me earlier, I forgave it. I'd give it another two dollars of my time.

Twenty bucks lighter, and not even twenty minutes later, I unfriended Meteor Storm. I suspected my player's card held some secret info, like "Hey machine, hi there, Tammy's been on you earlier and you gave her way too much money. Lighten up. Clean her out or something." I had a feeling that if I'd stayed on it another half-hour, I'd be out of money. I cashed out, telling the game, "For the record, I'm still not crazy about you."

I was back to my original twenty and back to feeling miserable. I was wandering about looking for an empty penny machine, one where my bet wouldn't have to be more than a nickel. I spotted Wheel of Fortune. It was a game I'd seldom played, since it seemed to be a punishing machine. It would absolutely not award bonuses unless you played over twenty cents. We battled, me playing my nickel and simply hoping for some good spins.

A guy sat down at the adjacent game. Within two minutes, he began speaking to me. Maybe I looked vulnerable because he was ever so sweet and rather humorous. I snuck a sidelong glance at him and saw that he was maybe a dozen years younger than me, very handsome and wore classy clothes. I saw he was playing forty cents a spin.

Now, normally I wouldn't give a gambler a second glance. Even though I was also gambling, I just didn't feel, deep down in my bones, that I was a gambler. I'm not an idiot - I know a larger bet would likely produce a larger win, but I had no desire to "make my money" that way. I was still old-school enough to think hard work and effort would lead the way to an eventual easy retirement.

But as I said, I was feeling low and decided that talking to this cute guy might perk me up. Our rapport would only last until one of us decided to leave our machine. Yet thirty minutes later, we were still there. He was winning some money, claiming I was the lucky charm as he'd been losing all night. Every now and then he honoured me by asking me to press the spin button for him. I was chagrined when I couldn't win him any money but he took it in stride.

Before long, it was established that neither one of us were married. CuteBoy asked me if I lived with anybody. I told him about my mother and that I also had to meet her in less than an hour. He said he lived with his ex-girlfriend but was looking for a new apartment. We shared a few laughs and when the coffee lady came around, he ordered us both one and covered the tip.

I was just starting to think that I wouldn't mind if this guy wanted to be my friend. Ever since I'd returned to Toronto, I hadn't had much time to reconnect with the few pals I did have. I didn't think CuteBoy was boyfriend material; for one thing, I didn't care for the age difference. His ex-girlfriend, he said, was still in university. But I sure would like to go places with someone other than my mother, that was for certain.

Out of the blue, CuteBoy suggested we go outside. I figured he was probably a smoker and needed a fix. I agreed, since I'd already lost half my money at The Wheel of Fortune. We cashed out and CuteBoy headed to the machine that gave you the money when you inserted your voucher.

Since I was there as well, I inserted my voucher and received $10.35.

CuteBoy led the way out of the casino, through an exit I'd never seen before. I remarked on this. "This is the closest exit to where I park," he replied. "Horse racing fans come in this way."

Once outside, I followed him into the parking lot. "Wow!" I exclaimed. "I didn't know this parking lot existed! It's ten times faster to get into the casino this way."

"Don't tell anybody!" CuteBoy joked. He continued to make light conversation as we walked, though he never lit up a cigarette. Suddenly he stopped at a rather dated red sports car. "You wanna get in?" he asked.

"Oh. This is your car?" I asked back. I had been wondering why we were walking in the parking lot. I hesitated a brief second, considering my safety. The multitude of security monitors I'd seen earlier assured me that, even if CuteBoy raped and murdered me, the cameras would surely have caught his image.

"Yeah, let's sit for awhile," CuteBoy said, unlocking the passenger door. I got in. He went around the car and got into the driver's side and started it up.

"We're not going anywhere, are we?" I asked. "Cuz I have to meet my mom in like twenty minutes."

"Just gonna put the heater on," he said, then turned to me. "Give me a hug. That'll warm me up."

Again I hesitated and then thought - sure, what's a hug between friends? I leaned forward and gave him one, patting his back. Then I stopped, feeling the gesture had been rather maternal. With a sweet smile, CuteBoy raised the stakes. "How about a kiss?"

Whoa. From platonic to romantic in record speed. "Are you kidding? I must be...uh...ten years older than you!" I laughed.

"What does age matter? We're just two people trying to make each other happy," was his response.

"Talking to you made me very happy," I conceded. "I'll give you a kiss. But don't let me forget, I have to meet my mom at eleven o'clock."

CuteBoy looked at the car's radio for the time. "Shit, that doesn't give us much time to get it on."

"Say what?" I asked. Surely I'd misheard him.

He reclined his seat and laid back. I watched him unbutton his jeans and slide down the zipper. "You can do this in under ten minutes, huh?"

My eyes bugged out and CuteBoy stopped before I could see anything swollen. I started to grab at the door handle. "I can't believe this!" I said. "I thought you were a nice guy!"

He gently took my arm. "Hold on, I'm sorry, I thought you'd be into it."

I looked hard at him. "I HAD NO IDEA this was going to happen. I thought we were going for a walk, get to know each other better."

He nodded. "Yeah, that's what we're doing. But we have to hurry because you have to meet your mom."

"I'm going back into the casino," I said. "This just isn't what I had in mind."

"I'll drive you to the entrance," he said. "I'm going home anyways."

Again with mistrust, I accepted. We didn't speak. As we pulled up to the entrance, I opened the door and gave him one last look. "Do you do this often?" I asked.

"Sure," he said. "It's how I met my current girlfriend."

I stepped out and said, "Thanks for the ride, uh….." And then laughed because I didn't even know his name.

He started to pull away and I slammed the door shut for him. This guy went from being a real gentleman to turning into a complete cad. I re-entered the casino with a look of disgust. I couldn't believe the guy wanted me to blow him without properly introducing himself first.

•••••••••

I was at the drum waiting for my mother to appear. I pulled out my cellphone to check for messages and saw one that had come in hours earlier. Of course, at the casino where everything was at an added volume, you couldn't help but miss the tiny ping sound of an email coming into your phone.

The email was sent from Sherman at Blast Records. In a nutshell, he moaned that Starburst was bringing a bad name to the record company. He warned me that trouble was afoot. I was in the middle of composing a letter back to him but saved it to draft form when Kitty arrived. She looked like she'd been through a battle. Her hair was sticking up, her blouse was misbuttoned, her pants were so twisted that the crotch part lay by her thigh. Her eyes were glassy, her lips chapped, her cheeks red.

"Whoa, mom, you look a mess!" I said.

She was talking fast. "I'm here and now I'm going back. I have my card in the Cats Machine and I'm starting to get my money back. But there's so many ruffians here tonight. I'm scared somebody is going to take my machine. I left my kleenex on the seat so they better not. See you in two hours." With that, she did an about-face and stormed off.

With the phone still in my hand, I felt the ping when another email came in. Glancing down, I saw it was from Sherman again. The subject line - 'THE SHIT HAS HIT THE FAN" - caused me to open it quickly. This time the email was terse. "Two bands in trouble. Will contact you first thing tomorrow."

I hustled to the Cats machine. I rather enjoyed the payout on that game when I played it, as well as the images of the 'cats' (lions, panthers, cheetahs). The only reason I rarely did play the machine was because it was next to my most hated game, Kitty Glitter, the biggest tease of them all. My mother had her chair pulled as close to the machine as possible. I tapped her shoulder and she jumped.

"Oh, I thought it was one of the hooligans trying to take my game," Kitty snarled, giving the surroundings an evil glance. I saw she was playing eighty cents and commented on it. "Of course," Kitty said. "I'm trying to win my money back before we leave. The bigger the bet, the bigger the payout."

She played five non-winning bets while I worked up my nerve to tell her we had to leave. "Mom, there's been some trouble at work," I began. "I need to go home and check on it."

"It's not a workday," Kitty said, not looking up from her game.

"Well, actually, in the rock and roll business, the weekends are workdays," I said.

"You brought your phone. Work off that," Kitty said, or rather, ordered.

"No, I want to go home and google stuff," I replied. "Anyhow, it's too busy in here. You said so yourself."

"I don't want to leave yet!" Kitty said. Just then her machine gave her a payout of forty cents. "See that? I'm starting to win my money back."

"You won half of what you bet," I remarked scathingly. "Besides, we've been here four hours already. Long enough."

"We were here eight hours on Monday," Kitty recalled.

"It doesn't mean we have to spend eight hours every time!" I almost yelled in frustration. "Today we spend four hours. Maybe next time we'll spend twelve hours."

Kitty finally looked up at me and made sure I saw her hand hover over the cash-out button. "Is that a deal?"

Deals, promises, they were all starting to amount to the same thing. "Yes!" I said. Kitty pressed the cash-out button. I felt I'd finally won one small battle until I saw the machine flash a sign saying 'Cash paid - .03'. She had used up all her money in the machine.

"I need to use the ladies room," Kitty said, pushing her chair back with some difficulty. A passing security guard kindly pulled it out for her and she rewarded him with a nasty sneeze. Kitty went into a stall, where she seemed to spend an eternity.

"What's taking you so long?" I called out, after fifteen minutes.

Kitty came out carrying her soiled diaper. "I thought I'd change this before we got in the car." I pitied the washroom staff who had to empty the garbage containers. I backed away from her and edged against the wall. My shoulder hit something and I glanced around to see a bin attached to the wall. Upon closer inspection, I saw it contained about a hundred needles.

"Oh my God, are people doing drugs in here?" I said aloud.

Kitty dumped her diaper into the trash and looked over. "Probably," she replied. "For their diabetes, I imagine. Most everybody at the old age homes had it."

"Well, let's get going," I urged my mother. "I've got work to do."

Kitty started searching the many pockets of her fisherman's vest. She withdrew her casino voucher from a wad of used tissues and held it up. "For those whose weekends are workdays," she intoned.

With a sneeze that echoed throughout the washroom and covered the donation box, Kitty made her three cent donation.

CHAPTER XIII

Kitty spent the next week in bed, fighting her cold. She may have gotten better sooner had I given her any attention. Don't get me wrong - I love my mother. The memories of growing up with her and her invaluable help in raising my children overshadowed my current constant annoyance at her. The reason for my callous attitude is that I had my own pile of problems.

Returning to the house late last night, I pulled out the laptop and immediately started googling the bands I represented for Blast Records. Twisted, the country band who brought in the most dough for the label, were (whew!) still out there selling out shows. If not for them, I'd be destitute. The Noise, my former band, were also still in business. They'd fallen way off the charts but had a never-say-never attitude. I noticed they were coming to Niagara Falls in the next couple weeks and I wondered if I felt like making the trip. Probably not - my feelings were still hurt. Starburst, the current bad boys, were all over the net but it was the same footage used over and over. Blurry cell-phone videos of the paramedics working over the singer. The ambulance arriving and quickly leaving with the overdosed musician. The guitarist's mug shots for his alleged trafficking charge.

So what two bands are in trouble? Obviously Starburst was one of them. They were my second biggest earners, but compared to Twisted, it was night and day. As for The Noise? I was lucky to get venues to accept fifty t-shirts to sell. Often they'd return forty of them. I went to bed, knowing I'd have more answers when I woke up.

Before I even got out of bed the next morning, I opened the email on my cell-phone and discovered I now represented only two bands. Sherman sent a letter saying they were dropping Starburst faster than a hot crack pipe. All the current news items were nothing compared to what was coming - namely that Starburst ran an ecstasy drug ring. I was told to stop selling the merchandise immediately and try to get as many returns as possible. That sucked. I'd just made a big sale of a hundred hemp hoodies to a chain of head shops. It also meant doing a shitload of work that would not benefit my bank account.

The email from Sherman was - while not rude - terse and obviously sent while in a vile mood. I didn't bother to reply anything more than "terrible news! Will stop selling. Anything else?" The last bit was to jar his memory; he did say two bands were in trouble. There was no further contact from Blast Records that day.

The next day, I was seated at the dining room table. I'd spent two days cancelling orders for Starburst and was contemplating the conversation I'd just had with a vendor.

"I was looking forward to seeing Twisted tonight," said Jared from a music store in Texas. "Why'd they cancel?"

"Twisted cancelled?" I asked. "I have no idea why." Not that cancellations were anything new - people were always getting sick or tour buses getting into accidents or equipment getting stolen.

"I thought you'd know," Jared went on, "being the president of their fan club and all."

I had to secretly laugh at that. I certainly didn't consider myself a fan, especially of Starburst, though I was president of their fan club as well. It was just a job I was given. "Well, nobody told me anything," I said. "But don't worry. I'm sure they'll reschedule. Sorry again about the Starburst order."

I was enjoying my quickly prepared supper of cereal and milk when I got a text from Sherman. Band number two was revealed and it was the worst of news. The text read 'Twisted breaking up. Can you believe this?"

I quickly texted back, "No!!! What happened?!"

The text back read, "Long story."

My text said, "I gotta know!"

Sherman sent, "Will send you an email in the morning."

We texted back and forth for a few minutes until I decided I had enough of modern technology. I picked up the house phone (free North American calling!) and gave Sherman an old-fashioned landline call. He answered on the first ring with a weak "Hello?"

"Sherman, it's me, Tammy," I said quickly. "What the hell? Twisted can't be breaking up. They're our main band!"

"Apparently it's a done deal," Sherman said. He sounded so down-trodden, his spirit seemed to slip into my bloodstream. "I got word there was a fight between a couple members of the band at Saturday night's concert. I thought, big deal, not like the first time bands got into fights. They kiss and make up. Then today, just before I left the office, I get the papers." Sherman paused.

"What kind of papers?" I asked.

"The legal papers informing us that we no longer manage them," he replied.

"I don't get it," I said. "They're dropping Blast? So are they still together?"

"No, they're done. They're history," Sherman confirmed. "The papers were just a formality. Still, it breaks my heart. I never thought this would happen, at least not when they're at the top of their game. Biggest act the label has managed in years."

"Can you at least tell me what happened?" I begged.

"Do you recall the girl who ran the Twisted fan club awhile back?" he asked.

"I never met her," I replied. "But I got her job, remember?"

"Yes, well, she left the club to be with Colby, the singer," Sherman related. "But it seems she was cheating on him with the lead guitarist. Colby found out on Saturday. Brett and Colby barely got along as it was, so I guess this was the straw that broke the camel's back."

Yeah, and my bank account, I thought. "And there's absolutely no chance of them getting back together?" I asked pitifully.

Sherman responded harshly. "After I finish cancelling their next hundred shows, you think I want them back? Which reminds me. Just like with Starshit, you're gonna have to cancel all of Twisted's orders. That's gotta hurt."

"Isn't that the gist of most country songs?" I asked miserably. "Lots of hurtin' and cheatin'. Welcome to their world."

Twisted was a big act. Cancelling their orders took a lot of effort and to make matters worse, it appeared I had caught Kitty's cold. I tried to slog through all my income-reversal calls and emails while still trying to fill anything for my remaining act, The Noise. This week, it looked like my commission from The Noise sales would amount to a measly sixty bucks.

On Friday, I just couldn't get out of bed. My fogged up brain declared I'd had a miserable week, my headache informed me I was sick and my lifeless body said I'd taken an emotional beating for days and deserved the rest. I slept soundly until noon when my mother tapped on my door. I struggled to awaken.

"I'm not going to the casino," I mumbled, still half-asleep.

"Don't be silly," Kitty said, carefully balancing a bowl of soup and a cup of tea on a tray. I took it from her before she could drop it on me. "We still have a week before we go again." She reached into the pocket of her housecoat and pulled out my cell phone. "You left this on the table downstairs."

"I don't care," I said, taking a sip of tea. "I'm not working today. I'm sick."

"I know," Kitty replied. "I could hear you coughing all night."

"Sorry."

"That's ok," Kitty said. "Tammy, I'm afraid I have some bad news. Your phone was ringing and ringing but I didn't want to wake you. I could see it was from the same person so I decided to answer it."

"Who called?" I asked.

"Sherman?" she replied. I slowly started to lower the tea cup. "I'm afraid your friend Bradley passed away."

• • • • • • • • • •

Bradley, the superstar in The Noise, didn't exactly pass away. He committed suicide. It was already all over the TV and the radio but details were still sketchy. I knew where to get the inside story.

With shaking hands, I called up BiBi, Sherman's wife. It had been months since I'd last spoken to her. Nevertheless, as soon as she answered, I began to cry.

"BiBi, I'm in shock!" I wailed. "What happened?"

"He committed suicide!" she wailed right back.

"Well, yeah, I know that," I huffed, my tone bringing me back to earth. "It's all over the news. But why?"

"He left a note," she whimpered. "Oh, I used to love him so much!"

"I know," I said. "You were wild about him."

"I was besotted, is what I was!" she affirmed. "And now he's gone!"

"Do you know what the note said?" I asked gently.

"It was terrible!" BiBi shrieked. "And his weird girlfriend? The one who's been road managing them? She found him. She finds the note and she fucking photographs it and TEXTS it to Sherman! I swear, she has no class!"

"What'd the note say?" I asked again.

"Hang on," BiBi paused. "I'm sending it to you right now."

"I hope he died peacefully," I sighed.

"If you consider hanging yourself peaceful," BiBi replied.

"Oh, God, no…he hung himself?"

"With a few of his stage scarves. Did you get the text?" BiBi asked. "Can you read it and keep me on the phone?"

I picked up my cell. "Yeah, I'm using the house phone," I said. "I'll look at it now."

The note was so brief yet so telling about Bradley. He had one obsession all his life and that was his hair. The note read: "Now the world will know Im going bald. I dont need your pity. fuck u all but rock on". Vain, arrogant and not the brightest of men, right up to the end.

Unbelievably, BiBi also sent a photo of the deceased rock star. I almost didn't look at it, but a quick glance told me it wasn't very menacing. Bradley had a thick scarf around his neck that almost had a stylish arrangement to it. He'd just come offstage and his clothes looked dark and dramatic. I was glad most of his face was covered. It appeared that when he jolted to an abrupt stop as he stepped off the dressing room chair, his hairpiece had jerked forward, thankfully covering any death-throe looks.

"He was going bald?" I asked. "I didn't know that and I was working with them less than a year ago. I mean, I knew he wore extensions and pieces to make his hair look bigger…but going bald?"

"Apparently," BiBi replied.

"And the note says 'now the world will know'? Why would the world know?" I sputtered.

"According to Trisha, Brad kicked everybody out of the dressing room after the show," BiBi explained. "He wanted to take a shower. He thought everyone had left and he took off his wig and suddenly somebody's taking a photo of him. Seems a news reporter was still there. He'd just come out of the washroom in time to snap a shot."

"Beeb, it's not like he was TMZ or anything," I said. "I heard this happened in Cochrane, Alberta. This was probably for some small-time newspaper!"

"Well, it's too late now," BiBi started to cry again. "The poor baby felt threatened! Trisha said she came back into the room and Bradley told her what happened. And that the reporter just ran away after taking the photo and that he was ruined. Trisha tried to console him but he'd have none of it. He ordered her onto the tour bus and said he'd be out in a few minutes. When he didn't show up after a half hour, she went back for him and found him... dead!"

"Man, this is fucked," was all I could think of to say.

"Sherman wants to talk to you," BiBi said. I was immediately transferred to him.

"Bibi showed you his suicide note?" Sherman asked bluntly. I confirmed I had read it. "Look, we're trying to keep it under wraps. Everybody knows he committed suicide, I think they found out it was from hanging, but nobody knows about the contents of the note. I don't want you telling anybody, ok?"

"I won't tell a soul," I promised. Maybe my mother, but only because I was always searching for dinner conversation.

"So let's recap," Sherman said in a bitter tone. "We got rid of Starshit, so you no longer work for them. Twisted broke up, so you can't work for them. And now The Noise has lost their singer and will probably fold. There go your three bands."

"Jeez, I just realized that!" I moaned.

"If you ask me," Sherman replied, "I'd say you're fucked."

• • • • • • • • •

The secret of the suicide note lasted until the 6 PM news. By then, the same photos I'd been texted suddenly appeared everywhere. I know it wasn't me who had notified the press and I highly doubted it was Sherman or BiBi. Neither would want to denigrate Bradley's memory in that way. I strongly suspected Trisha and figured she probably had earned a few thousand dollars with her posthumous betrayal.

On the day of the funeral, I stayed home. Suddenly unemployed, I didn't think I could afford to fly to Calgary, where Bradley's family still lived and where he would be buried. I knew that Sherman and BiBi would go. I'd read that many rock celebrities would be attending. Though Bradley Atwater was no longer with us, The Noise suddenly got tons of press. The usual silver lining of scandals.

I couldn't understand why I was crying so much. It wasn't like Bradley was a family member. I simply worked for him. The thing was, I saw Bradley at his worst and at his best and as annoying and narcissistic as he could be, somehow I guess I grew to love him. Not in a romantic sense - no, I never felt that way about him and I had a deathly fear of STD's as well. I just know I took care of that boy as best I could, but within a year of me leaving, he's dead.

The doorbell rang. I didn't care who it was; I was simply unfit to be seen by the human eye. Besides all the crying I'd done, my nose was running nonstop from the cold I still had. I yelled out at Kitty, "Mom! Get the door!" After a minute, the doorbell sounded again. "Mom! There's someone at the door!"

Kitty shuffled past my room. "I heard it the first time," she said. I heard her open the front door and call out to somebody. A minute later, she was coming back up the stairs. Pushing my door open, she entered with a huge box that read Zenith 60-inch Colour TV. I couldn't even see her upper body as she cradled the box in both arms.

"Jesus Christ, Mom!" I said as I tried to jump out of bed before Kitty could give herself a hernia. I heard a voice behind the box remind me to watch my language but at that point, I was twisted in my blankets and only got as far as the floor. With quick panicked glances between Kitty holding what must be a sixty-pound box and the blankets that I was trying to kick my legs out of, I finally succeeded in freeing myself. "Don't move! I'm coming!"

"I'll just set it on your bed," Kitty said, moving past me and holding the box out at arm's length. I was astonished at her sudden superhuman strength.

The only thing I could think of to say was, "I wonder who sent us a TV?"

"I doubt it's a TV," Kitty replied. "I think it's just a box somebody used for whatever is inside."

I gingerly approached it. I saw my name and address on it and Special Delivery Express Post stamps all over. I didn't think it was a bomb but still, I picked up the box with a very delicate touch. I gave my mother an astounded look. "It doesn't weigh anything!" I said. "It feels empty."

"There's only one way to find out," Kitty said, reaching into her house-coat pocket and pulling out a nail file. She held it out to me but I backed away.

"I'm scared," I declared. "It's too creepy, getting sent a box that weighs nothing. If you want to see what's inside so badly, you can open it."

Kitty went to work on the box with her little nail file while I rear-ranged my bedding. A quick intake of breath made me look at her. She stared frightfully at the sight within the box.

"Tammy, you were right to be scared," Kitty spoke softly, backing up slowly. "You got mailed some kind of animal!"

· · · · · · · · · ·

The interior of the box held mounds of human hair. Locks of Brad-ley's hair, to be precise. There was a scrap of paper inside with the words - "Sorry. Mailing this in a rush. Give me a call when the dust settles. Dawn." A phone number was scribbled down.

Dawn! I hadn't talked to Dawn in years. Ever since Bradley and he/she had their falling out, Dawn kept his distance from anybody connected to The Noise. I wasn't about to wait for dust to settle; I picked up the home phone and dialled the number.

After a couple rings, Dawn answered with a muffled hello. I had a flash of panic when I wondered if I called while the funeral was in progress. "Dawn, it's me, Tammy," I said quietly. "Did I call at a bad time?" Like, during Ava Maria or something?

"Oh, sugar, it's a sad time, is what it is," Dawn replied.

"I know," I said, stifling my tears. "I wish I could have gone to the fu-neral."

"I just came from it," Dawn said woefully. "I'm in the cab going back to the hotel."

"Yeah, I thought you'd go," I replied. "You two had a real connection. I never saw Bradley act so...real...so normal as when he was around you. Was there a big turnout?"

"Oh, yeah, befitting his Canadian rock god status," Dawn gave a brittle laugh and then added, "You've got a lot of big rock stars in this country. They took it pretty hard."

"So how you been, Dawn?" I asked. "The last I really remember, you and Brad were starting up ManMakeup together. How'd that go?"

"Still the top seller," Dawn replied. "You haven't seen the products?"

"I don't really shop that aisle," I confessed. "And Brad was still involved? Even after you got so mad at him?"

"For a couple years he was, although he didn't do much of anything," Dawn recalled. "So then I made him a good offer and bought him out. Back then, I wanted him out of my life forever."

"Aawww, don't you wish you guys had made up before he died?" I asked. "Isn't that always the way?"

"Hun, Bradley didn't tell anybody but about five years ago, he made a trip to New York to see me," Dawn said. "He had a problem that was literally driving him mad. Remember how he thought I was the only one who could cut his hair? Well, five years ago, he got it in his head that again I was the only one who could help his hair."

"He went to you for a haircut?" I asked in disbelief. "That was probably an excuse. I bet he just wanted to make up with you."

"Sugar, he's been wanting to make up for years," Dawn replied. "But then he came to me in tears one day, begging me to stop him from losing his hair."

"How the hell could you do that?" I snorted. "You gave him hair plugs?"

"I gave him everything but that," Dawn answered. "I gave him extensions, hair weaves, hair pieces he could attach with combs...but he was going bald so fast. Maybe a couple years ago we went to a full-on wig. And we became friends again." She let forth a big sob. "Who kills themselves over hair loss?"

"Yeah, I know! And speaking of hair loss, it seems I've gained some," I led into the reason for my call. "I got this box of hair from you today. I don't get it."

Dawn let forth another dramatic wail. "Oh, Tammy, maybe I sent that in my grief, but I have to make a confession to you. You know how I used to cut Brad's hair and send you a bunch? Well, I don't know why, but I kept some for myself. And for some reason, I felt like I was cheating you by doing that. Really, Tammy, I'm sorry, you probably could have made more money if you'd had more hair and....I was a bad friend to keep it. It's been bothering me for years and now, with this happening, I just wanted you to have what's rightfully yours."

"Seriously, Dawn? I never noticed, shall we say, 'product' missing," I said. "So stop beating yourself up over it. It's ok."

"Oh, that's a relief," Dawn replied. I heard her ask the cab driver to wait.

"Where you off to now?" I inquired.

"There's a bunch of people going to the Hard Rock Cafe," Dawn replied. I could hear him huffing as he entered his hotel. "We're going to toast the memory of Brad. I'm wearing a chic black dress, but I wore flats to the funeral and want to change shoes. Bradley always liked me in heels."

• • • • • • • • • •

That night, as I was drifting off to sleep, my eyes suddenly flew wide open. A few words of Dawn's conversation had drifted into my subconscious...made more money if I had more hair....That phrase, compounded by my dread of having zero income for the next foreseeable future, put a fuzzy idea into my head. Why not sell A Lock of Bradley's Hair?

I wondered if this wouldn't be macabre, selling the very thing Bradley would have spent a fortune on - his hair. Opening my laptop, I quickly googled any mention of Brad's recent passing. He was trending at number two on top sites. Bradley Atwater had never been so popular.

More importantly, I gauged the reactions of his fans. There was plenty of grief. A blog's post caught my eye - it was a story of how one fan bought a lock of Bradley's hair off the road manager. I never was the road manager - that was Sherman's job until recently. I was the assistant road manager, working for probably a quarter of the pay Sherman received. Hence the reason I was trying to make a second income with the hair! She claimed she bought four locks of hair that day and was willing to sell it on eBay. A link was supplied.

I clicked on the link, which put me onto an eBay listing. I immediately recognized the bag and my hand-written note declaring it as official. It looked like it came from my original offerings; it may have been one of the first. I saw she'd listed two locks starting at $100 each - five times what she'd paid! She had many offers already and they were currently at $170 apiece.

There were two other listings for Brad's hair but they were both in a frame and missing the sticker with my note on it. Both owners claimed it was truly a lock of his hair. They mentioned where and how they'd obtained it, with both instances ringing a bell. I was always on high alert for security when I sold my wares and could recall the most minute details. However, they had discarded the thing most valued by collectors - the original packaging!

I printed out the eBay notices, as well as the posting on the blog. Hhmm, so it seemed there was money to be made if a person had some of Bradley's hair. Collectors would pay dearly to own such an item, especially if it was perversely connected to his suicide. I had an eBay account; I'd sold band items often from my dwindling collection. I hadn't been selling hair lately; that had run out long ago. But now, suddenly, I had stock. And better, I had provenance. Hell, I WAS provenance!

So since I had product, did I have packaging? Everything I owned in San Diego had been shipped home. I unpacked the stuff I needed on a daily basis and had Rain put the rest of my boxes into the basement. Sliding into my slippers, I quietly made my way down the hallway. I peeked into Kitty's room and saw her fast asleep, her bedside table lamp still on. Not wanting to wake her, I left it that way.

Rarely do I go into the basement. The top two floors of our house are fine but the basement, in all the years Kitty had owned the house, had never been renovated. It was chilly and dark and filled with furniture I didn't recognize. She had trunks packed with nothing but paperwork and knickknacks. The only time I came down here was if I had to check the fuse box or shut off the water, which was maybe three times in my entire life. Plus there were spiders down here that were mutant in size.

I poked around, wondering where Rain may have put the few boxes. I banged my kneecap on a piano bench that was almost invisible in the corners of the room. "What the fuck!?" I yelped. "Who the fuck even plays piano?"

I shoved it aside and continued the search. I debated calling my son but I'd left my phone upstairs. Sighing, I headed back to the steps when I saw a rickety desk against one wall. A large overstuffed antique office chair sat next to it. My items crowded the old desk. On the chair was the box I was specifically looking for, marked Office Supplies.

Grabbing the box, I made a beeline for the upper floor, not wanting to spend another minute in the basement. I shut the door to that dungeon and turned around to head up to my bedroom. I almost had a heart attack when I came face to face with Kitty.

"Holy shit!" I screeched. "You scared the living daylights out of me! What are you doing awake at this hour?"

"Who could sleep with all the bad language going on in this house?" Kitty replied. "What are you doing up?"

"I'm looking for some stuff of mine," I retorted. "Geez Louise, what's with all that crap downstairs? How many dressers and trunks do you need? I swear, we're gonna have one hell of a yard sale."

"We'll do no such thing," Kitty said firmly.

"Then I'm gonna get somebody to cart it all off to Goodwill," I countered.

"Over my dead body," Kitty said. I hated that kind of talk so I backed down.

"Mom, there's some nice stuff down there, but most of it is garbage! Just boxes of toys and trunks of clothes..."

"It's mostly stuff I picked up when I was with the kids," Kitty said, also changing her tact. She took on a hangdog look. "I miss them. Don't you? Anyhow, Rain knows what to do with all of it. Can we just let him take care of it when he comes home?"

That wouldn't be until his Christmas break, which was still three months away. I huffed but figured I'd give in. It had been there fifteen years, what was a few more weeks? "Fine," I said. "Go back to bed."

"You're not?" she asked.

"I don't think so. I'm working on a project," I answered.

"Can I help?" Mom asked. "I'm awake anyway."

"Nah...well, maybe," I said. "Since you're awake...wait a second." I placed my Office Supplies box onto the dining room table and ran upstairs. In a moment, I was back with the big TV box. "OK, here's what I'm working on," I said to Kitty and explained the plan.

Kitty scrunched up her face. "You think you can make money at this?"

"Mom, I need to make money at this," I said. "I don't have a job anymore. How am I going to live? And put kids through school?"

"Tammy, if you need money, why don't you ask me?" Kitty implored. "We don't have to call it a loan. I can make it a gift."

I shook my head. "You need your money, especially the way I see you gamble." Kitty smiled, as if I'd given her a compliment. "And who knows how long you're going to live? The doctor says you're fine, as far as old people go. I may end up supporting you as well one day."

"I have the government to look after me," Kitty said. I knew she received some money every month from an agency that had to do with my dad's old job. Probably his pension and I thanked God for that every time I saw it arrive.

"Well, I'm a big girl now, Mom," I reminded her. "A mother of three who's got to make a living." With that, I opened up the Office Supplies box and it was like I was transported back to one of my hotel rooms. Afternoons spent filling bags with Bradley's hair, affixing a sticker to each one attesting to its validity.

At first I allowed Kitty to help me, but with her bad eyesight, she couldn't discern a lock from a lump of hair. I tried to get her to be precise as to what went into each package, but within minutes she was easily persuaded to give up the task. Her gnarled fingers were incapable of pulling off a sticker when I requested one and she was only too happy to give up that job as well. She was invaluable when it came to making tea.

"Shall we have some music?" Kitty asked. She went into the living room and returned with the ghetto blaster I kept there. She had a CD in her hand. Anticipating The Best of Perry Como, at best hoping for Elvis, I was astounded when she put on an early CD of The Noise.

"Where did you get that?!" I asked, pausing in my work. "I don't even have a Noise CD!"

"It belongs to the twins," Kitty replied. "They always listened to it."

At first I wasn't sure I wanted to hear the CD - I was afraid I would get too emotional. However, the first song to play made me laugh aloud as a memory came to me. "Ha! The crowds always wanted the band to play that song but Brad was so sick of it! One time in Sweden, Brad insisted they not do that song. Well, the audience refused to leave the building at the end of the concert. They kept chanting Shock Me! Shock Me! The Noise had to come back on and sing that song and... ha, ha...Bradley wasn't singing the right words...ha, ha...he was singing 'fuck me' and I don't even think the crowd noticed 'cuz they were singing over him..."

I stopped and looked at my mother's expression. She didn't seem angry. "My, cursing in such a public forum!" was her response. Then she asked, "Were you two close?"

Those four words were all I needed to hear. While I worked, I related stories from how I first met Bradley Atwater, lead singer for The Noise, until the final time I saw him. I cried without shame, telling my mother how familial I felt with Bradley. After two hours of spilling my guts, my project was completed. Almost four hundred neatly packaged locks of Bradley's hair. I tidied up while Mom took the cups over to the sink.

"Hey, Mom, thanks," I said.

"For what?" she asked.

"Just for listening," I replied. From the moment I heard of Bradley's death, I'd barricaded myself into my bedroom. Kitty left me alone but had seized this opportunity to let me know she was still my mother and there if I needed her.

"You knew Bradley walked that high wire all his life," Kitty said. "You must have known it was going to end badly."

"Yeah, but I always expected a drug overdose, maybe a high-speed car crash," I said, near tears again. "Not him taking his own life! And he was going bald when I was still working for the band. Why didn't I know? Why wouldn't he tell me?"

"Oh, Tammy, what could you have done?" she asked.

"I don't know! What I always did! Give advice! Take action!" I barked.

Kitty remained stoic. "Let's pretend I'm Bradley," she said. "I've come to you and I say, 'Tammy, I have a big, big problem. I'm going bald and there's no stopping it.' And what would you have said?"

"Off the cuff?" I asked, taking just a second to give a suggestion. "OK, knowing Bradley's personality, I'd try something like this - Brad, don't fight it. Embrace it!" Kitty gave me a questioning look so I continued. "I'd say, nobody can rock a new style like you. So you ditch the same ol' same ol' and try something wild and crazy. I'd say, Bradley, shave it all off and make headlines with your new BALD look."

Kitty nodded and sagely said, "You know, that may have worked."

•••••••••

After a rejuvenating grief-induced sleep, I woke up resigned to the fact that I was going to capitalize on someone's downfall.

I set up one of my packages in a pretty yet tastefully sombre setting. I took close-up photos of the hair, as well as the bag's sticker and a note of authenticity, all attesting that this was primo shit. My writeup for the eBay site was respectful and honoured the memory of the dead musician. I made no reference to the fact his missing hair had a lot to do with his suicide. Any idiot could read between the lines.

I put the sale up on eBay, giving people a week to place their bids. I checked the other girl's bid and saw she was approaching $200. I made that my minimum offer. Surely, with my verifiable time spent with Bradley and The Noise, that would enhance sales. I may never have been an actual rock star myself but I was in their inner circle.

Worried that I might saturate the market, I made sure that the words 'limited quantity' were highlighted. Even more concerned that interest may fade within a week, I thought about other potential markets. I placed the exact same ad on Kijiji and Craigslist, two internet sites that would allow me to place an ad for free as well as keep all of the profits. I placed the ad locally, thinking I'd save on shipping charges. When I realized shipping the package would cost about the same as the price of a stamp, I refigured the ad so that it would appear in every city the sites had listed. Next I posted messages on a dozen Facebook sites. I had decided $250 would be my asking price. I surfed the net, responding to various rock n' roll websites, Canadiana collectors and music blogs.

With an air of a job well-done, I shut my laptop, only to open it up a second later. As an afterthought, I decided to post the sale of limited locks onto the site of Blast Records Fan Club. It was there I saw an announcement. The Noise had been scheduled to play in Niagara Falls, Ontario in two days time. The show would NOT be rescheduled NOR would it be cancelled. The show would go on.

Confounded, I decided to call Sherman. As I picked up the home phone, my cell chirped, conveying I'd received some sort of email. Since the computer was open, I logged onto my email and saw that someone had seen my eBay ad and had a question.

"So, how do I know for sure that this is really Brad's hair?" said iheart-brad@gmail.com.

I thought I'd put enough information into the eBay proposal to ensure buyers would believe they were getting authentic goods. What more could I say? I conveyed this to the customer. Knowing my letter could be seen by other eBay shoppers, I added a kicker. "PS, iheart, let me guarantee it to you this way - if technology ever advances enough, you can take the DNA from this hair and have Bradley's baby."

I clicked send and then called Sherman. "Yo, Sherman," I greeted him. "How you doin'? How was the funeral?"

"The funeral was really sad," Sherman said. "Everybody crying. You should have seen BiBi. But the after-party was great. I wish you could've come."

"Me too," I agreed. "I spoke to Dawn. He said he was there."

"Yeah, she was. He was. Whatever," Sherman said. Dawn always stupefied him. "He was bawling at the funeral and then he comes back to the party, looking like a million bucks. Like so beautiful, he had half the guys in the place trying to jump his bones."

"Hey, Sherman, I was looking at the fan club website," I began, "and I saw the announcement that The Noise is still playing Niagara Falls? I don't get it."

"Yeah, I was going to call you," Sherman said. "I just finished putting that up on the site. Looks like you still got a job."

"Are you saying The Noise is going ahead without Brad?" I sputtered out. "That's unbelievable!"

"Believe it."

"But Bradley WAS The Noise!" I went on. "The band should have been called Bradley Atwater and The Noise."

"Tate thinks they can still make a go of it," Sherman said. "I tried to talk him out of it. Told him we'd come out with a Greatest Hits CD soon. But he wasn't interested. Said he's going to be the new singer. At the funeral party, he was telling all the TV and news reporters that the band would keep going."

"I give them a month," I said cynically. "Tate knows music, he knows the business, he just doesn't have Bradley's sex appeal."

"Tell me about it," Sherman oddly said. "But that's where you come in. Before they realize they're nothing without Brad, before hotshot Tate throws in the towel, we need to unload all the damn Noise product we have. I'm shipping everything to your house in Toronto. I'm sending you their schedule too, though that's subject to change." He gave a sarcastic fake laugh.

I asked him to give a hug to BiBi from me and disconnected. About to shut the laptop, I glanced quickly to see if my reply had been posted to the eBay site. Instead, I stared at a different box that held the figure of $220.

I had gotten my first bid.

· · · · · · · · · ·

From the moment Sherman told me to expect a shipment, I waited at home, not more than a few feet from my front door. I didn't want any impatient delivery man leaving me a note saying they'd attempted to drop off a package. The concert was Friday night - I needed to sort through the merchandise as well as find a delivery service to get them to Niagara Falls.

Friday morning I was just about to call Sherman to tell him we had a disaster on our hands when Kitty said, "Tammy, a brown van just pulled up to the house." I had the front door open before the NowEx man was out of his vehicle. He pulled out a dolly and loaded three boxes onto it. Wheeling them to the front door, he asked for Tammy Canseco.

"That's me," I said. "I'll take them." I wanted the man to hurry and started unloading the dolly myself. I signed for the delivery and bid him adieu. Hauling the boxes onto the kitchen table, I said to Kitty, "Take your oatmeal into the living room, Mom. I need this space. I've got mega work to do and I need to get it done pronto."

"Is this the package you've been expecting?" she asked.

"Yeah, all the fan-wear stuff for The Noise," I replied. "You know, hats, t-shirts...let's see what Sherman sent." I ripped into the boxes and saw exactly what I'd described. Much of the clothing had the band's stylized name on it. Some of the t-shirts showed images of the band. My heart lurched when I saw Bradley's face. Selling these shirts at a concert where Brad wasn't even performing felt more morbid than selling his hair. "Now I just have to figure out how to get this stuff to Niagara Falls."

"Niagara Falls?" Kitty asked. I began sorting the merchandise into piles of ten. According to an email Sherman had sent, there were ten shows coming up in the Ontario region. Ten years ago, The Noise had a 'Playing the Planet" world tour happening. This year, they had a 'Rockin' Ontario' provincial tour. Yes, how the mighty have fallen, but at least they were still working, had still been plying their craft.

"It's the first show on their tour," I responded. "The band didn't want to cancel. I don't know how it's going to go. But I can't talk right now. I have to make some calls and find a delivery service to take this to the show. It needs to get there in the next few hours!"

"Where's the show?" Kitty ignored my request for no conversation.

"I told you!" I snapped. "Niagara Falls! At some resort."

"Probably The Falls Resort," Kitty said, smiling.

"Yeah, that's it, The Falls," I recalled.

"Why don't you just save yourself the aggravation and drive the stuff out there yourself?" Kitty asked.

I looked at her in amazement. "You know, that makes sense. And this way, I know it's getting there safe and sound. Thanks, Mom, brilliant idea!"

Kitty stood up. "I'm going to get changed. I'm coming with you."

"Mom, stay home. I'm just going there and back," I said. In case she got any funny ideas.

She paused at the foot of the stairs. "If you want to use my Town Car, you'll let me come with you."

Whoa, this was something new! Since when had the car she couldn't possibly drive become a bargaining chip? "It's just another rock concert," I warned. "You won't want to be tagging along."

Kitty started up the stairs with a spring in her step. "Don't worry about me. I'll find something to do."

"Yeah, well, I guess there is the Falls, one of the seven natural wonders of the world to see....," but Kitty had already disappeared into her room.

I finished packing up the merchandise and then had a eureka moment. Where was my brain? If I was now going to the concert, why didn't I bring a few of my A Lock of Bradley's Hair to sell? My eBay sales were going ok - it looked like $300 would be the maximum I'd get - but it was my Kijiji sales that were raking in the dough. I'd already sold twenty locks - $5,000 directly deposited into my bank account. A couple grand immediately went to pay off a big parking ticket as well as catch up on some bills. The $3,000 I was left with was more money than I'd had in a long time.

I ran up to my room and took twenty bags from my stash. I put them all into a backpack that hopefully wouldn't draw attention to me. I chose my outfit carefully - I wanted to look hip and cool if I ran into any of the band, but I also wanted to be able to melt into a crowd. Black was always a good go-to colour. As I made my way back down the stairs, I saw Kitty in her chair by the front door.

"I'm ready to go whenever you are," she called out.

"What the hell?" I asked, confused. "You've got that crazy fishing vest on. You're wearing your gambling clothes!"

"Yes, you said we could go to a casino in two weeks and two weeks is up," she announced.

"Uh, having a senior moment?" I asked. "I've gotta go to work."

"You go to work and I'll go play the slots," Kitty almost quivered in ecstasy. I looked at her in puzzlement and she responded by saying, "Didn't you know? The Falls Resort? That's where the bus trip from the seniors' home would drop us off. That's where The Falls Casino is!"

• • • • • • • • • •

"Jesus on a popsicle stick," I roared, "I'm not paying twenty bucks for parking!" I'd circled the giant layout of the The Falls Resort, looking for a cheaper lot.

Once again, Kitty urged me to enter the parking garage. "I assure you, Tammy, it won't cost you a penny."

"It flat out says, Casino Parking, twenty dollars," I said. "Maybe your eyes can't make that out."

"Just take my word for it," Kitty implored.

I swung the Town Car into the garage. "OK, have it your way," I told her. "But you better not blow all your money. You're paying for parking if you're wrong."

We arrived in plenty of time for the show. I kept the box of merchandise in the car while I went to find my sales contact. I left Kitty in front of the casino with strict instructions to meet up with me in two hours. Making my way to the concert venue, I encountered a member of the security staff. He was kind enough to find my contact, Boris.

Boris appeared harassed. The Noise was scheduled to arrive at any moment, he had press anxiously awaiting their arrival and there was a problem with the sound system. The sale of thirty ball caps and fifty t- shirts were the least of his worries. "The people you want to give them to aren't here yet," he said. "Where's the stuff? I'll show you where you can drop it off."

"I didn't bring it in," I responded. "I wasn't sure where I had to go... didn't want to be lugging it around with me."

Boris looked miffed. "Well, you can go and get it. I'm not sure where I'll be when you return..."

I interrupted. "Just show me where you want me to leave it," I suggested. "I'll come back with it and I won't have to bother you again."

"Follow me then," Boris said, already heading off.

The security guard had caught the entire exchange. Just to be on the safe side, I looked him in the eye and said, "So I'll be back, ok? I'm dropping off a box of stuff. I'm...I'm with the band." It felt so good to utter those words again, though I didn't know if I wanted to be associated with this new version of The Noise. The guard nodded his understanding.

Boris led me through the small yet elegant lobby of the venue. We entered the actual concert hall which could probably hold a thousand people. A few seats were already filled with a motley crew of assorted reporters and photographers. A couple female newscasters were primping while their cameramen checked equipment.

We passed the stage and walked into the backstage area. Another member of the security staff stood guard in front of the dressing room, still empty. We passed another dressing room, where a member of the The Falls catering team was pouring pretzels into a bowl. I saw another lady carefully laying out cheese and crackers. I ran to keep up with Boris, who was speaking to somebody on a walkie-talkie.

It looked like we were going to go outside when we came to the backdoor exit. Boris opened the door, glanced out and then reported into his handheld device. "Still no sign of them," he said. He then pointed to a door next to the exit. A sign on it read 'Supply Room'. "That's where you'll leave your fan-wear," he said, punching at a few numbers on the control panel installed next to it. "The code's easy to remember. 1, 2, 3, 4. Got it?" I nodded. "The sales staff will come pick it up when they get here. Seems everybody's running behind schedule today."

"Ok, well, I'm good to go then," I said. "Thanks. You go take care of business."

"You can find your way out?" he asked. "I told the Hamilton Observer guy I'd be right back to finish our interview."

I assured him I could manage and he scurried off, but not before taking another look out the backstage door. I returned to my car in the parking garage and pulled out the box of merchandise. I saw the same security guard on my way back into the venue. He simply nodded and moved the red velvet rope aside so I could enter. I manoeuvred my way down the stairs, seeing Boris taking a smiling photo and then turn and glower at a couple guys working feverishly over a sound board. I'd seen a hundred sound board failures in my time. I always found that somehow, come showtime, they managed to get fixed.

I'd just laid my box on the floor of the supply room when I heard a big whoosh of air brakes come from outside. My heart skipped a beat when I realized The Noise had arrived, only to resume it's normal pace when I remembered Bradley wouldn't be with them. Even though I always got along with the rest of the band, Bradley was the one who kept it interesting.

A burly guard had opened the backstage door and Mickey was the first to enter. He saw me but didn't really see me. "Hi, Mickey," I said. He gave me another look.

"Hey, look who's here!" he said. "It's Tammy, right?"

He instantly lost a lot of lustre right there. "Yup, same name you've called me for fifteen years," I replied.

He didn't get the dig. "Come to see the concert?" he asked. Stan walked in. "Yo, Stan, look who came to see the concert!" He pointed at me.

"Hey, it's the old lady who used to tour with us!" Stan yelled, coming over to give me a little hug.

"You make it sound like I was a groupie," I chastised him. "I worked for you guys."

"What work?" Stan crowed. "You had nothing but fun travelling with the likes of us." I smiled benignly but wanted to punch him. Sure, there were fun times, in between late-night runs for cigarettes and cleaning up puddles of vomit weekly. Tate was the next to walk in. Stan passed me on. "Tater, look who's coming to see the show tonight!"

Tate looked like he had the weight of the world on his shoulders. "Hey, Tammy," he said, as if we'd just seen each other this morning. "I hope you bought a ticket."

I don't know if he meant it as a joke or was serious but either way, it came off sounding rude. "Actually, I'm just here to drop off fan-wear," I said. "Good luck tonight," I added.

A beefy man in his thirties, wearing a loud Hawaiian shirt, came through the door. "Oh, man, this is happening," he said. "I don't know if I'm ready...."

"You sounded great at the audition," Tate reprimanded him sharply. "You'll do fine. Stop worrying already!" His clipped words didn't inspire calmness.

Boris came running down the hallway, welcoming the band. I stepped aside and almost backed into a young man in horn-rimmed glasses, wearing a three-piece suit. "Who are you?" I blurted out. He didn't fit the rock image at all.

"I'm the assistant road manager," the kid said, all full of himself. "Who are you?"

"I used to be the assistant road manager for The Noise," I answered.

"You're Trisha?" the kid asked in amazement.

"Trisha? No, I'm Tammy."

"Like that was so last year," the new roadie said. I agreed, saying he was precisely right. "I can't say I heard about you, but I've only just started. Trisha though? Wow, I heard she was quite the number. Anyhow, gotta run, big show. Lots to do, you know."

Yeah, I knew exactly what your duties entailed, Mr. New Assistant Road Manager. Run along. Tate probably needs his stage pants ironed.

· · · · · · · · · ·

I left the concert venue once again and asked the security guard where I could find a coffee. He indicated there was a Tim Horton's shop on the level below.

"Great," I said. "Can I get you one? I still have another box to unload," I lied. Fortunately he said he couldn't drink while on duty. I rode the escalator down and joined a long line-up waiting for their java fix. Once I'd finally gotten my coffee and took the first sip, my tastebuds informed me that this had to be the best coffee I'd ever tasted.

I went back to my car and removed the backpack. There was a big black garbage bag destined for Goodwill, filled with Kitty's shoes worn before her bunions got too bad. I emptied it and put the backpack inside. I know I told the security guy I had another box to bring in; hopefully he'd think I'd said a bag.

It was time to meet Kitty. I returned to our meeting spot right on schedule and saw a pink pixie inside the casino. It was dodging around customers, sidestepping and pirouetting like a whirling dervish. As the brightly-clad bobbing figure emerged from the casino, I saw it was my mother. She had a wild grin on her face.

"Looks like you're having fun," I remarked when she scurried up to me.

"I forgot how big this place was!" Kitty said in a too-loud voice. "There's so many machines! I want to play all of them. Don't tell me we're leaving now. I left my card in a machine. I'll have to go back for it."

I figured that was all part of her usual plan to stay longer. Right now, it didn't matter. "No hurry, Mom," I said kindly. "I was going to ask you, if you don't mind, if we can stay a few more hours? I was thinking I might watch the concert."

Kitty grabbed me in a quick hug. "Oh, I was hoping you'd say that! I'm not winning but I'm having the time of my life! So we'll meet in two hours again?"

"If it's ok, can we make it three hours?" I asked. "Are you going to be alright for the next bit? If you're hungry, there's a Tim Horton's in the level below."

Kitty nodded. "I know, that's where the bus drops us off. So I'll see you in three hours!" I nodded, wished her luck and started to move off. Kitty called my name and I looked back at her. She was pointing at a litter barrel. "There's a garbage can if you want to throw that out."

I was glad she'd brought my focus back to the garbage bag. As I made my way back to the concert area, I manipulated the bag to make it look fuller than it was. I approached the same security guard who was now supervising a growing line-up of people, many in their declining years. Were they taking advantage of a free ticket? I acted like the bag had some serious weight to it. In reality, it weighed about a pound.

"Me again," I said as I walked up to the guard. "Last load of merchandise to bring in." He nodded and moved the red rope aside. I kept up the act until I entered the actual concert area. The seats were now devoid of press but the stage was a beehive of activity. The same two guys were working over the soundboard and I could hear a faint hiss emitting from some speaker. I wished they'd speak to Tate; he knew everything about musical instruments and speakers and the like. But now he was too busy trying to be the new superstar of the band. Don't bother the genius.

With a faint feeling I was in enemy territory, I continued my charade of delivering fan-wear to the supply room. At this point, the t-shirts I'd already delivered were probably in the venue's lobby, being prepared for sale. I pretended I was hard at work, carefully descending each stair with the non-heavy bag in my arms.

"Can I help you with that?" a voice startled me. I looked behind me and saw a security guard descending the stairs. I quickened my pace ahead of him.

"No, it's ok, I got it," I said, clutching the bag. I reached the bottom step one second before he did.

"You know where you're going with that?" he queried.

"Oh, yeah, I've been here before," I replied, then gave him my tried and true line. "I'm with the band."

It was as good as a get-out-of-jail-free Monopoly game card. "K, have a good show," he said, veering off to his right. I veered left, glancing up quickly at the roadies working on stage. I didn't see anybody I recognized, though the youngest of the crew looked vaguely familiar. If memory served me, he was Mickey's latest wife's son. I'd seen photos of him from the wedding which took place at the Ice Hotel in Quebec. I remember the event made headlines; Bradley got out of hand and almost melted the entire structure. If the kid was now working for The Noise, I assumed Mickey was still married to the French chanteuse.

I made my way backstage. There was a commotion in The Noise's dressing room. I could hear Tate yelling at the new band member. "That's a C chord! Why do I keep hearing G-Flat? C chord! Repeat after me. C chord." If I'd still been assistant road manager, I'd have stood up to Tate and told him to quit being a bully. Rock star or not, people still had to have manners in this world.

"C chord," I heard the new guy say. "Don't worry, Tate, I'll get it right when we get on stage."

"Sam!" Tate barked. "We're ready for another reporter."

I kept my head down as I lumbered past the reporters, but I cast a sidelong glance into the room. I saw the new assistant road manager say to Tate, "It's not Sam, it's Samuel."

"Oh, fuck off," Tate said. "And Sam? Bring back a good-looking reporter this time."

There were only men in the hallway and I didn't want to get chosen out of default. I saw the empty dressing room and quickly ducked in, shutting the door firmly behind me. With speed, I withdrew the back-pack and threw the black garbage bag into a sparkling clean waste container. With less than thirty minutes to go before showtime, I pulled out my cellphone.

It was time to try a new marketing strategy called social media. Due to my job, I was on seventeen different programs, from Twitter to Facebook to MySpace. I rarely used them but I did know how to post an announcement. Rather than send it to my small list of contacts, I made it public for all to see. Twitter only allowed a limited amount of characters to be used, so I had to be succinct.

"Tonite! The Falls Casino Backstage door. Locks of Bradley's hair 4 sale after show. Hair bona fide real. $200. Look for girl with Hello Jiffy backpack." I meant to put $250 but decided to leave it that way. The tweet went out into the world.

That same message worked for the other sites. I could have proceeded further but I heard an announcement for the crowd to welcome The Noise. Caught up in my work session, I hadn't even heard the band leave their dressing room next door. I was about to make my exit when two different sounds emitted from my cell phone. A ping (a Facebook message) and a chirp (Twitter) indicated I'd already received feedback.

I opened the Facebook message first. My mouth downturned when I saw the respondent didn't 'like' my message. His comment was "$200? A bit steep, no?" I was about to comment but then looked at the Twitter message. "Oh no! At concert but didn't bring $200. I would love to have a lock of B's hair. I miss him!!!"

I could hear the band launch into their usual opening number. To my ear, the sound system had been fixed. The music came through loud and clear, if at a somewhat diminished pace. I considered the messages I'd received. Obviously the price wasn't going over too well. I quickly re-tweeted a short note "New price - only for today. $100 for A Lock of Bradley's

Hair. Guaranteed real. Backstage door. The Falls Casino, Niagara." After I sent that, I put the same words into my comment box on Facebook.

Just as I was putting my cell into my pocket, another chirp alerted me. I glanced at the Twitter message that read, "Perfect! $100 I have! Forget tacky t-shirt. I'm buying Brads hair. See u after concert! Girl with dreads/ Marvin the Martian tattoo."

I tweeted back "C U L8R" and put my phone away. That tingly feeling came over me. I had a potential customer. I was back in business!

•••••••••

The first song was just ending as I made my way up the short hallway. A security guard spotted me and I just gave a disinterested nod and said my usual greeting, "I'm with the band." This time the security guard gave me a second look, especially at the Hello Jiffy backpack I was wearing.

Fortunately Samuel was hovering just out of sight. He heard my voice and lunged around the security staff. "Oh, thank God you're here!" he yelled. "I need your help!"

The guard stepped aside. Over Samuel's shoulder, I could see the front of the crowd. Usually these were the true fans - the ones who belonged to secret clubs and got to buy pre-sale tickets. Or the ones who didn't mind paying top price, as long as they could get up close to the act. With their cheers and wild dancing, they often inspired the band to get crazier.

What I witnessed were looks of confusion and mostly stone-still bodies. There were a couple guys gyrating but they were obviously inebriated as they didn't stop when the song ended. Half the crowd politely applauded and maybe a dozen walked out. They weren't senior citizens either.

"What was that you said?" I asked the assistant road manager, adding sarcastically, "I couldn't hear you over the roar of the crowd."

"Yeah, it's a rough start," Samuel said. "I think they miss the old guy."

I looked startled. "What old guy?"

"The dead one," he replied.

"You mean Bradley," I said with a solemn face. "He was the leader of the band. Damn right the fans are going to miss him."

"Well, sorry, I didn't know. I never heard of these guys until Tate hired me a couple days ago," Samuel said defensively.

"How'd you get the job?" I asked. "What's your background?"

"I was doing psychic readings for a living," Samuel said. "I don't even listen to this kind of music. I'm more into new age kind of stuff. I gave Tate a tarot card reading and it went well. So well that he ended up offering me a job. I thought it'd be a nice change."

"Are we having fun yet?" I asked.

"Well, the bus ride down was pretty fun," Samuel said. "Mickey ended up bringing a couple girls and they got a little crazy." Samuel was red-faced relating this. "But as soon as we get here, the big guy starts whining about how nervous he is and then he throws up. Everybody got away from the mess and then Stan tells ME to clean it up."

"Yeah, get to the point of the story," I said. I could hear The Noise start up their second song, play a few bars and stop. Tate sang out "C Chooorrrd" and a mumbled but amplified voice responded, "Yeah, yeah, shit, sorry, Tate."

Samuel said, "That is the point! I didn't vomit, why would I be the one to clean it up?"

"Because that's your job."

"So disgusting! I did it, but do I look dressed for that kind of work?" he asked, displaying his natty suit. "And what's with Tate's attitude? One minute he's super nice and the next minute he's making you feel like scum."

"Yeah, that's Tate," I agreed. "Passive-aggressive. Each one has their quirks. You have to know how to deal with them."

Now his face was cherry tomato red. "And here I am now, standing at the front of the crowd, scanning the women..."

"Let me guess," I cut in. "Stan's in the mood for love."

"For an early thirties busty blonde," Samuel said. "Not enough I have to look at their faces, I have to look at their chest as well. Should I be doing this for him?"

I shrugged. "It's your call." The band had started up the song again, and once more screwed it up. The two dancing bears booed them loudly. The third attempt seemed to work as they played on.

"This is my first day, you know," Samuel seemed to be looking for pity. "I don't know what to expect next."

I pretended to get a phone call, pulling my cell out of my pocket and squinting at the blank screen. "Let me tell you, the fun has only just begun," I said to Samuel. "Would you excuse me while I take this call?" He stepped aside and I moved toward the guard. "I'll be back," I said.

I walked towards the newly-vacated floor seats near the front of the stage. Sliding into a chair, I had a weird sensation something was visually off. I realized that, even in the waning years of The Noise, the people in the floor seats never sat down. They were always up and dancing. It was only up in the angled seats that people rested their tushies. Tonight, everybody sat. I directed my gaze up to the stage.

Mickey was on bass guitar, working his usual one-foot circle. Didn't he see the mega stage he could cross now and then? Tapping his foot to the music was as physical as he got. And it was painful to watch the new guy as he bent over his guitar. He was wearing the same ludicrous Hawaiian shirt and was seated on a stool, hunching over his instrument. Every now and then he'd stand up, try to act like he was in a rock show, but fear got the better of him and he'd plunk back down onto the stool.

As for Tate being the lead singer? Give it up for him - he knew the lyrics. But where he used to be a dynamic showman himself, known as one of the top rock guitarists in the world, now he preferred to present himself as Bradley's replacement. Where Brad used to caress and simulate sex with the mike stand, Tate's awkward impression resembled a dog humping someone's leg. And where the former singer would traverse the stage umpteen times while ferociously belting out a rock tune, this new singer assumed a Crouching Tiger karate pose and screeched into the microphone. Where all eyes used to be on Bradley, the entire audience could not bear to look at Tate.

Stan, the drummer? He was like the Ringo Starr of The Beatles. The least known, least handsome, least amount of fans...tonight he was the shining star of the group. And for Stan to stick out says a lot about how sorry a show this was turning out to be.

I skipped out of my seat when I heard what I recalled as the band's last song. There were two held in reserve for the encore. I wasn't the only one leaving, as I waited for a huge woman to extricate herself from her seat beside mine. My attention went back up to the stage when I heard the song grind to a halt. Tate stormed over to the new guy and pulled the guitar off his body.

"Watch and learn, Chubbo," Tate said. A gasp went up from the crowd. Tate began playing guitar and the rest of the band joined in, but then stopped when Tate did. "Shit, I forgot. Now I have to sing and play guitar!

Hey, this song goes out to Bradley," Tate said to the crowd.

A voice cracked, "You should have let The Noise die when he did!" That got a round of applause.

Tate responded by saying, "Next weekend we have a show at the Fort James Arena. Spread the word! Guys, from the top..."

The band played out their song as I slipped around the side of the stage and encountered the security guard again. "Watch out," I warned him. "The boys are gonna be in a nasty mood when they come offstage. Not their best show."

"I saw them play last year in Nova Scotia," the guy said. "That's where my family's from. They were amazing. What's with them tonight?"

"They're missing a singer," I replied. "Well, gotta go take care of business."

He turned back to the show and I casually made my way to the backstage exit. I could see the band come off the stage to a very noticeable smattering of applause. As usual, they stood off in the wings, taking a breather before responding to the crowd's anticipated demands for an encore.

Tonight, the boys huddled just inside the entranceway to the stage. "We won't make them wait too long," Tate said. "Maybe half a minute."

"Dude, I don't even think they're clapping anymore," Mickey said.

Stan had been jogging in place but stopped. He said, "Nope, that's the sound of people leaving."

"Sorry for fucking up, guys," the new guy said feebly. "I'll practice all week, I promise."

"Come on!" Tate said to nobody in general. "We always do encores! We haven't even sung our biggest hit!"

The security guard approached the band and with one arm outstretched, he asked, "Would you like me to escort you to your dressing room?"

"Oh, fuck off," said Tate. As they headed down the hallway, I slipped out the door. Time to find Marvin the Martian.

• • • • • • • • •

There was a small crowd waiting outside the back stage door. I was certainly glad to see The Noise still had some fans, but they were here awfully early. I didn't see how they could have even left the concert hall yet.

I had the door open, wondering if there was a way to prop it so that I wouldn't get locked out. As I turned my back to look for anything that might do the trick, I heard a voice yell out, "There it is! The Hello Jiffy backpack!"

I turned to see a dozen people start clamouring for my attention. Not wanting to draw attention to myself, I slammed the door shut and hustled off a few feet. "Come on, I got what you want," I said to them. "Just follow me." I led the way down the alley until I found a secluded area. Leaning into the small indent of the building, I took the Hello Jiffy bag off my back.

"Your tweet said a hundred, right?" said a middle-aged woman. She looked like she still had traces of a red dye around her hairline. Waving a crisp hundred dollar bill, she added, "And thanks for doing this. I'm Bradley's biggest fan!"

I plucked the money out of her outstretched hand and withdrew a bag out of my backpack. I held it aloft and made a short sales pitch. "I want you all to know I have a very limited supply of these. I worked with The Noise for fifteen years and whenever Bradley got a haircut, he let me keep the locks." I was pushing the brand. "You will find these on eBay, going for about three hundred right now. You guys are getting a bargain, the spur-of-the-moment social media deal."

I'd no sooner shut my trap than five people came forward with money in their hands. "Is it ok if I buy two?" asked a man on crutches. "One's a gift for my girlfriend, she's still crying over his death, and one for me, so what?"

"Sure," I agreed. "Two hundred please. Take care of your leg."

A big guy swaggered in front of a mother with a sleeping baby harnessed in a sling across her hip. "I'll give ya fifty bucks," he bellowed.

"Sorry, it's a hundred," I replied. "Rock bottom price." I reached around him and took the two fifties out of the mother's hand and handed her A Lock of Bradley's Hair. The mother immediately started to cry and I gave her a heartfelt pat on the shoulder. I may have even given her a hug if that brute wasn't still in front of me.

"Ok, eighty bucks and that's my final offer," the guy said, shoving the money into my palm. I refused to close my hand, so that he couldn't get the cash to stay.

"I believe I said a hundred," I stated firmly, standing my ground. I saw a teen-aged boy come down the alley, deftly riding a skateboard. He held out a clearly discernible hundred dollar bill. I could see he was wearing a vintage Noise T-shirt and my emotions swelled even more. In what could have been a perfect YouTube clip, his hundred and my bag of hair exchanged hands in one fluid movement. We even gave each other a look of awe, knowing we'd never be able to pull that off again.

I turned my attention back to the brute, who now clearly held five twenty-dollar bills fanned in his hand. I scooped them up and without a word, gave him his bag.

"You're sure this is for real?" he had to go and ask.

"You want to return it, go ahead," I said, ready to hand him his money back.

"Ah, it's only a hundred bucks," the man jeered. "I lost that in five minutes at the slots."

I still had one more customer. The guy was about thirty and had an aura of lonesomeness about him. "Is it OK if I pay with American money?" he asked. "Sorry, I saw the Facebook post and I got here as fast as I could. I had no time to change it."

"You're from the States?" I asked. "You didn't see the show?"

"Nah," the guy said. "If Brad had been here, yeah, for sure I'd have bought the ticket. But I just can't imagine The Noise being the same without him. I couldn't bear to go."

"You're a big fan?" I asked, withdrawing a bag.

"A big fan of Bradley Atwater mainly, though I don't mind the music," the guy said. "Ten years ago, I had a crap job at The Buffalo Auditorium, working in the concession booth. We got a call that the pop machine needed refilling in the dressing room and I went down there with a bunch of sodas. The Noise were playing that night. I remember you."

"You do?" I asked incredulously.

"Brad's bootlace had snapped and you were tying the ends together and trying to make it work, but Brad wasn't any help...he wouldn't take off the boot," the guy softly laughed.

I barely remembered that incident. I didn't remember this guy at all. But while that night may have been run-of-the-mill, the man before me apparently had a life-changing evening. "So you got to see Brad up close and in person?" I asked reverently.

"For some reason, I added a couple cans of Grape Crush, and Bradley saw them and told me I had good taste. He told me to come back to the room after the show. I had to work but I snuck away and went back to the dressing room. You guys had some strict security but Bradley allowed me in."

"So you partied with them?" I asked.

"Just till they had to leave the building, not long," he admitted. "But I took the can of Grape Crush I saw him drink and by his table, I saw his black eye-liner, so I took that too. And on his chair was a beautiful long strand of his hair! I snagged that. But best of all, I saw the boots he wore on stage. And don't ask my why, but when nobody was looking, I took out that broken lace. I may have lost my job that night, but it was worth it. I found a new passion."

He reached into his jeans pocket and withdrew a small satin pouch. From this pouch he took out the old bootlace and held it out to me. I took it and admired it and when I saw him just looking at me, I asked, "You're not giving this to me, are you?"

"No," he said, taking it back. "It's part of my growing Bradley Atwater collection. One night they played in Toronto and I went to the backstage door and I saw Bradley throw a cigarette to the ground. I actually had to tackle somebody to get it. First fight I ever was in."

"Eww," I replied. "I could have collected a billion cigarette butts." Who would have known?

I completed our transaction and was about to step away when a man in a mismatched business suit walked over. I'd noticed him the whole time I was selling. At first he distressed me - I wondered if he might be under-cover casino security - but his whole persona told me he wasn't. This man had brown pants, a grey blazer, black running shoes, three days growth of beard, hair that needed a trim two months ago and tired eyes.

He walked over wearily. I saw a woman come careening around the corner on high-heeled boots, her black mini-skirt jacked up dangerously high. She wore a large multi-hued hat and her breasts heaved through her skin-tight The Noise tank top. She slowed when she saw I didn't have a line-up. The man saw her as well and spoke quickly.

"How many you got left?" he asked.

"Why?" I asked.

"I want to buy them," he replied.

"All of them?" I asked. He nodded. "Are you a collector?"

"You could say that," he said. I looked at him dead-on and his bleary eyes looked back at me, giving nothing away. I had a feeling the guy was going to buy Brad's locks at a steal and turn around and sell them at a great mark-up. Still, a sale was a sale. Since it didn't look like a backstage crowd was going to appear for this version of The Noise, it would mean getting rid of all the product I was currently carrying.

I opened the backpack and started to count them. I had exactly half of what I'd brought. "I have ten left," I said. "A thousand bucks. No deals." The guy immediately started to count out his money so I began taking out the bags. An unusual feeling came over me, a guilty sort of apprehension. Wasn't I supposed to meet someone? It would be nice to dump all of the hair on this shylock but I didn't want to break someone's heart with my greed. I gave the man a look of dejection.

"I'm sorry," I lied. "I miscounted. I only have nine left."

The woman had reached us just as I said that. The man clipped a hundred out of his money and said, "I'll take them!" He thrust the cash into my hand and started to bundle up the bags.

The girl behind him wailed. "That was your last one?" She didn't give me a chance to speak. "Fuck me! I got here as fast as I could! Fucking concert sucks and now this! Fuck my life!" With that, she reached for her Rasta cap and ripped it off in anger, throwing it to the ground. Her dreadlocks fell down to her waist. I stared at her.

"You wouldn't be Marvin the Martian, would you?" I asked.

She turned sideways, swiped her hair aside and displayed her tattoo of the Warner Brothers character. I reached into my knapsack and pulled out the last bag of hair. Holding it up, I said to her astonished face, "This one has been reserved for you all along."

•••••••••

With the backstage door locked, I couldn't figure out how to get back into the casino. I saw The Noise tour bus pull up so I knew the band would be coming out shortly. I hoped to somehow make my way back inside without being seen by them. But before I could work out my plan, the door opened and a guard popped his head out.

"Yeah, you've got fans out here," he yelled and then took a second look and called out a correction. "You've got a fan out here."

The door burst open as the four members of the band came out. Stan had a big grin, Chubbo didn't want to be seen, Mickey looked sheepish and Tate's glowering face and stiff-armed wave made him look like he belonged in Hitler's army. When they saw it was just me, they collided into each other as they stopped.

Chubbo looked around. "Hey, where's the big crowd you guys said you always get?" he whined. "One girl makes a crowd?"

"It's our old assistant road manager," Tate said. "Does little Tammy want her cushy job back?" I stared at him, shocked at his rudeness. And the fact he thought I had a cushy job. "Too bad Brad's not here rooting for you anymore, huh?"

I said the only thing I could think of that may sting. "Nice show, Tate." I turned and headed directly for the open backstage door. Samuel was just coming out, his arms full of band junk.

"A little help?" he called out to the boys.

Stan spoke up. "Hey, new guy, run back and see if there's any girls left in the lobby or something. Tell them they're invited to a party back at the hotel."

Samuel looked dismayed at this task and saw me over the baggage in his arms. He whispered, "You want your job back? You can have it."

I gave one more look at the boys and felt absolutely zero appeal. It was then that I knew the rock n' roll life was over for me. I gave Samuel the saddest look ever.

"You must be delusional," I said.

• • • • • • • • • •

When I caught up with Kitty, it didn't take much for her to talk me into signing up for a Player's Card. I felt like being around noise and bright lights; inside I felt raw. With a smile tinged by sorrow, I was happy to accept the ten dollar new-member gift. Sure I had a backpack with two grand in it, but that was my paycheck. This was free money. The counter clerk also informed me that as long as I swiped my player's card when I left the parking lot, then I would get free parking. That $20 bug in my bonnet over the posted parking fee flew away.

Kitty and I agreed to meet at one in the morning. My ten bucks disappeared in a flash. Again I had to suspiciously wonder if the machine knew I was playing with the casino's money? I left my machine and decided it wouldn't hurt to spend my own money. I withdrew a twenty from my backpack and was looking for a slot machine when I spotted Kitty.

She was standing at a bank machine, making a withdrawal. An elderly gentleman was standing beside the machine, engaging her in conversation. I strode up in time to hear him say, "I'm Bill McAllister. I live in Niagara Falls, but on the US side."

"I'm Kitty," my mother said. "Kitty Casino."

"Come here often?" the man asked.

His line seemed to work as my mother giggled. "Not as often as I'd like," she responded.

"How's it going, Mom?" I asked. "Taking money out, I see."

"I maxed out my limit for yesterday," she said. The ATM spit the money out and Kitty took it, stuffing it into a zippered pocket of her fishing vest. "But it just passed midnight - it's a new day!"

"You took out your whole limit?" I asked.

"Oh, Tammy, how often do I get to come here?" Kitty asked. By my estimation, we'd been here six hours or more, and Kitty acted like we'd just arrived. I'd figured on leaving when we were to next meet up.

Instead, since we'd accidentally connected, we changed our meeting time to 2 AM. By then I'd lost my twenty and had decided to mourn the loss of Bradley by living as brazenly as he did; I splurged another twenty. When I next saw Kitty, she was with her newfound friend Bill, so I agreed to meet her at 4 AM. To celebrate the success of my sales, I took out twenty more dollars. I managed to win a six dollar jackpot, but the rest of my winnings were negligible.

At four, I was waiting on Kitty. I had played out my cash voucher, whiling away the last ten minutes by playing one cent bets. Maybe my fatigue was causing me paranoia, but I swore the slot machine was toying with me. Because I'd strayed from my usual five cent bet, the machine started acting like it would have paid out huge if I'd stuck with my wager. Screens full of matching penguins would appear and I'd win four cents, whereas I may have won eighty bucks with a nickel bet.

I saw Kitty walk up ten minutes late. This time she had her dentures gritted. "I know I'm late," she said. "My money's in a machine and the voucher won't come out. The attendants are looking at it."

She turned around and marched away. I wearily followed her. Though the casino was still filled with gamblers, it wasn't as congested. Kitty was easy to spot - like following the bouncing pink ball. She approached a casino worker guarding her chair at Puppy Parade.

"It's out of paper, that's why your voucher wouldn't print," he said. "It's good now. You can cash out."

I saw she had less than two dollars in the machine. "How about you play that out and then we leave?" I suggested.

"Already?" she asked.

Kitty decided to stay at the same machine. She played her usual forty cent bet and came up with zilch. "Come on," Kitty said, rubbing the screen. "I went to a lot of trouble for you. Time to pay up."

Her next forty cent bet went nowhere. Same with her third spin. She was down to less than sixty cents and I started to look for the car keys. "One more bet," Kitty said. "Then I'll cash out."

And of course the machine heard her say this, or so I imagined. She won twenty bucks. A few spins later, the exact same sequence came up, rewarding her with another twenty dollars. I never saw this coming. Kitty looked over at me with a smile that was somewhat crazed. I mean, the old lady had been up for probably twenty-four hours by now.

"We could be here awhile, Tammy!" she crowed. "If you have any money left, you may as well spend it."

I reluctantly pulled another twenty from my knapsack. What a way to celebrate - by throwing away more money.

• • • • • • • • • •

At 6 AM, after following Kitty from machine to machine, I put my foot down. "You've been here twelve hours, Mom. That's HALF A DAY," I stressed. "We're leaving." Kitty had just won her biggest jackpot ever and I was irked by the faint pang of jealousy I felt. I should be happy for her; instead I was down a hundred bucks and felt sick about it.

"I guess I've had enough for one day," Kitty said, cashing out. "And we can always come back on the bus. You need a player's card for that and now you have one."

"We'll see," I replied.

We exited the parking lot and I was thrilled to see the gate swing up when I inserted my player's card into the machine. The attendant didn't glance at me nor ask me for money. "Well, that's good, that card saved me twenty bucks," I said, yawning. "Wow, what a long night. Now we have ninety minutes of travel ahead of us."

Kitty already had her eyes closed but she said, "Drive carefully."

I replied, "I wouldn't mind some conversation to keep me awake. Good Lord, the sun's up already! So what happened to your friend?"

"Bill? He has to be home by three or his wife worries," Kitty said.

"So you had a good time then?" I asked.

"I met some nice people and I won six hundred dollars today," my mother answered drowsily. "We'll have to come here again."

I was quiet for a moment, digesting what she'd said. I knew she'd maxed out her bank limit yesterday - she told me so herself - and who knows what other money she'd brought. I saw her take another five hundred out at midnight. She won six hundred off that, so yeah, today she was ahead of the game. I guess yesterday no longer counted.

I was about to point this out but then shut my mouth. She had a good day; this should hold her for awhile. Kitty slept with a smile on her face, her snores sounding like the lions on the Wild Safari machine we last played.

• • • • • • • • •

Next stop for the Noise - Fort James! Seeing as how Kitty had enjoyed herself so much last time, I googled the Fort James Arena to see if I could find a casino in the area. I knew it'd be safe to drop her off for a couple hours - it appeared to be the only place where she wouldn't get into trouble. I almost fell off my chair when I saw there was a casino about two kilometres from the arena!

We arrived super early so that Kitty wouldn't complain about leaving too soon...though it was always too soon for her. Discovering that this casino wasn't affiliated with any of the other three casinos we'd been to, we had to sign up for a new player's card. I didn't mind; by now I associated that with a monetary reward. Sure enough, I had ten dollars to freely waste before I left for the arena. I was astounded at the points my gameplay was rewarding me. Unlike the other places, the Red Willow Casino was very giving.

Just like the week before, I entered the venue with the merchandise I had to drop off. I lingered in the lobby, talking to the staff who would be selling the t-shirts. They had four bright and cheerful girls awaiting the customers. I told them to cool their jets; the Niagara Falls concert had returned ninety per cent of their fan-wear.

I acted like I was sauntering out, but ducked into a ladies room where I sat on a toilet and conducted my business, meaning my tweets and Instagrams and whatnot posts. I had put out soft hints earlier that there would be collector's merchandise available...just not what it was or where it was being sold. Now I typed in the nitty gritty details and sent them out.

Once the concert began, I moseyed out and caught about ten minutes. The sluggishness of the show, as well as hearing audience members wishing they had vegetables to throw, made me repair back to the washroom. Best seat in the house for this current incarnation of The Noise.

As soon as I recognized the band's last song, I left the arena. There were a dozen people standing out front and I looked over at a security guard. "Isn't there some kind of back door exit here?" I asked him.

"Nah, everybody comes in through the front," the young man said. "We got a side door, but that end's under construction right now."

"Who are all these people then?" I asked.

"I dunno, maybe they couldn't get tickets to the show, though there's plenty of seats left," the guard shrugged. "I don't know why they're here."

I hoped they were there to see me. I started towards the side of the arena, where I figured I could hide behind some fencing or something. As I passed the crowd, I barely whispered, "If you want a lock of Bradley's hair, come with me."

En masse, the whole group turned and followed me like sheep. A man came up to me and I recognized him from Niagara Falls; the man who'd bought nine bags of hair.

"Shall we do this now or shall we do this later?" was his opening line.

"Well...how much are you going to want this time?" I asked.

"Whatever you brought," he replied.

Once again I'd brought twenty bags. I had a rush when I realized I wouldn't have to work very hard tonight. Still...."Let's make it later," I said. "I'd like to sell a few to some actual fans."

He didn't argue, just got to the back of the line. I made my spiel and handed out bag after bag. One heartsick fan raced from Ottawa the moment she read I'd be there. Another claimed to have slept with Brad when she saw The Noise play a show in Barrie. When it was Mr. Shylock's turn, he took the remaining dozen bags and gave me twelve crisp hundreds. I didn't know if I should have held out for some fans from the concert but it felt better this way. Get rid of the shit and get out of Dodge.

Two thousand smackeroos again in my bag, but no desire to dip into it. I found Kitty back at the casino and she asked if I was hungry. I suggested we pick up McDonald's on the way home but she had a different idea - why not eat at The Red Willow?

"Because casino food is like airport food," was my quick reply. "Way over-priced."

"It's ok, we can pay for it with my points," Kitty said.

"Mom, this casino is not affiliated with the other ones we play at," I reminded her. "You haven't accumulated enough points yet."

"I checked," Kitty said. "I have enough for two meals at the Snack Shack."

"Already?" I squeaked. "This is our first time here!"

"They've awfully generous with their points system," Kitty agreed.

I'd say. Two hot dogs, fries and a drink worth. Kitty managed to convince me to stay another four hours. The pleasant staff, the new machines and the fact that I only managed to lose ten dollars...compounded with the realization that this particular gambling establishment was no more than an hour away from home....yeah, I rather liked this Red Willow Casino. Heaven forbid my mother found out.

• • • • • • • • • •

Checking the schedule for The Awful Noise's next date, I saw I was going to have to make a journey. They were playing an outdoor concert in Stoneland, Ontario. In the old days, they would have been the headliners. Now they were scheduled to start at the supper hour.

My next stop on the information highway was Mapquest. I plugged in the location of the upcoming concert venue and for the destination, I entered 'nearest casino'. As Kitty's luck would have it, it was less than five minutes to the Stoneland Casino. I knew I'd be taking her.

It was Wednesday morning when Kitty brought her laundry downstairs. Her pink clothes were visible on top. She left the basket of laundry in my sight half the day until she finally got around to doing it. As I was trying out an unfamiliar recipe for dinner (making use of my newfound time), Kitty folded her dried clothes.

Holding up her pink blouse, she said, "Good thing I remembered to wash this. You never know when we might go to the casino again."

It was a broad hint, but I played along. "You never know," I replied. "It could be as soon as this Saturday."

Mother stopped what she was doing. She didn't say a word, just clasped her hands and looked up at me with the most hopeful expression. I scraped the sauce that was sticking to the pan, pleased to know I was about to make Kitty very happy. Good thing, because her burnt dinner wouldn't.

"The band has a show in Stoneland," I explained. "And there's a casino not far away. The problem is, it's an all-day concert. I'm not sure how long we'll be there. Could be a long time."

"You can leave me at the casino," Kitty replied. "However long it takes, you know I'll be fine."

I nodded. "It's about the only place I feel I can trust you. But I'll still be able to check in with you."

"You do what you have to do, Tammy," Kitty said. "I'll be just dandy. So can I plan on Saturday then?"

"Yup."

"But not before?" she tried.

"Nope."

In the few days before the event, I worked the social media, letting the public know that A Lock of Bradley's Hair would be sold - location to follow on the day. Sales on eBay the first week were solid and the second week, I sold my limit for $250 each lock. This week, $200 was still the asking price and I had yet to get a bid. I could feel interest waning. For the first time ever, I had money sitting in my bank account. It wasn't like I had become wealthy, but I was still socking away a few bucks until I could find another job.

The Stoneland Casino was quite a surprise. Again, the drive was not intolerable - maybe ninety minutes. I wasn't prepared for such a large casino either. The exterior looked welcoming, though it was the usual long walk to the front door. You would have thought I'd taken Kitty to Busch Gardens, the way she was reacting.

"Look at all the flowers still in bloom!" she exclaimed. "I've never been here, though some of the seniors told me about this place. And they were right, it's glorious!"

"We haven't even been inside yet," I said. "I liked the one last week-end, the Red Willow one. It wasn't small, but it wasn't big either. I could always find you."

That wouldn't be the case today. As we walked in and rode an escalator up to a second level, I saw slot machines splayed out to the left and right of me. Kitty gasped and then spotted a game she liked right in front of her. She rushed to the More Hearts game.

"Look!" she yelled over her shoulder. "It's a penny game here! I've never seen it as a penny game before."

"Hang on," I said, "Let's go sign up for a player's card."

Kitty was pulling her card out of her vest pocket. "Didn't you bring your OGG card?" she asked. "It's the same one you use at Five Star."

I gave her a questioning look. "Even though we're all the way in Stone-land?"

"The 'O' in OGG stands for Ontario," was Kitty's reply.

Damn. I was looking forward to some free sign-up money. Instead, I had to sign up to get a replacement card. I played out ten dollars and then tried to locate Kitty before our scheduled meet time. I spotted games I'd not played at other casinos, only because they were two cent machines or more elsewhere. Not today! I didn't know if Kitty would attempt to talk me into staying after my work was done - I rather hoped she would. Besides, I hadn't reached my limit yet.

Right at the appointed hour, Kitty came barrelling down the hallway, two vouchers in her hand. "Look!" She shoved them in my face, an inch from my eyes. Maybe she thought we all looked at things the same way she did. "I put in a twenty and I was almost out when it paid me twenty dollars back! So I took that out, put in a new twenty, and look! I won twenty again on my first spin!"

"Good girl!" I congratulated her on her...skill? "Now I gotta go, but I'll be back in a couple hours to check on you."

I arrived at the concert grounds just after noon. The parking lot was already half-full with early arrivals. The opening act, The Stoneland Boys, were not yet big and judging by what I was hearing, would never be. However, the next act, The Barstools, had a song on the radio that was climbing the charts, so they were drawing a crowd.

I threw on the vendors' badge that would allow me entry into the place. Usually us working stiffs would drop off our Pepsi or Johnny-On-The-Spots and get out of there. It wasn't a free pass to the concert. However, these days Tammy Canseco was playing by different rules.

Opening the trunk of the Town Car, I saw my Hello Jiffy backpack next to the box of fan-wear. I realized I'd forgotten to bring something to hide it in. Hoping for the best, I grabbed the box and headed for the front gates.

Security was checking the purses and knapsacks of every concertgoer. I imagined I'd get waved through and was astounded when the young, well-built guard asked me to open the box. "But I'm making a drop-off," I said, pointing to my badge that read 'Vendor - Blast Records Fan Club'. And then of course I added, "I'm with the band."

"Which one?" he asked.

"Which one?" I repeated. I again pointed at my badge, while also looking at it myself. "Oh," was my sodden reply, when I saw it could mean anything. I set the box down and opened it myself, pointing to the t-shirt's logos. "I'm dropping off fan-wear for The Noise."

He dug through the box, satisfied that it was stuffed with legal product, not secretly hiding heroin or locks of hair. "Alright," he said, closing the carton. "You'll want to go left when you get inside. All the sales booths are set up at the back."

"Thanks," I said. "You'll see me again. I have another load of stuff. This was all I could carry." I was laying out the groundwork of my plan. He simply nodded as a line-up was forming behind me.

As soon as I entered, I put the box down and scoped out the place. The stage was at the far end and before me lay a massive open space, half-filled with people on blankets . Behind me were rows of stadium seating which only had a few people. I could see little tents, snack trucks and open-air booths to my left, though not all were open for business yet. To my right was a row of latrines.

The main thing I was looking for was a discreet place to sell my own wares, if I could even figure out how to get them in. I squinted from the high noon sun, wishing I'd brought my shades. I wasn't prepared to be so out in the open, working in such broad daylight.

My concerned thoughts were interrupted by a goth-dressed woman who appeared in front of me. I stared at her; she seemed attired for the middle of the night. With her make-up so severe, I worried she may be supernatural. "Hi!" came a friendly voice out of those black lips. "You're with Blast Records?"

"Yeahhhh," I responded.

"We've been waiting for you," she replied. "You have some fan-wear?"

"Yeah, you know where I have to go?" I asked.

"Come with me, I'm selling the stuff," she said, already walking off.

I picked up the box. "I hope you didn't miss any sales," I said.

"For The Noise? No," she replied. "They were a last minute replacement anyhow. Starburst was scheduled to play but they went down in flames." She gave me a look. "But I guess you know that?"

"Do I ever," I said. "Look, we have a tiny problem....," I began my lie. "Half the stuff I brought is the wrong thing. I'm going to go back to... uh, the hotel and get the right stuff and be back with it soon as I can. Is that ok?"

"Sure," she replied sweetly. "I don't plan on them being my big seller today. I hope you brought ball caps though. Those will sell, just to keep the sun outta people's eyes."

I left her with all the ball caps and half the t-shirts. Taking the box with the remaining shirts, I headed back for my car. There was a different way to get out and though there was another guard there, an elderly gent, he didn't do anything but smile as I walked past.

I went back to my car and opened the trunk. I placed the box in it and emptied it of t-shirts. The Hello Jiffy backpack went on the bottom and with the t-shirts put back on top, the box appeared full again. Looking out over the parking lot, I was reluctant to give up my somewhat decent space. Who knew how far I'd have to walk when I returned from meeting Kitty?

The Stoneland Casino lot was filled to near capacity as well. After driving in ever-increasing circles, I finally found a spot and walked up to the the entrance. Coming out the front door were an unlikely twosome - Tate, from The Noise, and his new assistant road manager, Samuel. I recognized Sam before Tate. In his casual clothes, a windbreaker hiding his tattooed arms, Tate resembled just a normal guy badly in need of a haircut.

"Hey," I said to the guys. "Fancy meeting you here," I added.

"Coming to see another show?" Tate asked, a rude pitch to his voice.

"I'm coming to gamble," I said proudly. I wanted him to think I had money to blow and didn't need his stinking job. "I had to drop off some of your fan-wear but I didn't need to stick around, so why would I?"

"Well, there's word out that somebody is selling pieces of our hair," Tate growled.

"Actually, I keep hearing it's Bradley's hair," Samuel cut in.

I shrugged. "First I heard of it," I bald-faced lied.

"It's that bitch Trisha, I tell ya," Tate punched the air. "This sounds like something she'd do, the conniving piece of ass."

I changed the subject. "Hey, Tate, when did you start gambling?"

"What are you, my mother?" Tate spat out. He stormed off.

"Who had to buy your size large BOYS underwear?" I said to his re-treating back. "Who went to the drugstore for your VD medicine? Who had to remind you to pack fucking mittens when we toured Russia?"

I could have kept going but he flipped me the bird without looking at me. Samuel spoke up, "Aw, he's just pissed. He lost a lot of money in there."

"Don't bother sticking up for him," I said. "He's always been a tem-peramental basket-case. What in the world are you doing hanging out with him?"

"I just caught a ride," he replied. "Talked to the management, spoke to them about me working here. You know, as a psychic."

"Really? Any luck?"

Samuel ruefully said, "Nah, they don't want someone telling a gam-bler they're in for a run of bad luck. It'll make them go home. I never considered that."

"Stick it out with The Noise," I advised. "There's only...what? Five more shows left?"

"I'll try," Samuel said unconvincingly. Then he startled me by saying, "Hey, I know it's you selling the hair." I opened my mouth to disclaim it but he gave me a rueful smile. "I'm on the net all the time, all the social sites. And I saw the posts about the hair and the provenance...come on, how many assistant road managers did The Noise have? But don't worry. You think I'm gonna bust you? Ha! Not to this ungrateful lot!"

In the parking lot, a loud voice boomed out. "Hey, ASS Road Manager, you want a ride back or not?" Samuel gave a soft whimper and took off at a trot.

I walked into the casino and didn't even bother to look around for Kitty. I found an empty two-cent machine and inserted a five-dollar bill, whiling away the time playing what was an almost useless endeavour - trying to get a win with a 1-line chance. In the twenty minutes I waited, my biggest win was a nickel. When I saw Kitty run up, right at two o'clock, I cashed out and put my voucher in my pocket. I knew I'd be using it later.

"How's work? Work's good?" Kitty asked breathlessly.

I teased her with, "How's casino? Casino good?"

"I may have to visit the ATM soon," she said happily. I'd have had the opposite reaction. "Are you staying?" she asked, her eyes searching the other side of the room. "I want to show you this new game; I still have my card in it. Oh, Tammy, you'll love it here! There's so many different one-cent machines!"

"Yeah, maybe I'll play a little when work is done," I said. "I'm going back there now and listen, I probably won't return for a long time."

"You take however long you need, Tammy," my mother said. "In four hours, I promise I'll turn on my phone."

No wonder she wasn't answering my calls.

• • • • • • • • • •

It came as no surprise that I'd have to park in the overflow parking lot. Luck was with me though; a bus was trawling the aisles, picking up concert-goers. I caught a lift. As soon as the bus dropped the thirty of us off at the front gate, I spotted the same guard that I'd seen earlier. I made sure to get into his line-up.

"Hi, just me again," I greeted him warmly. I put my box down on the table and opened it up myself. "Just more T-shirts and stuff."

He barely riffed through the top layer before glancing up at a couple boisterous guys behind me. His brow furrowed as he said, "Yeah, go on in."

I serenely walked past him but as soon as I entered the venue, I quickly made for the sales booth. I spotted my ghoulish sales associate, busy applying a second coat of black polish to her nails. "Got the right t-shirts here," I said.

She lifted up her hands. "I can't touch anything right now," she wiggled her fingers. "Can you just place them behind the counter?'

She didn't even notice me take out my Hello Jiffy backpack. I bid her farewell and pulled my cell phone out of my pocket. I posted that I was on the premises with the goods and that the next message would indicate my selling position.

I looked around and just didn't like my options one bit. For one thing, there were security guards everywhere, all of them looking fierce, as if they were working a political summit meeting. I glanced over to the stage area and saw there was no possible way I could set up shop there. And I didn't have a license to sell anything other than the fan-wear I'd delivered, so setting up amongst the vendors and sales booths wouldn't work. A sense that I was destined for failure came over me. I headed over to the outdoor washroom. As much as I hated those things, I had to take a pee.

I got a tweet while I was in the dark johnny-on-the-spot. I didn't read it as I wanted to get out of there pronto. While already midway through September, the day was hot and the sun was blazing. The crowds were making full use of the latrines and the smell was mindboggling. I opened the door and catapulted out, almost falling into the face of a young woman about to throw up. Her friend had her arm around her.

"Come on," the friend said. "It's free, let's go in. I'll hold your hair."

I gasped in disbelief. "She's gonna put her head in that hole?"

Letting them pass, I then looked at my phone. The tweet read, "I'm at the park. Can I buy the hair before the show? Where are you?"

I looked around. Where the hell was I going to do this?? The first thing to hit me was that I was standing in the only place where I couldn't see any security. I didn't blame them. I didn't want to spend any more time than I needed here either.

Wandering behind the johnnys, I saw there was a clearing. About a metre of space separated the bathrooms from the fence. Though the breeze seemed to be blowing the smell my way, the fence captured it, and the odour was ten times worse. As bad as it seemed, it appeared to be the perfect spot to do business. I tweeted my position.

Immediately I received, "I'm real close, be there in five minutes."

I bided my time by holding my breath and listening to the retching coming from one of the stalls. In about ten minutes, a guy came running behind the row of washrooms. "Oh, good! You're still here!" he smiled.

"Good God, it stinks!" he added.

I held out the bag of hair, wanting to make my exit as soon as we'd completed our transaction. "A hundred, please," I asked.

"A hundred is fine," he said. "They're going for a hundred and a half on eBay this morning."

"That's it?" I asked.

"I made a bid, but now I hope somebody outbids me," he said, handing over the bill and taking the hair. "Cuz now I already have a lock! Hey, my buddy would want one, I'm sure. Can I run back and get him?"

"Can you call him or something?" I asked, almost begged.

"Nah, he lost his phone," the guy said. "I'll tweet you soon as I find him."

I agreed to this and the guy ran off. I figured I'd give him five minutes and then I'd go find some clean air. I was just about to leave when I got the tweet that the two of them were returning.

As I made the sale, I received a Facebook ping asking me if I was at the concert in Stoneland. I posted my location as soon as the two guys left, one of them wearing his t-shirt over his face to cut the stench. I waited for the response and it came back immediately, asking me to save a bag. I pulled one out of the backpack and waited.

Two girls shyly came around the corner. They didn't look any older than fifteen. None of us said anything; we just stared at one another. Finally I broke the ice. "Did you girls Facebook me?"

They both smiled. The one with the ginger hair said, "You're the one selling the hair? We didn't know what to expect. You look so normal."

"Sorry to disappoint," I said.

The one with the blondest hair I'd ever seen said, "No, we thought you might be some shady con man or something. You look like our mom."

"You guys were fans of Bradley Atwater?" I asked.

The blond said, "We grew up listening to The Noise. My mom loves them."

The ginger girl said, "Mom loves Brad, you mean." Then she got a little bit of a sad look on her face. "Loved Brad, I should say. He's been dead, what? Like a month now? And she's still broken up over it."

Her sister spoke up. "This is my sister and..."

"We're twins, actually," Ginger said.

"Really?" I said. "I have twin girls too."

"We thought it would be nice if we could surprise mom with A Lock of Bradley's Hair," Blondie said.

"Is she coming to the concert?" I asked.

"Oh, no!" Blondie laughed. "She's too old to go to concerts!"

"Actually, she probably would have come if Bradley was here," Ginger said. "How often does The Noise come to Stoneland?"

I held out the hair. "It's a hundred bucks," I said.

At this, the conversation sputtered as the girls shared an embarrassed look. "We bought a stupid Noise t-shirt for Mom before we found out you were here," Ginger said.

"It has Bradley's picture on it," Blondie added.

"So now we only have....," she counted the money in her hand, as well as the cash her sister shoved into her palm "...eighty dollars. We were wondering if you would take that?"

Both girls looked at me with identical pleading faces. I wondered if my twin daughters had ever pulled that trick with Kitty. I smiled and handed them a bag. "Only because you remind me of my girls."

"Thank you!" they both said, their body language relaxing. They gave me the money and before leaving, Ginger said, "You might want to move away from here. I think this place could be toxic."

I nodded, about to follow them, when another couple of girls showed up. I backed up a few paces and withdrew a bag. "A Lock of Bradley's Hair?"

"Not for me," the tall one said. "I think that's gross. Hair from a dead man's head."

"He was alive when it was cut," I said, turning my attention to the short girl with the thick glasses. "I should know. I was there."

She held out two hundred dollar bills. "Never mind her. I'll take two."

"Smart cookie," I said, taking out a second bag. "Hey, the show's about to start soon. You guys got good seats?"

"I didn't come for The Noise," said the short girl, putting the hair safely into the zippered purse belted to her waist. "I came for the hair."

They left and I stayed put, debating whether I should leave my base of operations. So far, I'd sold five bags of hair and noticed I hadn't felt a moment's panic. I knew no security guard in his right mind would come back here. I could smoke a reefer the size of a cigar and the urinal's stench would mask the blunt's odour. The smell of money is what kept me there.

Just before 4 PM, a man sporting a wicked sunburn came around the corner. He looked relieved to see me. I could tell he had been drinking though he didn't come off as being an idiot. "You're the roadie selling the hair?" he asked in a British accent.

"Are you looking to buy?" I asked.

He swayed to and fro in front of me. "It's for me girl," he declared. "We're here on holiday. She's a big fan of The Noise. When we found out the band was playing here, we managed to change our flight and stay so we could see them. She'll love me forever when I give her this, eh?"

I handed him the bag and received a hundred American dollars in exchange. Instead of walking out the way he came, the British man walked further along the little corridor of grass. About ten feet away from me, he unzipped his pants and took a horse's piss. The odd stench of his urine wafted over but I wasn't about to give up my patch of dirt.

A loudspeaker blared. "Ladies and gentleman, take your seats. The next show is about to begin."

I said to the man, "Looks like The Noise is going on now."

The man looked at me aghast. "Oh, I've got to find Minnie! We've got seats right up front." He shook his penis, tucked it back into his pants and did up his button. I didn't bother to tell him his fly was gapingly open. "Thanks for the hair!"

The man went flying out of there. I heard the emcee come on with forced enthusiasm, asking everybody to give it up for one of Canada's leading rock bands, The Noise! I walked over to the outer edge of the johns, where I could see the stage. Though the band members appeared as tiny matchsticks, the Jumbotron screens let me see them up close.

And it was worse than before. Instead of their usual hard-rock intro song, they opened with a song Tate had written years ago. Bradley and him had battled over it, I recalled. Brad claimed it was too hill-billy. They played it at one show in Cincinnati and it went over to little applause. Today it had the exact same effect. The Jumbotron caught Mickey giving Tate a 'told you so' look.

Tate stepped up to the mike. "Here's a song you like," he assured us. "We changed it up a bit. I hope you like it even more."

Now The Noise went into the song usually reserved as the opener. Though it wasn't the same without Bradley, at least it was rock n' roll. But after the first chorus, as a few fists started pumping the air, I saw a roadie run on stage and give Tate an instrument. It looked like a mandolin. Suddenly the rock song turned into a dull dreamy dirge. Tate sang the lyrics as if he was in slow-motion. As the song came to a close, the audience booed their approval.

The third song, a massive hit for the band, was played the way it was meant to be played. If one closed their eyes and shut off half their hearing, it almost sounded like The Noise. However, these people came to SEE the band and by now, somebody should have gotten the party started. The new guy was still sweating buckets, sitting on a stool and refusing to look at Tate. Tate stood glued to the microphone stand, every now and then holding the mic out to the audience. He expected the crowd to sing back the chorus to him but he received only a couple off-key responses. Mickey never moved to begin with and Stan was attached to his drum set.

At the end of the tune, Stan threw a drumstick in the air, trying for his signature move of catching it. He miscalculated and tried to grab it, falling off his chair. Those who missed this couldn't be blamed; they were probably rooted to the sight of Tate's ludicrous pose at the song's finale. He probably thought he looked RockGod-like; instead he looked like he was going to take a dive off a swimming dock.

I went back to my sales spot. I couldn't bear to witness their performance any longer. I'd rather hunker down in the rank putrid space behind the shit-holes. Anyway, I was getting used to the smell.

"We're in luck, she's still here," said a voice I recognized, breaking my reverie. "I brought you some customers."

It was the English dude. "Hey, I thought you'd be watching The Noise!" I said.

He scoffed. "You call that The Noise? I want to rush the stage and punch that guy Tate in the face."

There were three others with him. We all crowded further into the enclosure so we wouldn't be seen. One girl in a Noise t-shirt, standing taller than the man next to her, wrapped her arms around him and nuzzled the top of his head. "First time I ever saw my baby cry," she said. "After we get the hair, we're going to see if we can get our money back for the show."

I made two sales there and then waited what seemed like forever until the next customer showed up. He sauntered in and saw me. "You still here?" he asked.

I could tell by the song playing that the band was mangling its closing number. "You didn't stay for the end?" I asked the stranger.

"Who did?" was his response.

"Are you looking to buy?" I asked, knowing that came out sounding like I had drugs for sale. "I mean, do you want some hair?"

"Yeah, I'll take one," he said. "You never know, I can sell it on eBay and probably make a lot of money."

I handed the bag over and took his money. "I sold a lock two weeks ago for three hundred dollars," I said.

"Wow, they're probably only going to go up from there," he replied in awe. "Man, it smells like shit back here!" He figured it was time to beat a hasty exit.

The band was nearing the end of their set when I decided to take another peek. I was appalled to see the crowds gathered at the food booths and sales tents, at the line-ups for the urinals, everywhere but in the seats watching The Noise. The security guarding the front of the stage looked embarrassed, as if they were just hanging out with nothing to occupy them.

If I had been anticipating a lock-buying crowd, this was a rude awakening. Any possible takers would have made their appearance by now. Damn damn damn. Sales had been way worse than I thought they'd be - not the sell-out I'd experienced earlier. I slung my Hello Jiffy onto my back and finally left the safety of my malodorous meeting spot.

As I made the long trek to my car, no courtesy bus in sight, I tried to fight the miserable mood that came over me. I still made a little bit of money today, didn't I? Too bad that mysterious collector didn't show up. He always helped me make my quota.

No sooner had I thought this when my phone chirped, telling me I had another tweet. I checked it. Though it gave a weird name (@fanconnected), I suspected it came from my big spender. It read, "Sorry I missed you. See you in Fulton. As usual, I hope to buy the remainder of your stock."

Perhaps next time I'd take a few more than my usual twenty locks of Bradley's hair.

• • • • • • • • •

The backlash to the new version of The Noise was so severe, the next show would officially be their last. The remainder of their Rockin' Ontario tour was going to be cancelled. Not just due to lack of ticket sales; people who had bought tickets were now trying to return them. To make life easier, Blast Records just cancelled the rest of the tour.

I'd never been to Fulton. I knew it was outside of Toronto and I anticipated it would take some time to get there. When I googled it on Mapquest, I was pleased to see it was less than an hour from home. I then mapped the distance from the Fulton Leisure Centre to the nearest casino. Tribes Casino came up as only ten minutes away. Man oh man, was I getting into Kitty's good books!

The Tribes Casino was just the size I liked. Not too gigantic but still big enough to find plenty of machines to play. It was also less than a minute off the main highway. To my chagrin, I saw it was another OGG joint so no free money. I told Kitty I'd play five bucks for an hour and then think about leaving for the concert. We parted ways since it was Saturday and the chance of finding slot machines beside each other were slim.

When I caught up with her at the Lucky Fountain game, I was up twenty dollars. "I love this place!" I trilled to Kitty. "I can't lose! I don't want to go to work."

Kitty gave me a stern look. "No, no, Tammy, don't let gambling interfere with your job. That means you have a problem."

I almost didn't give a damn if the concert got their fan-wear. Who cared? It wasn't like the band would be together after tonight. I doubted I would get into trouble if Blast Records didn't receive the pittance the sales would bring. And I was actually having quite a good time, gambling my nickel wager and winning winning winning. Five dollar wins! Nine dollar wins! The voucher in my pocket was just itching to be inserted into another machine.

On the other hand, damn my conscience, I wanted to appear the dutiful daughter. Besides, Tribes Casino wasn't going anywhere. They were open 24/7. I made a ticked off face and said, " Don't worry, I'm going. You stay and have all the fun."

Again I warned her it may be hours before she next saw me, but I was no longer apprehensive about it. Time stood still for Kitty when she was playing the slots. If I came back next Tuesday, I'm sure she'd still be awake and playing her forty cent bets.

I zipped back to Fulton and found their Leisure Centre. It looked like there was an auditorium as well as work-out facilities, a hockey arena and a swimming pool. I parked the car and grabbed the box of fan-wear. I threw on my vendor's badge and headed into the centre. Presenting myself to the security guard, I indicated the box I had and told him my business.

The guard must have been bored as he decided to open the box and give it a thorough search. "Hey, hey, try not to wrinkle everything," I advised.

"Do you have any bottles or alcohol?" the guard asked.

I pointed to my vendor badge. "I'm just here to work," I said. "Can I go in now and drop off this stuff? I...I'll probably be back with another load." That was my usual plan, but I was getting a bad feeling about this guy. He seemed to be one of only two guards in sight. The other was a buxom woman whose shirt buttons were straining; she was chatting up a janitor.

The guard, who had a tattoo of Satan playing drums on his inner arm, thumbed me in. I found a dinky table set up and a teen-age girl sitting behind it. "Excuse me," I said. "Can you tell me where I can find the booth where they're selling t-shirts and stuff?"

"Oh, it's right here," the gum-popping kid said. "Are you the lady with the band?"

"With The Noise?" I asked. In the old days, I'd have jumped on the chance to stake my claim to peripheral fame, but now? I wanted no association with Tate and his mess. "No, I just work for the record company. Here's your box of fan-wear."

"Don't get pissed off if I don't sell many," the girl warned me. "It's like nowhere near sold out. It's like not even half sold out."

"Is it a big space?"

"The auditorium?" she asked, eyes wide. "It's huge! I bet it holds like a thousand people."

And if not even five hundred were showing up, I didn't think that boded well for my own sales. As I left the card table/merchandise booth, I did a walk around the premises. I could see they'd closed off part of the Leisure Centre so that The Noise fans would not be mistaken for the hockey players. Past the barricades and down the hall, I could see guys arriving with massive bags slung over their backs. If one listened hard enough, you could hear slapshots being taken.

I popped into the auditorium and surprised a guard sitting in one of the seats. He jumped up and asked for my ticket. I just took a quick peek, saw it was probably the smallest venue The Noise had ever played and beat a hasty retreat. I walked over to a small snack shop set up, not yet open for business, and saw there was nowhere to go past that point. I considered using the washroom to conduct sales, but that would limit them to females only.

Giving the same guard a nod on my way out, I headed for my car, tweeting as I walked. "At The Noise's FINAL concert! The LAST locks of Bradley's hair to be sold TONITE!!! $50!"

I sent the tweet before I could change my mind. Yeah, that was quite the price reduction from before. However, eBay sales had stopped and I still had lots of product left. Maybe this would spike interest.

The concert was due to start in less than an hour and still the parking lot was empty. I started up the car and went on a drive-around. There were now a couple additional guards standing outside the venue. I drove around to the other end of the Centre where the rink was. The lot was filled with cars and guys standing around shooting the shit. I managed to drive behind the building where I encountered a mammoth pile of artificial snow. A Zamboni was dumping more of the white stuff, scraped off the rink's ice, onto the mound.

Driving back to the entrance near the concert, I saw a few cars starting to trickle in. My phone chirped and I saw I had a twitter message. "Where are u?" I knew it wasn't from my mother so it had to be a potential buyer. The problem is, where was I going to be? Inside was too small, too cramped, nowhere to hide. Somehow I'd known, once I'd spotted that unusual snowbank, that it would enter my scenario. I tweeted the location and that I would be there in the next few minutes.

I could have driven back there but I just didn't want to be seen in my personal ride. I lifted up the trunk of the Town Car and prepared myself for the awkward load I was about to deliver. Instead of the twenty bags of locks in my Hello Jiffy knapsack, I now had two large shopping bags full of hair. My plan was to sell more today so I initially packed double the usual. Those forty bags totally filled my knapsack but then I checked out

eBay and saw nothing had moved. It was the same with Kijiji and Craigslist. There were a couple lame requests from fan-sites but they looked like
more bother than they were worth. Hence, the new low price and my
trunk full of the remaining locks of hair.

As I walked up to the snowbank, I was pleased to see three guys standing there. I didn't give a thought to my safety; my mind was on making
enough money tonight to cover one year of one of my children's university education. A cool ten grand.

I laid the bags down. "You the guys who tweeted me?" I asked.

"I did," said one of the guys. "The Noise fucking rocks. I'm going to
make this the start of my collection."

I was about to speak but held my tongue, simply holding out a bag. He
held out a fifty and in a quick exchange, we made the trade. "How about
you guys?" I asked the other two. "Only fifty bucks."

"Nah, we're just here to keep him company," one of the buddies said.

"Well, thanks then," I said as they moved off. I couldn't hold it anymore. "You know the band's done, right? This is their last concert."

There were yelps of disbelief and a stricken look came over the new
collector.

I waited by the snowbank and only moved when the Zamboni came
out the rear doors and deposited more ice shards and snow onto the pile.
Once it had re-entered the building, I checked my watch and saw it was
nearly time for the concert to begin. Wondering if I hadn't tweeted my
location correctly - maybe I'd only sent it to that one guy! - I re-sent my
position.

I had barely pressed 'send' when I saw a woman walking up to me in
stiletto heels. She had on a black leather skirt and a black bustier. "Jesus!"
she yelled from far away. I looked around, wondering if His Holiness had
made an appearance. She came closer and repeated herself. "Jesus! Could
you have gotten any farther from the concert?"

"Are you looking for me?" I asked innocently.

She stopped short. "Oh please tell me you're the one who's selling
Bradley's hair."

"Alright, yeah, I can tell you that," I said, reaching into my bag and taking out a package. "They're on sale tonight. Fifty dollars."

"I heard, that's great," she replied. "I'll take two. My boyfriend and I were big fans of Bradley Atwater. I still can't believe he's dead. Jesus, I'm freezing and standing by this snow isn't helping. The concert is about to start; I'm heading back."

"OK, thanks for coming all this way," I said.

"No, thank you!" she said emphatically. "I really, really loved Brad and now I have something to remember him by."

Her kind words kept me energized for the next ten minutes. I heard the band start up and saw they now went with a completely new intro song. With another ten shows, it may have gotten good. Right now, it sounded under-rehearsed and lame. The second song was marred by feedback so bad, the band was forced to stop. A second start resulted in an earsplitting (even from where I was standing) screech from the amplifiers. A voice came over the loud-speaker, announcing a half-hour break for technical problems.

I immediately sent out a tweet. "Last chance b4 they're gone! Get them NOW during break! $50! Snowbank behind ice rink!" I awaited the throngs.

One person showed up. He could have been Willie Nelson's twin. I saw him coming, wheezing and puffing, stopping once to adjust a strap holding his fake leg onto his knee. I grabbed a couple bags and met him partway.

He withdrew a fifty from a wallet that was chained to his belt. "Sorry to make you come so far," I apologized.

"Hey, I understand," the ol' guy said. "I used to scalp Leaf tickets down at the Gardens. Always trying to avoid security."

"How many you want?" I asked. He held out a fifty so I handed him one bag and took his money. "Hey, you tweet?" I asked.

"What'd you call me?" he looked insulted.

"No, no, I mean...do you tweet? I sent out a message on twitter...," I tried to explain but he kept shaking his head. He was as old-fashioned as my mother. How I wished that Kitty would get with the times, if only to learn how to text.

"Can't say I know about that stuff," Willie said. "I don't even own a cell phone. I'm at the concert with my son and he got some kind of message on his smart-ass phone and he sent me out here."

I nodded but inwardly, I sniffed. Some son. Willie limped off and I resumed my post by the snowbank. I heard the announcement for everybody to take their seats again as the show was about to (re)start. I cursed aloud and then, because nobody was around to tell me to watch my tongue, I swore one more time - a choice word I had been saving up but had no occasion to use.

"Motherfucker!" I said, wondering if the word even fit. "Well, that's it! We are now closed...for good!" With that, I bent down to pick up my bags.

"Looks like you could use some business," a voice piped up.

I was so startled, I screamed and fell on my ass into the prickly, sharp snow. I jumped up quickly and faced the speaker. It was the guy who'd bought heavily off me before - the one who was probably flipping Bradley's hair for a quick buck.

"Sorry, didn't mean to scare you," he said. "I saw your tweet as I was pulling into the place."

"You just got here?" I asked suspiciously. "I didn't see you coming."

He gestured to the other side of the snowbank. "I came around that side. Closer parking lot. So you're quitting early? You're not doing the backstage door thing?"

I shook my head. "Too much security."

"You were busy tonight?" he asked, perhaps a bit warily.

"Oh, yeah!" I said, hyping the meagre sales. "The Noise may soon be quiet for good, but people still want A Lock of Bradley's Hair!"

I was waiting for it and he didn't disappoint. "How many you got left?"

"Two hundred, give or take four," I replied. "You can have the lot for ten grand. If not, I'm just going to sell them on eBay. It takes longer, but it's a bigger payday."

He looked at me for a moment and then said, "Give me a second." He walked off two steps and started sending out a message on his cell-phone. For someone dressed so dreary and rundown, he sure had a top-of-the-line iPhone. He came back to me moments later. "I'll give you five thousand and you'll never have to see my face again."

I debated with myself for perhaps a micro-second. "I hope you make a killing," I said. That was all he needed to hear as he counted out crisp hundred dollar bills. I took them and pointed out the two large shopping bags. "They're all yours."

He scooped them up and disappeared behind the snowbank. I made sure my money was secure, noticing I was in a dark abandoned area for the first time. I'd just taken a few steps to go back to my car when the guard with the satanic drummer tattoo came around the corner. "Hey, you!" he shouted.

In a jerky, cartoony manner, I started to run, because I was the bad guy and he was the good guy. But I stopped after one step when I realized I had no hair on me. And then a sad realization when I thought - I have no hair? I didn't even keep a lock for myself? I stopped my momentum and asked, "Who, me?"

"Are you the girl selling A Lock of Bradley's Hair?"

"Selling Alloca what?"

"Listen, did you see a girl with high heels and wearing all leather?"

I nodded. "Yeah...I saw her." Can't convict me for just seeing some-body.

"Please tell me she bought TWO locks of hair!" he implored, clutch-ing my shoulder.

"She did," I allowed.

The security guard almost collapsed in ecstasy. "Oh, thank God! We had a hundred saved up and then you go and sell them for fifty! So I texted her to buy two but I didn't know if she got the text. It'd be great to have two, in case we ever... you know ... break up. Then we'd both have one."

"Smart," I replied.

This time he clapped my shoulder. "I gotta get back to work," he said. "They think I'm patrolling the parking lot. But I just want to tell you, the band tonight - the ones calling themselves The Noise? They suck. There'll never be another Brad Atwater. He was one of a kind. Let me say this, what you're doing is righteous." A squawk came over his radio so he waved and took off.

I was back at Tribes sooner than I'd hoped. And though I had thou-sands of dollars at my disposal, I left it all in the car and took in my twenty dollar voucher. Six hours later, I was very ready to leave, but first had to cash in my ticket which had grown to forty dollars.

The Noise was finished, I'd gotten rid of all that hair, and I was com-ing home with money. I was a winner in all ways today. If only my run of good luck would last.

CHAPTER XIV

I lost that winning feeling pretty quickly. For two days after the Fulton show and Tribes Casino, I did nothing but sleep and watch feel-good YouTube videos. The truth was, I was glad to be finished with that lousy job. Being the fan club president of three bands I didn't care for had been draining me of my joie de vivre! I just wanted to relax and not have a single worry in the world.

On Wednesday, I received two emails, both from my twin daughters. They had to come up with the balance of their school tuition and submitted the amount needed. The figure was absurd. I went down to the living room, where Kitty was watching an old black and white movie.

"Hey, mom, the girls sent me their tuition notice," I said, laying the laptop in front of her. "Look how much Tatum is asking for! She's gotta be scamming me."

Kitty lifted up the laptop as if it was a bag of potatoes. She brought her eyes to the screen and then nodded. "Maybe she is scamming you," Kitty agreed. "It's three hundred more than last year." She giggled, thinking she'd really cracked a funny one.

I was in no mood for joking. "So I guess Sadie's is correct too?" I clicked to the other twin's message and held the computer in front of Kitty's face.

"If I recall, that's exactly the same as last year," she replied.

I slammed the computer shut. "That's just for school?!" I tried not to freak. "Never mind their rooms and food and...frickin'....nail polish!" I started to walk away and then wheeled around. "Oh my God, and then there's Rain! How much is he going to cost me?"

"Don't worry about Rain," Kitty said. "I paid his tuition in August. That's when his school required it."

"I told you, Mom, I'm home now," I said, rather harshly. "Time for me to start looking after my own kids."

Storming back up to my room, I pulled out my Hello Jiffy knapsack and counted all the money I had saved from selling hair. Whatever money I'd collected from eBay had already gone to my own bills. The cash in front of me just barely covered the twins tuitions. Obviously I'd have to find a job sooner than I'd anticipated.

I pulled up Kijiji on the computer and went to the help wanted ads. When it came to the box asking what type of job I wanted, I stared at it for a good five minutes. What did I do? What was I? Secretary? President? I typed in 'assistant road manager' and all sort of replies popped up. Road asphalt-laying workers needed, all sorts of assistants wanted at minimum pay and loads of qualified managers desired. I expanded my search and added 'rock band assistant road manager'. That came up with a grand total of 0 replies.

Did I even want that lifestyle again? I decided to make a cup of coffee and went downstairs. Kitty was dragging her laundry basket to the top of the stairs. "I'll take that down for you," I said. "I can throw it in the washer too."

"Thank you, Tammy," she said. "And I'm sorry if I made you mad about paying Rain's tuition."

"No, I'm sorry I yelled at you," I replied. "Actually, it's good you did pay it; I couldn't afford it. I had no idea schools cost so much! So now I guess I owe you."

"I can pay the girls' tuition too," she added. "You don't have to owe me."

"Mom! Please! Stop thinking you have to take care of us all the time," I said firmly. "I can make the girls tuition myself. I saved up some money," I added proudly. See how good I am, Mother? Kitty had always tried to instil a save-for-a-rainy-day mentality in me.

"It's just that I know your job doesn't pay a lot," Kitty said. "Oh, see my vest there?" she asked, pointing to her gambling attire in the laundry basket. "I spilled coffee on it at Tribes. Can you use some of that stain-release spritzer? I don't want to look grubby next time you take me somewhere."

Oh, yeah, I forgot to tell Kitty about my current predicament. I was about to break the news when she came over to show me the stain on the vest.

"It's right on the pocket where I keep my money," she pointed. "The zippered one. I can't wait to see where you take me this weekend, Tammy! I love going to these new casinos." She sighed with contentment.

"You know my job that barely pays anything?" I began. "Well...it's no more. All three bands are done. I'm out of a job."

Kitty froze solid. Just her mouth barely moved. "That can't be. There's four more weeks left on The Noise's schedule. You told me. Eight shows over eight weeks."

"The rest of the tour got cancelled," I replied, shrugging. "Nothing I can do about it. That's showbiz."

"So now what?"

"So now I have to find a new job," I answered. "Life goes on, right?"

• • • • • • • • • •

My flippant remark may have been the germ that made Kitty sick. Not in a physical way where she had a fever or was throwing up, but in a psychological way. Life goes on? Sure, but who said it had to go smoothly?

That very night, as I tried to get a good sleep in preparation for a job interview the next morning (at a Chapters bookstore as a shelf-stocker), I was awakened by the sound of the TV blaring. I went downstairs. Kitty was watching the same movie she'd seen earlier that day.

"Mom, it's too loud!" I said, turning down the volume. "And you watched this already. Go to bed!"

"I didn't see the ending," Kitty said. "You go to bed."

"Fine, just keep it down," I said. Two hours later I woke up, stifling from heat. I'd already kicked off all my covers and was still covered in sweat. Again I stormed downstairs and saw Kitty had turned the heat up and had it cranked to Texas summer temperatures. I went around looking for her to give her hell and found her snoring in her bed. I managed to fall back asleep, only to be woken again. Kitty was roaming the halls.

Once more I faced her. "Mom, please, the sun isn't even up yet," I said. "What are you doing?"

"Getting some exercise," was her answer. "I found my pedometer and

I'm trying to get ten thousand steps in."

"How about I take you for a walk tomorrow?" I asked, groggily turning back to my room.

"Where?" Kitty promptly asked.

"I don't know!" I yelled. "To Goodwill maybe. The bus stop and back. I don't know!" I slammed my door shut and went to try and grab whatever sleep I could in the last couple hours before my alarm went off.

The interview didn't go well. Being late probably had a lot to do with it.

Berating my mother over my lack of sleep, I forbade her to leave her bedroom that night. I had two interviews lined up the next day and I wanted to nail one of the jobs. The Starbucks manager one appealed to me the most. The Humane Society receptionist job would be OK only because it was just around the corner from home.

We both went to bed at midnight. At 1 AM., I awoke to a strange noise. As my ears tried to make sense of it, I crept cautiously out of my bedroom and into the hallway. The sound was coming from Kitty's room - a soft moaning followed by muted whimpering.

Knocking on the door, I asked, "Mom, is something the matter?" I walked on in. In the old days, I would have asked if I may enter, but these days I'd seen more of my mother's body than I care to express.

Kitty had old photo albums spread across her bed. She'd been looking at pictures of my Dad, something I'd rarely seen her do. She beckoned me over to look at a photo of my father in his scientist clothes. "Oh, Tammy, wasn't he so handsome? And such a brilliant mind!" she stroked the picture as lovingly as I'd seen her stroke the roses on the Golden Goddess slot machine. "I'm glad I chose him over anyone else. Otherwise, we wouldn't have had you."

"Yeah, like I'm quite the prize," I replied.

"He would have adored your children," she dismissed my remark. Patting the bed next to her, she said, "Sit, Tammy, you probably haven't seen these in a long time."

"Mom, I have to go to bed. I have those interviews tomorrow," I said.

Kitty turned a page in the photo book and then began the low moan as she saw the wedding pictures. "I was so in love with this man!" Kitty cried. Her tears spilled onto the page and I sat down and used the sleeve of my nightgown to wipe them off.

"I'll look at them for a minute and then I have to go to sleep," I said. The honeymoon, my birth, my first this and that, ending with the guests gathered at my father's - I guess you could call it - funeral afterparty. "That was the worst day of my life," Kitty reminisced. "Not the day he died but the day of his funeral. Having to be so sad in public. I didn't know half the people there. I just wanted to be alone to grieve him."

Mom seemed to get sleepy as the viewing session came to an end. Thank goodness, because I was barely keeping my eyes open. I picked up the photo albums and returned them into the box she kept under her bed. "Now go to sleep, Mom," I whispered, turning off her lamp.

One hour later, I again woke to a noise. This was almost animalistic in nature - a keening that went from a low pitch to a higher volume. The first place I decided to check was Kitty's bedroom again. I simply knocked and walked in.

Strewn across the bed were mementoes of my children's school years. Kitty had something cradled in her arms and was rocking back and forth. "Mom, it's three in the morning!" I complained. "I thought you went to bed!"

"Oh, Tammy, look what I found!" she hiccuped tearfully, holding out a large home-made Mother's Day card. It was a combined effort of all three of my kids; their school photos from early elementary years appearing as the centres of crayoned flowers. Inside, written in Rain's always-precise printing, was a poem. The gist of it was that there was no Grandmother's Day and since Kitty was just like a mother to them, she deserved recognition. The back of the card had about a thousand x's and o's on it.

"That's what's making you cry so much?" I had to ask.

"Did you ever see Rain's Grade Twelve report card?" she inquired. "His teachers wrote such glowing praise, he was such a good student. Tammy, read this...." She pulled out a report card and I dutifully read it, nodding.

"I always knew he was smart," I said, yawning. "Now, how about...."

Kitty thrust another report card at me. "And look at this one, at what it says about Sadie in Grade Three? Her teacher was spot on, don't you think? She's just like that now!"

I read how Sadie had a strong personality, would be a natural leader, would go on to great things. I'm sure the teacher wrote that on half the report cards. "OK, I read it," I said. "Now put this sh...stuff away and go to bed."

"Just let me show you a couple things," Kitty begged. A couple things turned into a couple hours. Kitty just wouldn't let me go to bed. Maybe I'm not the sensitive type of mother, but a Thanksgiving turkey made out of your handprint, or a self-portrait constructed from macaroni, would have been discarded long ago.

After we'd seen everything she'd collected over the past fifteen years, I was allowed to pack it back into the big suitcase she kept in her closet. It weighed close to fifty pounds and had to be wedged back into place. I wondered how she got it out.

Managing to grab a couple hours sleep, I showed up for my Starbucks interview. I was offered a cup of their delicious coffee and in my sleep-deprived stupor, I drank it down like I was dying of thirst. Seriously burning my tongue, I spat it out onto the clipboard in front of the interviewer. That was one quick interview and something told me to forget it. As for the Humane Society, I was told I could arrive anytime between 9 AM and 4 PM for the interview. I chose 3 PM and arrived after a quick afternoon nap at home. They'd already filled the position. Since the next day was Saturday, nothing was shaking. I ended up having to spend the day at home with my mother and there was some kind of black energy in the house. No matter what I said, what I suggested, I was met with a dark stare. She retreated to her bedroom and spent most of the day sleeping.

At supper, she picked the carrots out of her mixed vegetables, flicking each one off her plate with a sharp fork-stroke. She was making a mess and being very unlike the tidy Kitty Canseco of old. "I hope you're having fun," I said sarcastically.

"Most fun I've had all week," came her equally sarcastic reply.

"You've been cooped up in the house for days," I said. "Let's go out tomorrow and do something."

"Oh, yay," Kitty said in a condescending voice. "Whoopee. What do you have in mind? Do you want to take me out for a COFFEE? A stroll?" She pushed her plate away. "I'm not eating this excuse of a meal."

With that, she stood up and started to trounce out of the kitchen. Before she could go back up to her room, I said, "I thought maybe we'd try that bus to Niagara Falls."

Kitty knew damn well we weren't going to see the breathtaking water-fall. She whipped around and this time her "Yay! Whoopee!" was for real. She flung herself back down into her chair and pulled her plate of food towards her. She even made sure I saw her retrieve a carrot from between the salt and pepper shakers and pop it into her mouth.

I knew I made her happy just now and in return, Kitty was trying her best to please me. Sometimes she broke my heart.

•••••••••

This was a new casino adventure, so we arrived way too early at the bus's pick-up location. The Kato bus was always on schedule; we assumed it would be the same with this bus. With over half an hour to spare, Kitty regaled me with tales of her last visit to The Falls Casino. I totally recalled my cup of coffee and had a toonie already earmarked for it.

When the bus was fifteen minutes late, I began to worry, thinking that maybe it was full and neglected us. However, there was a gaggle of people standing around who didn't get on the City Transit bus; I assumed they were also going to the casino.

The bus eventually trundled along and we got on board. Finding a couple seats together, I was thrilled to hear we were the last pick-up - it would be highway sailing until we got there. And to boot, the bus driver put on a comedy movie I'd never seen. Kitty and I paid our five dollar tariff. I settled back to watch the flick; Kitty instantly fell asleep. What a pleasant way to waste ninety minutes on a Sunday afternoon.

The movie ended just as we were pulling into the entrance to the ca-sino. Sure enough, the Tim Horton's coffee shop was just inside. I realized it was close to the supper hour and urged Kitty to grab a bite. She wolfed down a twelve-grain bagel while I ordered my large cup of coffee.

At the entrance to the casino, we agreed to split up and meet in our usual two hours. Kitty took off like she knew where she was going. I with-drew five dollars out of my wallet and went to find a penny machine de-serving of my cash.

I remembered the game with the soothing sounds and delicate graph-ics. I knew it was near the corner of the vast casino and I set off to find it. With my head in all directions but straight ahead, I almost walked into a wheelchair parked at the side of a machine. I quickly averted it, though the man in the chair was oblivious to me.

The Lotus Flower was two machines away from the wheelchair bound man. A customer was playing it and I saw he still had over twenty dollars in the machine. He was wagering a dollar a spin so hopefully he'd be getting off soon. I didn't want to appear as a stalker so I edged away and looked at the machine the guy in the wheelchair was playing. It was then that I got a closer look at the big picture. There were not one but sort of two people playing the machine. I could see the gaming chair was bolted into the floor; thus the man had to play over to the side of it. There was a woman sitting in the chair next to him. She was just as old, both were probably in their late eighties, and I assumed she was his wife. I watched the way she tenderly lifted his hand and placed it on the spin button to make a bet, withdrawing it only to keep it warm in her two hands.

My eyes were riveted to the pair. My peripheral vision caught the man at my Lotus Flower stand up, but only to withdraw his wallet out of his back pocket. He opened it, glanced inside for a long moment and then angrily withdrew a ten dollar bill. He inserted it into the machine and started slamming the spin button. I hoped he wouldn't bruise my fragile zen-like game before I got to it.

I inched a bit closer to the old couple to see what kind of bet they were making. I don't know what's up with old people, but they all seemed in a hell of a hurry to get rid of their savings. I regularly saw senior citizens making bets equal to their age. When I saw the old lady, who was wearing bandages on her ankles as well as her arms, was limiting themselves to ten cent bets, I thought it would ease my melancholy over this couple. Instead, I worried if they could afford it. Or if the old guy had an addiction and in their declining years, the wife said, Fuck it, I'll be an enabler, if it makes him happy.

Suddenly the old gal let out a laugh. "Look, Rene, we won five of a kind!" She put the man's hands in his lap and then lifted his chin to face the screen. Images of spilling coins filled it and a horn blared. The words BIG WIN flashed at the top of it all. Their ten cent bet had won them forty dollars. I was so happy for them, I could have cried.

Moving away, I then stood behind the man playing Lotus Flower. He knew I was there. I suspected he had no money left. He won a couple bucks when he was almost down to nothing and instead of being grateful, he slapped out three more bets.

He lost and I moved into his warm seat. Inserting my five dollar bill, I mentally told the machine I'd treat it nicer. I placed a five cent bet, only to have the bonus come up immediately. For the rest of my time at the casino, that five dollar bill was the only time I used up any of my own money in a slot machine. I'd had it up to twelve bucks at one point, down to nine cents at another, but I managed to make it last.

Coming home, the bus driver announced our stop would be the first one. I smiled. We were always last on the Kato bus. I took a sip of my coffee, bought with the remaining $1.60 of my winnings. I didn't mind this bus trip one bit. Maybe I shouldn't have bought this third coffee of the night though, considering I still had a ninety minute ride ahead of me. I glanced up to see a man walking down the aisle. As he passed me, I craned my head and saw him enter a washroom at the back.

Now I was content. With all costs tallied, this trip today had cost me less than twenty dollars. With an on-board washroom included, who could ask for a more stimulating outing? I thought we might take this trip again one day.

• • • • • • • • • •

It had been my intention to make a grandiose announcement to Kitty. We would make The Falls Casino in Niagara Falls a weekly trip. I felt secure knowing that, if she had something to look forward to every Sunday, then she would behave like a proper little old lady the rest of the week.

On Tuesday I had an appointment near the airport - another interview for a receptionist position. This one was at the Special Touch Spa. As I sped north up Highway 422, I saw a sign posted on the side of the road. It simply announced that FiveStar Casino was coming up at the next exit.

Though there were quite a few job seekers, I felt I was engaged and charming in the interview. The bosses seemed interested and promised me they'd call me later in the day if they wanted me to come back.

At 4 PM, I got the call and yes, they did want me to come back - for another interview. Still, this was more progress than I'd made with my last few efforts at getting a job.

As I was tearing open a box of fish n' chips to pop into the oven for dinner, I looked over at Kitty. She was reading the newspaper's financial section, using a magnifying glass to help her see better. Look at her, I thought, she must be bored beyond belief.

"Hey, so I got another interview with that spa place," I said. "It's one exit past FiveStar Casino. They want me there at nine tomorrow. I'm going to have to leave early, what with rush hour..."

"So close to FiveStar Casino?"

"Not real close," I amended. "I just passed the sign. It's like fifteen minutes away."

"But it's on the way?" Kitty asked. I gave a grudging nod. "Maybe you could drop me off before your interview?"

"I don't know," I said. "I plan on leaving super early. I don't what to be late 'cuz of traffic."

"I'll be ready," she said calmly. "I was wondering when we'd go to a casino again!" I didn't bother to remind her we'd just been to one the day before last. As soon as my alarm clock sounded the next morning, I flew out of bed. I ran downstairs to put on a pot of coffee, only to discover Kitty dressed and ready to go. She'd already made coffee; her usual weak, barely brown batch. I wished I could mimic my kids, the way they jokingly forbid Kitty to make coffee. She jokingly obliged them. There was no way I was going to be the one making coffee all the time though.

I gave myself over two hours to drive what was normally about a forty-minute trip. I didn't realize I was going away from downtown while everybody else was driving in. The trip to the casino took less time than I expected.

"You're going to be awfully early for your interview," Kitty said. "That'll look good to your employers."

"It's a little too early," I said. "I doubt they're even open."

"Do you want to come into the casino for a bit?" she asked.

"Yeah, if only to grab a cup of coffee."

As I walked into the gaming centre and saw the security guard at the entrance, it suddenly hit me that it wasn't even eight o'clock in the morning. Who comes to gamble at that time? I couldn't even look the guard in the eye as I mumbled a good morning in response to his hearty welcome. I seriously felt like such a low-life; so addicted to gambling, I had to show up at the breakfast hour! I was glad I had my mother with me to lend me some respect.

The casino wasn't busy but as usual, there were still people every-where. At this hour, there appeared to be as many staff as patrons. The employees were polishing machines from top to bottom. They were spraying a vinegary smelling solution on chairs and wiping them down. Vacuum machines droned loudly. Many slot machines were barricaded off and were being serviced en masse.

Kitty and I sat at a couple empty machines - Thunderhorn and Bee Lucky. Next to Kitty sat a man looking dapper in a three-piece suit. We had barely sat down when he won a bonus on Arabian Fortunes. He had his machine on silent volume, but the flashing sign clearly read that he'd won almost a hundred bucks.

He looked over at us and winked. He really had a handsome rakish air and was about my age. If only he wasn't gambling, especially a $1.20 bet, I might have made a pass at him. "Maybe I should just take the money and run," he said, pressing the button to cash out. "I hope my luck is as good in court today!" He took his voucher out of the machine, picked up a briefcase by his feet and stood up. "Good luck, ladies," he said as he departed.

He'd barely disappeared when a woman plopped into his seat. "One more machine and then I must leave," she said to nobody in particular. I saw her placing forty cent bets. She'd barely let the machine finish its spin before hitting the re-spin button again. It seemed she couldn't spend her money fast enough. When the bonus came up, she didn't even notice at first; she was so busy pounding the spin button. It paid her next to noth-ing so she cashed out in a huff.

Instead of leaving, she jumped onto the machine next to me, Aloha Delights. "I don't really like this one," she said to me. "It doesn't give bo-nuses, like every other machine."

"Sometimes it pays pretty good though, " I said. Once it'd paid me ten bucks on four parrots in a row.

"Nothing is paying out this morning," she groused. "I should just quit and get to work already." She took twenty out of her purse and inserted it into the machine. "When this is done, I'm done."

I noticed she was dressed almost identical to me. I wore my sole busi-ness suit - what I considered a prim and proper receptionist would wear, complete with high-collared white blouse and stylish flats. Showing that I

was there to work and not make a fashion statement. "What do you do?"
I asked.

"I teach high school French," she said, conversing in a normal tone but
spastically hitting the spin button like she had a bad muscle spasm in her
hand. I had never seen money go down so fast. It was like the machine
knew this gal was going to spend her twenty bucks, no matter what, so
why not just get it over with. She was going twenty spins without winning. When she did, the amount was dismal.

On her final bet, probably three minutes after she'd sat down, it looked
like she was going to get a good win. However, the last piece didn't fall
into the order needed and her money was gone. "Shit!" she said.

"Merde," I corrected her.

She glanced at her watch and then took out her wallet. She stared into
space a moment and then threw her wallet back into her purse. "Gotta go,
I was late yesterday, can't have it happen again," she muttered.

"You can say you were stuck in traffic," I suggested.

She threw her purse over her shoulder. "I wish," she pouted. "Where I
work though? Not even five minutes from home and they know it. Yesterday I said I wasn't feeling well."

"And last week? What'd you say?"

I said that in jest but the teacher replied, "I said I couldn't find my
keys."

Once she was gone, I played alongside Kitty until my five dollars was
spent. It didn't take long on the two machines I tried. "I'm going to my
interview now," I told my mother. "I don't know how long it will take so
I don't know when we can meet up. Can you keep your cell phone on?"

She didn't even look up from her game. "Sometimes it's too loud in
here. I can't hear it when it rings."

"Well, then, how about you check it every so often?" I sighed. "If you
see a missed call and it's my number, then you call me back, ok?"

"Good luck, Tammy, I really hope you get this job," my mother said.
"Imagine! I could come here five days a week!"

When I arrived at The Special Touch Spa, I saw there were still more
applicants vying for the same job. Looking them over, I decided I was the
best dressed for an office job. One girl wore an overly low-cut blouse and
still felt the need to leave the top button undone. Another girl had on a

dress slit up to the thigh. The boss sat all the women in a big room before taking us in for separate interviews. He gave a little speech.

"We need two girls," Enrico began. "You all passed the first stage but we had a lot of qualified applicants. Before you decide if you want this job, there's a few things you should know." He looked around at all of us. "First thing, we often have people calling in sick or not showing up. What we need is a couple dolls who can come in on short notice."

A cute redhead spoke up. "I have two kids at home," she said. "I'd need time to find a babysitter."

"You can leave now," Enrico said. The woman laughed, as if he made a witty remark. He didn't continue speaking, just waited for the redhead to leave. She looked at the rest of us and then, snapping up her shoulder bag, she stormed out. "Anybody else have a problem?" None of us spoke a word. "On to the next thing - our clientele is 99% men."

"That's unusual," said a woman to my right. "Spas are usually for women."

"What are you, a racist?" Enrico asked harshly. "We get men from all around the world, thanks to us being near the airport. We also have a large local base of regulars. The more customers, the better."

The same woman spoke again, obviously trying to make amends. "I have a background in marketing," she piped up. "I can help you put ads in the paper, put out flyers..."

"Are you trying to cause trouble?" he retorted. "We have ads in the paper, right where everybody else has 'em...in the classified section. You know what? You can leave."

Once again, Enrico went silent. The marketing whiz did the exact same thing as the redhead - started off with a nervous laugh, saw the boss was serious, flounced out. I was starting to get a dislike for Enrico but I needed a job...and at this rate, my chances were looking better. I kept my mouth shut.

"Last thing," Enrico continued. "If you get hired, you've got to show up dressed for the job. You got that?" The boss now directed his full attention on me. "Dressed to kill."

I was pleased the boss made note of my attire. Compared to all the other applicants, I was by far the most professional looking. In my shin-length business skirt with matching button-up jacket, complete with the white blouse and the plouffe of lace at the collar, I was the epitome of a high-class receptionist.

My personal interview went well, I thought. I stressed that I needed a job and would be at their beck and call. Maybe I came across as a bit subservient but I was agreeable to their pay-scale as well as the ungodly hours I'd be asked to work. They were open 24/7. I batted my eyelashes and acted like Enrico was the most important man in the universe.

Before I left, Enrico said he had to look at a few more girls and that he'd make his choice later today. I shook his hand with the both of mine, wishing I'd remembered to moisturize them. I gave him the most brilliant smile I've ever used and headed back to the casino.

Unbelievably, Kitty was still sitting at Thunderhorn. "Have you been here the whole time?" I asked incredulously.

She nodded as she made yet another bet. "It had almost eaten up all my money, but then I got close to a hundred back." She made another bet and won a few cents. Not even enough to make her smile. "So then I thought my luck was changing, but it appears the machine is going to take it all back."

"So you're almost out of money?" I asked.

"No, dear, I haven't had to visit the ATM," she replied.

"You want to go?"

"Already?" Kitty said. "You don't want to play?"

I really didn't see the need to play. All I had planned on doing today was looking for a job. I was just back at the casino to pick up my mother. But perhaps I didn't need to break a hip looking for work today; chances were great that I'd be getting that receptionist job.

"Maybe I'll play five bucks," I told Kitty. "But that's it. Once it's gone, we're going home. Besides, I'm starving."

"Oh, let's eat then!" Kitty exclaimed. "Let's use up some of my points!"

Her points enabled me to gorge at the buffet. With the top button of my skirt undone, I walked back onto the gaming floor. I didn't think five dollars would last long so I agreed to meet my mom in an hour.

An hour later, my five bucks had grown by a dollar. I showed my voucher to Kitty. "You haven't lost your five dollars yet?" she asked.

I laughed. "Don't say it, I know what you're thinking..."

She said it anyways. "I guess we have to stay longer then."

Since I now had only six dollars, we again agreed to meet in an hour. I spent most of my time at a machine in the far corner of the casino. The music being played there was old time rock and roll, maybe from the fifties and sixties. It felt warm and secluded and I could have dozed off if Amber Rays wasn't being so benevolent. My six dollars ballooned up to twelve and when I finally had a two-dollar run of no significant wins, I cashed out and ambled off to find Kitty.

"You're still winning?" Kitty asked. "If you're having so much luck, you should increase your bets."

"Nope," I said strongly. "I'm sticking to my plan. I feel if I play larger, I won't win at all. It's like I'm working here. I'm an investor and my dividends are paying out quite nicely."

Kitty scrunched up her face. "I think you're making what they call low-risk investments."

"Oh, like we know what we're talking about!" I giggled. "I don't even know if what I said made sense. So one more hour and no matter if I'm up or down, we go home. After that, we run into rush hour."

When you played the Buffalo Spirit game, whenever the eagles came up to signify a possible bonus, it made the most pleasant noise. This machine was one that allowed you to control the volume and I had it cranked high. I achieved a bonus and rather than select five games at five times the payout, I chose twenty-four games at the normal payout. And though during the bonus I won an additional ten spins, the eventual payout was only slightly more than two dollars. Still, a tidy return on a nickel. Maybe my next interview should be in the financial world. I pulled out my cell phone to check the time and saw I had a missed call. I didn't recognize the number. As I was looking at the phone, it rang again, with the same number appearing. I quickly answered it.

"Is this Tammy?" a man asked. The person playing Buffalo Spirit a few machines away had their volume turned up loud as well. The eagles sounded their loud lovely sound.

"Yes!" I shouted. "Who's this?"

"Enrico from The Special Touch Spa."

"Hang on one brief moment," I said politely. With that, I cupped the phone to my chest, trying to muffle the cacophony of the casino. I bolted out of my seat and started to run out, only to dash back and pull out my player's card. Barely two steps were taken before I remembered to cash out my ten dollar voucher. I ran pell mell to the exit.

"Thanks for coming," said the security guard.

"I'll be back," I mouthed. I wondered if they saw this on a regular basis - the employee not wanting to be caught at the casino.

I ran over to the coat check area, where the noise of the slot machines could not be heard. Trying to catch my breath, I said, "I'm back! You still there?"

"Yeah, I tried you once already," Enrico said. "Left you a voice mail. On your home machine and your cell."

"Sorry, I didn't hear the phone ring," was my honest reply. "Are you calling about the job?" He called me twice so he must really need to talk to me!

"Yes," he said, then paused. I waited with bated breath for the good news before he continued. "We've narrowed it down to three girls. We want to see you all again. Can you make it here in an hour?"

"An hour?" I repeated. I'd have no time to run home and freshen up.

"I know it's short notice, but it's one of the job requirements we spoke about," Enrico affirmed. "Amongst other things, if you recall."

"I want the job," I said firmly. "I'll be there."

I had ten minutes to meet Kitty. I hustled into the washroom and re-set my make-up, fluffed up my hair. I was a minute late meeting my mom. She was five minutes late. As I tried calling her on her cellphone, I rocked side to side. After eight hours in shoes I rarely wore, my feet were on fire.

Kitty came shuffling up, looking miserable. "Oh, sh...shoot, Mom," I said, forgetting about her being a few minutes late when I needed to get out of there fast. "You look like you lost your mojo."

Kitty gave me a disgruntled look. "I know we have to leave," she grumbled. "Too bad. I'm up two hundred dollars."'

"Well, here's the deal," I said. "I know you probably want to get home by now but that job called. They need to see me one last time and I have to be there in the next hour."

You could see Kitty's recovery. Her eyes got a bright sheen back to them, her posture straightened, her cheeks brightened. "Do you want me to wait here for you?" she asked with her hands clasped to her bosom. "I can do that."

"If it's no bother..."

"No, I don't mind at all!" Kitty trilled. "Oh, I hope you get this job! You should, you look real pretty today."

"Thanks," I replied. "My feet are killing me though. I can barely walk anymore."

"You can wear my shoes," Kitty suggested. We were the same size.

I eyed her footwear and saw it was her usual black Hush Puppy shoes. They could almost double for slippers. Normally, I would never ever wear my mother's shoes. But my feet were aching so badly and what choice did I have? Besides, they were so flat and severe-looking, it would only enforce the idea that I was all business.

Agreeing to the change, we switched shoes. Kitty sat down at the Noah's Ark machine and instantly kicked off the shoes. She looked me over. "Now you look real nice," she said. "Like you're going to church."

I made it to my appointment and walked into the waiting room. Two other women sat there and immediately, I had an inkling I was overdressed. One applicant wore a net shirt with a leopard print bra underneath. Her booty shorts left nothing to the imagination. The other contender had on a skin-tight dress, which on me would have been a t-shirt. She wore thigh-high leather boots and a pound of make-up to cover all the acne on her face. There was a bandage on the inside of each forearm.

The closest I came to being sexy was the top button of my skirt still being undone. I did it back up and decided to undo the buttons of my jacket. I glanced down at my blouse and saw a dollop of barbecue sauce from the glazed chicken I'd had for lunch. It was nasty and crusting over my chest area, so I redid the buttons.

Enrico came out of his office and surveyed the three of us. He looked hard at my ensemble and said, "You. Tammy? Yeah, you can leave."

•••••••••

Kitty took the news hard. "But Mom, actually, it would be a long drive to make every day. Plus the boss was awfully mean and the whole place seemed shady."

"It would be somewhere you could take me every day," Kitty whined. "Then I wouldn't have to stay home and be so miserable all the time."

We weren't even home from FiveStar and I was on the phone making plans to go to Niagara Falls for the very next day. We switched it up this time - I put in a full fruitless day of job-hunting while Kitty slept through the daylight hours. We took an evening bus which pulled into The Falls Casino at 9 PM.

I got my usual cup of coffee and settled down at the Turtle Treasures machine. I knew that when you got a bonus on this, the chances of a large pay-off were good. On the first bonus I received, the game put a kibosh on that idea. It paid off nothing. I moved on. No more than two hours into the five-hour trip, I'd lost my twenty dollars. Sure, I had my bank card on me, never mind the extra sixty or so in cash. I didn't even consider it for more than a minute; I held fast to my belief that I had a limit. As well as no job.

I sought out my mother and proceeded to watch her gamble for the next three hours. Though she offered to give me money, I refused. Instead, I watched her blow over a hundred bucks. And though I suggested she wager less, she refused. It was close to two AM when she hustled over to an ATM. This time I was one step ahead of her and told her to forget it. The bus was leaving soon; we may as well head that way.

"There's still a few minutes time left to play," Kitty said, looking up at me with pleading eyes. "Why don't you go get a coffee? I'll meet you at the bus."

"Yeah, no," I said. I could just imagine holding up a busload of people, waiting while Kitty played out a fifty-game bonus. "There's always another day."

We didn't get home until 4 AM. The three coffees I'd had kept me up till 6. When I awoke at 1 PM, I joined an equally sleepy Kitty for a late breakfast. I was in no mood for conversation, but Kitty was obsessing over a strange piece of malarkey.

"I wish you had let me play," Kitty said. "I was going to play Incan Spirit. I never played that game before and I saw the man playing it lose a hundred dollars. I just know it was going to pay off."

"No guarantees, Mom," I mumbled through a bit of peanut butter on burnt toast.

"It was bound to!" Kitty said vehemently. "That's how those machines work!"

"Haven't you read any of the brochures they supply at the casinos?" I asked. "Everything works on a computer chip. It's all random."

"Says who?"

"Says the brochures!" I said forcefully. "They also talk about addiction. Maybe I'll pick one up for you."

"You're one to talk about addiction," Kitty said.

"Me?!" I snorted derisively. "What was I ever addicted to?"

"To having a good time! To being wild and free!" Kitty seemed close to crying.

Maybe we were both tired. I could sense a battle about to erupt. "Look, if it means so much to you, let's go back to Incan Spirit tomorrow, ok?"

The planned bus trip was to leave at noon. At 12:15, my cell phone rang. It was the bus company, informing us their bus had broken down on the side of the highway. I relayed the info to my mother.

"That happened to us before on the way to Kato," Kitty recalled. "Middle of winter and half the old people weren't even dressed properly. It took over an hour to get us on another bus."

She didn't seem perturbed, thank goodness. I started the car but as soon as I made a left hand turn to go home, she said, "I thought we were going to the casino. This is not the way to the highway."

I pulled to the side. Poor old lady probably didn't get it right the first time. "Mom, the bus trip is cancelled. They broke down."

"I know, you said that already," she said. "But you also said we're going to the casino. Since we're taking the day off anyways..." I considered it for a moment, but she cinched the deal when she added, "If it's money for gas you're worried about, I'll pay it."

I turned the car around and headed for Niagara Falls. I thought I remembered the route correctly but ended up missing my exit. I had to proceed a little farther and then turned down a street when I saw a sign saying 'FunTime Casino'.

"Look, Mom," I pointed out. "That must be an old sign. It just says FunTime Casino."

But lo and behold, at the end of the street was a building with the words FunTime Casino written in slightly cartoonish letters. Both our eyes bugged out and neither of us needed to say a word as I swung into their parking lot.

FunTime Casino was just as much fun as The Falls. Upon a quick interrogation of a security guard, I found out both casinos were partners.

He claimed this one was slightly smaller but I found it just as large as the other one. The bulk of the slots seemed to be penny machines and it even provided two floors of gaming fun. Unlike FiveStar or Tribes, or even The Falls, you didn't have to wait for a coffee server to come around. There were two areas where you could serve yourself.

When I caught up with Kitty and told her I was getting hungry, she thought she had enough points accumulated for a meal. Sure enough, my little gambling gal had points aplenty. I had a magnificent buffet meal - I swear these casinos must hire the highest calibre chefs around. Yet people would just dine and dash. The chefs were under-appreciated. Finally, though I was having fun, I admitted to myself I was getting sleepy. I kept rubbing my eyes, hoping to clear my bleared vision. Looking at my cellphone, I saw it was almost midnight, time to meet Kitty. I figured she'd be ready to leave by now too.

She was still sitting at the Wizard of Oz game where I'd last seen her. "I have to remember this game," Kitty said as I walked up on her winning thirty dollars. "It's my new favourite game."

"It's midnight," I said. "We've been here close to eleven hours. Time to go."

She cashed out and stood up. "Time to go to The Falls," she said.

I did a double-take. "The Falls? Haven't you had enough gambling for one day?"

Kitty gave me a patronizing look. "We came to Niagara Falls for a reason, remember?" she said. "Incan Spirit is still calling my name. And he's at The Falls."

• • • • • • • • •

Over the next three months, as the weather got colder, Kitty's health seemed to worsen. Only when she wasn't at the casino, mind you. She tried various tactics to get me to take her gambling. Her favourite was that she wasn't getting enough exercise and her bones were getting brittle, but she got a great workout when she was at the casino. I'd take her and often find her at the same machine for hours. She'd claim the arthritis in her fingers was acting up but if she could spend a few hours pressing spin buttons, that would ease the pain. And if any of the various casinos sent her an offer, how could she refuse?

I often gave in. We varied our trips to different gaming venues. Sometimes we'd take a bus, sometimes we'd drive. The amount of money I was spending worried me, though it wasn't extravagant. What really concerned me were the times we'd spend without going to a casino for more than four days. That's when Kitty's ailments seemed to have substance.

I'd waken to hear her prowling the house during the darkest hours. I'd inquire as to what she was doing and get an answer like, "Playing my pedometer. I can't cash out until I reach ten thousand." I worried again about dementia. Other times she wouldn't get out of bed, I wouldn't hear a peep out of her, but come the middle of the night and she's moaning and crying. When it became unbearable (for me), I'd tell her to put on her outfit and I'd take her to FiveStar. She didn't even bother with the whoops of delight anymore. She'd just get dressed fast, put her teeth in and be waiting by the front door. I knew that once we arrived at the casino, she'd be the same old Kitty I used to know, full of vim and vigour. I loved her that way.

One day I walked into her bedroom and found Kitty in a sound sleep. As I bent to place the blanket back on her exposed body, I saw a monstrous bruise on Kitty's shin. When she woke up, I asked her about it.

"I got that a couple weeks ago," she explained. "This man won nothing on his bonus and he pushed his chair away when he trounced off. I was sitting beside him and his chair hit my leg."

"Well, we should go get that checked out," I said. "It looks terrible!"

"It doesn't hurt."

"It doesn't matter," I asserted. "I'm booking you an appointment."

Her doctor could see her at his next available opening, which wasn't for another two months. Since it didn't appear to be an emergency, he suggested we visit a walk-in clinic. There were about a dozen to choose from within minutes from home but of course Kitty wanted to drive to one close to a casino.

The clinic was filled to over-capacity with patients. We stated our case to the receptionist, even going so far as to show her Kitty's leg. She agreed to slot us in, warning us that the doctor had a full caseload and the wait might take awhile. Taking awhile turned out to be going on three hours. Kitty's status as an old lady was having no effect here.

After we finally got in and the doctor took a fifteen second look at Kitty's shin, he prescribed some ointment to apply to it. Otherwise, it was healing on its own. The ointment was only because her skin was excessively dry.

"Hey, doctor, while I'm here, I may as well ask you something..." I began.

"If this is about you, you will have to go back into the waiting room," the Indian doctor commanded. "You will have to fill out the paperwork...."

"No, no, it's about my mom!" I interjected. Kitty gave me a curious look that I ignored. "She's been acting real strange lately. I'm worried she may be...how do you describe it...coming down with dementia?"

"Oh, Tammy, not this again," my mother sighed.

"You said you are here for her leg," the doctor said. "You can see I have a very full waiting room."

"Well, real quick, can you check her out?" I begged.

The doctor turned to Kitty. "What season are we in?"

"Though it feels like winter, technically it's still autumn," Kitty replied.

"How old are you?"

"Oh, who keeps track? But I was born in 1942."

"What are the names of your children?"

"Tammy. I just have one. But I have three grandchildren. Rain, Tatum and Sadie."

"What's your address?"

She recited that and the doctor looked at his clipboard. Something obviously matched as the doctor turned toward me. "Your mother is fine. She doesn't have dementia."

We left. I returned a few minutes later to retrieve my mother's forgotten gloves.

• • • • • • • • •

The Christmas season was upon us. Since I rarely went anywhere other than to a casino these days, and the thought of dragging Kitty around a mall didn't inspire me, I did all of my meagre Christmas shopping for my children online. I couldn't come up with any sort of idea as to what to give my mother and sadly resorted to buying her gift certificates to play slots at any OGG casino. How lame can you get?

All three of my kids were coming home. They had a nice two-week break and planned to spend it with Kitty and I. She gamely ventured into the basement and came up with all her decorations. I asked about a tree and was told that it was family tradition that Rain choose the perfect one.

We cleaned the house from top to main floor. Looking for a job had somehow gone onto the back-burner. The trips to the casino seemed to require a day to recover, both for Kitty and I. And she seemed to need me a lot more these days. She may have disagreed with that statement, but I strongly felt somebody had to keep an eye on her. I knew I'd get around to finding employment eventually; I just hoped I wouldn't have to put Kitty back into a senior's home so I could go to work.

When the kids arrived, there were a couple days of a joyous reunion. The twins' precious bedazzled iPhones chirped non-stop and they somehow managed to text like mad while maintaining a civil conversation. I discovered Sadie had a boyfriend she met in school who only lived a couple blocks away. He also had a twin. When Sadie asked her sister Tatum to a party, it turned out to be the boyfriend's family gathering. Tatum said she didn't mingle from the minute she laid eyes on the boyfriend's gorgeous twin brother. Both were single and they agreed to go on a double-date with Sadie and her guy. I barely saw the two of them after that epic date.

As for Rain, he spent the first couple of days colluding a lot with Kitty. I don't know what their deal was but they'd always been close. Rain was in a relationship with a woman from Mississauga; it had been going on for a couple years now. All I knew was that she was a tad older than him and was in some kind of master's degree program. Maybe in her sixth year of university, but Rain said she was going to be able to get a good job after that. She was due to arrive into Toronto any day from her apprenticeship at some Cambodian hospital.

On Christmas Eve, all my kids were decked out in their finest duds. The girls looked like they were going clubbing while Rain had on a suit and tie. They were all gathered in the foyer around 9 PM.

"Where you off to?" I asked, without adding, "It's Christmas!"

Sadie spoke up first. "Jeff and Jon are taking us to The Mercury Club. Tatum said she likes the DJ playing there and Jon said he knows the doorman and can get us in."

"He's so amazing!" Tatum swooned over her new beau.

"And you, Rain?" I asked. "You need the car?"

"No, Siobhan's coming to get me," he said. "She's picking up a couple friends on the way. We're going to a poetry recital over at the Halal House."

The kids left. Kitty and I sat in the empty living room. "You may as well turn on the fireplace channel," my mother said. I did. The festive sight of a fire burning did nothing to lift our spirits.

"We'll have a good Christmas," I said. "We never did anything but hang out on Christmas Eve anyhow. It's Christmas Day when we open the presents, you cook a big meal..."

"We used to always play games on Christmas Eve, remember?" Kitty said sadly.

"Yeah, but Mom, that was when the kids were younger," I reminded her. "Now they're grown up, they have friends, boyfriends...they don't want to sit around with a couple old ladies playing Yahtzee."

"So they go out and have fun and we stay home and be old," Kitty deduced.

I had no quick comeback for that. Actually, her statement drummed in my mind for a couple minutes while I stared into the fake TV fire. "You know, you're right, why shouldn't we have some fun as well?"

Kitty knew I wouldn't suggest going to midnight mass or maybe catching a late movie. She knew exactly that fun meant a trip to the casino. She hustled up to her room and came back down with her pink clothes on. She ran to her purse and started pulling things out, only to re-insert them into her fishing vest. We were about to leave, when she pushed me back inside. "Turn off the TV," she commanded. "We don't want to burn down the house!" Good one, Kitty, I thought, seeing the giddy mood she was in. Kitty Casino was ready to rumble!

As we drove to FiveStar Casino, I told her our plan. "We're going to stay out as late as we want," I told her. "Just like the kids. We have all day tomorrow to laze about."

"There's a turkey dinner to be made," Kitty reminded me. Usually she was in charge of that but I wondered if her culinary skills were up to the challenge. I was hoping for a big bucket of KFC.

As we pulled into the FiveStar Casino grounds, I was nonplussed to see the lot completely empty. "We picked a good day to come," I said. "Nobody's here."

"They're all probably celebrating with family," Kitty agreed.

To our utter amazement, the doors were locked. A passing security guard heard our knocks and came up to the door. Even though we snagged the best parking place in history, the weather was below freezing and we were shivering.

"You're not closed, are you?" I asked as soon as the door opened. The guard completely blocked our entry.

"Yeah, until 8 AM tomorrow," he announced.

"But you never close!" I said.

"I know, this is a first," he admitted. "Management said it's impossible to get enough people to come in to work. Just security is here tonight. Sorry, you can try Tribes." With that he shut and relocked the door. Kitty and I hustled back to the car.

"Well?" I said. "Shall we go to Tribes?"

I blared the heat to warm us up. I guess I let the car get overly hot as Kitty was lulled into a sleep punctuated by long expulsions of air. I stopped talking and just concentrated on the forty minute drive to Tribes.

I didn't bother waking Kitty up when we arrived. I drove into the parking lot and saw zero spaces. I did see fifty cars also driving about, looking for a place to park. Since the horses weren't racing, I knew everybody was here to play the slots. Hell, probably half of FiveStar's regulars were here as well. There was no way I wanted to subject Kitty to a crowd like that.

I turned around and headed back to the highway. Before I got to it, I pulled up 'nearest casino' on my GPS. Tribes was obviously listed, followed by FiveStar. However, the third was a place I'd never visited - Quint Times Raceway. Like FiveStar and Tribes, and maybe others I'd visited, these casinos also held horse races. I knew FiveStar had a giant area upstairs that we'd sometimes visit for a bite to eat. Though the space was gigantic, it was rarely filled with more than a dozen men as they raised their bored faces to various TV screens. Some showed horse races while others displayed basketball games or soccer matches or the like.

The GPS showed the Quint Times Raceway to be just under an hour away. That was starting to take me pretty far from home and we'd already spent enough time in transit. I glanced at Kitty, sound asleep, and wondered how mad she'd be if she woke up and found we were back at home. Ah, fuck, I'd probably ruin the whole holiday just by being lazy. And it made me happy to see her act like we were one of the kids, out to have our own good time. I decided to plow on ahead to Quint, Ontario, where the casino was located. Maybe this act of kindness would make up for my pathetic Christmas gift.

The snow was just starting to fall when the GPS directed me into the teensy weeny town of Quint. If my GPS had broken down, I would have had no idea how to get home. We'd left the highway long ago and I just followed the directions I was given. I turned down a long sideroad and saw a magnificent racetrack. My oohing and aahing over it woke Kitty up.

"Look at their nice racetrack!" I exclaimed. "It almost looks like one from the olden days."

"That's not the racetrack at Tribes," Kitty declared. "Where are we?"

"Yeah, Tribes was jam-packed," I said. "I thought we'd come to this place. Quint Times Casino; you've never been here before."

Kitty clapped her hands. "A new casino? Oh, this will be fun!"

Before we even got to the entrance of the casino, I could see cars parked on the side of the long road. Gamely I proceeded but a quick drive-through showed me there was not a parking place to be had. I idled in place for a few minutes, hoping to catch somebody leaving and then pulling the old Christmas-shopping-at-a-busy-mall trick. You know - drive slowly behind them while they get to their car and then wait for their space? Nobody was leaving the casino, though other cars were driving in, hoping to also nab a closer spot. I beat a hasty retreat back to the cars parked along the road and joined the end of the line.

Aghast, I looked over at Kitty. "Oh, sh..shoot!" I gasped. "I should have dropped you off at the entrance!"

"That's ok," Kitty said. "I always bring my hat and gloves. I hope you did too."

Of course I hadn't, but that bad habit hadn't changed since I was a kid. We locked the car and walked along the slick road towards the casino. The snowflakes were big and bold in the bright moonlight and the temperature was frigid. I held onto Kitty tightly, hoping she'd think I was being a conscientious daughter. In reality, my hands gripped her under her armpit, where they were kept somewhat warmer.

"Look at that lovely entrance," Kitty exclaimed. "I feel like we should be wearing petticoats and carrying a parasol."

As cold as we were, we did have to stop and admire it. It was so old-timey; I didn't expect it from a casino. "It sure is a tiny entrance though," I said. "Well, let's get out of the cold and see what this place is like."

The moment we walked in, a surreal feeling overcame me. Kitty and I stopped short and stared at the inside of the Quint Times Casino. "I must say, this is different," Kitty finally commented. "Size-wise, it's not much bigger than our basement at home."

"Are you kidding me?" I blustered. "They call this a casino?" I continued to gaze upon the room. The walls were painted with floor-to-ceiling scenes of running horses, of buggies and carriages, of ladies and gents in vintage clothing, sitting in wooden grandstands, happy and cheering. The large scale of the paintings contributed to making the room feel claustrophobic. The hordes of people milling about didn't help either.

"Let's take a walk around and see what kind of games there are," Kitty suggested.

I just nodded and started to follow her. I couldn't help laughing as we headed in one direction and reached that wall in no time. Making a square of the room took about a minute. "Let's go through the middle now," Kitty said. We managed to stay together as we dodged all the gamblers. Since it appeared most of the games were taken, quite a few people were simply standing behind players, watching them play.

"See anything you want to try?" I asked.

"I'll play anything that's available," Kitty replied. "Let's try to find me a machine."

She no sooner had said that when I spotted a man look at his watch and suddenly cash out. "I see one!" I said, making an instant dash for it. I narrowly beat an obese woman wearing a stained white t-shirt and stretch pants. She gave me a glower; I gave back an apologetic shrug.

Kitty came over and we looked at the machine I'd scored. "Oh, darn, it's a quarter machine!" I groaned. "I didn't even look when I saw it was available."

"It's not my favourite game either," Kitty said, though she was happy to have a seat. "I don't care for these sevens and cherries games. But who knows if there's even another empty seat in the house?" She proceeded to insert her player's card.

"I'm going to go walk around," I said. "Hopefully I can find a penny machine."

"Shall we meet up in an hour or two hours?" Kitty asked.

"Ha!" I retorted. "If I want to find you, I'll just call out your name."

Don't ask me what was up with this casino - maybe Quint was the unheralded home of many millionaires - but out of the maybe hundred slot machines they had there, perhaps twenty were penny machines. Out of those twenty, half of them required you to play a minimum of forty cents. I didn't care for those. The ten that I would have played at were obviously taken; a couple even had a line-up behind them. I continued to stroll around until I saw a seat become suddenly available in front of me. A woman had been playing next to her boyfriend; I saw her hit zero credits, pull out her player's card and jump onto the lap of her mate. I slid onto her vacated seat so quickly, you'd have thought we'd planned this sequence.

Glad to get off my feet, I glanced up at the game I found myself on. It was Red Rooster, which I never played as it was never a penny game. And it still wasn't here; it cost a dime to play one line. If I played my usual five lines at normal payout, that would cost me a cool half dollar each spin. No freaking way was I going to blow through my twenty dollar limit with bets that large. The only way I could afford to stretch out my money was to play one line at normal payout, something I hated to do. And still it was costing me twice as much as usual.

I stayed at that machine for quite some time, ignoring the withering glances of people who looked at my bet. Did they feel I had no right to play if I wasn't going to bet good and proper? Why did they even care how much I was spending? It should be nobody's business but for me and the slot machine.

After a hundred leisurely spins, I was rewarded with a win of four dollars. I was relieved to have won a little something and let out a small cry of delight. The woman playing on my right glanced over. "Try playing the max," she didn't suggest so much as flat out told me. "You would have been a big winner here tonight."

"I'd love to," I said somewhat haughtily. "If only I didn't have the three kids in school."

"Aren't they home for the holidays?" the woman asked.

I didn't want to get into it with this woman who'd obviously been drinking or was just plain stupid. I looked for Kitty and found her within thirty seconds; it wasn't hard in the intimate space. "Maybe this was a bad idea," I said. "I had no idea it would be such a small casino. And so crowded."

"If we stay long enough, I'm sure it will thin out," Kitty said. "Did you see they have a Wizard of Oz here? My favourite game? It costs more than anywhere else but I might spend a few dollars on it...if it ever opens up." She glanced wistfully at the far corner of the casino. "That's where I'll be." She walked off before I could suggest we call it quits.

Somehow my twenty lasted me most of the night. I knew I wouldn't leave with money, but every now and then I'd win enough to keep me spinning away. It was about four in the morning when I spotted Kitty finally playing Wizard of Oz. I walked over and saw, according to the screen, that she was almost out of credits. "How's it going with your beloved Wizard?" I asked.

"Not so good," Kitty replied. "You'd think I could win a few dollars. I certainly put in enough."

A couple people passed us, exclaiming loudly over the weather and how cold it was getting. I suggested to Kitty that we get going and she immediately pressed her cash-out button. A voucher was printed for seventy cents. "Good timing," she said. "I can say I'm leaving with money."

I cashed in my own two dollars and we stepped outside the quaint casino into a chilly snowstorm. I could see the Town Car parked far away on the road leading into the parking lot. I made Kitty stay in the entrance while I ran to the car, warmed it up and returned to pick her up.

As she got into the car, she said, "Oh, you've got it nice and warm. Thank you."

"So what'd you think of that casino?" I asked.

"It was alright," Kitty said. "Maybe we won't come back." She yawned. "Are you OK to drive in this snow?"

"Yeah, we're far from home but the roads don't look that bad," I noted. "Plus we have good tires. We should be fine."

"Then I'm going to take a nap," Kitty said, falling asleep instantly.

And I'm sure we would be fine, I thought as I drove along County Road 15 aimlessly. Just as soon as the heavy snowfall would allow my GPS to acquire a signal.

• • • • • • • • • •

Christmas Day was unlike any I had ever spent with my kin. For me, it felt like the first time we were celebrating as a real family. Sure, if the touring schedule allowed, I'd spend as many Christmases as I could with the Canseco bunch but it always felt like I was just there as an added decoration. Come two or three days after Christmas and Tammy would disappear with the mistletoe. This year, I felt like the matriarch of the house as I doled out the KFC cole slaw and mashed potatoes.

"I see you're tweaking our usual turkey dinner," Rain joked.

"Turkey, chicken, it's almost the same," I joked back. He was in my good books with the sentimental gift he'd given me. He'd bought me an electronic photo book and had inserted a hundred photos of the girls and himself. Some pictures had Kitty laughing along with them and there were even some of me and the kids when they were younger. I'd gotten him a desk plaque with his name engraved on it, for his future office desk. He swore he didn't have one and would use it the first chance he got.

I was pretty cheap with the twins too but they hid their dismay well. Incredibly, Kitty was thrilled with the five ten-dollar gift certificates I'd gotten her. Judging by what I often saw her lose, I deduced I gave her about an hour of fun. She handed me her gift with a look of shame. "I'm sorry, Tammy," she said, eyes downcast. "I don't know what you're into anymore so I had no idea what to get. This was all I could think of last minute."

The box she handed me was small and square. I figured it contained a bracelet, maybe a necklace. As I unwrapped the present and cracked open the lid of the box, a wad of crisp bills presented itself. They were the new plastic Canadian bills that can't stay folded. Kitty had tried to wedge them into the box by bending them. I don't know how she managed to get the lid on and wrap it, but she did. As soon as I took the lid off, the bills sprang out as if they had a life of their own and fluttered to the ground.

"Mom, you shouldn't have!" I said, counting the bills as I picked them up. She'd laid a cool grand on me. Cold, hard plastic cash. And what did she get in return? An unspoken guarantee that with some OGG gift certificates, I'd probably be taking her to the casino again.

•••••••••

New Year's Eve had my house in an uproar. The twins were going out with their matching set to a house party. They had friends over and it seemed that, at 4 PM, the party had already started. The music was blaring, wine was flowing and seven girls ran through the house in various stages of undress.

Rain came into the house with a case of beer. I saw him stocking the fridge. He had an annoyed look on his face. "The party I was going to got cancelled," he groused. "The girl's dad is in Mexico or Jamaica or somewhere. Anyhow, he got mugged and he's coming home and now she doesn't want to have a party."

"Too bad," I commiserated.

"Well, it's understandable she's worried about him," Rain said. "Still, that leaves me with nothing to do. Siobhan went with her parents to their year-round cottage. That's not my idea of a fun New Year's Eve."

"So what are you going to do?" I asked. "Maybe the girls can take you to their party?"

"I already asked a few of the guys if they want to come over here," Rain said. "There won't be a lot of us, just five or six. It's not like we're going to be having a party or anything. Just drink some beers, order a pizza, maybe play some cards. Is that alright?"

Like I would deny my son a party when he was rarely home? "You go right ahead," I told Rain. "Since it looks like you'll be drinking, I guess you won't be needing the Town Car?"

He pulled the keys out of his pocket and put them on the table. "You're going out?" he asked almost incredulously. That only spurred my decision.

"I was thinking about it," I said coyly. "You don't want two old ladies hanging around."

"Thanks!" was his reply. Good thing I was his mother.

I went in search of Kitty and found her in her bedroom, completely under the covers. "Are you cold?" I asked. "Want me to turn the heat up?"

"No, I'm just trying to block out the sound of all those girls yammering," Kitty said, poking her head out. "Listen to them! I swear they're all talking at the same time."

"It's only going to get louder," I warned her. "Rain's plans got cancelled so he's invited some guys over."

"Aaagh," Kitty groaned. "Maybe I'm getting old but I can't take all this noise anymore." She sat up in bed and pointed at her dresser. "Tammy, if you could open my top drawer?" I did as she asked. "In the right hand corner, buried at the bottom, is a little plastic case. It has ear plugs in it. I don't use them often...."

I stopped looking. "Hey, why don't we avoid all the ruckus and just go to FiveStar?" I asked.

Kitty removed the blankets and swung her legs off the bed. "We haven't been to a casino in a week," she stated. "It didn't seem right, what with the kids here."

"They won't even notice we're gone," I laughed.

"But it's New Year's Eve," Kitty went on. "I'm sure they'll have a big crowd at FiveStar."

"I'm sure they will too, but we'll leave now, get there by the dinner hour...It probably won't get busy for a few hours yet. We'll stay until you decide you've had enough."

She walked over to the drawer I'd left open and rummaged through it, pulling out the five OGG gift certificates. "Or until I've spent all the money you gave me!" I hoped her eyesight caught on that they were only ten dollar denominations.

I dressed in some glitzy clothes I hadn't worn in five years. The Noise had been booked to play a celebrity wedding and I needed something with razzle dazzle. I'd only worn it once. Since it was New Year's Eve, a little glitz wouldn't be out of order. I even added a mini-skirt. Sure I was too old to be wearing something that short but I've seen sexier outfits on some of the octogenarians at the casino.

En route, Kitty was talking a mile a minute, but she was all over the map. In one breath, she was talking about the exact moment she laid eyes on my Dad, the next she was gibbering about the battles they'd fought over naming me.

"I wanted to call you Judith after my aunt but your father forbade it," she reminisced. "He wanted to call you Ali McGraw after some movie star he liked."

"You would have called me Ali McGraw?"

"It would have been Ali, of course," she corrected. "We finally settled on Tammy, named after no-one. I hope you've been liking your name all these years."

"I've gotten used to it," I said lightly. "How about you? Do you like when people call you Kitty Casino?"

"Why not?" she asked. "It's my name."

Then she went into a monologue about the time on her honeymoon when they played the slots on the cruise ship. "I knew they were my destiny," she said, laughing way too loudly. "Maybe not for a few years, but I knew we'd meet again!" She then segued into how foolish some New Year's resolutions were. "Just listen to how many people say tonight that they're going to give up gambling," she giggled. "Not me! I'll go to the casino as long as the good Lord allows! How about you, Tammy? Any silly resolutions?"

"Yeah. To get a job in the New Year."

Kitty finally stopped with her chatter. We drove a moment in silence before she said, "Yes, I guess you would feel the need to work. I would stay at home?"

I avoided the subject; we were out for a good time, weren't we? "We'll deal with that when the time comes," I said. "Look, we're here already." And though it was early, the casino had plenty of business. We checked our jackets at the coat check and headed over to the entrance of the casino. In the lobby before the entry point was a woman dressed up as a showgirl. She was manning a huge spinning wheel and asked if we'd like to give it a spin.

"Why not?" I said. I took a spin and once the wheel stopped turning, the arrow pointed to a question.

"Answer this correctly and you get a prize," the showgirl said. "If you continue to put money into a machine, are you guaranteed to win?"

I answered like a good schoolgirl. "No, it's random, it's all the computer chip."

"Correct!" the showgirl beamed. "You win a prize!" I was hoping for free slot play but she handed me over a tube of lip balm. "Would you like to play?" she asked Kitty.

Kitty stepped up to the game. Her attempt at a spin caused the wheel to move about four spaces. She landed on the question 'If you play long enough, will you win back the money you lost?' Kitty read it aloud and then answered the question. "Oh, I'm sure you would! I never have the opportunity to stay as long as I'd like..."

"Mom!" I interrupted. "You know that's not the answer!"

"Computer chip," Kitty declared. "That's the answer for everything - it's all in the computer chip."

The showgirl perhaps took pity on Kitty or maybe she was instructed to give out lip balm to everyone. She handed one over and Kitty took it and tucked it into a small pocket in her fishing vest.

"Look at that," Kitty said as we headed for the main entrance of the casino. "I'm on a winning streak! Come on, Tammy, I can hear Incan Spirit calling my name again." She was almost skipping as we joined a small line-up of patrons waiting to get in. There were two guards working there, one manning the entry point and the other the exit. They stood probably ten feet apart.

The entry guard was checking the ID on a couple guys ahead of us. To me they looked like they were in their late twenties but these guards took no chances. I was about to breeze by the boys but Kitty held back. The exit-point sentry glanced at her and motioned that she could bypass the two men being scrutinized.

Flirtatiously, Mom asked, "You're not going to check if I'm old enough?"

The guard, a handsome elderly gent, winked at Kitty and said, "Well, little lady, now you've got me worried. Maybe I better check your ID after all."

A wide smile enveloped my mother's suddenly girlish face. The guard's overly flattering remark seemed to melt twenty years off Kitty as her eyes lit up and she threw her head back to laugh. In a flash, her body seemed to visibly stiffen. Instantly the chill that raced through me told me this wasn't right. "Jesus Christ, Mom! Are you OK?"

But I knew she wasn't. There were three clues in quick succession. First of all, even if she was being suffocated by a boa constrictor, she'd stop struggling long enough to tell me to watch my language. She didn't do it. Using the Lord's name in vain? To her, that's a big sin. We weren't a real church-going family, but Kitty had her priorities.

The second thing - I'd noticed her eyes earlier, how clear they were, how bright blue. As soon as she'd stiffened, I could see her eyes immediately lose their spark and start to cloud. Though her eyes were open, I sensed it was final act, curtain closing…

And the third clue? If the massive heart attack hadn't instantly killed her, Kitty falling backwards, her head crashing onto the hard marble floor, would likely have done the trick.

After a moment in which the elderly guard, his female counterpart, the two guys being ID'd and myself seemed rooted in place, all organized hell broke loose. The female guard spoke into her walkie-talkie and said some code word that required emergency personnel immediately. The two guys were waved in but instead they moved back to take in the scene. Other people began to arrive and I wanted to get close to Kitty, but the elderly guard was shielding her for all he was worth. In about a minute, some emergency staff came running. I saw one take her pulse and shake his head at his partner.

He looked up at the guard. "We're moving her to the side," he said. "Ambulance is on its way."

"Is she going to be ok?" I asked. He didn't say a hearse was coming, he said an ambulance. He gave me a strange look so I added, "I'm her daughter."

The man, wearing an OGG Emergency Personnel uniform, had the grace to look me in the eye and say solemnly, "I'm sorry for your loss, ma'am."

I jolted, now that I'd received actual confirmation. Another team of emergency personnel came running with a gurney. The four of them lifted my mother onto it and covered her with a sheet. I could hear an ambulance siren in the distance as a crowd swelled around us.

"Nothing to see, folks," said the old security guard. "Go on in, have fun, Happy New Year's."

Through the big windows, an ambulance could be seen speeding into the casino lot. I approached the emergency guy who had declared my mother dead. "Could I just be with her for a minute before they take her away?"

The four emergency staff parted and then formed a protective cocoon around me. The first thing I did was close her eyes. I wanted to recapture the memory of them sparkling as bright as a big jackpot win. I wished I could close her mouth but didn't touch it. What had appeared to be a captivating final smile in life turned out to be a grotesque grimace in death. Instead, I laid Kitty's head to the side. Had Kitty been alive, she would have been staring into the bright lights of the casino. An unwanted macabre thought hit me - she's probably going to the wrong light. But I figured she'd be pleased with either choice.

As I saw the ambulance men enter the casino with their own gurney, I reached into the largest pocket of Kitty's fishing vest. Discreetly, I removed her spare diaper. Kitty was leaving the casino for the final time and she'd do it with some class.

CHAPTER XV

The kids took it hard, way more than I did. After the initial spate of shock and tears, we all sat down at the kitchen table. A box of tissues was within reach.

"I don't even know where to start," I began, "but we have to think about planning her funeral."

Just saying that word made the twins start bawling again. Rain and I waited for their wails to subside before Rain said, "She didn't want a funeral."

"You have to have a funeral, Rain," I told him. "It's the law, I think."

"No, you don't," he said. "And she wanted to be cremated."

"How do you know?" I asked.

"She told me," he replied. "Cremation and then just a memorial service. She called it a Celebration of Life. It's all in her will."

"Well, great, if we can just find the will...."

"It's in her safety deposit box," Rain replied. "She told me."

I looked at him a bit dumbfounded but didn't quit. "Great! I know where she keeps the box. I just don't know where she keeps the key."

"I have it," Rain said. "And she has a spare one in her top drawer in her bedroom."

"Ok," I decided. "Let's get through the cremation first and then we'll deal with the lawyers and banks and stuff." I wasn't looking forward to any of it.

I chose the cheapest way of doing everything. I had no idea how much this was going to cost me. I chose a simple urn for the ashes, but then had to splurge on three necklaces for the kids. Each one had a pinch of Kitty's ashes kept in a little miniature jug held centred in the middle of a knotted satin string. They cost almost two hundred apiece.

The kids had to get back to school soon so we decided to hold her memorial the day before they left. Kitty had not been dead three days before Rain sat me down at the kitchen table. "I hate to do this, but you know I've got to leave. We'd better get to the bank and look at her will."

"Lots of things we have to do," I said, making my fifteenth coffee of the day. "Do I stay in this big place by myself? Do I sell the house? Did you see how much shit Kitty has in the basement? Hello, Goodwill!"

"First of all, I don't want you in for any big surprise when you look at the will and find out I'm the executor," Rain said.

I blinked. "I'm already big surprised," I said. "Why you? Why not me?"

Rain gave a phoney shrug that let me know he had an idea why level-headed grandson was executor and not flighty ditzy daughter. "Who knows?" he dismissed it. "As for the basement, don't you dare touch it. A lot of that shit is mine."

I had to smile. In the past couple days, more swear words had been uttered in the house than probably in the past thirty years. "I know, Kitty told me you had some stuff there from one of your dorms."

"I got more than that," Rain corrected me. "Most of what's down there are different things we collected over the years. At auctions, at yard sales..."

"I saw!" I said. "Bunch of old crap. There's that old desk and lumpy chair, for example."

Rain's eyes widened. "That's Lincoln Alexander's desk and chair!" he exclaimed. "Remember I told you when Kitty and I bought it at a yard sale?"

"Big deal."

Rain shook his head. "Do you even know who Lincoln Alexander is?"

"I dunno," I said, exasperated. "You said you got it at a yard sale. I figured he was a neighbour or something."

"He was governor-general of Canada, Mother," Rain informed me. "Pretty famous guy."

"Sorry!" I retorted. "Well, you can get rid of that old bed and mattress you have down there. Nobody uses a twin bed anymore." Rain agreed.

"And that piano bench that I banged my leg on. We don't have a piano. That's gone."

Rain laid his head on the table and groaned, saying, "No, no, no. I distinctly remember telling you when we found it. Kitty took us kids out for a walk. It was garbage night and she liked to see what she could find. On this night she spotted a piano bench. And yeah, since we didn't have a piano, she wasn't that interested. Tatum was the one who figured out that the seat opened up. Then I saw it had a false bottom and I worked it up and there were a bunch of music papers under that..."

"Yeah, yeah, I remember," I said. "Listen, you were just a kid when you told me. If I recall, you were going on a mile a minute about discovering some musician's long-lost songs...."

"His name was Glen Gould."

"Yeah, yeah, Glen Gold!" I misinterpreted. "I remember thinking that was a pretty cliche stage name. I wonder if he ever went anywhere?"

"Mom, he's a famous pianist, known all over the world!" Rain said. "And it's not Gold, it's Gould."

"So what else is down there I can't give away?" I asked.

"I wouldn't say everything has value, but I'd like to get it checked out," Rain said. "She bought such unusual things. Original art deco pieces, old hat pins....There's a big chest down there? It's like from the 1800's, used to belong to a sea captain. Inside it are a bunch of books, all first editions."

"Wow," I said. "I saw a trunk full of clothes; I don't think I saw the books."

"Those clothes? You know that movie 'White Noise' that won the Oscar? It filmed in Toronto; the studio is not far from here. They were having a sale of props and clothes from the movie but on the day of the sale, there was a blizzard. Kitty still took us and she came home with a bunch of costumes dirt cheap."

"So you're telling me that, in your opinion, we could be living above a gold mine?" I asked.

Rain shrugged. "I'm thinking, we appraise all the stuff down there, sell it off as fast as possible, and use the money to pay for the cremation. I know you didn't go all out, but still, it had to cost money."

"Almost six grand," I said. "God, what if we'd booked the viewings and the church funeral and the burial grounds ceremony? Can you imagine what that would have cost?" I shook my head in wonder. Dying didn't come cheap.

•••••••••

Quickly selling the goldmine below got pushed to the side once we went to the bank and saw the contents of Kitty's bulging safety deposit box.

Rain and I sat alone in the small room provided next to the vault. He placed the locked box onto the table. "Well, let's hope for the best," Rain meekly offered as he inserted a key and opened the lid. The first thing I saw was a familiar yet jarring sight - a small bag containing a lock of Bradley's hair.

Brad lifted it out and looked in the bag. "I don't know what this is about," he muttered, placing it aside. "Why would she have hair if it's not from one of us?"

"I don't know. I thought the same thing when I saw the piano bench," I replied, reaching for the hair. "I know who Bradley is though. Is it ok if I keep that?"

Rain had already moved on to a thick envelope and he simply waved his hand for me to take it away. I put it in my purse, feeling a surge of gratitude to Kitty for thinking this lock of hair would have any value. She proved to be right; though A Lock of Bradley's hair may not be worth much money anymore, it still held sentimental value.

Rain had spread the contents of the envelope over the table and looked concerned. "I think we need to hire somebody to take a look at all this. It's beyond my scope."

"Great," I complained. "Let's hope Glen Gould can pay for that too."

"Judging by what I think I'm seeing, we should be able to afford it ourselves," Rain softly said, his voice sounding like he was witnessing a miracle. "These all appear to be stock certificates. Look!" he pointed to a few in front of me. "That one is for a thousand shares in Microsoft. Here's a local one - Rogers, bought years ago...they're a giant company now. Here's another thousand shares for...." and Rain guffawed as he read the company title.... "for Facebook! Do you think she even knew what Facebook was?"

"I didn't even think she knew what stocks were," I murmured.

"The girls and I would tease her when we saw her reading that section of the paper," Rain recalled. "We figured she was bored."

"Who knew?" I said. I certainly didn't.

Rain pulled out another envelope with a return address that I saw monthly. "This is from your Dad's old job," Rain said.

"No, that's from the government," I corrected him. "Kitty got a cheque from them every month. It's how she got by."

"Yeah, Grandpa worked for the government," Rain informed me. "Grandma said he invented some kind of bolt that can withstand intense temperatures. They use it in outer space on all the satellite dishes."

I felt a long belated pride in my father's accomplishments but I still didn't get the whole picture. "So what were those cheques she was getting? His pension?"

"All that went into her bank," Rain informed me. "Two, three years ago, I helped her with a bunch of paperwork for the bank. Direct deposits for everything except the cheque she got from these guys." He indicated the envelope he was holding and then opened it.

As he silently read it, I was startled to see tears stream down his face. "Rain, you're crying!" I was startled. "From a government letter?"

"I wish I knew Grandpa," Rain said. "He must have been a brilliant man."

"I wish I got to know him longer," I said. "He passed away way too soon."

"According to this letter, upon Grandpa's death, Kitty would continue to receive his patent profits. Upon her..." and here Rain winced... "her death, the profits will continue to go to whoever is named in her will."

"We have to find the will," I stated. Rain reached into the box and pulled out a jewellery box. "I recognize that from when I was a kid. I haven't seen it in years."

Rain passed it over to me. Opening the box should have come with that giant ray of light you see happen in the movies. Inside were her engagement and wedding rings which she'd eventually had to remove when her arthritic fingers got too plump. There was a gold bracelet with an engraving, "To my love Kitty - you're a good woman. Happy Anniversary." I was glad to know Kitty was appreciated by someone in her life. I was suffering severe pangs of guilt over my shoddy treatment of her the past year.

"I've got her bank statement, Mom," Rain warned. "Did you know what she had in her account?"

I shrugged. "I have no idea. Obviously enough to go gambling every second day. I imagine she had some money saved up...we were planning on keeping her in a senior's home for a few years, remember?"

"You weren't here much when all that retirement home business was going on," Rain said. "I was worried about how we were going to afford it and Kitty said the government would take care of it. She said there was no need to disturb her savings."

"She was always so secret when it came to her personal shit," I said. "So she has some money?"

Rain laughed then tried to speak. He started to laugh again and I let him get it out of his system. "Some money?" he managed to repeat. "Let me tell you, Grandma Kitty sure pulled one over us." He reached over and moved the box of jewellery aside. I hadn't even looked at the brooches or the diamond studded necklace. I could see yards of gold chains twined at the bottom. One thick piece had an attachment that oddly read DISCO KING. Laying the paper in front of me, he pointed to a numerical figure. "What does that say?"

I took a look and said, "Two thousand...."

"That's two million, Ma."

I couldn't even read what number came after the two, comma. My body temperature went cold and then hot; my eyes began blinking uncontrollably. My heart started banging so hard in my chest, I feared I would collapse. It was the first time I felt a swoon coming on.

"You ok, Mom?" Rain asked. "Maybe I won't show you the part where it says how much she has in RRSP's."

"Is it anything like her savings?" I barely managed to get out, fanning myself with the government letter's envelope.

Rain nodded and laid the statement aside. "Maybe you can look at that later," he said, "when you've recovered from this shock." He lifted out a manilla envelope and took a peek inside. "She had a life insurance policy. Did you know that?"

I was starting to whimper, though whether it was from grief, happiness at this windfall or the massive subterfuge Kitty had pulled, I couldn't say. "No, I didn't know that! It seems like I didn't even know who my mother was at all! I never saw her wear jewellery - look! A whole box of it! She picks garbage and buys stocks... that's not the Kitty I knew! My mother made me cookies and made sure I did my homework..."

"She did that with us too," Rain said. "And she just got interested in collecting stuff after you moved to San Diego. She said she was bored and it was something to do while we were in school."

All the energy had been zapped from my body. I sat in the chair provided in the room, my hands clutching the arms. "Is there anything else in that box?"

Rain pulled out a long box that looked like it may contain more jewellery. I was wrong. Inside were multiple keys, each with a little note attached saying what lock they opened. "Oh, thank goodness we found this," he said. "These are for all the storage boxes and suitcases in the basement. Look," he pointed out a note that had been masking-taped to a key. I saw my mother's shaky handwriting. "It says 'Suitcase of Old Jazz Recordings'. I can't wait to find that one!"

"You didn't find the will?" I meekly asked.

Rain looked into the box. "There's one more thing at the bottom." He pulled it out and I saw a law firm's emblem on the corner of the envelope. He looked at the front and then solemnly turned it around and showed me. Stamped on the front were the words 'Last Will and Testament.'

He began to open it but I stopped him. "Rain, let's take this home," I said. "Let's read it with the girls."

•••••••••

By the time my daughters came home, with their boyfriends in tow, I was totally involved in preparation for the next day's celebration of Kitty's life. Rain had been in the basement since we'd returned and I never saw him for the rest of the evening, though I did hear the occasional hoot and holler.

I went to bed at 9 PM. The day had exhausted me. I had made six kinds of cookies, I cleaned the entire main floor, I took care of the safety deposit box and I'd gotten rich. I didn't have the money in my hands, but I knew I was going to be well-off. For the first time ever, I didn't feel any guilt as I put the three hundred dollar liquor tab onto my MasterCard.

The morning of the "party", I woke up shivering. The furnace had managed to shut off during the night. Rain looked at it and said I'd better call a repairman. I simply said OK and picked up the phone. Man oh man, look at me splurging Kitty's money! In the old days, I'd have worn a snowsuit in the house for days before coughing up the cash needed to fix the furnace.

I sent the twins to the local grocery store for last-minute supplies for our fete. They took forever and it was a mad rush to get everything ready for our 3 PM - 6 PM celebration. The furnace guy had left and heat was coming back into the house.

Rain came into the kitchen, removing his hat and scarf. "Whew, you can feel the heat blaring!" he said. "It'll be toasty warm when the guests arrive."

I pulled a tray of appetizers out of the oven. "Looks like we never got around to reading that will," I said. "We have to do it before you kids leave tomorrow."

"Tatum has an 8 AM flight," Rain noted. "We have to be there for six or so. We're running out of time."

"How about after everybody leaves?" I suggested. "If we can pry the girls away from their boyfriends?"

At ten minutes to three, the first guests started to arrive. They were elderly friends of Kitty's though I hadn't seen them in eons. They didn't stay long but sure had a lot of questions about Kitty's death. How did she die? Did they do an autopsy? Was her will up to date? Was she cremated? Unless they were trying to work out their own impending demise, I had no idea why they were so curious.

It wasn't a big crowd and I knew almost nobody. The twins stuck to their dates, Rain and Siobhan worked the room like an old married couple and I acted like the hired help. In between running for another bottle of wine and looking for more napkins and replenishing the food trays, I'd mumble a few thank you's to the "I'm sorry for your loss" type of comments. Eventually I was murmuring "Thank you for coming".

At 6:15 PM, Rain called a cab for the remaining two people at the party. They were a married couple I vaguely remembered as being neighbours at one time. The kids knew them better than I. I didn't remember them being such voracious drinkers. As Rain and the twin's dates helped the couple down the stairs and into the waiting taxi, the woman almost slipped.

"Oopsy daisy, maybe I had too much wine!" she giggled.

Her husband grabbed the roof of the car to steady himself and then turned to Rain and grabbed his hand. Shaking it, he said, "It was a wonderful party. Thank your Grandma for us."

Rain shook his head as the cab drove off. "Thank Grandma?" he repeated. "They didn't realize Kitty wasn't there?"

The boys came back into the house and we all congregated in the kitchen, where I was washing some pots and pans. The twins were wiping and putting them away. "Well, that went alright, don't you think?" I asked everyone in general.

"Boring as fuck," was Rain's comment.

"Rain, watch your language," his long-time girlfriend said. All the Canseco family heads swivelled to her when she said that. Siobhan looked at us, a worried look on her face. "What? What'd I do? Was I too bossy?"

She didn't know that while we liked her well enough before, she suddenly became a member of the family right there. I couldn't help myself; with wet soapy hands, I rushed over and gave her a hug. "You just took us by surprise," I said. "That was the exact phrase Kitty always used."

"Speaking of Kitty, Mom...," Rain drew my attention, his eyes pointing over to the twins.

"Right, yes," I replied, turning toward my daughters. "I know you two have probably made plans for tonight...."

"Just gonna hang out here," Sadie cut in. "All of us."

"But why?" I asked. "Don't you want to see your friends before you head back?"

"It's our last night here, Mom," Rain said. "We want to spend it with you. It'll be months till we see you again."

I didn't know what to say. Maybe other maternal types hear this kind of comment all the time but it was probably the first time I truly felt like I was on board as their guardian. "Thank you, kids," I proffered. "You make me feel so loved...."

"Duh, I hope so, you're our mother," was Tatum's reaction. "So what shall we do tonight? A never-ending Monopoly game or maybe Trivial Pursuit?"

"I think we need to take a half-hour or so and read Kitty's will," I said sombrely.

"You didn't read it?" Tatum asked, a pained look on her face. "I'd rather play crazy eights than hear it."

Sadie joined in. "Can't you and Rain read it? I don't want to hear how poor Grandma was."

"It's been a sad enough week," Tatum affirmed.

"She wasn't poor," I said.

"You should see the stuff in the basement," Rain said. "I made a list."

"You and Grandma and that stupid basement!" Tatum cried out. "You guys always adding to the junk!" She started to cry and her beau took her in his arms.

"You think it was all me and her?" Rain asked, unaffected by his sister's tears. "I was down there for twelve hours yesterday. She added stuff I never saw before! You guys have to see it!"

"I'm not going down there," was the response from all three living Canseco women.

I turned to Siobhan and the twin boys. "I don't mean to insult you, but if maybe you guys could sit in the living room? I think this should be a family matter."

"I don't mean to insult you," said Jon, one of the twins, "but would you mind if me and Jeff ran out to buy beer? We've had some wine but the two of us are more beer drinkers."

"You've been drinking," Siobhan said. "I'll drive you over to the beer store." They immediately got up and left us to our business.

Once the front door had closed, Rain pulled out the sealed envelope containing Kitty's last will and testament. He motioned for all of us to gather around the kitchen table. I poured us each a glass of wine; this was my first one. I sank into a chair, glad to finally be off my feet.

"Fasten your seat belt," Rain told the girls. "Because in a few minutes, you're going to be tripping."

• • • • • • • • • •

Out of the manila folder, Rain took out two envelopes. In big block letters, one envelope stated OPEN ME FIRST. My son did as he was told and slit open the smaller envelope. "As executor of her will, I guess I should be the one to read it," he said, then looked down at the letter. "Oh, shit, it's in her handwriting. I can barely make it out." He studied it a moment longer and then looked over to me. "Mom, care to try?"

I'd received enough chatty letters from Kitty over the years to be able to decipher her shaky handwriting. I reached for the letter, took a sip of my wine and upon seeing the date on the paper, said, "This was written less than a year ago!" I took another sip of my wine, hoping Kitty hadn't been pissed off at me that day. "OK, as Rain said yesterday, here goes nothing..."

The letter began "This is my last will and testament. Making a will means leaving anything I own to loved ones. As for the testament? I imagine it means I should testify as to the reasons why I'm doing so.

The second envelope contains the actual will, complete with the legal jargon, and all typed out cleanly in black and white. This letter is to tell you why you are receiving nothing compared to what I'd like to bestow on you. My family meant the world to me and brought me only happiness and pride my whole life. This letter is to also beg you to forgive me for my actions while you were all growing up."

At this point, the four of us exchanged confused looks. What had Kitty done that we should be forgiving her for? I had a three-second run-through in my mind of how many times Kitty had wronged me and came up with nothing. I continued reading. "To Rain, Tatum and Sadie, my beloved grandchildren. Your Grandma Kitty shortchanged you on a normal childhood. I should have taken you bowling and to the movies. Instead I made you pull paintings out of garbage cans and lug home century-old couches from Goodwill...."

Tatum interrupted to say, "I didn't find our life so bad. I played little league soccer for six years."

"I asked to take ballet and she signed me up right away," Sadie said.

"I'm glad she didn't take us bowling," Rain added. "I hate bowling."

I went on. "I told you we'd have to stop eating out for six months if you wanted to go to Disneyland. And I made you help pay for your schooling. I didn't need to do any of this. The government was taking care of me quite nicely. I started dabbling in the stock market and found out I could make wise choices. I had your grandpa's pension and his patent profits and I could have taken you to Disneyland every month. But I wanted you children to know about money - how it doesn't grow on trees and how you have to finance. I could have spared you the sorrow of student loans and paid it all upfront, but what would you learn from that?"

"I'd learn how to get eight hours sleep," Rain answered. The girls nodded in agreement.

"To my dearest grandchildren, I leave....," and looked up to ensure I had their attention. Did I ever. "I leave the contents of the basement."

Sadie pouted. "Oh, no, I don't want any of that junk. Not unless there's like a first edition of a Dr. Seuss book. I always liked Dr. Seuss."

Rain said, "Sade, there's a first edition of Green Eggs and Ham."

"Shut the front door!" she exclaimed. "Dibs!"

"I'm telling ya, I made a list," Rain said excitedly. "You're not going to believe it."

"She goes on about the basement," I said. "She talks to you here, Rain." I again returned to the letter. "Rain, you know about most of the stuff down there, but often while you kids were away at school, I'd walk over to Goodwill and the old stores on that street and see what I could find. I showed you a lot but you were young, maybe you didn't understand their value, so I packed them all away in trunks and storage boxes and suitcases. I hope you found the jewellery box with all the keys!" Rain nodded in the girls direction; we'd found the box.

"I know the basement is a mess but Rain, I trust you'll make a list. I can't recall offhand what is down there but I know most of it has value. Keep what is rightfully your's, Rain, like that Lionel train set you urged me to buy. I know we got it for a steal and I knew it was worth money, but I still made you pay for half out of your newspaper job. Remember when we went for a walk and you saw a box of old-fashioned girlie magazines? We went through them and sure enough, there was a number-one edition of Playboy Magazine. That's down there somewhere. Look in that vintage Louis Vuitton suitcase.

What else do I have down there? I could go and look but a big spider landed on my blouse last time I went down and nearly gave me a heart attack. Just sell it and use the funds to pay for any student loans you may have left. I've been updating my will every couple years so if you're reading this now, I imagine you're still in school.

I hope the basement will be enough, but in case it isn't, I have an account in each of your names at my bank. There's not a lot, maybe a hundred grand each, but I always worried about the house burning down and thought I'd better have a Plan B for you kids.

Finally, the money from the government. I'm not talking about my old age pension or the pension money I was receiving from my husband's job. Those will both end upon my death. I'm talking about the money Mr. Canseco earned every month with his invention. So much money for such a little bolt! And the government will continue to pay it to any living heirs or until they no longer use it. Don't worry, kids, they'll use it forever or until outer space is no longer utilized. This means your children's children could reap from Grandpa's gizmo. I am leaving this money to Rain, Tatum and Sadie to be split equally."

I stopped at this point to take a gulp of wine and saw my kids looking at me sadly. "Don't worry, Mom," Sadie said. "We'll split everything with you."

Tatum was amazed. "From what you're reading...is my school being paid for?" I nodded but Tatum didn't seem to comprehend. "I don't have to work two jobs anymore?"

"Not even one job," I said, putting down the wine glass and returning to the letter. "To my daughter Tammy," I began then stopped. "Oh, oh...it doesn't say beloved or darling or anything....."

"Probably because you already know how she felt about you," Sadie deduced.

"Mom," Rain said in a carefully modulated voice. "You saw her safety deposit box. You know she has money."

"I know, but what if she left it to some animal shelter or something?" I cried. "We never thought about that! What if she left it to those drunken neighbours?"

"How about you just read what she wrote?" Sadie suggested. With a shaking hand, I nervously picked up the letter to see what punishment Kitty planned on dealing me from the afterlife.

"OK...to my daughter Tammy," I said, clearing my throat. "Please contact a lawyer and have them walk you through this." At this point, my face reddened and I glanced at my kids. They seemed to be in accordance with Kitty. "I had a whale of a time with the stock market and opened up all sorts of accounts. Except for the old Nortel stock, they are doing splendid. You will find them in the thick manilla envelope in the safety deposit box. Sell it all but you may want to keep Facebook - they're only going to go up."

At this point, the kids all started laughing. "Kitty was on Facebook?" Tatum asked. She seemed to be less ebullient than the other two.

"Kitty owned a piece of it, but I doubt she ever went on it," Rain said. "Remember how we tried to teach her to Skype?"

"Can we get back to me?" I asked, before continuing. "Besides the stocks, I leave you my savings account as well as my RRSP's and any other investments listed in the will. Don't forget about the life insurance policy. You are the beneficiary. In the case of you pre-deceasing me, your children will inherit it."

At this, I shuddered. Rain said, "See, Mom? Grandma Kitty wouldn't have cut you out of her will."

I gave a shaky laugh. "There's a bit more, we're almost done." My voice seemed to be echoing in my ears; I didn't know if it was the wine or the will. "All told, there should be over four million dollars. I'm sure taxes will take a big chunk of it, but try to make the rest of the money last for awhile.

I always meant to leave you something, Tammy. Nobody knew how much I wanted to come home and you rescued me. As I write this letter, I'm back in my marital home, surrounded by photos of my grandchildren and being looked after by my only child. I may not have been the best mother for you, Tammy. I let you run wild and have children out of wed-lock and I didn't continue the path your father had chosen for you. When you left me with your kids to raise, I probably went overboard. I forced them to study every single day of their lives...."

"Poor me," Sadie said. "I only got straight A's all through school."

"Poor US," Rain corrected. "We all got partial scholarships because of our grades."

"...just to make amends for my negligence with you. I leave you my house and all my belongings, except for the basement's contents. You always hated the basement and I have armies of trained spiders waiting to attack you if you try to throw anything out.

In closing, I love you all so very much. Tatum and Sadie, you could be brats but you both had your heads on straight and always showed me respect. Rain, you were my confidante and I could trust you implicitly. I wish you all the best in your futures. Tammy, you came back to Toronto and I was just one more problem you had to take on. You did it. I want you to know this - even though I'm dead now, I was already dead when I was at those seniors' homes. When you brought me back to live with you, you gave me back my life. That's worth four million and then some. Love, Kitty Casino aka Katherine Canseco."

I stopped reading as I'd come to the end of the page. I almost felt sick, knowing that I would likely have returned her to a home once I'd found work. But maybe Kitty would have divulged her wealth. Who knows? We were all silent until Tatum murmured, "There's more on the other side."

I flipped the page over. "Oh, there's a PS! It says 'Speaking of wedlock, Tammy, it's my hope that you find yourself a good man and settle down. You're not too old to have kids still. I saw on TV how some movie stars are having children into their mid-forties. You'd make a good mother.'" I put down the letter. After a beat, I asked, "Was she getting a final dig in at me?"

Rain jumped up so fast, his chair almost fell over. "Who cares? You're rich, Mom! I mean really stinking rich!"

Sadie grabbed the wine bottle and refilled all our glasses. "Four million? The house? Life insurance? I couldn't keep track! Do what she said, Mom, hire a financial guy."

Rain hugged Tatum. "Can you believe this, baby sis? We're set for life! Thanks, Grandma! Thanks, Grandpa!"

Tatum pushed Rain away. "It doesn't feel right!" she cried. "We're all so happy because suddenly we're rich? Grandma Kitty just died!"

Sadie picked up a wine glass and put it in her sister's hand. "I think Grandma would want us to be happy," she said. "This is her fault. Blame Grandma Kitty."

Rain walked over to the girls with his glass. "Here's to Grandma Kitty for making all our school problems go away," he said.

Tatum was silent before a small grin started to spread over her face. "You mean I won't be struggling with that stupid physics course anymore? I'll get better grades?" She raised her glass in the toast.

Moments later, the assorted romantic interests of my children returned with the beer. There was enough wine left that all seven of us got thoroughly sloshed. Rain kept going down to the basement and venturing up with boxes or suitcases.

"Check out this crate!" he said, carrying a large box rather easily. He laid it on the floor and the twin boys instantly darted over.

"Oh man, my dad collects this stuff!" Jon said. "These are as old as the toys he has."

Jeff ever so gingerly lifted out a piece. "This is older than Dad's," he said. "Look, it even has the driver still."

"What are you guys talking about?" Tatum said. "Toys?"

"A whole box of old tin toys," Rain confirmed. "Some from Japan...

look, Jon, that one there says Occupied Japan....some from Germany... Jeff, that one's German, pre World War One..."

"And you think they're worth something?" Sadie asked.

The twins both turned to her then back to Rain. "You've got to get this on eBay," Jeff said.

"Well, hang on, there's another box," Rain said. He'd obviously brought it up with the other, as it was still sitting at the top of the basement stairs. He opened it and pulled out a vintage Barbie Doll, still in its packaging. "These aren't cool toy cars and trucks...these are all dolls and action figures.... "

"Chewbacca!" Jon oddly blurted out, dashing to the carton. "Still in the box! Dude, with this, you wanna go to a fan convention...."

"I remember that!" Sadie announced. "Grandma got it at a yard sale. Man, how many yard sales did we go to? And I wanted to open it up on the spot but Grandma Kitty wouldn't let me touch it. I thought she was so mean."

"So smart is what she was," Jon said. "Look, she has more! Was she a Star Wars fan?"

Oh, how we howled at that. Then we shared stories of how wise Kitty could be at times and then how innocent and naive. The party we held earlier was a sham; this was the real celebration of Kitty's life. Rain brought up a strange lot - a bunch of papers held loosely together with elastic bands. "Knowing Kitty, this could be the Declaration of Independence," he joked. He took the band off one and unfurled the paper.

"Just an old map," I noticed. "Not even anywhere special. Plain ol' Toronto."

"Hey, I'm going to school to be a city planner," Jeff said. "I had to study a bunch of maps last year." He took a closer look. "This is interesting...it's dated the first year the city changed its name from York."

"Toronto was called York?" I asked.

"What else you have there?" Jeff asked Rain.

Some were a designer's dress sketches, some were building blueprints, but most were maps. Maps from everywhere in Canada it appeared. One was so old that it began to rip before it was half opened. Jon pointed to a visible date - 1858 - and Rain reverentially just folded it up again.

"Ya know, I may have had too much to drink to handle this with care," he said.

Siobhan stood up. "I think it's time I put you to bed."

"You two have to leave in the morning," Jeff said to my daughters. "Maybe we should get going."

"Wait, wait, wait," I said, none too sober myself. "You've all spent enough time with your mother. I'm the one going to bed and nobody bother me until it's time to leave for the airport. Is that clear?"

"Sheesh, yes, rich bitch," Rain said. Siobhan smacked him on the arm.

"It's OK," I told her. "I like the sound of that."

Up in my bedroom, I crawled into bed and grabbed my laptop. Opening it, I wondered what to look at. An unbidden laugh trickled out as I recalled Kitty buying Facebook stock and I remembered I had a Facebook page. I decided to post some kind of tribute about Kitty onto it.

To my surprise, I had messages. There was one from Dawn, from BiBi, even condolences from Samuel, the assistant road manager of the now-defunct The Noise. I don't know how Blast Records found out about Kitty passing away but the word had gotten around.

There was even a message that warmed my heart. It was from Kerry, the guy I had a one-night affair with a few months back. The message read 'I'm so sorry to hear about your mother passing away. I recall meeting her that night at the Kato Casino. She seemed very nice. All my condolences - Kerry (ex-manager of Living Large).'

The message had only come in a few minutes ago. I was dwelling on a reply, was definitely going to thank him for thinking of me, but was wondering how to respond to the 'ex' part of his recent job. A posting from Kerry suddenly popped up. This one read 'Just FYI, I now work as the manager for the Escape label. Got myself an office job and relocated to Toronto. In an overpriced condo not far from you actually. Again, my sympathies on the loss of your mom."

I was grateful for his pity, but more curious as to how he knew where I lived. Was he interested in me? I remembered he had come out of a rough breakup, but that was over a year ago. Lord knows I'd often thought about him since our one-night stand. It wasn't the sex I fondly recalled though; it was the way he made me feel like I was the most important person in the world.

With my fingers poised above the keyboard, I wondered if I should reply cautiously or add some flirtatious hints to my message. How to play it in case I was reading too much into his words? Perhaps he'd already hooked up with a new woman and was just keeping in touch.

Another message popped up. It didn't contain any notes of consoling words; rather, it read "This may sound inappropriate but maybe, when everything calms down, we can meet for a coffee?"

For Kitty's sake, I quickly responded to this message. I asked Kerry, almost ordered him, to meet me at the local Starbucks the next evening. Kitty would have approved.

CHAPTER XVI

The thousand bucks Kitty gave me at Christmas saw me through all of January. Then I slowly started selling off the jewellery. It turned out the DISCO KING trinket was solid gold and the man offered me eleven hundred for it. I had been prepared to dicker but that price was so outrageous for such a gaudy piece of jewellery, I snapped it up.

It appeared that I was going to be a rich woman, once the lawyers finished probating the will and the banks got around to deciding that Kitty was really dead and they simply had no choice but to release her money. In the interim, I lived frugally. The kids, on the other hand, had no time to sell the basement contents. They still had school and lived away from home. I convinced Rain I had skills with eBay and he allowed me to sell off a few pieces. The kids were making out like gangsters.

For some reason, I still hadn't properly grieved my mother. I shed tears, but I certainly didn't carry on like my daughters did. There was even a month where I was more angry at Kitty than I'd ever been in my life. Inner conversations kept repeating themselves in my mind. We talked about taking a trip to Vegas, did you forget? You were scheduled for eye surgery in a month, remember? How about Rain's graduation? You already had your dress picked out!

The thought of death just disgusted me now. You have goals and aspirations but who comes knocking at the most inopportune time? The grim reaper. Hello, death, I wasn't expecting you. What's that, you say? Too damn bad? One wasn't allowed to be prepared, to be dignified, to have lipstick on. To wear clean underwear, for God's sake! You had absolutely no say in the matter. Here I am, the bastard says, come with me, no time for good-byes. I was scared of dying before. Now I had no respect for death.

Finally, mid-August, all the moons and stars aligned and I received my inheritance. As Kitty had warned, taxes took a chunk but I could still say I was a millionaire several times over. I never had to worry about money again. For the first time, I took my kids on a holiday. For some reason I thought they'd want to go to Disneyland. They chose New Orleans. My twins were still dating their twins, so I took them along as well. Siobhan couldn't make it; she was working in a country I never knew existed.

Though I had the best of times in The Big Easy, I immediately fell back into a strange funk when I got home. One night, Kerry got out of my bed to find me standing by the fireplace. I was holding the urn containing Kitty's ashes.

"What's the matter, hon?" Kerry asked softly, his large bulk looking ridiculous in my housecoat.

"I don't know...," I said. "I think I should get some professional help. I can't seem to get over Kitty's death."

"It hasn't been that long," Kerry consoled me. "And Tammy, maybe I'm stepping out of line here, but I don't think having that urn in plain view is helping any. I mean, you see it every day."

"I didn't plan on keeping it there this long," I replied. "Kitty wanted us to spread her ashes. I just don't know where." I put the urn back on the mantle. "I bet that's why I'm so sad. I've been procrastinating over this. Don't worry about me, Kerry, I'll be OK. I'll work it out."

Kerry held out his arms and I snuggled into his girth. "Let's go back to bed," he said. "In the morning, I'll make you bacon and eggs."

He was such a good man. See, Kitty? I'm following your will to the letter, still trying to be your dutiful daughter.

••••••••••

As I was drifting off to sleep, my sentence "I bet that's why I'm so sad" replayed itself in my mind. The phrase kept getting shorter until finally, the words "I bet, I bet, I bet" were the last thing I remembered hearing. The plan must have worked itself out while I dozed.

In the morning, after a thumbs-up breakfast, I kissed Kerry goodbye as he prepared to leave for work. "Got any plans for today?" he asked. "Do you want to meet for lunch?"

"Sure," I said. "But I do have plans. I'm going to take care of my mother."

• • • • • • • • •

FiveStar Casino, though the place of her death, was also Kitty's second favourite place in the world. Kato was first but it was a long drive and I had a lunch date. I'm sure Kitty would have understood. That's where I decided to spread her ashes - at FiveStar Casino.

At 10 AM on a Wednesday morning, the parking lot gave up a space just a minute's walk from my valued side-door entrance. I marvelled at how warm the day was; the last time we were here, we'd checked in hats, scarves and mittens. Come to think of it, I'd never retrieved Kitty's belongings. I hope they went to Goodwill.

The urn containing Kitty's ashes was secreted in my large shoulder bag. I entered the building and quickly walked up the escalator. I passed a man standing still, looking at his cell phone. Shouldn't he be at work, I wondered, not taking in that we were about the same age. Not considering that he may also have come into a few mil himself.

As I heard the noise of the slot machines resound in the casino ahead of me, I got a residual feeling of anticipation. I shook that off; I was on a mission. I breezed past the security guard, who gave me a bright smile and said, "Good morning! I hope you have great luck today..." But I was already past him. Though I've never had my purse searched at a casino before, now would not be a good time for it to happen.

I hustled into the casino's gaming room and then jolted to a stop. It was like the roof closed in on me and suddenly my chest felt constricted. I slowly gazed around and then started gasping for breath. I figured I may be having an anxiety attack, maybe even my own heart attack! When it hit me what was going on, I knew I had to run to a washroom. I was in the throes of a huge wave of grief.

When I'd entered the casino, the first sight to greet me was a lineup of little old ladies waiting at the Players Place counter. As I tore my eyes from them, I landed on the bank of machines located near the big drum. All were being played by white-haired little old ladies. Over to my left were seventeen more, it seemed. Everywhere I looked, I was seeing Kitty Casino.

As I raced for a washroom, trying desperately to hold in my pent-up mewls, I rather brusquely shoved past an elderly couple holding hands. From my periphery I saw the old geezer try to make a scene about it but his partner held firmly to his hand. "Let it be," she said in a smoker's voice. "She probably lost everything she has."

As I finally reached the washroom (my only complaint about Five-Star's layout; not enough washrooms!), I collided with the woman emptying the needles container. The bin got bumped hard enough to make a dozen needles fall to the floor. "I'm sorry!" I said immediately. "Let me pick them up."

"NO!" said the dark-haired lady. Other than her hair, she had a kind, grandmotherly look to her. "You could get sick," she advised. "Let me do that. I have gloves."

"Be careful," I said as she gingerly picked them up. "I shouldn't have been running like that."

The cleaning lady glanced up. "Maybe you had to use the washroom badly?" she attempted to remind me.

The sobs bubbled to the surface. "No...my mother died...here at the casino," I whimpered.

The cleaner stood up quickly. "Just now?" she asked.

"No."

The woman put a consoling hand on my arm. "Ohhh, was she the lady who died here yesterday? In this washroom?"

"No...it was New Year's Eve..like eight months ago?" I offered. I began feeling I might look stupid; it had been long enough to start getting over it, but my brain forgot to tell my soul.

Still, the woman continued to stroke my arm. "You poor thing," she said. "I lost my mother three years ago and I think about her every day still."

With that, I tore away, dived into a stall and just leaned my back against the door to close it. I cried hard for five minutes and then wound down for the next ten. I used up most of the tissue in the stall and at one point, enough clarity came back to me to flush the toilet before I clogged it.

I'd finally broken out of my snap and mourned my mother. As I prepared to leave the stall, my heavy bag clunked against the door and I remembered the urn. The same cleaning lady was at the far end of the washroom. I really didn't want to face her and was relieved when she respected my unspoken need for solitude. She didn't even glance my way; simply acted like I had just taken the usual piss.

As I left the washroom, I put on invisible blinders. I didn't want to see or speak to anyone unless they were under the age of sixty. I took a walk around the whole casino, wondering where I could spread these ashes. I passed the Lucky Fountain, a pet game of Kitty's, but I couldn't see myself dumping the urn over the machine. I'm sure security would have me out of there in no time. Part of me thought it was a chance I was willing to take, if only there wasn't a tattooed biker already on the game. I wandered out of the casino and decided to take the escalator to the upper level. It was a thousand times more private than downstairs. Instead of joyful gamblers, I encountered sullen off-track bettors. This level would only be packed on horse racing days and today wasn't one. I gazed out the windows at the track.

There were a few horses being exercised. Some people sat in the stands but they looked like they were simply assessing the horses' ability. A couple took photos and a couple more were holding stopwatches. I figured I could spread the ashes outside and immediately took off to find a way to get out there.

I almost missed it but near an elevator there was a discreet door that said EMPLOYEES ONLY. I revived my old trick - to act like I belonged to the organization. I put on a false face of an non-uniformed employee and opened the door. A short set of stairs led down to another door that was made of glass. Bright sunlight shone through and I hoped the door was unlocked.

And why wouldn't it be? On the job employees didn't have time to unlock doors all day, especially if they were in a stated EMPLOYEES ONLY zone. I cautiously opened the door and stepped out onto a deck filled with unoccupied tables and chairs. There was a railing at the far end and I walked over to it.

As I gazed at the scene in front of me, it seemed I was looking into a patch of heaven. On this side of the casino, the traffic sounds were completely muted. Acres of green training fields stretched before me. The three horses gliding by looked like they should sprout wings; the clip-clop of their hooves a soothing note. Full fluffy white clouds filled the sky and the warm sun shone almost directly overhead. The silence was so complete, I felt I was in church. I'd found my spot.

Laying my shoulder bag onto a nearby table, I pulled out the urn of Kitty's ashes. As I unscrewed the lid, I wondered how I should go about it. Do I just tip it over and dump them out? Do I make to and fro motions with my arms and empty it in five swings? Do I say something?

I couldn't think of something to say aloud. My mind was full of thoughts though. I still hadn't been able to rid myself of guilt. Guilt over my less than golden treatment of Kitty, of how I badgered her about her declining health and her spending habits. At that I had to scoff. The scenes I'd almost caused when she dared to gamble over a half-dollar. How I'd constantly drill into her brain about knowing her limit. God damn it - she always knew she could play two bucks a spin all day long and she'd still have money to burn. She felt content with her usual forty cent bets and though I accused her of throwing away her money, I had no choice but to allow it. It wasn't my money; it was her's to do with as she pleased. And it pleased her to be able to leave her family a ton of dough.

With these thoughts in mind, I gripped the urn by the opening while the other hand held the bottom. I threw out a spray of ashes, only to discover the wind wasn't working with me. The ashes seemed to float out four feet then stop in the air, before reversing onto me. I stood still a moment, aghast at how I could always manage to screw things up when it came to my mom.

"Can't do anything right, can I, Mom?" I asked the urn. "Couldn't be a proper kid growing up, couldn't be decent when I came back home. And what do you do? You reward me for my bad behaviour with FOUR MIL-LION FUCKING DOLLARS!" With this I threw another batch of ashes to the wind. My voice was rising visibly and it came out ragged, marred by growing sobs.

"I'm sorry, Mom," I cried, the tears on my face cutting through some of the ashes that had been blown back onto it. "I'm sorry for swearing just now, I'm sorry for being so selfish all the time, I'm sorry...." I only took a pause because I didn't know what to say next out of the thousand regrets flooding my brain. "I'm sorry I gave you no choice about taking care of my kids, for just having up and left you with three babies...."

Another hard toss with another blowback that I managed to sidestep.

I continued my diatribe. "Oh, hey, I don't think I ever said thank you for raising my children so...," and I flung some more, "...so thank you." I yelled, my mouth open, ashes flying onto my tongue. "Thank you for a roof over my head, thank you for returning three great kids to me, thank you for staying alive long enough so I could spend one more year with you...."

I almost collapsed against the railing in my anguish. I could feel the urn was almost empty. After today, I knew I would be able to find my equilibrium, to go on living my life as before. NO! Better than before. Now I wouldn't have to search for a job with my non-existent work skills. I wouldn't have to budget carefully or use coupons or worry about paying the hydro bill ever again. I could go back to school, I could volunteer at a food bank, I could travel the world again without a bunch of rowdy rock stars.

I tipped the urn over the railing and watched as the last of the ashes slid out and drifted downwards. With a big sniffle, like a preacher over a gravesite, I intoned, "You said I gave you a new life? Well, Mom, you SAVED my life. Go now. Go find Dad. I love you, Kitty Casino."

With that, I let forth such a wail, it probably threw off the horses timing. I looked up into the blinding sun, eyes wide open and keened the loss of my mother. I was taking a breath for another sob when I heard "...the matter?"

I jumped and almost dropped the empty urn over the railing. I wheeled about and saw a member of FiveStar Casino's security staff. I'd probably appeared a lunatic howling at the sun. My first instinct was to grab my purse and run - blame it on the old A Lock of Bradley's Hair days. However he was standing in front of the glass exit door.

Stuttering, I said, "N...no, nothing's the matter, I just needed some air."

The guard looked at the urn in my hands. I looked at the urn and then met his eyes. I couldn't hold back the hiccup that comes after a big cry that escaped from me. He backed up and opened the door. "Employees only down here," he said.

I picked up my bag and crossed the deck and went through the door. He shut it behind me and walked away. I was so glad he didn't arrest me or take me in for questioning. I considered his circumspect behaviour and came up with the likely reason.

I was probably not the first person to have done this.

• • • • • • • • •

It had been my intention to make a left off the escalators and head for my car in the parking lot. Instead, at the bottom of the stairs, I changed my mind. I was going to go and play one spin at a slot machine in honour of my mother.

I re-entered the casino and the guard manning the entry desk said, "Hi, there, hope you have..." and then stopped as he looked at my face. I assumed I had a somewhat, shall we say, ashen appearance? I simply lifted up my black vintage The Noise t-shirt (sort of a funeral/casino look) and tried to wipe my face.

As I walked toward Lucky Fountain, I could see it was still being played by the biker. He was snarling so I wasn't about to ask him if I could make one teensy tiny spin on his machine. There were a couple Wizard of Oz machines here, but Kitty really didn't care for them. She only liked the one at FunTime Casino. I found myself in the same place where I'd made my first wager on a slot machine - Kitty Glitter.

As I looked at the machine sitting unplayed, I recalled how I origi-nally thought it read 'Kitty Litter'. I would often call it that or even Kitty Litterbox. I hated that game. You could spend your entire paycheque hop-ing for that bonus. When it finally appeared, the payout could be spec-tacular...or it could win less than the wager you placed.

I stepped up to it. "Well, Kitty," I said aloud, not caring if the woman playing Noah's Ark could hear me. "For me, this is where it started. And this is where it will end." I inserted a five dollar bill and without thinking, made my usual nickel bet.

I knew the three diamond-encrusted catfood bowls would pop up. I just knew they would. And sure enough, Ding! Up popped the first dish I needed for the bonus. Ka-ching! Up jumped the second one. I sat back with a sure smile on my face.

And then the wheels spun with nothing else. I won diddly squat. Like many of the patrons who'd come before me to this game, and like many who would follow, I pushed away from the machine as I angrily cashed out. "You always were a piece of shit, Kitty Litter!" I told it.

In disgust, I headed over to the red machine that would give me cash for my voucher. It was out of order and I was directed to one deeper into the casino. That one had a line-up of ten people so I went in search of another. A slot machine caught my eye. It was one I'd never played though I'd seen it often. It just didn't appeal to me. It was the name of it that grabbed my attention.

Miss Kitty. With its childishly drawn pictures of blue birds and yellow fish and the big purple wildcard cat. Some of the characters almost appeared to be stick figures. I preferred the glitzy games with the loud squawking parrots or the handsome smirking pirates. Miss Kitty looked sweet and innocent nestled between Tigress, with its ferocious tigers and Oom Papa, with its dancing cuckoo clocks.

I saw a man slide off the stool in front of Miss Kitty and move over to the next game. For a moment he played both slot machines but when his credits ran out, he quit playing. I stood a moment longer and then decided to sit down on the vacated stool. I looked up at the game and saw the man had been betting a buck twenty. It was none of my concern.

Again I looked at the name of the machine. "Miss Kitty," I said aloud. "That sounds a lot more classy than Kitty Litter. This is going to be my last bet."

I inserted the voucher and noticed I had ashes all over my fingers. I had to smile, glad I was able to leave some of Kitty inside the actual casino. I looked at the button needed to make a five cent bet and then held back. Why play my usual bet, I thought? This isn't about me! I inwardly felt a stab of shame, knowing I'd been a self-absorbed incorrigible brat my whole life....and still my mother loved me.

"No, this is in your honour, Mom," I said. "It might hurt a bit but I'm going to play forty cents." I punched the buttons and then hovered my finger over the cash-out button, knowing this wouldn't take long.

Purple cats, each meowing seductively each time they appeared, sprang up all over the screen. I couldn't see any of the birds or fishes - just beautiful purring smiling purple cats. "What's going on?" I asked aloud. I'd never seen a screen fill with so many identical symbols.

The man playing next to me stopped his betting and watched my machine. "That's going to be a big win," he said. "You would have won more if you'd played the maximum."

Images of coins spilling from some unseen bucket appeared, along with the joyful sounds that came with scoring a jackpot. Under the Win lettering, I saw numbers quickly start to rise. I was happy to see five dollars blow by and my smile got bigger when it went past twenty. Then my mouth formed a huge 'O' when it started approaching a hundred.

A few people gathered behind me. I was congratulated on my win, I was asked why I only played forty cents, I was told I was so lucky I should move on to the nickel slots. I ignored them all. I didn't bother explaining I had three kids to put through school. I didn't mention I wasn't here to make my fortune. I didn't inform them that forty cents, even though I was now a millionaire, still went against my grain.

The machine finally went silent and I stared up at my winnings. Three hundred and eighty dollars. I hit the cash-out button.

There was still time to kill before I met Kerry for lunch. I could have stayed longer at the casino. But I felt absolutely no desire to be there anymore. I did need to use the washroom before I left though.

I did my business and then headed to the sink to wash up. I saw my appearance in the mirror - smudged face, bloodshot eyes, wild hair. I washed my face thoroughly, splashing water all over the sink's counter. Figuring I should find the red cash-out machine, I pulled my voucher for $380 out of my back pocket. I was about to walk out of the washroom when I spotted the little plexiglass container bolted to the wall.

It was the bin less than a third filled with cash vouchers that you could donate to the housekeeping staff. Though I played my credits till I hit zero, Kitty would always donate if her credits were under forty cents. I remembered the last time she'd inserted her ticket - it showed twelve cents. I could see a few slips of paper for under a nickel. There was a voucher clearly visible for two dollars and I felt a wave of gratitude for that kindly soul. I looked at the voucher in my hand, for more money than I'd ever won in my life, and simply added it to the small pile in the bin. I was glad to see it land face up, the amount loud and proud.

I bid a fond farewell to the security guard at the exit. I knew I wouldn't be back. It wasn't that I disliked FiveStar Casino or any of the casinos for that matter. I'd had plenty of fun. But it wasn't my thing; it was my mother's hobby. I liked movies, I enjoyed dancing, I wanted to go to auctions and visit my kids. I had a boyfriend that I wanted to stick around.

And besides, it just wouldn't be the same without Kitty Casino.